IN THE AUTUMN WIND

To Bonnie,
   who's really going to
that mythical city, Nahodka!
      Best wishes,
         Dorothy Stroup

8/9/87

IN THE AUTUMN WIND

A NOVEL

Dorothy Stroup

CHARLES SCRIBNER'S SONS / NEW YORK

For Kan Katayanagi and Tomio Abe

This novel is a work of fiction. Any references to historical events; to real people, living or dead; or to real locales are intended only to give the fiction a setting in historical reality. Other names, characters, places, and incidents either are the product of the author's imagination or are used fictitiously, and their resemblance, if any, to real-life counterparts is entirely coincidental.

Library of Congress Cataloging-in-Publication Data

Stroup, Dorothy.
In the autumn wind.

1. World War, 1939-1945—Fiction. 2. Hiroshima-shi
(Japan)—Bombardment, 1945—Fiction. I. Title.
PS3569.T735I5   1987   813'.54   86-10075
ISBN 0-684-18642-X

Published simultaneously in Canada by
Collier Macmillan Canada, Inc.

Composition by Westchester Book Composition, Inc.,
Yorktown Heights, New York

Manufactured by The Haddon Craftsmen,Inc.,
Scranton, Pennsylvania

Designed by Susan Lu

Map by David Lindroth

First Edition

Acknowledgments

During the early sixties I spent three rich and rewarding years teaching English at Hiroshima Jogakuin, a women's high school and college. It was one of the peak experiences of my life.

I did not begin the novel, however, until a decade later, when Michael Rubin suggested that I expand into a novel the story I had originally read in his class at the University of California Extension. Without his criticism and encouragement and that of all the members of the Tuesday Writers' Group in Berkeley, I could not have finished the book.

I was also helped immeasurably by Kanji Kuramoto and the other members of the Committee of Atomic Bomb Survivors of the U.S.A., by Steven Okazaki and Frances Politeo's documentary, *Survivors*; by Barbara Reynolds, founder of the Hiroshima/Nagasaki Memorial Library Collection at Wilmington College, Wilmington, Ohio; and by Kyoko Tokuno Buswell and Yoshiko Miyakoshi, who helped me with translations of Japanese sources.

Eventually I knew that I needed more information and, in 1979, returned to Japan, where I interviewed more than forty people in all walks of life. I could not have made the trip without the generous travel grant I received from Masaru and Hiroko Kurahashi of ISAJ (International Student Advisers of Japan). Nor could I have accomplished the task without the help of many friends, especially those associated with Hiroshima Jogakuin: Kikuyo Abe, Akiko Aoyama, Sakae Edamatsu, Fusako Ueno Fujiwara, Doris Hartman, Hamako Hirose, Hideo and Chizuko Ikeda, Masayuki Imaishi, Keiko Ishido, Midori Kai, Satoshi Kawamura, Yoshiko Kimura, Mary McMillan, Miyoko Matsubara and Shozo Uno of the Hiroshima Peace Culture Center, Sadami Naganishi, Kaizo and Toe Odagiri, Kanako Saruta, Dixie Setoyama,

Eiko Suhama, Chisa and Kiyoshi Tanimoto, Tetsuko Teranishi, Nobuko Ueno, Kaeko and Gaku Yamamoto, Yasuko Yamaoka, Nobuyuki Yuasa, Tokiko Yoshida, Motoko and Yoshi Yoshioka and Yoshi's father, who was imprisoned in Siberia and Yoshi's mother, who waited for him.

Two *Yomiuri Shimbun* reporters, Shigeru Fujiwara and Munehiro Okumura, helped me understand the special vocabulary of the *genbaku* (atomic bomb) experience so that I could do my interviews in Japanese when necessary. The *Yomiuri Shimbun* staff in Osaka gave me copies of their nine-volume series *Senso* (The War) and led me through their annual War Exhibit, which depicts the horrors and hardships of that time.

Minoru Ohmuta of the *Chugoku Shimbun* spent his off-work hours giving me ideas and new leads to follow. Minoru Yuzaki of Hiroshima University, whose research for the book *Genbaku Bakushinchi* (The Epicenter of the Atomic Explosion) was a project to re-create on a map the old neighborhood of Nakajima (now the Peace Park), took me to a reunion of fifty-year-olds who had been elementary school students evacuated to the country before the bomb.

Yoshiteru Kosakai, chief of the Hiroshima City Library and editor of the five-volume series *Hiroshima Genbaku Shizai-shi* (The History of the Damage to Hiroshima), introduced me to many survivors, including Hisato Nishida, the eighty-three-year-old former mayor of Inokuchi, and the late Yuichi Sasaki, who lost thirteen of his relatives in the bombing and dedicated the rest of his life to photographing the devastation of Hiroshima and its gradual resurgence. Shikoku Goro showed me his sketchbook created from a pictorial record of his experiences in Siberia and brought home in a tiny notebook he had concealed in the sole of his shoe.

In Maizuru, I met Yoshimasa Yoshida, a city official who had been in charge of the repatriation from China and Russia, one of the largest movements of population in history. Afterwards, he answered with careful documentation the long lists of questions I wrote him.

Many others helped with this book. Roberta Pryor has been the best imaginable agent, and the editors at Scribners have been conscientious and attentive. Special thanks go to my family and close friends, who gave their unflagging support and encouragement, especially Dick Stroup, Sarah Young, and Alan Geller.

Among the women whose spirits pervade this book are: the late Hatsuyo Ikeda, who survived the bomb husbandless and worked as a maid to bring up her children; Yasu Sato, also husbandless, who supported her three children by creating knickknacks for sale in souvenir shops; Mrs. Haru Tanaka, who tended the sick and dying in a vacant lot across from her house; the late Kuniko Jenkins, a nurse at the time, who listened to the stories of the wounded before they died; Yuriko Kaikawa and her mother, Asako Akiyama, who lost the other five of her six children; and Masuko Abe, who lost her youngest son and cremated her father near Hiroshima City Hall on August 7, 1945.

Principal Characters

THE FAMILY

The Haras

Chiyo Hara, *a housewife living in Hiroshima*

Shintaro Hara, *her husband, a middle-school teacher now in the army*

Kenichi Hara, *her elder son*

Yoko Hara, *her daughter*

Hiroshi Hara, *her younger son*

The Ogawas

Isao Ogawa, *Chiyo's brother, who lives in the suburb of Inokuchi*

Kazuko Ogawa, *Isao's wife*

Fusako Ogawa, *their daughter*

The Nagatanis

Akiko Nagatani Fujiwara, *Kazuko's sister*

Mrs. Hana Nagatani, Grandmother, *Kazuko and Akiko's mother*

The Fujiwaras

Kikuo Fujiwara, *Akiko's husband*

Koichi Fujiwara, *their son*

THE NEIGHBORS

The Ikedas

Mrs. Ikeda, *a neighbor whose husband is the captain of the* Tonarigumi, *the Neighborhood Association*

Mr. Ikeda, *her husband, an employee of City Hall*

The elder Ikedas, *Mr. Ikeda's parents*

Kyoko Ikeda, *Mr. and Mrs. Ikeda's daughter and youngest child, the same age as Yoko Hara*

Yukiji Ikeda, *their younger son*

Ichiro Ikeda, *their elder son*

Haruko Ikeda, *Ichiro's wife*

Takeshi Ikeda, *Haruko and Ichiro's elder son*

Kunio Ikeda, *their younger son*

The Yamamotos

Mrs. Yamamoto, *Chiyo's next-door neighbor*

Captain Yamamoto, *her husband*

Sachiko Yamamoto, *their daughter, age sixteen at the time of the bomb*

Yasu Yamamoto, *their son, the same age as Kenichi Hara*

The elder Yamamotos, *Captain Yamamoto's parents, who live in Ujina*

The Kasamas

Mrs. Kasama, *the oldest member of the* Tonarigumi

Colonel Kasama, *her husband*

Tetsuo Kasama, *a man claiming to be the Kasama nephew*

Hanako Kasama, *his wife*

OTHER CHARACTERS

Mr. Takano, *Kenichi's favorite teacher*

Mrs. Takano, *his wife*

Hideo Nakayama, *a shop owner on Miyajima who sells* kokeshi *dolls*

Yuki Sasaki, *Nakayama's nephew*

Morishita-san, *the delivery man and later foreman at Asahi Enterprises*

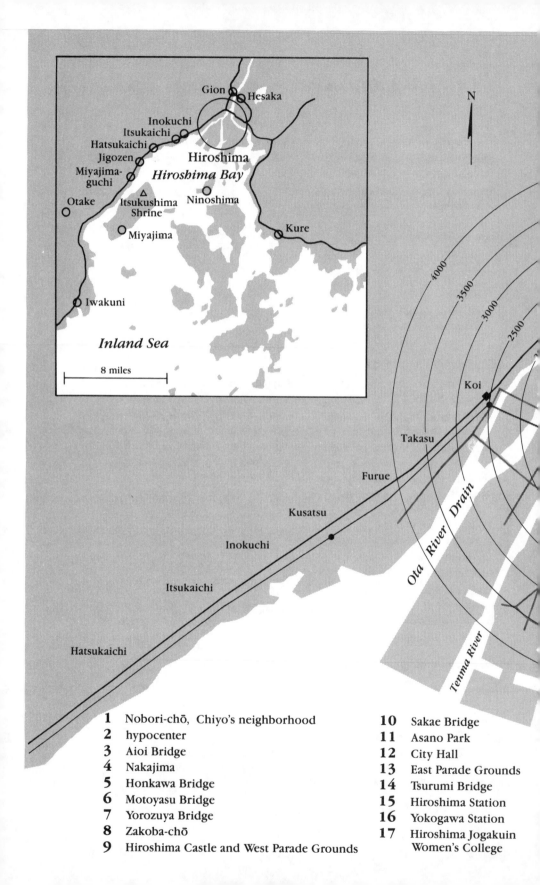

N

Gion
Hesaka
Inokuchi
Itsukaichi
Hatsukaichi
Jigozen
Miyajima-
guchi
Hiroshima
Hiroshima Bay
Otake
Itsukushima
Shrine
Ninoshima
Miyajima
Kure
Iwakuni
Inland Sea
8 miles

Koi
Takasu
Furue
Kusatsu
Inokuchi
Itsukaichi
Hatsukaichi

Ota River Drain
Tenma River

4000
3500
3000
2500

1 Nobori-chō, Chiyo's neighborhood	**10**	Sakae Bridge
2 hypocenter	**11**	Asano Park
3 Aioi Bridge	**12**	City Hall
4 Nakajima	**13**	East Parade Grounds
5 Honkawa Bridge	**14**	Tsurumi Bridge
6 Motoyasu Bridge	**15**	Hiroshima Station
7 Yorozuya Bridge	**16**	Yokogawa Station
8 Zakoba-chō	**17**	Hiroshima Jogakuin
9 Hiroshima Castle and West Parade Grounds		Women's College

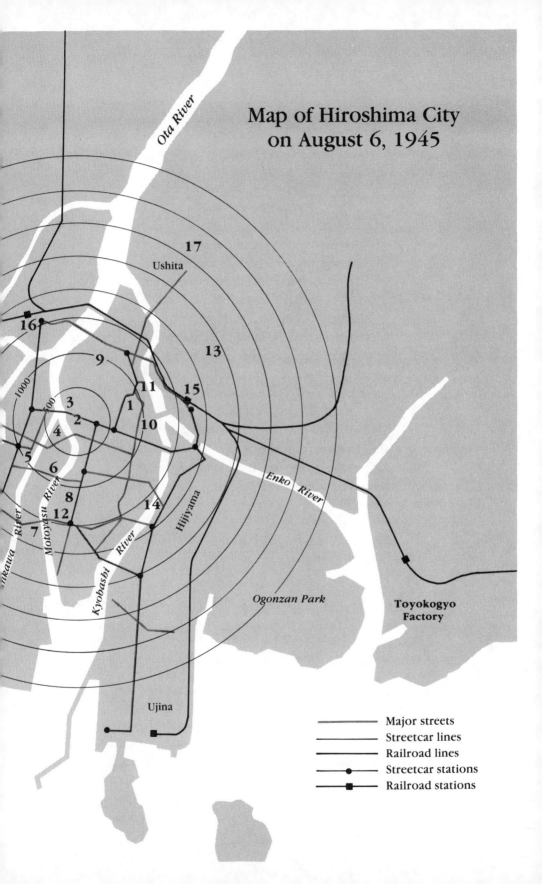

Map of Hiroshima City
on August 6, 1945

Ota River

Ushita

17

16

13

9

11

15

1000

3

500

1

2

10

4

5

6

Motoyasu River

8

14

Hijiyama

12

kawa River

7

Kyobashi River

Enko River

Ogonzan Park

Toyokogyo
Factory

Ujina

Major streets
Streetcar lines
Railroad lines
Streetcar stations
Railroad stations

EXPLANATORY NOTE

In the pronunciation of Japanese words the consonants are read as in English (with the "g" always hard) and the basic vowels (a, e, i, o, u) as in Italian or Spanish. There are no silent letters. However, when any vowel is sandwiched between two aspirated consonants, the vowel is half devoiced. The word "sukiyaki," for instance, is pronounced "skee-YAH-key", and *hibakusha* is "hee-BAHKH-shah".

Except in dialogue, Japanese names are rendered here in the Western order with the given name first and the family name last.

Part One

Chapter One

WAITING FOR DAILY RATIONS OUTSIDE Mrs. Ikeda's porch, Chiyo Hara stiffened her shoulders against the raw March wind that penetrated her cotton blouse and baggy *monpe,* her wartime work trousers. Ten women stood in Mrs. Ikeda's formerly well-groomed tea garden, huddled in clumps of two or three, thin and anxious, their cotton-padded air raid hoods covering their heads and partly obscuring their faces.

"Hara!" Mrs. Ikeda, wife of the Neighborhood Association captain, stood at the edge of the porch calling out the family names, holding up the rations. Two half carrots, a handful of soybeans, a small *daikon* radish, a tiny piece of salted shark. Who could live on that? Especially with the appetite of her teenaged son, Kenichi. She could have eaten the whole portion herself, standing right there, the soybeans raw.

"*Hai,*" Chiyo answered. She bowed, holding out her basket, stared at the pitiful contents plunked down there, then smiled at Mrs. Ikeda, a tiny knot of a person, hard and gnarled at the knuckles like the carrots she was passing out.

The other women stood waiting, their faces expressionless, but the anxiety and exhaustion showing through. The same women,

3

wearing the same baggy *monpe* every day, carrying the same despair. All of them wondering how to get enough to eat, how to keep their families together.

Chiyo decided to make her escape right after the ration distribution. Before Mrs. Ikeda made the day's announcements. There was nothing to depend on but rations. No more secret rice from her brother's acquaintances. And the forages into the country not worth the time and energy. Farmers getting greedier, not even trusting money anymore. Only expensive kimonos and antiques would do.

And now Yoko, her only daughter, being evacuated to her uncle's. All upper-grade schoolchildren had been ordered to go to relatives if they had any and deep into the countryside with their teachers and classmates if they didn't.

"Send her out here immediately before they change their minds," Chiyo's brother, Isao, had warned. "They might decide tomorrow that nobody can leave at all."

First her youngest son, Hiroshi. Gone a year ago. Now her daughter Yoko's turn. And next—

She was lucky having a brother who lived in the suburbs. Mrs. Ikeda's country relatives were stingy and small-minded. "I'd much rather have my Kyoko out in a temple with her teacher than with those terrible relatives," she'd said. "But anyway we don't have to choose because they haven't invited her."

Chiyo felt guilty when she thought of her own generous family. But everyone in the neighborhood had someone to help. A relative in the country, a soldier quartered in the household who turned over his rations, a husband with a government position like Mrs. Ikeda's.

"Kasama!" Mrs. Ikeda called out.

There was one without any blessings. Old, retired Colonel Kasama, Kenichi's ethics teacher, mobilized to teach because he was too old for the army. But staunchly loyal to the emperor and the army's rules, refusing every offer of extra food. If they couldn't live on the rations the government gave them, he said, they should all die. It was traitorous to buy food on the black market, he said. The soldiers needed it to fight the war.

Chiyo watched Mrs. Kasama's tired, drawn face when she went forward with her basket and bowed, graciously receiving her bounty. That face had once been serene and smooth under the cloud of white hair she bore with such dignity. It was hard for the rest of them to watch her, hard not to give her some of their own portion, knowing how she had to struggle to feed the colonel without letting

4

him know how she'd done it. Did he ever loosen up from that stiff military bearing of his? Even in bed?

Why was everyone staring at her now instead of at Mrs. Kasama? Had she said all that out loud? No, they were looking at her carrots, comparing them with Mrs. Kasama's. Exactly equal. Mrs. Ikeda did a good job dividing them up.

Now their attention was on Mrs. Yamamoto, the last person on the list. Then it was over.

"Oh!" Chiyo exclaimed. "The embers in my hibachi. I forgot to check them before I came down here. And Yoko to pack."

"You're lucky," said Mrs. Ikeda. "Having a generous relative in the country."

Chiyo waited for Mrs. Ikeda's familiar harangue, complaining that the Ikedas were worse off than the rest of them. Actually Mrs. Ikeda really was worse off. Not just because of her daughter being evacuated to the temple. There were her two sons in the army, the youngest somewhere in the South Seas and no letters for months. And her parents-in-law living with them. And a grandchild. And the daughter-in-law pregnant again and her husband, their eldest son, a pilot in the Kamikaze Corps. Nobody even dared talk about that.

Lately, they'd hardly dared talk about anything. The Americans were coming closer and the official explanations getting flimsier. She'd hardly noticed the first defeats at Coral Sea and Midway in 1943. Then Guadalcanal two years ago. Saipan and Guam last year. Manila this year in February. And just a few days ago, the Imperial Army on Iwo Jima almost annihilated. The commanding general had asked his few remaining soldiers to fight until the last man, then committed suicide. Okinawa was next. The Imperial Navy had declared they would defend it to the death. After that was Japan itself. And who would defend Japan to the death? Already, they said, Tokyo had been obliterated by the B-29s. Osaka was a pile of rubble. Nagoya and Kobe were next. Then . . .

"Yes, we are lucky," Chiyo breathed, interrupting Mrs. Ikeda's complaints. "But I must go."

She bowed again, not even looking at Mrs. Yamamoto, her closest friend and neighbor. They knew she didn't have any burning embers. Nobody had even seen a piece of charcoal in the last year, and the cow dung they were using for fuel hardly made embers.

Never mind. Everybody took turns escaping. She was entitled to it once in a while. And Mrs. Yamamoto would tell her later what went on.

Just beyond the gate, out of sight, Chiyo grabbed the fence, steadying herself against a sudden spell of dizziness, faintness from hunger. A dazzling vision of cherry blossoms loomed before her, their fragrance enveloping her. They were the cherry blossoms of her youth, stretching along the banks of the wide, lazy Ota, the source of Hiroshima's seven rivers, which branched out like fingers flowing through the fan-shaped breadth of Hiroshima on its way to the Inland Sea.

Chiyo had walked along those banks every spring with her parents and brother, Isao, the perfume of the blossoms mingling with the fresh sea breeze coming up from the river. Or they had gone on picnics up on the hill, Hijiyama, to the southeast, where they would sit under the blanket of white blossoms formed by the trees and gaze at the city stretched below them, counting the rivers — the Enko behind them, the Kyobashi just below them, then a wide stretch of land to the Motoyasu, which flowed on one side of Naka-jima, where Grandmother lived, the Honkawa on the other side, the Tenma beyond that, and finally, farthest away, the Ota River drain that entered the sea just above her native place, Inokuchi.

The rivers were silver under the sun, coursing their way past the tiled roofs of the houses and the few tall landmarks, the castle on the hill to the north, the stately Gothic tower of Nagarekawa Church in Nobori-chō near Chiyo's present house, the railroad station on the east bank of the Enko. And along the streetcar tracks in the main part of town, the proud eight-story Fukuya Department Store that stood like a prince among the other concrete bank buildings, the Shimomura watchtower on the Hondori shopping street, the Chamber of Commerce by Aioi Bridge, the huge Western-style Industry Promotion Hall with its turrets and domes.

Her dizziness was gone. What if the others came through the gate just now and found her here, clutching the end of the fence, showing her weakness and lack of restraint?

She let go of the fence, shifted the weight of her basket and took two steps forward to test her steadiness, trying not to think about the past. They would have cherry blossoms in abundance again this spring. But no food. No clams either. Everyone searching for them along the beach and the riverbanks. And no fish. Even if they caught one they were supposed to give it to the army.

She walked slowly past the Miyamotos' tiny stationery shop, past the massive, clipped hedge that held the snobbish Ishibashi family aloof from the rest of them, toward the Kasamas' modest house across the street from her own. But afraid of meeting old, wiry

Colonel Kasama, she crossed the street and passed in front of the house of her next-door neighbors, the Yamamotos.

The memories lingered. Spring fragrances and the fresh smells of Hiroshima's seven rivers. And out in Inokuchi the view of the sparkling Inland Sea with the oyster beds lying out across the horizon in front of the house which had belonged to her great-great-grandfather and now belonged to her brother, Isao.

They would swim out from the shore on long summer afternoons to Miyojin, the tiny island with the lonely pine tree on top which always stood, beckoning to them, just a few meters beyond the house.

Once Isao had caught an octopus, digging his hand through a hole just above the water on the island. He pulled it out, squirming and alive, with its arms clutching up toward his elbow. They both ran screaming toward the kitchen door, and their mother, shrieking, called to their grandfather. He knew what to do. He took it back to the shore and killed it, and they ate it afterwards for weeks.

Fresh octopus. And *asari,* the short-necked clams they dug in Inokuchi and along the riverbank in Hiroshima near the Girls' School.

She smiled. Really, it was the food that made her nostalgic, not the cherry blossoms. The big, beefy mushrooms, the *matsutake* that grew wild and huge under pine trees in the fall. And right after that, the bright orange persimmons they called *kaki,* with stress on the last syllable to distinguish them from *kaki,* the fat, juicy oysters.

In Hiroshima, autumn was best; that was when its two famous products, both kinds of *kaki,* were in season.

Almost at her front gate now.

She tried hard to remember the taste of a fresh oyster, even a dried persimmon. Isao and his delicate, well-bred wife, Kazuko, carefully guarded the tree in their garden and dried the harvest for special gifts.

Or rice. Pure, polished white rice. And crisp green beans and peas, taro root, bamboo shoots. At least with Yoko gone, there would be only two to feed, and she didn't have to eat much herself, just enough for energy to search for food, sew clothes for the army, help with the other endless tasks of the Neighborhood Association. It wasn't like the heavy work Kenichi was doing, tearing down buildings to make a fire lane for when the bombs came. Nothing they did took as much energy as that, not even the *takeyari* practice they had to do, defending themselves with flimsy bamboo swords. She flinched at the vision of herself stabbing a red-haired American giant. No matter how terrible the Americans were, she would rather take her chances surrendering. Better than the constant, hopeless foraging for food, the screaming air raid sirens, and the stream of B-29s passing overhead every night while they waited for the bombs which did not drop, constantly waiting for Hiroshima's turn to come. And wondering when Kenichi would go into the army. Boys only fourteen were lying about their age and running off to join the kamikaze pilots, which meant certain death. And defending their homeland with bamboo swords, which also meant certain death. Why not surrender? At least her husband might come home and end his long, gnawing silence.

Once inside, she stepped out of her *geta,* her wooden sandals, onto the sitting room, which was covered with *tatami,* the thick straw mats they used for sitting and sleeping. Then she walked back to the kitchen and out to the storehouse, cold and musty and half dark in the late afternoon. She lifted the lid of the huge pickle barrel and saw the last yellow radish floating on top. Better save it for Kenichi's lunches. She could slice it thin to go with barley rice and make it last at least another week. What she needed now was bulk. The secret rice buried under the floor in the living room for serious emergencies? She couldn't justify that. But peering into the box where the sweet potatoes had been, she discovered two round shapes wrapped in wilted leaves. How could she have missed them before? Kenichi, of course. He had kept the potatoes hidden somewhere all this time, saving them for Yoko's special dinner, then slipped them into the box before he went to school.

She put one of them back. One tonight for dinner. The other for some future desperate time.

Inside again, she saw a shadow out beyond the *genkan,* her entranceway.

Yoko home from school already? The door opened, harshly jangling the bell.

"*Gomen kudasai!*" Their old postman, long past retirement, was still going his rounds in worn khaki work clothes, his old leather bag strapped on to the rack of his bicycle. He was waving a letter.

She held her breath. "Not now," she prayed. "Not while I'm at home alone."

She bent forward, her knees unsteady, then knelt on the edge of the *tatami*.

"From China," the postman said pleasantly. "Must be your husband." He looked at her hands folded tensely in her lap.

"It's not an official army letter," he said gently. "See? It's in his handwriting." He had delivered letters in the neighborhood all his life and had known Shintaro as a child.

She took the letter, not at all sure it was his handwriting. He had died, she decided, and they had cremated him and buried his ashes on a lonely hill in China.

"Thank you," she breathed.

He grinned and bowed, then withdrew, jangling the bell of his bicycle in noisy retreat.

His shadow disappeared beyond the *genkan*. She stared back into the house, trying to decide where she should read the letter. The small sitting room? The kitchen and bathroom behind it? The room across the hall from the sitting room where they slept, or the formal guest room beyond that?

She looked again at the envelope. Bold brush strokes made with charcoal ink. The address, then the family name HARA in one large character, then her name and each of the children's. He'd written each name with tender care, expressing his longing for them.

Sitting on the edge of the *tatami* with the *shōji* doors open, letting in the cold air of the *genkan,* she opened the letter. The paper inside was light and thin. Two pages.

> Greetings. I have neglected writing you for some time now, only falling asleep exhausted every night. But today is New Year's Day, and we have declared ourselves a holiday. We are in the dead of winter here, always inside, but at least there is time to write. I imagine that when you get this, the plum blossoms in Hiroshima will have faded and perhaps the cherry trees will be blossoming.

Chiyo's spirits sagged. January. It wasn't going to be recent news.

> Here, of course, there is no possibility that anything could bloom until June. It is much colder than in Japan, and there is not even a hint of the coming spring.

Kenichi would spend hours reading the letter and looking at the map, deciding where his father was stationed. Kenichi listened to all the war news on the radio, read all the announcements and notices tacked on public walls, plotted where the Fifth Army was, the Second, the Ninth, the Kwantung.

> Don't worry about me. I have been working hard, but am quite healthy. Continue your good work at home. Tell the children to study hard. We will fight until victory comes. Then I will return to you and Kenichi and Yoko and Hiroshi.

Quite healthy? What did he mean by that? Why hadn't he just said "healthy"?

It didn't mean anything. She wasn't going to worry over every word.

> I wish I could see how the children have grown. I am keeping track of their ages. Kenichi will soon be thirteen. Yoko is eleven, and Hiroshi is eight. Correct me if I'm mistaken.
> Has Ken-chan taken the entrance exam to Rijo Middle School yet? Tell me his score as soon as you know, and tell him to give all his attention to his studies.

That was disappointing. She had written twice, telling about Kenichi's success. He had taken the second highest mark in the entrance exam. They were all proud of him, but it was his father's praise Kenichi was waiting for.

Shintaro would be surprised if he knew the students studied only on Sundays and the rest of the time did their demolition work, tearing down houses to create fire lanes.

> Tell Yoko-chan that everyone says there will be *hagi* flowers, the purple daisies, blooming here in the spring, the kind they make incense from in Japan. Does Yoko still make necklaces from them when you go to the island?

Did Shintaro think they had even a moment to go out to the island nowadays?

> And tell Hiroshi that I have found a special Chinese toy to give him when I return home.

She laughed. Hiroshi considered himself an adult. Beyond toys. But secretly, he would be excited.

> And as for you, my wife, remember that I think of you and the children, always, during all my waking hours and in my dreams when I sleep. I am praying for the day when I can come home. My nostalgia is boundless.
>
> To my beloved wife and children
> Hara Shintaro
> the year of our Emperor, Showa 20
> 1st month, 1st day

The tears flowed down her cheeks, his presence so strong that she ached for him, her loneliness boundless and intolerable. That last part. He'd managed to get all of it through the censors, who hated sentiment. They wanted machines for soldiers, not human beings. And machines for soldiers' wives.

She was reading through a haze of tears when Yoko appeared.

"*Tadaima!*" Tiny, compact Yoko. Her energy and eagerness intense like a bullet. What would she be like if she had all the nourishment she needed?

She stepped out of her shoes and climbed onto the *tatami*. "What's that?" she demanded. "From Father?" She saw her mother's face, wet with tears. "He's all right, isn't he?"

Chiyo nodded; then Kenichi arrived.

"It's a letter from Father," Yoko shouted. She took it from Chiyo and held it close.

Kenichi stood a moment on the dirt floor of the *genkan* and grinned at them. The half-open door let in the faint light of the late afternoon sun which shone behind him. His arms extended beyond the sleeves of his worn student-soldier tunic, but the Rijo Middle School cap he wore proudly over his nearly shaved head was new.

Yoko reluctantly surrendered the letter to him, and he turned it over, feeling its thickness, pressing it to his forehead, looking carefully at the calligraphy.

"Father's beautiful handwriting," he said.

Shintaro had taught Chinese literature and calligraphy at Rijo Middle School. Chiyo was always praising his brushwork to the children.

"Read it out loud to us," Yoko demanded.

In the kitchen, cajoling the flame to cook their dinner, Chiyo thought of Shintaro's military quarters. On a hill overlooking a Chinese village, he had written. In spite of Kenichi's efforts, they couldn't really tell where he was. The first letter had referred to some sort of headquarters. Manchuria, Kenichi decided. But in a later letter, he said he was moving south with a company of men. He told them about a sheet of ice on the road shining like silver under the sun, a tall mountain that looked exactly like a painting by the Japanese artist Sesshu, who had been in China hundreds of years ago. In the next letter he mentioned the view of the sunset across the hills and the flowers blossoming in the valley.

She liked to imagine him sitting up late at night, writing a letter to his beloved family, a candle lighting his serene and classic face, accenting his high cheekbones and casting a shadow of his chiseled profile against the wall.

She had married him for his classic face and his bearing. Her family had given her only two pictures to choose from. One was of a man in a dark, Western-style suit, looking too proud and self-assured. Chiyo had refused him after the first meeting. But Shintaro. His picture showed him wearing a traditional Japanese kimono with *hakama,* the formal samurai-style skirt, and his grandfather's sword, trying to look taller and older than he was. There was something about his eyes.

She had come to love him for his poetry, for that sense in him of suppressed hunger never quite satisfied, and for his inexhaustible store of curiosity and desire. Now he was in that distant, foreign place, enduring fear, hunger, cold, who knows what else? If she could appear one night, unannounced, touch his shoulder, divert his attention from the candlelight. She would reach her arms around his shoulders and press his cheek to hers, pull him down. They wouldn't even talk.

"Mama!" Yoko called, then drew in a sharp breath. "Can't I wait until the cherry blossoms come out? Just at least until then? I don't want to go, Mama. Please." Yoko held her breath, biting on her lip. She was small for her age, but explosive. Thick bobbed hair, silken and shining in spite of her poor diet. And a delicate but rounded face, all eagerness, openness, and honesty. She said things directly. At age eleven she was not interested in nuance.

"We have to do what the government tells us," Chiyo said gently. "You don't want to leave after all the other children have gone, do you?"

"Why can't we all go to Inokuchi, then? Or why can't I go with Ikeda Kyoko?"

"You're closer to home if you go to Inokuchi."

Yoko was at the point of tears. "At least until the cherry trees bloom," she said. "Please."

Chiyo climbed onto the *tatami* and pulled her daughter into her arms. "All right, then," she said. "Until the tree in the garden blooms. Or until the other children go out to the temple. Whichever comes first." She pressed Yoko's head against her shoulder and looked up at Kenichi. "Take the kitchen knife out to the storehouse and cut off half the *daikon* in the barrel. We're having a special dinner for Yoko tonight."

She and Kenichi stared at each other over Yoko's head.

"I found a surprise out there today," she said. "Two beautiful sweet potatoes appeared out of nowhere."

He grinned, then went out to the kitchen to find the knife.

Chapter Two

THE CHERRY BLOSSOMS CAME AND WENT unnoticed. Everyone's attention was on stretching the food, mending the clothes, getting snatches of sleep between air raid sirens. At the end of April, a single B-29 dropped an incendiary bomb in downtown Otemachi, killing eleven people and bringing new urgency to plans for the children's evacuation.

"It's only the beginning," breathed Mrs. Yamamoto, walking home from ration distribution. She turned toward Chiyo with her usual tragic expression. Chiyo was accustomed to that look and to the gaunt, tall presence of Mrs. Yamamoto, whose face sometimes startled people who didn't know her. But at any moment she could break into laughter, revealing the gold tooth in her mouth. Chiyo loved her for those unexpected bursts and for the bright flash of gold that came with them.

But there was no hint of laughter in Mrs. Yamamoto's voice today. "I'm thinking of moving out to my in-laws in Ujina," she continued. "Only it's probably worse out there, being a port. I don't know. Inokuchi's safe, though. Why don't you go out to your brother's?"

"I think about it," said Chiyo, "but I just—Hiroshima isn't

much of a military city, you know. Why would they waste any bombs on us?"

Her brother, Isao, stopped briefly on his way home from the Toyokogyō factory near the port of Ujina where he worked as an engineer. Before the war he had designed heavy machinery, three-wheeled trucks, and for one glorious period in 1939, a Ford-like passenger car. Now they were making guns, under military orders.

"Don't wait until the rest of the school evacuates," Isao said. "Send Yoko now. The sooner she gets used to things in Inokuchi, the better."

"We'll bring her this weekend," Chiyo said.

"Send her tomorrow. I've made arrangements for her to enter school immediately. Postponing it will only make it harder."

He was sinewy like an electric wire and much thinner than Shintaro. He sat before her now, his legs bent under him and his hands on his knees in formal position, back straight, neck erect.

"Tomorrow morning," he urged. "Pack her things later. And come yourself with Kenichi as soon as you can. You're sitting on a tinderbox."

"Yoko has to have another day in school to say goodbye, at least," Chiyo protested. "And Kenichi, you know, he's only just entered Rijo Middle School. He can't stop now. He worked so hard on the entrance exam."

"Then he can take the streetcar in. At least he'll be safe at night. Being alive is more important than being in the right school, isn't it?"

Chiyo stared at her lap. "They always give us air raid warnings," she said, "and there's the shelter just down the street."

He gave his attention to the barley tea she had served him.

She lifted her head and looked at her firm and decisive elder brother. It was difficult to disagree with him. "I'm just not ready to abandon my husband's house yet," she said. "Even if I weren't considering what Kenichi wants."

Isao nodded. "I know. But you may have to do it, so be ready. We'll expect Yoko in two days."

Yoko looked small and vulnerable on the Hiroshima station platform. Her navy middy blouse and trousers moved in the breeze created by a departing troop train. Then her own train lumbered into the station, and Yoko bowed to Chiyo, then to Kenichi, then to Kenichi's best friend, Yasutaka Yamamoto, whom they called Yasu for short, or sometimes Ya-chan. Kyoko Ikeda had cried so hard the night before that her mother wouldn't let her go to the station and risk another tearful farewell.

"It won't be for long," Chiyo said.

Yoko's lips were quivering.

Kenichi pushed his way onto the train and stuck his head out a moment later. "Found a window seat!" he shouted. Chiyo and Yasu pushed Yoko forward through the door and handed the luggage up through the window.

Yoko's head was sticking out when the train pulled way. Chiyo warned the children against doing that. She motioned frantically to Yoko, but it was no use. Finally, when her tiny head was just a speck in the distance, she pulled it in.

Chiyo saw the soldier when she turned to go. He was sitting on the platform in a wheelchair, dressed in white, one leg resting on a foot board, the other tucked under him. No, it was gone. Amputated.

She turned away. Every wounded soldier looked like Shintaro. They'd sent this one home because he was used up and nobody wanted him around anymore.

"Mama!" There was urgency in Kenichi's voice. She forced herself to look at the soldier again. Too young and frail to be Shintaro, of course. But there was something—

Behind him was an even younger army private no older than seventeen, wearing winter-issue khaki with cap and leggings.

"*Oku-sama!*" the private called to her. "Honorable housewife, do you happen to know the whereabouts of the house of Ikeda Yukiji?"

"Who?" she asked, coming closer.

"Ikeda Yukiji," he repeated patiently. "Do you know where his house is?"

Yukiji, the Ikedas' youngest son. Gone off to war so proudly a few years ago.

"It's Ikeda-kun!" Kenichi repeated, still not sure his mother had understood. Kenichi and Yasu stood at attention, saluting Yukiji.

"Welcome home, Private Ikeda," said Yasu, slapping his hand down smartly as he finished the salute.

Chiyo knelt in front of Yukiji's wheelchair. "Ikeda-kun," she said. "Is it really you?"

He stared at her, his face stiff. The white military kimono encased him like steel armor. For a moment, Chiyo was afraid he wouldn't recognize her. He had been a little boy like Hiroshi so recently, but now maybe he had lost his memory as well as his leg.

He looked at her with deep concentration. Then his muscles relaxed. *"Oku-sama!"* he exclaimed. "The wife of teacher Hara!"

Something of Yukiji, the child, touched his face.

"Yuki-chan," she said, using his childhood name. "Does your mother know that you're coming?"

"I wrote her," he said. "Let's see now. I don't— Well, I can't remember."

His eyes misted over.

She looked at the young private. "I'll show you where he lives," she said. "I'm going there now. Ken-chan, you and Ya-chan have to get to school. I'll take him home the other way."

"I have orders to deliver him to his family and then return immediately to my duties at headquarters," the private interrupted. "If you can give me directions, that will be sufficient. You needn't accompany me."

"I will go with you," she said firmly. "He lives just down the street."

Officious young recruit. She kept far enough ahead so that he had no choice but to follow, then wondered whether she should run ahead and warn Mrs. Ikeda.

Instead, she slowed her pace to keep even with Yukiji. "When did you arrive back in Japan, Yuki-chan?" They were going toward Sakae Bridge, which led down the street past her house to the Ikedas'.

"Well, I came on a hospital ship," he pondered, looking puzzled. "I don't know how long we . . . it's strange how everything . . . it's hard to remember."

"You came two weeks ago," the private told him, keeping his voice official but with an edge to it, as if he had told Yukiji many times before.

"Oh, really?" Yukiji twisted his neck nervously to look back at him. Chiyo still wasn't sure how Yukiji's mind was. Maybe just fuzzy from drugs.

"Aren't you going to ask me how I lost my leg?" Yukiji demanded. It was his child's voice again. She looked at the private for a clue, but he stared straight ahead.

She leaned toward Yukiji, speaking softly. "Well, shouldn't we wait until your mother can hear it, too? You don't want to tell it all twice, do you?"

They stepped off the bridge into the street, passed the greengrocer's, the vacant lot next to his shop, the Kasamas' and Chiyo's house across the street. Chiyo spotted the unmistakable shape of Mrs. Yamamoto, who had emerged from her door and was doggedly plodding along on her old wooden *geta* toward the neighborhood meeting at the greengrocer's house.

"*Oku-sama!*" Chiyo called. "Look, here's Yuki-chan home from the war. I've just found him at the station. Could you go and tell his mother so she can get ready?"

"Ikeda-kun!" Mrs. Yamamoto gasped, catching a glimpse of the stump. "I'll tell Mrs. Ikeda right away." She turned abruptly and headed in the other direction.

The Ikeda family was waiting at the *genkan* when the home-coming soldier arrived. Tiny Mrs. Ikeda stared, with tight-lipped ferocity, at Yukiji's face, not even looking to where his leg had been. Yukiji's grandparents leaned over their canes and peered out, resembling the old man and woman of the folktales.

At their feet, almost crawling off the edge of the *tatami,* was Yukiji's nephew.

Great-grandfather, leaning on his cane, caught the baby at the back of the diapers and grabbed him up, hugging him and pointing to Yukiji.

"See, here's your Uncle Yukiji coming."

"I'm so glad," Mrs. Ikeda breathed, wiping a tear away with her apron. "Our Yukiji home."

The private pushed the wheelchair over the threshold onto the dirt floor of the *genkan,* and Mrs. Ikeda moved forward, ready to touch her son, but instead wiped her hands again and again on her apron.

"Your younger sister's at school. She's being evacuated to the country, but now that you're home, she'll get to see you before she leaves." She looked at him anxiously. He hadn't said anything yet. "Your sister-in-law is at the air raid drill." She paused again, waiting for a reaction. "And your father," she added. "He'll be—" She took another deep breath. "Surprised."

"I am Private Tanaka Yutaka of the Fifteenth Artillery Division of the Second Army," the soldier declared. "And I have been charged with the duty of accompanying Sergeant Ikeda and his belongings to his house, where he has been ordered to recuperate from his injury until further notice."

So. Yukiji had become a sergeant. That was something.

The boy soldier snapped the heels of his army-issue boots together and saluted Mrs. Ikeda as if she were a military officer. Then he handed her a large brown envelope full of papers. "Here are the details of his injury and the doctor's reports."

"Wait," Chiyo said. "How are we going to get him up into the house?"

Private Tanaka stood wavering, not sure what his duty was. Finally Grandfather and Private Tanaka lifted the chair from behind while Chiyo and Mrs. Ikeda pulled from the front.

Yukiji was ecstatic, wheeling his chair around in circles. Chiyo winced, watching the wheels, dirtied by the street, pressing against Mrs. Ikeda's pristine *tatami*.

"Everything's the same!" Yukiji shouted.

His mother sighed with relief and smiled. "You're the same, too, Yuki-chan!"

Yukiji beamed at her, then at his young nephew.

Chiyo felt better. Soon they would outfit him with an artificial leg and he could walk.

She and Mrs. Ikeda followed the private outside, bowing and thanking him. "All of our good fortune is due to you," said Mrs. Ikeda. "We will never forget your kindness. We will be forever in your debt."

Standing at the gate, Chiyo felt a sudden urge to go back and ask Yukiji if, just by chance, he had seen Shintaro somewhere in China. But not yet. A foolish question anyway. Still, she would ask him sometime just to satisfy herself.

She bowed to Mrs. Ikeda. "Congratulations, *Oku-sama!* For having him home safe and alive."

"*Okage-sama de,*" Mrs. Ikeda said, bowing back. "It is all on account of you and the shadow of the Buddha that we have been so fortunate."

"Not so," said Chiyo. "I just happened to be at the station seeing Yoko off."

"*Oku-sama!*" Yukiji called. "I have news of your husband."

It was the voice of the grown-up Yukiji, not the child-man hovering on the edge of reality, and it was like ice water freezing around her heart.

Chiyo retraced her steps. "You have news?" she asked. "You've seen him recently?"

"No, not for a long while. But I met somebody who came from the north, and he told me— No! That's not right. He said maybe he'd seen—" Yukiji drew himself up, shaking his head. "No, that wasn't it, either. That was somebody else. Oh, it was *terrible!*" He stared at her, then shifted his attention.

"Mother! Aren't you going to ask me how I lost my leg?"

Mrs. Ikeda scurried over and knelt before his wheelchair.

"Is my husband all right?" Chiyo asked, hoping to divert him. "He's not wounded or dead, is he?"

"Who?" Yukiji asked.

"My husband, Hara-sensei. You said you had news of him?"

His eyes were blank. "Mother, I'm so tired," he said. "And thirsty. Do you have any tea?"

Mrs. Ikeda looked from her son to Chiyo.

"It's all right," said Chiyo. "Let him rest. I can ask him later. I should go now."

Mrs. Ikeda nodded.

Chiyo, perspiring and desperate, stepped quietly out through the gate into the street.

Chapter Three

C HIYO WAITED THREE DAYS BEFORE
going back to see Yukiji. She did not want
to intrude on the family and in any case had to finish her allotment
of soldiers' shirts by the end of the week.

When she finished, she tied them in a heavy cotton *furoshiki,* the
wrapping cloth she used for delivery to Mrs. Ikeda, who collected
and accounted for the neighborhood. Then she searched her closet
for a suitable gift for Yukiji.

On a shelf above the *futon,* their sleeping quilts and mattresses,
she found a stack of Shintaro's calligraphy poems written on thick
white cardboard meant for display in hanging scrolls. Not a practical gift, but Yukiji had been one of Shintaro's best calligraphy students.

She chose Shintaro's favorite, a classical Chinese poem of the Tang
Dynasty about a languid river surrounded by blossoming spring
flowers and reflecting the moon on its way to the sea.

After wrapping the gift in her best silk *furoshiki,* patterned with
white cherry blossoms on a dark rose background, she started down
the street feeling almost lighthearted.

But as she walked through the Ikedas' front gate, her dread returned.

"*Gomen kudasai!*" she called hesitantly, sliding open the door and stepping inside. "Excuse me, but is anyone at home?"

She called again, twice. Finally a small voice floated out from behind the sitting room.

"*Hai.* Ikeda *desu.*"

Was he going to invite her in?

"In here," he finally called.

In one of the back rooms by the garden, Yukiji was lying on a *futon* in the center of the room. He looked wan and disconsolate. Even as a child, he had been thin. And restless, and finicky. But now, perhaps because of inactivity (certainly not an excess of food), he had begun spreading around the middle.

"Did I wake you?" she asked. "I called several times."

"Oh, did you? I didn't hear you." He sat up and hit his ear as if it were a recalcitrant machine. "Maybe I did doze off. It's getting so I can sleep better now. Not so many nightmares. I—"

"Nightmares?" she asked softly.

He looked at her anxious face. "Well, not really nightmares. Just sometimes, you know, dreams keep me awake."

She nodded, thinking of her own dreams about Shintaro. "Where is everybody?"

"Oh, they're out. Grandparents off at the black market searching for something to eat. And Mother's somewhere, you know, with the *Tonarigumi* business." He sighed, then looked up, beaming his sunlit childhood smile.

"You're looking much better," she told him.

He sat up. "Here, hand me that *tanzen,*" he said, pointing to the padded winter robe hanging on a hook on the wall. "I'll put it over my shoulders. It's a bit chilly."

She brought it to him, then knelt, making her ceremonial bow, and offered him the *shikishi* calligraphy, pleased when she saw him gaze at it with such delight.

"How wonderful, *Oku-sama,* but you'll want it yourself, won't you? These things are so precious."

"No, my husband has written several copies of this poem, and I'm sure he'd want you to have one. It's one of his favorites." She hoped the mention of Shintaro would remind Yukiji, but he seemed lost in the past, gazing at the dark, bold calligraphy strokes. "Hara-sensei taught us that poem our first year in middle school," he said.

He read the poem aloud in *kanbun,* the Japanese-style pronunciation of classical Chinese.

"I'm glad you like it," Chiyo said. "I know my husband would be pleased." She paused before continuing. "You were on the same ship with him going overseas, weren't you? I remember when you wrote your mother. Was that the last time you saw him?"

He looked at her sharply.

"Yes, at least two years ago. I didn't see him again. We were separated as soon as we got off the ship."

"But you told me you met somebody who might have known him."

He tucked his hands inside the sleeves of his *tanzen*. "It's getting warmer now," he said.

She waited expectantly, but he only stared at his blanket.

"Why don't I make you some tea?" she suggested.

"No, not just yet. Grandmother will be back soon, and she enjoys making it. First, I must tell you—Oh!" His back stiffened and he sat upright.

"What's the matter? Can I get you some medicine? Didn't they give you something for the pain?"

"No." He caught his breath and held it, feeling along his back with his left hand. "I guess it's gone now. They did give me some medicine for it, but I don't like to take it much, you know. I always feel groggy afterwards and kind of helpless."

His mind was all right, then.

"Yuki-chan," she said, calling him by his boyhood name. "When you were a little boy I watched you chasing dragonflies along the riverbank. In those days, every time you scratched your knee, you came and told me about it. And now you've come home from the war—"

"With my leg blown off!" he shouted. "Blown off!"

"Yes," Chiyo said. "Blown off. Tell me how it happened."

"I think I'll lie down."

She rearranged the pillow behind his head. "Would you like to go back to sleep?" she asked.

"No! I have to tell you—" He seemed compelled to talk. He turned his head on the pillow and gazed plaintively at her.

"There was a land mine," he began, "and it blew up right in front of us. We were in Burma. Americans and Chinese were following us, and the British were up ahead. We were always moving, pushing through the jungle, and it was so hot and steamy and sweaty, *Oba-chan*."

He had switched to the familiar title, *Oba-chan,* Aunty, the name he'd called her through childhood. "And then one night, after we'd been marching for maybe twelve or thirteen hours, we found a cool campsite. It was flat and had grassy ground with trees all around and even a breeze floating toward us through the palms. It made us feel so safe, *Oba-chan*. The Americans were very far behind, the British way ahead. And we were so tired. We even built a fire and then sat around it and sang the national anthem."

Chiyo saw a tear tracing down Yukiji's cheek. She looked at her lap again so he could wipe it away without her seeing him.

"And we were eating meat. For the first time in months. It was monkey meat. One of the men said he shot it when he was bringing up the rear flank.

"You know, *Oba-chan*," he said, "I don't think it was monkey meat. I think it was—" His lips quivered. "I need some air," he gasped. "It's so stifling here, all of a sudden."

Chiyo slid open the doors to the garden, letting in the sun and a view of blue irises.

"Everybody was sick and hungry. We had been retreating, marching for so many days. All of us muddy and no way to get clean. Everyone was dreaming of a hot *ofuro* to sink into, up to the neck, soaking out the pain. A Japanese bath is such a miracle, isn't it?"

She nodded. "And so what happened next? You were telling me about your leg."

He looked puzzled.

"You said it was a land mine."

"Oh. That's right. We were sitting around the fire eating that —*monkey meat!* Then one of the men thought he heard a noise, so he went over to investigate and—well, just beyond the campfire, just a few meters away from me he—he stepped on a land mine. That's why the campsite was so comfortable, you see. The British had lured us there. It was a trap."

He shook his head, remembering. "After that, the sky lit up. And everyone was floating in the air. It was like, you know, like we had all the time in the world, and—it was so strange—I could see— Everything was absolutely clear. All the scruffy, ugly faces and their shaggy beards. Like a magnifying glass, *Oba-chan*. Even their muddy uniforms and their skinny arms. Their mosquito bites —and—well, everybody just smiled at me. Bright, angelic smiles. As if they were about to tell me something secret and beautiful. We were just hanging there in the air, looking at each other and looking down at the trees.

"Then when we came down to the ground again, nobody was whole. My foot was gone. But the others—" He looked away.

"They didn't have faces or ears, or they were broken in half, or—

"I don't know why I'm the only one left, *Oba-chan*. I didn't do anything to keep myself from dying, but I didn't try to kill myself either. I just—"

"Of course not," Chiyo said. "Of course you would have acted honorably, and in the service of your emperor."

He did not hear her. He went on talking, telling her how he had awakened in the dark under the moon, lying on the bed of a truck, then heard a skirmish up front, more shooting and running, but his leg hurt so badly that he couldn't push himself up to look. The bodies were all around him on the truck, most of them dead, but some, he thought, still alive.

His commanding officer, Lieutenant Okata, pulled him and some others off the truck and whispered for them to run. The Americans had attacked from the rear. "Only a few jumped off. And I lost track of everybody because my foot was gone. I kept stumbling and falling in the bushes. But when I saw the lieutenant I got up and ran away, just on the stump. I was afraid he'd leave me behind.

"I don't remember anything after that, except we got to the coast. The lieutenant must have carried me part of the way. We found a navy hospital ship going to Singapore.

"Then the doctors discovered gangrene. So they put me to sleep and cut off my leg just above the knee." He stared hard at Chiyo.

"The lieutenant was there. He was standing next to my cot just before the operation, but when I woke up he was dead, *Oba-chan*. He was stronger and healthier than I was, and he saved me, and then he died. I'm the only one left of all those men, and I didn't do anything brave and I didn't die for my country and I'm no good to anybody anymore. I didn't deserve to be sent home alive. But the ship was coming anyway, so they just left me on it. They knew I couldn't fight anymore. And now I'm nothing but a shame to my family."

"Yuki-chan," Chiyo said, taking his hand. "You are *not* a shame to your family. Or anyone else. We are proud of you. Whatever you did in that jungle, and afterwards, even if you don't remember it all, was very brave. Otherwise you wouldn't have survived. What will happen to Japan if all the young men die? There are so few of you, and you are so precious. We need you at home. Never, never say that we are ashamed of you. We are proud of you. It is far braver to survive than to die."

She placed his hand carefully on his chest, rubbing it gently. He had closed his eyes and seemed to be dozing off. She waited, hoping he would wake and talk about Shintaro. But it was no use. He'd shared enough bad memories for one day.

"Yuki-chan, I've made you tired. You need lots of sleep to grow strong again. I'll let you rest now, but I'll come back and visit soon."

His eyes fluttered open a moment. "All right, *Oba-chan*. Thank you for bringing me the *shikishi*."

She went to see Yukiji the next day and the next, but even when she was alone with him, he wanted to talk only about his school days and his childhood. And so she sat next to him, patiently looking at his old photograph book.

Early May. Standing before the Ikeda porch, they could see the sprouting of new green leaves on the tips of trees in Asano Park to the north and on the Hijiyama hill to the south. Then in the midst of the freshness and the balmy days, the radio informed them of the death of Hitler and, two days later, of the fall of Berlin.

If Shintaro were home, Chiyo thought, he would suggest to someone somewhere that this particular moment, with the enemy victorious in Europe, was a good time to ask for peace. She wondered if anyone in Tokyo was thinking of that.

Crowds of khaki-clad soldiers appeared. Privates, colonels, generals, all busily moving about on foot, on horseback, in army transport trucks, or crowding onto streetcars, all of them either very young or very old. And ill-equipped. They were wearing faded, threadbare uniforms that didn't fit.

The Second Army had moved its headquarters to Hiroshima, Mrs. Ikeda said. She heard all the rumors at City Hall from her husband and repeated them at neighborhood meetings, increasing the anxiety.

On May 8 Germany surrendered unconditionally, and soon after the Americans warned that if Japan did not surrender unconditionally, destruction would rain down upon them.

"With the Second Army here, Hiroshima is a prime target now," Mrs. Ikeda said.

Chiyo realized that she didn't mind being a prime target as much as she minded not knowing about Shintaro. Almost a month now since Yukiji had come home, and still he had not told her.

Every day, she trudged doggedly down to the Ikedas, taking small gifts each time. Tiny rice balls of rice-substitute barley, a piece of the last dried persimmon, a slice of *daikon* pickle.

When the *Tonarigumi* gave out a larger-than-usual ration of sweet potatoes, she boiled one, slicing off a few pieces, arranging them on a plate as if they were tea cakes. On impulse, she brought along one of her own books of photographs. She was getting tired of examining his.

Yukiji exclaimed over the sweet potato slices, which he ate with his tea.

"We didn't have much food in the army, you know, but it's even worse here at home. I never believed sweet potatoes could be this delicious!"

He leafed through the photographs. "*Oba-chan,* look at this! Here we are by the river on a picnic. All that wonderful sushi— *makizushi* wrapped in seaweed with those cool cucumbers inside, and the *tekkamaki* with raw tuna, and *inarizushi* stuffed into the fried tofu shells, and—" He looked up at her. "No, let's not remember the food," he said. "There were other good things, too. We always sang and danced on those picnics. Remember Ken-chan that day? He was so small, and he wandered off and almost fell in the river."

Yes, Chiyo remembered that sunlit spring day and Kenichi, her only child then, sitting beside her, gnawing on a huge rice ball. But the next moment he was on top of the riverbank, his clean shirt dangling out of his tiny shorts. He had squatted down to examine a bug. His summer hat was strapped firmly under his chin, making a dark profile of his face. He hadn't quite mastered the art of walking, and he lurched toward the river when he stood up. Chiyo had jumped up and run forward, shouting, but Yukiji had gotten there first and caught Kenichi just in time.

She laughed, remembering. "Yes, so many things. It was good to have you always an older brother to Ken-chan."

They turned more pages. "I guess my husband wasn't at that picnic," she said. "But he did go on a lot of excursions with you boys. Look here. All of you on a fishing trip. His five favorites. And you were the most favorite, I think. He used to talk about what a good student you were."

Yukiji peered at the picture. "He looks different now, I imagine."

"Really? You mean he looks older now?"

"Well, I haven't seen him since the ship, you know. I just heard—"

Again, that same nervousness. He jerked his head away from her.

"If you have any news of him, I'm very anxious to know. Even if it's bad. Don't worry. I'd rather know."

"Yes, I remember now what I was going to tell you, but I decided I ought to wait until—well—until I feel better so I can tell the story right."

"Is it so terrible?"

"Not so bad. It's just that I want to tell you exactly the way I heard it, and—it seems so long ago now. It isn't direct news, anyway, you know. It's just a rumor."

"Won't it be even harder to remember the longer you wait?"

"Yes," he admitted. "But I want to get it right in my head."

"Just tell me if he's been wounded. Or at least tell me if he's alive. If he's been killed, I want to know now."

"He's alive," said Yukiji.

"Then has he been hurt?"

"I don't think so. Not badly, anyway."

"It isn't good news, then, is it?"

"Well, not exactly. But not bad either. Just a little puzzling."

"Then why—?"

"I'd better tell you now," Yukiji said suddenly. "Maybe I'll forget if I don't tell you."

"Oh, yes," Chiyo breathed. "I'd appreciate it so much."

"Well, as I said, it's just a rumor. He was up near the border somewhere."

He told her about the hospital ship and the man in the next bed, Sergeant Yamaguchi, who was having nightmares, shouting in his dreams about an explosion.

"So we began exchanging stories," Yukiji said, "and that's how I found out he knew Hara-sensei."

Their platoon had been protecting a Chinese village from the Communists, and they were surrounded by guerrillas, constantly being sabotaged, and always on guard.

"Sergeant Yamaguchi admired your husband, *Oba-chan.* He said it was difficult for a thoughtful, well-learned man like him to have to take orders from those puffed-up young officers with a higher rank. But he did it without losing any of his dignity."

Shintaro had been the liaison between the soldiers and villagers because he was the only one who could understand Chinese. He had tried to help the villagers, and had comforted the young Japanese soldiers, too, always listening to their troubles.

The Chinese living in the village were suspected of collaborating with the Communist guerrillas even though the villagers were always friendly, sometimes bringing the soldiers food. Some of the Chinese women even had affairs with the Japanese soldiers. But just below was barbed wire separating the Communist Chinese side from the territory the Japanese controlled.

"One night the sky lit up," Yukiji said. "Just like it did for me in Burma. A land mine."

When the sky was at its brightest, Yamaguchi saw two figures with their hands up, their guns in the air. Then it was dark again. In the morning, only Yamaguchi and two other men were still alive, and Yamaguchi himself had been blinded.

"And my husband?"

"Well, that's the strange thing. Hara-sensei and one of the privates were the only ones missing."

Yukiji explained about the Red Army propaganda, the leaflets written in bad Japanese, urging the soldiers to come over to the Communist side with their guns and other equipment. If they did that they could become officers and receive good food and warm clothing.

"Of course, only young soldiers believed that. Your husband, Hara-sensei, wouldn't have been tempted by things like that."

"You mean everybody thinks my husband surrendered to the Red Army or deserted?" Chiyo demanded.

"That's the evidence, but nobody understands it. Of course, Sergeant Yamaguchi doesn't know for sure if it was Hara-sensei he saw in the dark. Have you received any notice from the army about him, *Oku-sama?* A letter that says he's missing or been taken prisoner?"

"Nothing like that," said Chiyo. "Only a letter from him, telling me he is fairly healthy. And that was written New Year's Day. When did this explosion take place?"

"Well, it must have been in February. It was after New Year's anyway."

"So the letter was written before all this happened. And now he is missing. Or maybe dead. And if he has gone over to the other side, he might as well be dead. He's supposed to kill himself before he's captured. He can't come home."

She clasped her hands tightly, angry with Yukiji for bringing such terrible news. And yet she had pressed him to tell her, insisted on it. But it wasn't true. "My husband would never desert. It would be impossible for him to do that. And he wouldn't surrender either. There must be some mistake."

"I know," said Yukiji. "I think so, too, and I wasn't sure

whether to tell you or not. It's only a rumor, and Sergeant Yama-guchi was delirious part of the time just like I was."

"No, I'm glad you told me. I can be better prepared if the secret police come to question me about him."

"I just know there's some explanation, *Oba-chan*. Somehow, somewhere, he's all right. And there's a good reason for what he did. You'll find out eventually."

"*Tadaima!*" The door opened abruptly. Yukiji's grandparents. There would be at least five minutes of bowing and pleasantries before she could get out the door.

"Thank you again for telling me, Yuki-chan," she said. "I know how hard it was, and I'm relieved that your mind is as sharp and clear as ever."

Yukiji lay, not speaking, watching her as she started toward the door. "'Bye, *Oba-chan*," he finally managed.

"*Okairinasai.* Welcome home," Chiyo said to the grandparents when she got out to the sitting room, treating them as if they were the guests and she the hostess.

"Ah, *Hara-sensei no Oku-sama!*" said the grandmother, taken by surprise and still standing in the *genkan*, bobbing up and down, bowing. "Taking your time out from such a busy day to visit our poor, foolish grandchild. It is thanks to you and to the honorable shadow of the Lord Buddha that he is faring so well."

"Not so. Not so," said Chiyo, on her knees now, bowing her head so that it almost touched the *tatami*. "It is my pleasure to visit him and see that he is becoming healthier and stronger, and to hear the stories of his bravery."

The grandparents stepped up onto the *tatami* and knelt, both of them bowing to match Chiyo's bows. Yukiji's grandfather was nod-ding his head, mouthing phrases in a voice too low for her to hear, but the murmur was polite and comforting.

"Stay and have some tea with us," the grandmother urged when the bowing was finally finished. "It will take only a minute to brew."

"Oh, I'm sorry," said Chiyo. "I can't just now. I've stayed talk-ing to Yuki-chan much longer than I expected, and I'm very late for the air raid drill."

She stood up, backed off the *tatami*, stepped into her *geta*, kept moving, facing them, until she got to the door. They continued to praise each other's virtues, compliment each other for Yukiji's well-being, honor the Lord Buddha, the emperor, the nation. One more elaborate bow, and she was beyond the gate, out of sight, then scurrying down the street, and finally inside her own house.

She closed the doors, then went into the sleeping room and buried her face among the quilts. Lying there, alone and barricaded by walls, she screamed.

Chapter Four

CHIYO, SLEEPING IN THE SMALL BREAK-
fast room by the front *genkan*, awakened to
the dull sound of bombs thudding relentlessly in the distance.
Kenichi brought his *futon* from the sleeping room across the hall,
laid it by hers, and sat hugging his knees. "Almost morning," he
said. "Shall we go to the shelter?"

"I don't think so. They haven't sounded the alarm."

The bombing stopped, and the roar of planes died away. They
looked at each other, relieved, then fell asleep again. But she awoke
at dawn, crying out at an explosion that surrounded her and the
dark shadow of Shintaro running through a blaze of fire with his
arms and his gun in the air.

"What's the matter, Mama?"

"Nothing. Just a bad dream."

She went about her daily tasks in a stupor, not caring what happened around her, not paying attention even to the jagged pain in
the pit of her stomach.

Each day at ration distribution, the neighborhood women collected their portions and bowed to one another, repeating the proper
phrases as if by rote. There was no time now for gossip or pleasant-

ries. They had shortened their greetings to one word and the bowing to brief nods.

"Eh. Eh," Chiyo would respond, nodding, sucking in air through her teeth, betraying the tension she was suffering. They were all like that, compelled to suppress their fear and doubt, even their anger, behind mindless actions. It made them faceless and nameless. But hopeless, too. They were part of the suicidal masses who were going to stand together in one body and repel the enemy forces when they came to Japanese shores. Chiyo did not want to think about that. She attended the required *takeyari* defense drills, thrusting her bamboo sword through the hearts of imagined enemy soldiers; Chiyo pretended that she was attending one of Grandmother's classical Japanese dancing classes and that the motions she made had been choreographed to fit some unsung melody.

The Neighborhood Council distributed sweet potato shoots to each household. But they had already filled their gardens with *kabocha*, pumpkin plants. So they pooled the extra shoots and, with night soil and meager garbage, fertilized the small lot next door to the Kasama household, saving room to plant whatever might be distributed next. They went home exhausted, with no extra nourishment to compensate and with another day of hard labor ahead of them when the soil was fermented enough for the actual planting.

Expecting another allotment of cloth to sew into soldiers' shirts, they gathered for the usual distribution at Mrs. Ikeda's, but there was none.

"Huh!" Mrs. Yamamoto commented, folding her arms in front of her. "The arsenal's out of gunpowder and metal, they say, and now even the cloth is gone?" Everyone shrank from her gaze.

Middle of May. The military presence was everywhere now, the Second Army Headquarters firmly established at the East Parade Grounds just beyond the railroad station. They were inducting forty- and fifty-year-olds into the army, anyone who could stand on two feet, even some who couldn't. Maimed men with only one arm or crippled legs were drilling on the West Parade Grounds behind Hiroshima Castle.

"Better not let Yukiji get too healthy-looking," Mrs. Yamamoto said quietly to Mrs. Ikeda. "The army will be sending him off again."

Every day at ration distribution the *Tonarigumi* listened to the news on Mrs. Ikeda's radio. They carefully read the association's notices handed around in the neighborhood and watched the ones posted on bulletin boards, always trying to second-guess the official announcements. "We have suffered a slight setback," the radio had informed them after the defeat of Guam a year earlier. "But if everyone makes the same sacrifices as our soldiers, we can easily win the war."

They made their sacrifices and the enemy kept coming closer. "Yes, the Americans have taken Luzon," the army admitted, "but the important thing is to continue the struggle, to work harder." When Manila was taken in February, the radio announced that the Philippines were of little importance anyway. In March, Iwo Jima had fallen, and in April came the long, hard struggle for Okinawa. "We will never give up Okinawa," the radio announced. "We will defeat the enemy in Okinawa and turn the tide of the war." By May it was clear that the navy and army, fighting desperately, were losing ground. "We must intensify preparations to meet and repel the enemy when he attempts to invade the Japanese homeland," the radio said.

"Well, from the look of things," Mrs. Yamamoto said, "they'll be coming to Hiroshima first. Otherwise, why all these soldiers here?"

No one answered Mrs. Yamamoto's questions anymore.

They looked over their shoulders when they talked now, even in groups of two or three. The *Tokubo* thought-police were everywhere, listening. Chiyo's former teachers at the Girls' School had been called up and questioned about their old ties with American Christian missionaries. One of them had been asked whether he placed loyalty to his Christian God higher than loyalty to his emperor. No one wanted to discuss the subject, especially not Chiyo, who had been a student there and whose husband's situation might be under investigation at any moment.

In June it was Chiyo's turn to be *Tonarigumi* assistant captain, a job passed around to each household. It meant standing in line at the grocer's each day waiting for the neighborhood's share, carrying the rations back to Mrs. Ikeda's, helping her divide up the allotment, notifying the other households that the rations were in.

There was always a crisis. One morning Chiyo received an unexpected allotment of eggs, but only eight to distribute to ten families. "We can cut up carrots and turnips," she protested to the grocer. "But how can we divide an egg?"

The greengrocer's shop was at the end of their *Tonarigumi* block, the household closest to Sakae Bridge and only five houses down the street from Mrs. Ikeda's. The proprietor, Mr. Kateyama, was a frail old man who had hoped to retire before the war began. Instead he was dealing daily with disappointed and angry customers. Carefully wiping the perspiration from his brow with a big handkerchief, he explained patiently that each neighborhood had been asked to do with one or two less.

The *Tonarigumi* drew lots and Chiyo lost her egg, which was a relief. No one could accuse her of taking favors. But Mrs. Tamioka, a chronic complainer, was the other loser. She was quick to point out that for the special New Year's distribution her family had gotten one less mandarin orange. Mrs. Ikeda gave up her egg, but resented it so much that Chiyo stayed after the distribution to comfort her.

"Our household is much larger than hers," Mrs. Ikeda complained. "And they haven't allowed us extra rations for Yukiji because Kyoko is in the country. Yukiji is supposed to be getting army rations, but the army says he doesn't get them because he's not on active duty. Well, he still eats. And twice as much as Kyoko." She sighed, suddenly looking sharply at Chiyo. "We did reduce your portion because of Yoko, didn't we?"

"Yes." Chiyo nodded. "And not only that. They're saying now I'll have to provide housing for a soldier because our upstairs is empty."

"Well, that's good," Mrs. Ikeda said. "At least you can get the soldier's army rations. They always eat lunch and dinner at the barracks, you know. You only have to serve them breakfast."

"I don't like it," said Chiyo. "I don't want a stranger in my house." She wanted a comforting word, but Mrs. Ikeda's mind was still on Mrs. Tamioka and the egg.

"That woman never thinks of anyone except herself and her family. She never volunteers. She just comes and takes what's hers, then she goes away."

"Well, let's keep a record," Chiyo said. "We'll note down she got the egg this time and point it out next time she complains. We should have told her to ask Mrs. Kasama for her egg. That would have embarrassed her."

Mrs. Ikeda laughed. "Too late," she said. "Colonel Kasama's eaten it by now."

They both felt better, and Chiyo got up to go, taking a side glance into Yukiji's room. It was empty. Chiyo had stopped visiting him as frequently and she felt guilty about it.

"He's at the hospital today," Mrs. Ikeda said. "They're fitting him with an artificial leg so he can go back to work. Then we'll get the rations. At least until they decide to send him overseas again."

"Surely they won't do that!" said Chiyo.

"They're recruiting everybody," Mrs. Ikeda said grimly. "But you've cheered him up a lot. And really, you shouldn't bring him so many nice gifts."

Chiyo stepped down into the *genkan,* denying that the gifts were nice.

"Well, with things coming to you from your brother all the time, they may not seem nice to you, but they certainly are treats for the rest of us."

Chiyo smiled and bowed, holding in the resentment. "Not so many things coming my way," she breathed, wondering what the neighborhood would think if they knew about Shintaro. Mrs. Yamamoto would continue to be her friend, but she wasn't sure about Mrs. Ikeda or the others.

Anyway, if it made Mrs. Ikeda feel better to complain, then let her. She had the right. Her daughter, Kyoko, was still out in the country, homesick and wanting to come home. Mr. Ikeda had decided she must stay out at the temple and that they shouldn't visit her anymore.

They were ordered to turn in their china and metal to the government, keeping only daily dishes and a cooking pot for themselves. They had already given up their unneeded utensils twice before, but now they were pressed to surrender more, even glassware, jewelry, anything they didn't use constantly. Everyone had to produce something. Otherwise the government would think they were holding back. Chiyo, trying to think of something else she could sacrifice, stumbled out of Mrs. Ikeda's gate and walked silently beside Mrs. Yamamoto, both of them following behind Mrs. Ishibashi's maid.

"How are they going to make bullets out of my teapot?" Mrs. Yamamoto whispered after the maid had disappeared behind the Ishibashi hedge. Chiyo smiled at her, catching a sudden glimpse of her gold-toothed grin.

In the morning, while she was sorting through her remaining possessions, Isao stopped at the entrance, his usual brisk self, hurrying off to work, refusing to come in for tea. "Pack up everything else and bring it to Inokuchi before it's too late," he said. "Don't let the authorities have anymore. They've taken enough already."

"Well, there's nothing left. Just metal rings on the photograph book."

"Bring it," he said. "Come Saturday afternoon as soon as Kenichi finishes his work. We have to finish rice planting by Sunday night."

He started to leave, then turned back. "And bring Grandmother. She's still refusing to be evacuated, so we'll have to convince her."

"Grandmother still won't leave?" Chiyo expressed mild shock, but she wasn't surprised. Grandmother. Chiyo and the children had always called her that even though she was not their relative. She was the mother of Isao's wife, Kazuko, and the only grandmother the children had. Chiyo herself felt closer to Grandmother than she had ever felt to her own mother.

"She's lived in that house for sixty years, you know," Chiyo said. "She wants to die there. Maybe it's no use to—"

"She's been out on the West Parade Grounds practicing *takeyari*," Isao interrupted. "Defending her homeland with a bamboo sword."

"Really? Her *Tonarigumi* is forcing her to do that?"

"No." Isao shook his head. "Nobody over sixty had to do it. You know that. And she's seventy-two."

"But why—?"

"Who knows? She says it's her duty."

"Kenichi and I will bring her," Chiyo said firmly. "At least for a visit. You'll have to do the persuading after we get her there."

They planted the rice on the terraced plots near the foot of the mountain across the road from Isao's house, standing under the warm sun, their feet deep in the mud, thrusting the young seedlings under the water. At the end of each row, Chiyo stood and straightened her back, looking at the scene stretched out below her. First the terraced rice fields, then the county road, then the railroad and streetcar tracks, the houses along the shore, and finally the Inland Sea traveling out toward the sky and embracing the distant islands of Miyajima, Enoshima, Ninoshima, Nomishima, Etajima.

Inokuchi, her native place, the tiny town which hugged the end of the land, its houses gathered in clusters. It had been a seaside resort when she was a child, always filled in the summer with families walking on the road behind their house, carrying beach balls, pails and shovels, towels slung over their backs. Now no one swam or boated. And there was only surreptitious clamming. But the rice planting continued. She had missed it only once in her life, when she had gone to Tokyo on her honeymoon with Shintaro. Today, in the familiar surroundings and with Yoko in the row next to her keeping the same pace and rhythm as her mother, Chiyo's fear diminished.

At the end of the next row, she and Yoko looked at Isao's house, their ancestral place which had belonged to their family for fifteen generations. It was the house closest to the sea, its wide veranda jutting out on stilts beyond the shore.

"It's beautiful, isn't it, Mama?"

Chiyo smiled at her daughter, feeling the pain of her absence more deeply now that they were together again. She had grown accustomed to Hiroshi's absence, not to Yoko's.

Here on the hill her senses were sharper. She could almost hear the rising and falling of the tide as the sea slapped gently against the sturdy cedar stilts that supported the *engawa,* the porch surrounding the house and extending to the veranda, her grandfather's moon-viewing platform. They had sat there those August and September evenings, feeling the breezes and watching the full moon rise up behind their tiny private island, Myojin, the place where Isao had caught the octopus. On full-moon nights the island hovered in the sea just beyond them, its lone pine tree silhouetted against the sky. Sometimes, to match the mood of the evening, they had created haiku poetry.

"Come on, Mama!" Yoko handed Chiyo a new bunch of seedlings, and they turned into the next row. Select from the left hand, bend over, THRUST, stand up, select, bend over, THRUST! Under their breath, keeping the rhythm together, she and Yoko hummed the old tune. Not like the time before the war when they all sang together. In those days it had been a festival time, coming together and sharing their labor and food and the gossip. Now singing took too much energy.

In quick succession they planted each plot, moving on to the next neighbor's and then the next. Even Grandmother, coerced into coming because Chiyo said they couldn't plant without her, had climbed the hill and helped for a short time, and later had sat with them on the riverbank while they ate their meager lunches.

When they finished, the village members gathered at Isao's house, everyone settling on the wide veranda.

To mark the special occasion, Kazuko served them each a precious dried persimmon to go with their tea, and they sat for a time, munching slowly, talking of the old days when the clams and fish and berries were everywhere, easy to find. They remembered the fragrances of flowers and the first taste of strawberries in the spring. Those old days when people belonged to their land and would never leave, never go off to war.

"At least it's better here in Inokuchi than anywhere else," a neighbor said. And they cast stealthy glances at Grandmother, who sat sternly silent, gazing out across the Inland Sea.

When the light began to fade and after the neighbors had left, Isao turned to Grandmother. "With those air raid sirens going every night, you can't get any sleep."

Grandmother sat, imperial, unmoving. "I am needed by my *Tonarigumi,*" she said. "I cannot give up my war work."

"But you can do that here. There's plenty of war work wherever you go."

"I want to remain in my house," she said. "I will not move again in my lifetime."

Isao looked at her sternly. Two stubborn people confronting each other. There was an uncomfortable silence.

Kazuko moved among them quietly, stacking teacups on the tray. She stood up, her profile dark against the fading light. Even in her *monpe* work clothes, no one could mistake Kazuko for a country woman. She always held a tea tray as if she were ready to serve the Sun Goddess.

"It's almost time for dinner and then a good hot bath," she said. "Fusako and I are building a fire. Heaven knows, we need a long soak tonight after the work we've done." Soft, delicate Kazuko had not been brought up to plant rice or to build fires.

They sat languidly in the huge tiled bath, one of the special pleasures of Inokuchi. Isao and the boys had finished their bath, and now there was enough room for Grandmother, Kazuko, Chiyo, Fusako. And of course Yoko, who cuddled close to her mother, asking endless questions about Hiroshima.

Chiyo stepped out of the bath, leaving the others to soak longer, hoping to catch Isao alone to tell him about Shintaro. She found him in the sitting room, pensively smoking. Kenichi and Hiroshi were already asleep in the next room. But she could not bring herself to speak of the rumor. Not even to her brother. Maybe if they had been alone a bit longer, she could have hinted that she had something to say.

Isao left for work at dawn. Kenichi and Fusako went to school, accompanying Grandmother. Kazuko and Chiyo, after sending Yoko and Hiroshi to school, selected for barter the spring kimono they had worn on their last prewar excursions to view the cherry blossoms. They journeyed far into the country, looking for food.

End of June. Bombs pounded down on the shipyards at Kure to the southeast, destroying it in a merciless shelling that lasted all night. Chiyo and Kenichi huddled together in the dark, listening to the roaring planes and the ugly thud of bombs, wondering if the B-29s would fly back over Hiroshima to dump their extra loads. Kenichi, ready to spring for the air raid shelter, clutched their rucksack of emergency supplies. The bombs came closer, then receded, then came closer again. There was a burst of light. The whole ground shook.

"We'd better get to the shelter now while there's a lull," said Kenichi, standing up on his knees.

"But the planes will come while we're in the street," said Chiyo.

Now the planes were overhead, roaring with a sound so deafening that Chiyo and Kenichi could only clutch each other wordlessly, not breathing until they were gone. Chiyo stared at Kenichi's profile in the gray of dawn, watched him gasp for breath, hold in his fear, stiffen his resolve. He turned and smiled brightly at Chiyo. "Well, we're alive for another night, huh, Mama?" And he fell immediately asleep. Chiyo cursed the monster B-29s that were making a soldier of her child.

In the morning, the neighbors gathered in front of Mrs. Ikeda's *engawa*.

"When are they going to bomb Hiroshima?" asked Mrs. Ishibashi, who had come to ration distribution that morning instead of her maid. "Tokyo's been razed to the ground, then Osaka, then Kobe. Now Kure."

"They won't hurt us," Mrs. Kasama said. "The Americans have relatives here. We're in the safest place in Japan."

Chiyo was glad to listen to the woman's too-bright optimism, glad to believe anything anybody said.

"That's not the reason," said Mrs. Tamioka. "It's not just any American. It's President Truman who has the relative here. I've heard it from an absolutely reliable source."

"Those are all foolish rumors," said the greengrocer's wife. "It's because we produce mostly sake and tinned beef. No point in wasting bombs on us for that."

"We make guns, too," Mrs. Ikeda pointed out, "and the Second Army's here." Her voice was foreboding. "My husband says it's because they're saving Hiroshima for something special."

"I like the first rumor," Chiyo told Mrs. Yamamoto, walking home. "I think I'll believe that one."

Mrs. Yamamoto's laugh was especially cynical that day. Lingering at Chiyo's gate now, ready to say goodbye, she leaned forward. "How could it be any worse even if we surrendered!" she breathed. "Okinawa defeated. And have you heard about those poor young

Okinawan girls in the Lily Brigade? Pledged to defend their island to the death. No older than my daughter, Sachiko. The army had two thousand of them holed up in a bunker, each with a hand grenade, ready for the last defense." She leaned even closer to Chiyo's ear. "And then they blew themselves to smithereens," she hissed. "Even after that the army won't admit we're losing. Just keeps using up our energy on air raid drills and the *takeyari* practice. They want us all to die like that."

Chiyo sucked in her breath. No jokes from Mrs. Yamamoto today. Just outrage. And her remarks so traitorous that the secret police would put her in jail immediately and never let her out.

They stared at each other, then heard behind them the footsteps of Colonel Kasama, probably a member of the secret police himself. They turned and bowed respectfully, mumbled greetings, breathing freely only after he was gone.

"Have you heard from your husband?" Mrs. Yamamoto asked her urgently.

"Nothing," Chiyo said. "Just nothing." She wanted to put her air raid hood over her head and hide her eyes. "I'm afraid he's—" Her voice choked. "But why are you asking? Have you heard something I don't know?"

"The *Kempeitai,* the military police. They're in the neighborhood, I heard. But nobody knows what they're trying to find out."

"Oh, then they know—?" She caught her breath.

"It's all right," said Mrs. Yamamoto. "We all feel the same way. We're afraid it's us. Or our husbands or something. I just heard from mine yesterday, did I tell you? He's still in Manchuria in the Corps of Engineers. You'll hear soon, too. And just be calm if they come to question you. Don't act afraid, that's all."

Did Mrs. Yamamoto know something she didn't know? Maybe the whole neighborhood knew, and they didn't want to tell her.

She stood shivering in the warm morning air long after Mrs. Yamamoto had gone.

Every day, the search for food, the air raid drills, and *takeyari* practice. And at least every two weeks all of them mobilized to go to the station to see off the new conscripts, poor pitiful old men, young boys, men on crutches. Chiyo, bowing to them, thought of Yukiji. The ammunition was gone, so they were using humans instead. Putting them in suicide squads. They would have inducted Isao if he weren't making guns.

Every night, planes overhead and the bombs coming closer. Koji had been bombed, and Okayama, Fukuoka, Kagoshima, Sasebo. Eighteen cities all around them. And still no bombing of Hiroshima. And still no word about Shintaro. And no word either from the *Kempeitai*. She wished they would come and ask her any kind of question. Get it over with.

She and Kenichi had moved their *futon* permanently into the small sitting room so they could be together when the bombers came. Sometimes Chiyo sat in the dark after the all clear sounded, watching Kenichi sleeping, unable to sleep herself, tears streaming down her face.

Maybe because Shintaro loved Chinese literature so much, he was too sympathetic with those villagers. Back in 1931 he had hated the hotheaded young army officers who had bombed the Manchurian railroad. So they could start the war with China, he said. But when Shintaro's red card came for military induction, he refused all suggestions for getting himself excused. He said if his emperor needed him, he would go.

She hugged her knees to her stomach and prayed to Kannon, the Goddess of Mercy. "Just keep him alive. It doesn't matter where he is or what he did. Send him home wounded like Yukiji. Even with his leg cut off if you must."

Lying down again, she would conjure up a vision of the tall, stately statue of the Kudara Kannon in the museum at Nara, its delicate, all-knowing smile comforting her. And sometimes it helped. Sometimes she could sleep.

More and more there were two or three warnings in one night, and they would have to decide each time whether to go to the shelter. Kenichi would sit up, stare at her in the dark, then reach around wordlessly for the rucksack. Or he would just sit.

"Let's not go tonight, Mama. It's too much trouble. I'd rather just die here." He would fall back on his *futon,* both of them listening for the all-clear signal.

The authorities began giving out a new kind of substitute for the rice ration, flour made from sweet potato vines, mulberry leaves, pumpkins, and horse chestnuts. At least that was what Mrs. Yamamoto said it was, and she had been a home economics teacher before she married. Not that it mattered what it was. It tasted terrible. Mrs. Tamioka declared it inedible. Chiyo tried making a kind of bread with it. She mixed it with water and fried it like pancakes. She thickened the soup with it. But each time it gave them diarrhea, and they had to wait for each other, standing in the hallway outside the toilet.

Some evenings in the middle of July, if the heat continued unabated and they heard the antiaircraft fire and the bombs, Chiyo and Kenichi would collect their food, the cooking pot and some sleeping mats, cross over Sakae Bridge, which led to the railroad station, then go up toward the mouth of the Ota River. Sometimes Mrs. Yamamoto, her son, Yasu, and her gentle sixteen-year-old daughter, Sachiko, would go with them. They would sleep outside all night in the cool by the river, away from the danger of the city, the two boys excited and whispering to each other in the dark. Other nights, if the overhead roar was especially loud, they would go farther out across the East Parade Grounds toward Mt. Futaba. And Chiyo slept better those nights in the cool and the comforting presence of the Yamamotos, even with the worry that she might spill out in her dreams her shame and fear for Shintaro. Still the *Kempeitai* had not come.

Soon the whole neighborhood was going to the river at night, lying on their mats along the bank, returning across the bridges in the morning to the constant miracle of an unbombed city.

But one evening, soldiers were standing at Sakae Bridge, pointing bayonets at them. "Go back!" they shouted. "You're needed in the city. Who's going to fight the fires if everyone is gone?"

The soldiers were in a line stretched across the bridge, five or six of them wearing leggings and high boots over their khaki trousers, their legs spread apart to balance their bayonets. And so young. In a few years, if the war continued, it would be Kenichi standing there holding a bayonet.

Chiyo and the Yamamotos stepped back off the bridge. But Kenichi refused to move. He stood in front of the youngest soldier. "Hashimoto-kun!" he exclaimed. "Is it you?"

The soldier stared at him. Yasu broke away from his mother and stood by Kenichi, saluting the soldier. "Hashimoto-kun, remember Rijo Middle School?" he asked.

The soldier still didn't answer.

"It's all right if we go out there to sleep," insisted Kenichi. "We can run right back into the city and put the fire out. And we can work harder if we get a good night's sleep up there where it's cool."

The soldier took a step forward, holding his bayonet sideways like a barrier, almost shoving the boys away. "Go back!" he shouted again. "I have orders to send you back!"

They walked home, too discouraged to talk. "Maybe it wasn't Hashimoto-kun after all," Kenichi said at last. "Maybe it was just somebody who looked like him."

* * *

Now it was too late to evacuate. In ordinary times, it would have been summer vacation and the family would have been at their summer house on the island of Miyajima. Instead, Kenichi was with the demolition crew from early morning until night, the twelve- and thirteen-year-olds all working as if they had already been drafted into the army. They were caught up in the final big push to tear down the designated houses so they could complete the wide fire lane that would stretch through the city across the seven rivers from one mountain to the other.

Grandmother's house was in the way of the fire lane and would be demolished in a few days. Not necessary now to persuade Grandmother to evacuate. There was no other choice. And Grandmother's youngest daughter, Akiko, was on her way from Tokyo to help her move to Inokuchi. Chiyo did not have time to pay Grandmother a sympathy visit. Everyone in the city was pressed to work harder. The older students had been assigned to tasks with the military or in factories, but the twelve- and thirteen-year-olds struggled on with the *tatemono sokai,* the clearing away of buildings. They were taking off the roof tiles, clearing away the rubble after the men pulled down the buildings, all of them tugging on the rope. Soldiers, government workers, housewives, people from the suburbs, all had to take their turns giving voluntary service.

An early typhoon visited them on the second of August. Chiyo sat sewing army shirts under a dim light with the blackout curtains pulled, listening to the rain beat down, some of it through a leak in the roof to a pot she had put in the sitting room. In spite of the noisy rain plopping in the pan, Kenichi had fallen asleep over his beloved science book, which he tried to study at night even though there was no time for classes at school.

Deliberately Chiyo put down her sewing and got up to pull out an old photograph book from the shelf. She leafed through the photos to the one of Shintaro in uniform, taken shortly after the red draft card had arrived and turned their world inside out.

Then the photograph for the spring of 1944. Without Shintaro. Chiyo and the children standing before the blossoming cherry trees. She seemed so young then, only two years ago. In those days she still had her placid, quiet face, a bit too round to qualify for the enlongated classical look that Kazuko had, but it was gentle and warm, Shintaro had told her. She was a short woman, perhaps a bit too plump in those days. Not now.

Through angry tears, Chiyo stared at her quota of cloth distributed yesterday, lying on the table still waiting to be sewn into shirts. What was the use of finishing them? And the women in Grandmother's neighborhood going to the arsenal every day to make bullets even though there was no gunpowder. Even though none of them wanted to kill anybody. What was the point of this useless, senseless, hopeless war? Even if they won, what was the point?

A fly crawled on Kenichi's neck. He jerked, then woke up and slapped, but missed the fly. He grinned at his mother, ashamed of being asleep. Then he rubbed his eyes, red from the dust raised by the demolition crews.

"Rice is ready," she announced.

He raised his eyebrows. "Real rice?"

"Well, some of it. Enough so you can taste the rice flavor."

"I think I'd just rather have pure white rice and have it less often." He saw her crestfallen face and smiled at her, closing his book and coming to the table. "Anyway, it's better than the flour we've been eating."

"There's a surprise," Chiyo announced. "I found a pumpkin in the garden, not quite ripe but big enough to cook."

"Pumpkin!" He grinned. She set the bowl of supposed-to-be rice and the *kabocha,* the pumpkin, in front of him. He had always hated pumpkin as a child. Now he lifted his bowl, shoveling in the contents with his chopsticks, stopping just long enough to spear a piece of *kabocha* and shovel that in too. He put down his empty bowl, leaving the last piece of yellow pumpkin for a while, saving it to make the meal longer.

"Mama," he said suddenly, "suppose I died. And Father did too. Would we be able to find each other in the Pure Land, do you think? Before our souls transmigrate?"

She set down her chopsticks and stared at him. "Ken-chan, what a strange thing to say."

"Well, you know, if I died, wouldn't I meet all the ancestors?"

Chiyo clasped her hands together. Had he heard something about Shintaro, too, and was afraid to tell her?

"Ken-chan, I refuse to believe that we won't all be together again on this earth. In this house. We just have to keep healthy and keep working and—" She closed her eyes and swallowed hard. "Where did you ever get an idea like that?"

"Nowhere, Mama. I was just wondering. That's all."

"You haven't heard anything about your father, have you? Any rumors in the neighborhood, any news I don't know? Any—" She turned away, pretending to search for a grain of rice she had dropped.

"No, Mama. I was just using Papa and myself as an example. No other reason. I don't expect anything like that to happen, Mama. Of course not. I didn't mean to upset you, Mama."

She picked up her chopsticks and speared her last piece of *kabocha,* stalling for time until her voice felt steady again. "Well, of course, nobody knows the answer," she said calmly. The danger of tears had subsided now. "But I've always believed the dead can gravitate to the people they want to see again. Don't you feel it, during the *Obon* festival in August, that your grandparents are there, visiting us?"

"Yes," said Kenichi.

Absentmindedly he handed over his rice bowl for a second helping. There was no second helping, but since he wasn't noticing, she scraped some from her own bowl and handed it back.

"You know," Chiyo said, "I think it's because we get reincarnated eventually, but not right away. Not until we all get together once more."

He shoveled the rice into his mouth, plopping in the piece of pumpkin at the end. "If we have to work so hard, why don't they give us more to eat?"

Chiyo began to clear the table. "Think of the soldiers in Southeast Asia. Like Yuki-chan. Eating grass all the time and that—" She thought of the monkey meat. "At least we're home here together."

He nodded vacantly and reached for the book he had abandoned earlier.

When Chiyo came back from checking the bath, he was deeply absorbed, his scrawny neck and shaved head bent over the table, his feet tucked under him in a lotus position. He did not look up.

She decided that when the war was over, he would go to Tokyo University and study physics and be a famous scientist.

Chapter Five

S HE WAS IN A BUNKER ON A HILL IN
China and someone was shouting at Shin-
taro. "Wake up, Hara-kun! Get up!" Chiyo nudged him but he
wouldn't move. He was lifeless. Why wasn't anybody helping
her? She rolled off her *futon*. It was Yasutaka Yamamoto calling.
The lifeless lump was Kenichi, still asleep. She got up and went
out to the *genkan*.

"We must have overslept," she said. "What time is it?"

"Late. We've missed the opening ceremony at school."

He looked anxious and tired, even thinner than Kenichi. And
his face was sallow. She hoped he wasn't coming down with flu.

"I'll get Ken-chan," she said, then turned and saw that Kenichi
was already sitting up, a startled look on his face. His hair had
been cropped so close (as a prevention against lice, the school authorities said) that what remained was a soft caterpillarlike fuzz.

"Ya-chan, you'd better go on without him."

"No, I'm coming," Kenichi insisted. He stood up and pulled on
his pants, then ran his fingers through the fuzz, trying to press it
down.

"You haven't had your breakfast yet. You'll have to eat something."

46

He stopped off briefly in the toilet, wrapped the gaiters around his legs, grabbed his rucksack and air raid hat.

"I'll bring your breakfast and lunch together," she said.

She stared after them. Already Yasu was laughing at something Kenichi had said. They broke into a run. Where did they get the energy?

She stepped back into the *genkan* and closed the sliding door. Friday. Akiko would be down from Tokyo today, and Chiyo had promised to help her pack up Grandmother's things. But the last army shirt wasn't finished, and now Kenichi's lunch to make and take to him.

She reached the stop at Hachobori just as a streetcar ground to a halt in front of her. She had crowded in among the soldiers before she remembered the ban against civilians riding it. But no one seemed to notice her. The army shirts were finished and delivered; Kenichi's lunch was under one arm, a small pumpkin for Grandmother under the other. If her luck held, she would find Kenichi's demolition crew along the Honkawa near Grandmother's house.

She got off at the stop for Aioibashi, her favorite of the forty-nine bridges of Hiroshima, then walked across it, high and wide, to the center, where another smaller bridge jutted out like the stem of a T, reaching to the pointed nose of Nakajima, Grandmother's island, in the very center of Hiroshima's seven rivers.

She stood a moment gazing at the lazy Ota River, which divided just below the bridge into the Honkawa on the west and the Motoyasu on the east, forming an upside-down Y around Nakajima's nose. Fishing boats still dotted the shores, but the restaurants and excursion docks were silent now. On the west bank of the Motoyasu stood the concrete square warehouse of the Japan Red Cross. And beyond that the huge Hiroshima Prefectural Industry Promotion Hall, spread out at the edge of the river, winged with bay-windowed turrets and topped in the center with a sturdy dark dome that could be seen from anywhere in the city. It dominated the low tiled roofs around it, even the Chamber of Commerce Building and the temples on Nakajima across the river.

Under the emerging sun, the rivers flowed majestically on their journey south to the sea. She looked behind her toward Hiroshima Castle, which lifted its proud head above the trees behind the castle walls. They called it Rijo Castle, the Carp Castle. Kenichi's school was named after it. Now the sun was shining on the two bronze carp, their tails sticking up from each end of the roof, their heads diving into the castle keep, reflecting the sun's rays.

She walked onto the smaller bridge that led to the tip of the island, then followed along the west bank toward the Honkawa Bridge. Before reaching it, she caught sight of Kenichi's teacher Takano-sensei standing on the street and looking up toward the roofs. Boys stood at intervals along the ladders propped against the houses, handing down roof tiles one at a time to the students on the ground, who stacked them.

Chiyo shaded her eyes, looking toward the sun. Two dark figures were on the roof. Kenichi and Yasu.

"Come back down," Takano-sensei shouted. "It's time for the next crew to spell you."

They started toward the ladder. One gave the other a light punch and for a moment the silhouette that was Kenichi floated in the air. Chiyo gasped. But the next instant, the two boys were slamming their feet down against the ladder rungs. They were both all right. Maybe the angle of the sun had been playing tricks on her eyes.

"Oh, Mrs. Hara, you here?" Takano-sensei asked when he turned around. "Assigned to work on the roof today, are you?"

"Well, no, I'm just"—she held up the *furoshiki*—"bringing lunch."

She apologized for not getting Kenichi to school on time.

"Not so important," he said. "All he missed was the opening ceremony. The rest of the boys were nearly asleep anyway. I hate to see them working like this instead of studying." He removed his big handkerchief from his back pocket and wiped the perspiration from his brow. He had aged. The war had dried him out and wrinkled him. But he still had that same disarming air of bewilderment. He wasn't stern enough to be a teacher, people said. Just worried and kindly. He had been Shintaro's teacher once, then his colleague, then a teacher emeritus. And like Colonel Kasama and the greengrocer, he had been called back into service from retirement.

"I'm the one who gave the talk this morning." He smiled sorrowfully. "These days, words aren't important. Just action."

Chiyo wanted to touch Kenichi when he came down off the ladder. Instead, she handed him his lunch. Mr. Takano pulled out his handkerchief again, wiped his nose, blotted the perspiration that had formed on his brow. It was already very hot.

Chiyo pulled out her own lunch, six rice balls which she had been planning to share with Grandmother and Akiko. "Here's a little something for each of you."

She passed them around quickly, surreptitiously, keeping one for herself, deciding she would eat it now with the others and save the extra two for Grandmother and Akiko.

They stood in a huddle, not speaking for fear someone might discover what they were doing, savoring the taste of the tiny strip of seaweed wrapped around each rice ball, chewing the rice grains carefully, tasting the faint hint of a pickled plum inside.

"Essence of Japanese spirit," Takano-sensei exclaimed, bowing deeply. "I cannot express to you what pleasure this has given me."

"It was nothing," Chiyo murmured, delighted that her gift had been so well received.

She did not want to see Kenichi dancing again on the top of buildings. So she waved to the boys, bowed goodbye to Takano-sensei, then turned quickly and followed the riverbank into the narrow street in the Zaimoku Machi district, surrounded by huge old wooden temples, where Grandmother lived.

Akiko appeared at the door, still clad in her kimono, looking wan and rumpled from her train trip. She knelt, bowing in the correct, careful manner girls her generation had been taught. The war could not dilute the strict formalities of Grandmother's household.

Chiyo climbed onto the *tatami* and knelt beside Akiko, remembering the slim, graceful child they called Aki-chan who could sit for hours with her legs tucked under her, watching her mother's dancing lessons, her profile like a classic sculpture of rose-colored ivory. She had begun dancing at three, performed five recitals by the age of eight, received her credentials as a *natori,* teacher of the dance, before she finished the Girls' School. Chiyo had wanted to be a *natori,* too, but her own dancing lessons had begun too late.

Now, here was grown-up Akiko, still slim and graceful, still with classic, perfectly proportioned features. But the high color and the delicate, smooth complexion were gone, the skin around her mouth and eyes drawn and tight. They had not seen each other for at least five years.

Akiko wept, her face buried in her kimono sleeve. "How's everyone?" she finally managed through her tears.

"We're all right," Chiyo said. "At least the children are all here. And you?"

Akiko dried her eyes. "Well, surviving. Husband's still in Indonesia, and my son Koichi's out in Chiba with his grandparents. Tokyo is a burned-out desert. I'm sure you've heard. But now it's getting bad in Chiba. Every day new refugees come, and there isn't enough food. We're better off than most with the old family house, but Husband's parents are getting weaker. They can't make the trip down here. I'll have to stay in Chiba with them. But at least Koichi—" Her voice became a whisper. "I was thinking of sending him to Mother. There's more food down here, but now with Mother being evacuated I—"

They looked at each other, both knowing that Grandmother was sitting just on the other side of her *fusuma,* the thin sliding partition. She affected deafness, but always managed to hear when she wanted to.

Akiko slid open the *fusuma* to reveal Grandmother in formal position on her knees, waiting to greet Chiyo. She was a tiny woman. Yet a person standing or kneeling before her always had the sense of being presented to a mountain.

Chiyo felt the stern resolve in the room around her. The *byōbu,* the six-paneled silk screens which Grandmother used for backdrops, were folded up in one corner. The curtain was pulled open in front of the bare dancing stage. Grandmother's favorite string instruments, her samisen and koto, in their brocade covers, leaned like ghosts against the far wall, ready to go into their packing boxes. The house had been almost denuded by previous packing, the valuables sent out to Inokuchi. Now the things Grandmother held most dear had to be packed, and she would be separated forever from this stage where she had taught dancing for almost forty years.

Chiyo knelt and bowed formally to Grandmother, murmuring politeness. She proffered the tiny pumpkin, wrapped in one of her best and oldest *furoshiki.* "I'm sorry to have to offer you such a small, insignificant gift. It may not even be ripe enough, but at least it is fresh. It has been growing in our garden until just this morning."

"The honor of your presence is pleasure enough," Grandmother said. "No need for a gift." But she unwrapped the pumpkin and exclaimed over it.

"This is only a small expression of the deep sorrow I feel for the loss of your house," Chiyo said.

Grandmother's face stiffened. "The sacrifice is nothing compared to your husband's or any of those other men off in foreign places. If tearing it down can save someone's life, I will be more than compensated. I will build a new house after the war."

The house could never be rebuilt the way it was, not even under the most ideal circumstances. They all knew that.

Akiko went to the kitchen to make tea.

"Any news from your honorable husband?"

She had prepared herself to respond with a noncommittal nod, but it did not come. If she told, Grandmother would remember some wife of some ancient hero in a *kabuki* play, or in *The Tale of Heike,* who had suffered the same experience. Grandmother would be able to quote the passage and Chiyo would repeat it and ponder over it, comforting herself. And yet Chiyo could not tell. A good samurai wife was supposed to endure in silence everything, including the sight of her son's decapitated head wrapped in a *furoshiki* or her husband disemboweling himself. Grandmother never shared her own pain with anyone. She would not allow herself to become a prisoner of war, and the question of desertion would be beyond her comprehension. She would take her own life, staring straight at the enemy, cut her heart out without making a sound.

"I have heard a rumor," Chiyo said, hardly believing her own ears. Akiko had come back with the *mugi-cha,* the barley tea.

"A disturbing rumor?" Grandmother ventured.

"Well, Yukiji Ikeda, one of the neighbor boys, came home from the war. And his leg—" Chiyo thought of Yukiji's leg, bloody, bones jutting out, and all those miles he had tried to walk on it. "Yukiji's leg was blown off," she said fiercely. "So they sent him home, and on the ship back, he met a man who saw Shintaro, in the light of an explosion, running off into the enemy lines with his hands up."

Akiko gasped. Grandmother picked up her teacup. "Tell us the whole story the way you heard it."

Chiyo reviewed every detail of the rumor which, for two months, had invaded her thoughts and dreams.

Grandmother's face broke into a smile. "He is safe, then," she said. "Nobody is shooting at him or planting bombs under him. He is cold and hungry and miserable, probably, but he is safe. Under the circumstances, it is the best thing that could have happened to him. Surely we all know by this time that he is better off as a prisoner than he would be in the Japanese army."

Chiyo stared across the table at Grandmother, the woman who practiced defending her homeland with a bamboo sword, whose samurai code was stronger than the whole governing council of the Emperor Meiji.

"But, Grandmother, he never should have allowed himself to be taken prisoner. He was supposed to commit hara-kiri with his sword or blow himself up with a hand grenade. And what is worse, maybe he did." Chiyo reached inside her blouse for her handkerchief, accidentally pulling out Shintaro's worn-out letter, which she always carried with her. It dropped onto the table, and she left it there, covering her face with the handkerchief, pressing back her tears.

Grandmother reached across the table and touched Chiyo's hand.

"Let us examine the situation," Grandmother said. "First, discount any thoughts of his being a deserter. We all know your husband would never do anything that would bring dishonor to his country or his family. And if he did surrender, we have no idea why. Maybe he was taken by surprise. This man Yamaguchi only saw two figures by the light of the explosion. Maybe there were captors he didn't see." She paused. "Or maybe he was wounded and became unconscious. Then when he woke up, he was in a prison camp. Or there's the chance, too, that he was just confused by the bombing and went the wrong way."

"Then why were his hands up in the air?"

"Well, who knows what gestures a person makes in the middle of a bomb?"

"There's another possibility," Akiko said. "My husband, Kikuo, says we have spies, you know, to watch enemy activities. Maybe the Japanese army sent him across as a spy, and they told him to act as if he were deserting. He knows Chinese, after all, and they'd want to use a well-educated person like your husband for the best purposes."

"I never thought of that," said Chiyo.

"It sounds a bit farfetched to me, Aki-chan," Grandmother said, "but I suppose it's possible. There are endless possibilities. The rumor is so vague, after all. The whole story could be untrue. You might get another letter tomorrow that would prove none of it happened at all."

"That is the thought I cling to most," said Chiyo. "But I have been waiting for a long time now."

Still, their words lessened her anxiety. "I feel better now, having talked to you," she said. "And I'm ashamed of taking your time, telling you my fears when you are about to lose your house and there is so much work to be done. I came to help you, not talk about my troubles."

"A house does not compare with a husband, Chi-chan," Grandmother said quietly.

Chiyo began to sob. Not from despair, but from relief, for having unburdened herself, finally, after months of carrying around the knowledge and the pain.

Grandmother and Akiko sat in silence on either side of her,

touching her shoulders with theirs, each clasping one of her hands. They stared out at Grandmother's garden. The sun was strong now, pushing away the threat of more typhoon weather. She saw the tiny fruit of the pumpkin plants where once only flowers had grown. The pumpkin she had brought wasn't such a prize, really. Grandmother was growing it, too, and they would be eating it interminably, turning yellow from it, inside and out.

"You know, Chi-chan," Grandmother said. "There is no question that in any situation Shintaro's response would be a correct one."

"Yes," said Chiyo. "That is my worst fear. That he killed himself right after he was taken prisoner."

"No," Grandmother said. "I don't think so. Your husband is admirably imbued with the spirit of Bushido. He would be willing to make any sacrifice for his country. But he is also sensible. Once he was captured, what would be the point blowing himself up? He might admire the idea of an honorable and noble suicide in literature, but he wouldn't be impractical enough to do that to himself."

Grandmother took a sip of tea. "If he's been captured, there's a good chance he's safe. If he's dead, you would have heard from the army. And if he's deserted, the *Kempeitai* would have visited you by now."

She stood up and went to her nearly empty cupboard, pulled out a box, and arranged on her saucer three thimble-sized tea cakes made of pure sugar in the shape of delicate white roses. She passed them nonchalantly, as if eating them were an everyday occurrence.

Chiyo had not seen, much less eaten, a sugar tea cake for at least three years. She felt the sweetness spread through her.

"There's one thing certain," Grandmother said. "It will soon be over. We are losing the war."

"Oh, Mother," Akiko said. "It won't help to believe that, will it?"

"But we might as well get used to the idea," Grandmother said. "It would take a miracle to save us. We need another kamikaze, a divine wind, to blow off the enemy the way it did when Genghis Khan came to our shores in the thirteenth century. That is our only hope.

"Oh, I go out and practice with those bamboo spears whenever Mrs. Aoki asks me to. After all, we need the exercise, and it makes those army trainers feel useful, but we all know a bamboo spear isn't going to hold off the red-haired barbarians for more than a few seconds. All we can do is try to be someplace safe like Chiba or Inokuchi. Or China even. He's alive, Chi-chan. I can feel it in my bones." She smiled, then pointed to the letter. "Read it to us," she demanded. "We haven't heard it yet."

"Here, you read it," Chiyo insisted.

Grandmother read it through, out loud, and it sounded more beautiful and hopeful that day, as she sat on the *tatami* and stared at the tattered garden, surrounded by the samisen and koto and the few remaining objects of the past, than it had ever sounded.

They were ready by late afternoon when Isao arrived. They hardly spoke as they loaded the boxes and bundles onto the back of the truck, moving quickly back and forth in the fading light.

Grandmother and Akiko would sit in the cab in front with the driver, the samisen and the koto on their laps. Isao would ride in the back to watch over the other possessions.

"Wait!" Grandmother commanded. "One more look around."

"I'll come with you," Akiko said.

"No! I will take only a moment."

They waited until it was almost dark. Chiyo could imagine her going from room to room, remembering the recitals and banquets, the special moments with her husband and children.

Finally, Chiyo and Akiko went back inside to look for her. She was sitting in formal style, in the middle of the stage, a white cloth spread out beneath her. In the half dark, Chiyo thought she saw the glint of a silver object in Grandmother's hand.

"Mother!" Akiko gasped, climbing onto the stage. "What on earth are you doing?" She opened her mother's hands, then felt up the sleeves, but there was nothing there.

"I will not be useful to anyone in Inokuchi," Grandmother said calmly. "You must send Koichi from Chiba so that he can be well fed and nourished. He needs to live his life."

"Mother, it's not a question of that!"

"What's this?" said Isao, staring at Grandmother on the stage. "We have enough food. We've always had enough. We could manage it even if Akiko and her husband and in-laws all came along with Koichi. And Chiyo and Kenichi too."

"I appreciate your hospitality," said Grandmother. "But I have decided that I will stay in this house until Monday when it is torn down."

"You must come now," Isao said firmly. "Government regulations. Everybody has to be out the weekend before."

"Mother, please," Akiko took her by the hand, but Grandmother pulled it away. "Be reasonable," Akiko pleaded.

"The lights have been turned off," Isao said softly. "And the gas." Grandmother did not answer."

Isao climbed up on the stage next to her. "Come with us for the weekend, then. Be with us while Akiko is here. I promise to bring you back early Monday so you can see the house before they tear it down. Then if you really want to remain in Nakajima, we can arrange for you to live with someone in the neighborhood."

"Or you can stay in Nobori-chō with us," said Chiyo. "We have room, and it will prevent us from taking in a soldier."

"Anyway, come with us now," Isao said, standing up and stepping outside the door. He waited for them on the path.

Chiyo waved at Grandmother, safely ensconsed with Akiko in the cab of the truck.

Grandmother nodded, then turned her head away. For a moment, Chiyo thought she caught the glimpse of one glistening tear, but in the dark and at that distance she couldn't be sure.

Chapter Six

BRIGHT SUN FILTERED THROUGH THE *shōji* paper and spread its warmth on the feathery quilts her mother had made. Chiyo loved to lie in this room closest to the sea and listen to the waves lapping against the rocks below. Even during typhoons the sea was a moat against the outside world.

She pushed open the *shōji* just far enough to see the sun splashing on the *engawa* beyond.

At Inokuchi, she could always see the image of herself as a child and measure it against her adult self and against each of the children. Once, watching Yoko on the shore digging clams, she was so overcome with the idea of herself as two people that she felt the division physically. One of her was down at the edge of the sea and the other standing behind, looking at herself. Like a double exposure. It had taken her breath away.

Inokuchi made her feel whole again. But she could survive only small doses of Kazuko's perfection. Like her sister, Akiko, Kazuko had been trained for dancing. But Kazuko's talents were painterly. Before the war, she had orchestrated the hints of luxury: the finest tea from Uji, handwoven dark *kasuri* cloth for the *yukata,* the cotton kimono they wore on cooler summer evenings, bath salts perfumed with pine needles and rose petals, carefully chosen patterns and fabrics for the covers of her cushions, or *zabuton,* flowers arranged in heirloom vases in the entranceway where a *kakejiku* always hung as complement to the flowers—an old charcoal brush painting or a poem written or copied out by an ancestor. At the first hint of spring, she replaced the painting of a snow-covered branch with one of plum blossoms, in summer with one of irises or a locust clinging to a stalk of grass. In the fall, there were red maple leaves painted in watercolor instead of charcoal ink. And the next year, she displayed a different set of *kakejiku* for each season, always accented by fresh flowers or branches from the garden which Kazuko supervised. She carefully balanced the shape and color and size there, too, even paying attention to the number and color of the carp in the pond.

At tea there were sugar cakes in the shape of ocean waves, colored with a tinge of blue, arranged on a plate with thin red maple leaf cakes for contrast. Or *mochi,* pounded rice cakes, filled with bean paste that was yellow instead of the usual brownish red.

Not anymore. At the beginning of the war, Kazuko was cited by the *Tokuho* civil intelligence for wearing clothing that was too dressy and looked too expensive. It was demoralizing for others, they told her. She must wear wartime clothes like everyone else. Kazuko donned *monpe,* but the cloth and pattern were carefully chosen, and the police couldn't see her delicate silk underkimono.

Chiyo looked at Yoko asleep on her *futon.* She had been near her mother every night since she was born, and now for almost four months they had lived apart. Her face was pressed sideways against the pillow, her black shiny hair encasing her face like a piece of lacquer. No question that she would be the beauty of the family. Even more so than Akiko. She was the Moon Princess of the folktales, all the noblemen in the world attempting impossible feats to win her hand.

By now Kenichi would be awake and out walking with Hiroshi on the shore below. When Hiroshi had first been evacuated, he couldn't wait for Chiyo to visit, promptly moving his *futon* next to hers in the room by the sea. But now he was eight, and if the war ever ended and he came back to Hiroshima, his childhood would be gone.

Chiyo's niece, Fusako, slid open the *fusuma.* "What a good sleep you've had, Aunt. But now you can't spend any more of our beautiful Sunday in bed." She set down the tray of steaming tea, closed the *fusuma,* lifted the tray, stood up, bore it to Chiyo, knelt down again, set down the tray, poured the tea. Exactly the way Chiyo herself had been taught. But Fusako moved with the grace of nobility. Except when she thought someone was watching her. Then she was shy and self-conscious, even awkward.

Yoko awoke when Fusako pushed the *shōji* wide open, letting in more sun and a wider view of the garden, with the few lonely gold and silver carp swimming in the pond. The rest had been eaten.

Kazuko entered, bringing another tray with steaming bowls of *miso* soup, a lacquered container for rice, paper-thin pieces of seaweed. Even one egg.

"Breakfast here?" Chiyo said. "I feel like the empress."

Kazuko smiled. "Breakfast for the four of us. Grandmother and Akiko are still asleep, and Husband and the boys have already gone down to the shore."

She placed the soup before them, then began dishing up pure white rice. Chiyo held her bowl with both hands, letting the steam and the fragrance surround her before she began to eat.

The egg. Kazuko whipped it, dividing it into four bowls. "We still have three hens, you know. And every now and then we get an egg. But yesterday we got three! Can you imagine?"

"So the men divided theirs three ways, we're doing it four ways, and Aunt Akiko and Grandmother each get half of one," Fusako explained.

"You should join our *Tonarigumi*," Chiyo said dryly. "We need your kind of genius."

They began to eat, pouring their egg portions over the hot rice, picking up the seaweed with their chopsticks, then gathering a helping of rice inside the ring of seaweed and into their mouths. Only Shintaro's sudden appearance could surpass the ecstasy of it.

Kazuko removed Chiyo's bowl and filled it with a second helping.

"I know we should save this rice," Kazuko said. "Some army official gave it as a bonus out at Toyokogyo factory to encourage production of more guns, but of course there isn't any metal. Husband gave some of his share to the *Tonarigumi* to distribute, and he's saved some for you to give to Mrs. Kasama. He says we should eat the rest now while we can enjoy it."

"You know, they've been eating locusts," Chiyo said.

Lately, Mrs. Kasama had been up along the riverbank looking for special kinds of grass, catching locusts, which she said were good if they were fried crisply in a little sugar. Lean and gaunt, the Kasamas were shadows imprinted on the back of Chiyo's mind.

Chiyo set down her bowl and sighed. *"Mah, Nē-san,* Elder Sister. I will remember this lovely breakfast for the rest of my life."

Isao appeared, pacing in the garden with his arms folded inside his summer *yukata*. "What do you say we take Grandmother and Akiko out to Miyajima for a picnic?" he said. "We can see how the renters are doing in the summer house. Miguchi-san's been itching to take his fishing boat out, and I've gotten my hands on enough low-grade fuel to get us to Miyajima and back."

Chiyo held her breath. She had not dared to hope she would ever see Miyajima again.

They stood silent at the prow of Mr. Miguchi's boat, gazed at the sacred, misty island ahead, listened to the sound of the lapping waves and the even, grumpy muttering of the engine. Lying there behind the famous red *torii*, Miyajima beckoned, wearing its mantle of cedar trees, balancing its pagoda on top of the hill.

Miyajima was Chiyo's island. Not only because she had first met Shintaro there. Because of the summers, too, at the family house on the shore of Sugi no Ura, the Cedar Inlet. And beyond the shore the two-pronged rock, one end sticking up higher than the other like a mother protecting its child. When the tide was out, a stretch of white beach appeared between the rocks. She and Isao and their playmates had swum there and built castles and fortresses from the clean sand swept up by the blue salt water. They had taken oaths that they would defend to the death this secret place. Now, three of those five old playmates had gone off to war, and two had been killed.

In the late afternoon, they lay, sated, under the shade of the huge cedar tree, the swim out to the rocks accomplished, the lunch consumed, the well-being of the renters asked after, the house inspected along with the memories of earlier times. She and Isao had repeated what they knew and remembered of the legendary story of General Nogi, home from victory in the Russo-Japanese War, staying overnight as a guest at their house. Their father had been a young man then, and Isao just old enough to remember the general's uniform and war medals. Chiyo hadn't been born, but she knew the story by heart. He had stayed with his soldiers in the wide *tatami* room upstairs that looked out over the cedar trees and the sea. That room was unlived in now. Everything just as it had been when she was a child. Pictures of the Emperor Meiji with his white mustache and the Emperor Taisho as a young man in military uniform, mounted on a white steed. But mostly she loved the picture of the Emperor Showa as the young boy Hirohito, probably Kenichi's age when it was taken. Wearing his navy-blue high-collared school uniform.

The room was too intense with memories. Chiyo had retreated quickly to the beach, where she was lying now with the others, gazing lazily at the blue expanse beyond them. There was no division between the end of the sky and the end of the sea.

The younger ones were out on the rock, standing in descending order, all profiles. Fusako and Kenichi like mastheads, Yoko nested against the second rock, and Hiroshi just below her, digging through the sand for seashells.

Watching them, Chiyo felt the strength of Isao, sitting next to her, his lean, craggy profile carrying the hint of a smile.

She was seized with the desire to get Shintaro home and freeze them all in this moment.

"Stay the night with us," Kazuko suggested to Chiyo as they sat on the streetcar returning to Inokuchi station. "I'll wake you at dawn."

"I am returning to Nakajima to sleep one more night in my house," Grandmother announced firmly. "I have our things in my bag here, and we left Akiko's luggage in the neighbor's house. Besides, I think I've forgotten a box I stored under the stairs."

"Mother!" Akiko said. "We don't even have electricity."

"We don't need it. I always sleep in the dark anyway. Don't you?"

"What if the police find us?"

"They won't look. They're too busy."

Grandmother was settled firmly into her seat, and it was only a few minutes before the Inokuchi stop. "I'll come back to Inokuchi tomorrow afternoon," she promised. "Right after Akiko gets on the train."

There was an uncomfortable silence.

"We'll go along with them, then," Chiyo said. "In the morning I'll go with Grandmother to see Akiko off, then come back to Inokuchi with her. How would that be, Grandmother?"

"Fine," she said placidly.

Kazuko's anxious face relaxed. Then the streetcar came to a halt.

Chiyo hugged her two younger children goodbye, felt the anguish of parting from them again, watched them disembark with Isao and his family, then waved, watching them standing on the platform until they were out of sight.

Part Two

Chapter Seven

CHIYO WAS AWAKE AT DAWN, ANTICI-
pating news of Shintaro. Some formless
dream had made her feel his presence, though she had barely slept.
Two air raid warnings in the night, one turning into a full-scale
alarm. Each time she and Kenichi had considered the trip to the
shelter, had heard the all-clear signal, and had lain back down in the
motionless hot night air hoping for sleep. It did not come.

Out in the kitchen early she heard someone pushing open the
front door. It was Sachiko, Yasu's sixteen-year-old sister, so quiet
and gentle that people seldom noticed her presence.

"Younger Brother is sick," she said. "He's had a cold all week,
and now he's got a fever."

Kenichi appeared, already dressed. "Shall I go for Dr. Iwamura?"

"No. Mama can go. Just explain why he's absent, will you?"

Kenichi nodded. He was already wrapping leggings around his
ankles.

There was another air raid siren.

"I'd better get home," Sachiko said.

"Can I come over and see him a minute?" Kenichi asked.

"Later," said Sachiko. "After the fever's gone. You don't want
the flu, too." She ran off down the street.

By the time Kenichi stepped outside, looking lonely, Sachiko was back, ready for the day's work. Recently she'd had her assignment changed from the communications bureau at army headquarters to a demolition crew with the younger girls near Kenichi's worksite. She and Kenichi started off together, then turned and waved at Chiyo. She watched them fade into silhouettes against the cloudless sky, then turned back into the house. So much to do. See Akiko off, then accompany Grandmother to Inokuchi. And the Yamamotos to check on.

By eight o'clock she had cleaned the house, set soybeans on to soak, divided the rice for Mrs. Kasama and some for the Yamamotos. She was ready to leave when the siren sounded. The all-clear came moments later. She stepped outside. The sky was azure blue. Crystal, perfect, speechless day, calm and majestic, but too hot. No clouds or mist to protect them from the relentless heat. She saw the silver streaks of a B-29—"B-san," Kenichi called them. It was dancing high in the air, glinting in the sun, dangerous and beautiful. Strange, they'd already sounded the all-clear. And strange, too, that the B-29s flying over them never dropped any bombs. She thought of Mrs. Yamamoto's joke. "Maybe those American pilots want an aerial view of Mrs. Kasama and her husband in bed," she'd said, clapping her hand over her gold teeth. "Very important military secret!" Chiyo had laughed, thinking how hard it would be to endure things without Mrs. Yamamoto.

She decided the last two *asari* clams might cheer up Ya-chan and went back to get them.

A brilliant, blinding light surrounded her, jabbing itself into her body with the force of a thousand electric suns, all echoing a huge, ghostly roar. A wind ripped the bowels of the earth.

The wall collapsed. Dark silence enveloped her. The earth stopped breathing. An excruciating pain throbbed in her arm. She was pinned under a dark, heavy shadow.

Tilting her head backward, she saw slanting beams of light and a gray ceiling with a hole in it leading into an endless twilight sky. With her other arm, she lifted the shadowy weight above her just enough to slide herself out. Then she sat, breathing hard. It must have been a direct hit. But why would they want to bomb her neighborhood, Nobori-chō?

In the murky light she could see that the shadow above her had been her *tansu,* the chest her mother had used. It had toppled over and fallen against the crumbling wall, knocking her down and imprisoning her in the triangle of space beneath. Suddenly it crashed to the floor where she had been lying a moment before. She shivered, then stood and moved away from the wall.

Nothing was where it usually was. The table was in the next room, the dishes broken and spread across the floor. The wall behind the kitchen was gone, the beams caved in. Outside, the Kasamas' house had completely disappeared, the brick wall around it a pile of rubble.

Two people peered at her through the door opening, one with white hair almost standing on end, the other with a torn student tunic, splotched with blood. Both were sooty and dirty.

"Your face," one of them said. It was Yasu's voice.

She felt her cheek, squishy and wet, then took her hand away, covered with blood. No feeling there. Only her arm hurt.

"Your whole cheek is burned," Yasu said.

"But there's no fire."

"I hurt my back the same way," said Yasu.

The other person stood mute like a ghost. It was Mrs. Yamamoto, whose hair had been black the day before.

"You're all right?" Chiyo asked, stepping outside through the broken glass on the *genkan* floor. Mrs. Yamamoto nodded, shaking dust from her head, revealing that her hair was still black underneath.

Chiyo was surprised by her own harsh laughter. "It's dust!" she said, touching Mrs. Yamamoto's hair. "Not fright!"

But Mrs. Yamamoto was looking across the street. "The Kasamas!" she said. "The bomb must have fallen directly on them!" They started across the street to peer through the crumbled wall.

"Look!" Yasu pointed toward the center of the city. It was shrouded in smoke, new smoke pushing up, billowing higher into the sky. Nagarekawa Church slanted forward. Fukuya Department Store stood, battered and alone. Everything around it was gone. And beyond that, toward Aioi Bridge, she could see nothing at all.

"It's even worse down toward Nakajima. Kenichi's in there! And Grandmother!"

"And Sachiko," said Yasu.

The younger Mrs. Ikeda came carrying her baby in her arms, its face crushed and bloody, but staring at them with wide eyes. He wasn't crying.

"How did it happen?" asked Chiyo.

No one answered.

They stood in a huddle, young Mrs. Ikeda almost naked, her

blouse in shreds and her *monpe* trousers torn. Her face was vacant, unseeing.

"We'd better take you and the baby to Dr. Iwamura's," Mrs. Yamamoto said.

"Yukiji!" young Mrs. Ikeda blurted out. "He's back there pinned under the house! I can't get him out. Mother's already gone and Grandparents started off to Otemachi a few minutes ago. And nobody's—"

"You go to Dr. Iwamura's," Yasu ordered her. "We'll get him!"

It occurred to Chiyo, stepping through the rubble to the Ikeda house, that this morning it was Yasu who had needed to go to the doctor.

They couldn't find where the street was.

"Help me!" Yukiji's voice was barely audible from under the collapsed house.

"It's on his chest," said Yasu. "Here, you both pull him while I lift up the beam."

But he couldn't raise it high enough. They tried again, Chiyo and Yasu lifting and Mrs. Yamamoto pulling. They got it higher, but not enough.

"Just pull my shoulders," said Yukiji. "I can move a little now."

Chiyo pulled while Mrs. Yamamoto and Yasu lifted, but the beam settled even more heavily on his stomach, and he shouted in pain.

People were walking along the street, some with their hands stretched out as if they were blind and feeling their way.

"Help us!" Chiyo called to them. "He's pinned under here!"

None of them responded. They were wounded themselves, blackened faces and clothing hanging from their arms and shoulders. One person walked close by and Chiyo saw that it was not clothing hanging down, but skin. They kept walking, mindlessly, staring straight ahead, like ghosts.

"Come on," said Yasu. He had a heavy post in his hand. "Let's try again. I'll pry up the beam with this. Mama, you help me, and Mrs. Hara, you pull on his shoulders. Ikeda-san, the moment we lift it, you move! Understand? As fast as you can!"

They took a deep breath and everybody heaved and pulled. They did move the beam. At least a few centimeters. Chiyo pulled and Yukiji squirmed under it, his face screwed up tight with pain. She was afraid it would drop on him. But he turned sideways and shoved himself far forward before the beam dropped on his good leg. He was still caught underneath as high as the thigh, and he lay there, gasping, his chest heaving.

"Your wheelchair!" Chiyo shouted at him. "Where is it?"

"In the house," he said faintly. But there was no house. How could they carry him with both his legs damaged? Wisps of flame appeared around them, coming closer.

"Ikeda-san, pull your leg out! Just pull it!" Yasu shouted.

"I can't," he screamed. "How can I?"

They tried to reach the beam, but the flames were licking at it, and they couldn't get near him.

"Fire's coming! Just jerk yourself out!" Yasu ran in among the flames and took hold of Yukiji's arm.

"Ya-chan! Come back!" Mrs. Yamamoto shouted. "Everything's burning around you!"

The fallen beams and walls were engulfed in flames, and Yasu ran out just ahead of the fire. Flames were everywhere now, and they couldn't see Yukiji anymore. They were running up toward Asano Park near the castle, leaving Yukiji far behind, alone in the flames.

Masses of smoke swirled around them in the park and Yasu sat with his knees under his chin, his hands covering his face. Chiyo lay under a tree near Mrs. Yamamoto. The ground was strewn with people, burned crisp, calling for water, some of them already dead. The trees were charred, though there had been no fire here.

Yasu took off his student tunic and put it in the ground, then turned on his stomach to lie on it. Chiyo could see the dark pattern of his summer sleeping kimono burned onto his back. A terrible, numbing dread filled her. It was not an ordinary bomb. It was something nameless. Beyond human control.

Somehow Yasu had grabbed a canteen and first-aid kit from their ruined house. Chiyo washed his burns with the canteen water, then found some salve and bandage in his first-aid kit. Mrs. Yamamoto put a bandage on Chiyo's face. There were no burns on Mrs. Yamamoto, and no one had any idea why.

Another group came toward them, one with the skin of his back peeled completely away and dangling down from the waist over khaki trousers. They sat on the ground nearby and she could hear the skinless one talking.

"The top of the castle blew away. I saw it moving in the wind."

Chiyo stared at him. He was addressing no one in particular. They must have all gone mad. The three-hundred-year-old castle borne off in the wind?

She sank into unconsciousness, then awoke to see a woman propped up against a tree quietly breast-feeding her child. But the mother was dead and the child, unaware, still sucked at her breast.

"Don't look," Mrs. Yamamoto said. "We can't help. What can we do?"

Heavy black raindrops splotched Yasu's shirt and Mrs. Yamamoto's face. Chiyo looked down and saw them on her hands. She tried to rub them off. A new crush of people fleeing the fire pressed into the park, moving like a wave toward the river, catching Chiyo among them, separating her from the Yamamotos. People were falling into the river and being carried off by the current. Another crush behind her pushed her forward. She pressed her hands into the edge of the river to keep from falling in, then struggled desperately back up the hill toward the Yamamotos, finally collapsing on the ground next to them, exhausted. Her hands were still covered with the black spots even after being in the water.

"Where did they come from?" she asked. They stared at the spots, too tired to move, not knowing what to do.

The sun was coming out again, hot and relentless. Yasu passed around his flask of water. She was desperately thirsty and drank gratefully, feeling the coolness course through her stomach. The Yamamotos were watching her. She pulled the flask away from her lips and returned it. Yasu offered it to the skinless man but he took no notice. He had died.

After the water, she was weak and unable to move. More smoke came into the park, acrid and searing. The ancient pine trees were bursting into flame, and the bamboo groves exploding. A new wave of people pressed toward the riverbank.

"We can't stay here," said Mrs. Yamamoto.

"The only way out is across Sakae Bridge to the East Parade Grounds," said Yasu. "It's not burning over there."

"But we have to find Ken-chan and Sachiko," said Chiyo. "They're in the other direction."

"It's the only way to get through," said Yasu. "Everything in Nobori-chō is burning."

A vision of Yukiji's face billowed up in the smoke before Chiyo, almost smothering her. He had lived through the nightmare of the war in Burma to come home to this. And they had deserted him, left him in the flames to die.

And the Kasamas. Caught up with concern over Mrs. Ikeda's baby and Yukiji, they'd left them buried under their house. They had burned by now.

Yasu nudged her. "Come on. It's the only way out."

Yasu, only twelve, sick with the flu, making all the decisions.

They moved back out of the park toward Sakae Bridge. The river was clogged with people swimming among the bodies. A man on a raft leaned over to pick up a small boy, pulling him by the hands, but the child's skin came off like gloves, and he slithered back into the river.

Tiny devil-tongue flames stretched out along Sakae Bridge, licking at the railings, disappearing and reappearing somewhere else. People, lined up, followed each other across, unquestioning, unseeing. They did not notice the flames.

"See the fire on the bridge?"

"Where?" asked Mrs. Yamamoto.

Chiyo looked again and it was gone.

They hesitated.

"It's hot again. I'm so thirsty, Mama." Yasu, ashen-faced, a child again, too sick to go to school, and now his back injured and hurting him. He clung to his mother's arm while they gazed across the bridge. They drank once more from the canteen. Chiyo saw a girl Yoko's age sitting by the parapet at the edge of the bridge, her head a black tulip, skin peeled down around her neck.

"Water," the child whispered. Chiyo knelt and offered her some from the canteen. Her own mother would not have recognized her. She felt the Yamamotos behind her, silent, accusing. Hardly any water left.

"Yoko-chan?" she tried. But surely Yoko was safe out in Inokuchi. The child drank, then stared back, uncomprehending, out of her puffed black face, still clutching the canteen. Chiyo took it gently away from her and they joined the others walking in dazed silence across the bridge.

In front of Hiroshima station, a line of people waited for the bus, fingernails clutching each other's shoulders. When she came closer, Chiyo saw that they were corpses leaning against each other, burned to a crisp where they stood. Beyond were two gutted streetcars, bodies inside still clinging to the straps.

The station was an anthill. Streets in front of it were on fire; the Enko Bridge, which led back into the city, was burning. They went around to the back of the station. Trains were loaded with people, but not moving. A stationmaster lay dead on the tracks.

They pushed onto the East Parade Grounds, overflowing with people, all fleeing the city. All injured. She saw a cart piled high with belongings, a child sitting on top, and a woman aimlessly pushing it and carrying a suitcase. How foolish to think of possessions at a time like this.

Finally across the parade grounds, they turned south in along the streets again. Houses were not burned here; some were even standing, but they were occupied only by a deathlike silence.

Water gushed from a broken pipe, and Yasu filled his canteen. They drank and sank to the ground, weak again.

They saw that Taisho Bridge was passable, leading back into the city's center across the Enko River. After that were the Kyobashi and Motoyasu rivers to cross before they could reach Nakajima, where Grandmother lived and where Kenichi and Sachiko had been working. But instead of Nakajima, all they could see was a writhing, towering cloud spreading out at the top like an umbrella, a giant mushroom, rising higher and higher, the fire inside the column full of colors and raging.

"It's so beautiful," Mrs. Yamamoto breathed. "The most beautiful thing I have ever seen."

Chiyo stared at her, then looked back at the cloud. Yes, it was beautiful. And Kenichi and the others were there in the middle of it, surrounded by flames as Yukiji had been.

Once across Taisho Bridge, they followed the streetcar tracks south in front of Hijiyama, the hill where her family had gone to view cherry blossoms. When they reached Tsurumi Bridge above Kyobashi River, they saw that the railings were gone. People thronging across the bridge were almost pushing each other off. Bodies were piled on the edge and floating in the river, most of them middle-school students like Kenichi.

"Don't go in there," people said. "Turn around and go back up Hijiyama. Up on the hill. It's the only safe place."

The smoke and heat were more intense. They huddled at the end of the bridge, unable to decide.

"I'm going in there," Chiyo said. "I'll look for Sachiko. Go back to your in-law's house in Ujina. Follow the streetcar tracks. I'll get word to you. Yasu's sick. There's no need for all of us to go."

"No," said Yasu. "I'm going, too." He pushed ahead through the throng and onto the bridge, out of hearing, so that they had to follow. A wide expanse of land and smoke lay between them and the Motoyasu River. And the fire beyond raged furiously, relentless. They struggled on, stumbling over rubble, not daring to look at anyone or anything. Mrs. Yamamoto's white *tabi* socks were torn and black with dirt, one of her *zōri* sandals gone and both her feet bleeding.

"Shouldn't we stop and wrap a bandage around the bottom of your foot so you can walk?" Chiyo asked.

"No. If I stop, I can't go on."

Everywhere, tiny bonfires started on the ground from nowhere. No streets or landmarks were left to help them find the way. Only the fire ahead. The wind changed and the black smoke surrounded them. They stood, unable to see or breathe, almost suffocating, covering their faces with their hands. When the smoke cleared, Chiyo saw that Shinbashi Bridge had broken in half and fallen into the Motoyasu River. Nakajima, across the river, was billowing with flames and the river itself was choked with bodies. So many were middle-school students.

"Kenichi! Where are you? Kenichi! Can you hear me?" Chiyo shouted again and again into the smoke and the ruins and at the bodies in the river.

Yasu stared at her, startled, then shook his head. "It's no use. We can't get in there."

Chiyo looked north to where the fire was even worse. She could just make out the shape of the sturdy, concrete Motoyasu Bridge, still standing, even though the railings were gone and the lampposts twisted. She tried to see beyond to the Aioi Bridge, the city's biggest and strongest, but the smoke was too thick. If it hadn't collapsed yet, she decided, then Kenichi was alive.

An unbroken line of people came across the Motoyasu Bridge toward them, away from Nakajima and the flames. Nobody was going in.

"Let's go south," said Yasu. "Maybe we can get across the Meiji Bridge."

They poured the precious water from the canteen onto each of their handkerchiefs, soaked their faces, then followed the streetcar tracks in the direction of City Hall.

"Look at that!" Yasu said.

Chiyo was afraid to follow his gaze, but she turned and saw the old Kokutaiji Temple grounds, the tombstones toppled in every direction, and the huge old camphor trees, national treasures, four hundred years old, uprooted and turned over on their sides, their massive roots and stripped branches pointing upwards to the sky.

A bomb of that force. Strong enough to destroy all their houses, peel off their skin, lay waste concrete bridges and buildings, lift up a huge, ancient tree by its roots and lay it on its side. Yet the three of them were still alive.

She sat down, suddenly, in the rubble, weak and sobbing. Yasu musn't see her cry. And Mrs. Yamamoto without even a sandal to walk on. She stood up again, then stumbled against a cistern filled with swollen corpses, one a pregnant woman floating on the water and another a man hanging over the edge. His eyeballs had popped out of their sockets and they dangled, staring up at her. She cried out in fright.

Mrs. Yamamoto pulled her away, and for a moment they stood huddled together, Chiyo staring at Mrs. Yamamoto's unshod and bleeding foot.

"Please!" Chiyo pleaded. "Let me just bandage your foot. Stand there and put your hand on my shoulder. I'll fix it."

Mrs. Yamamoto obeyed and Chiyo knelt down close to the hot, scorched earth, winding the bandage around, padding the bottom. Yasu waited, erect and tense, then went ahead of them toward the Meiji Bridge. They followed dumbly.

A line of soldiers stood along the bank.

"You can't go in there," one said.

"Our children are at the Honkawa Bridge with a demolition crew," Chiyo insisted.

The soldier shook his head. "Nobody can go in there," he said. "You can see for yourself."

Beyond him, she saw two silhouettes of humans running toward them. Then they disappeared again back into the smoke.

"Have you seen any middle-school students coming out?"

The soldier's grimy faced dripped with perspiration, and he wore a bandage around his head. But he was not burned. It encouraged Chiyo to see someone almost whole.

"Go look up on Hijiyama," he said. "They're setting up a first aid station there." Some compassion had crept into his voice.

"We just came from there!" She glared at him, not moving.

"Go back up there again, then. Fire's coming. You can't stay here."

Chiyo saw Yasu ready to spring past the soldier into the smoke beyond. He stood rigid, fighting with himself, then looked accusingly at his mother. "Why didn't you let me go to school today? I should have been with them!"

She didn't answer.

Smoke pushed toward them again, hovering dangerously close, carrying intense heat.

Chiyo moved back. "We've got to stay alive ourselves," she said.

They stared at her.

"We shouldn't have come!" Chiyo said angrily.

"No," said Mrs. Yamamoto. "We had to try."

They went back across the Kyobashi River, this time on Hijiyama Bridge to the south of the Tsurumi. People were clinging to the edge where the railings had once been. But Chiyo did not look at the bodies she touched with her feet, nor at the ones floating in the river below. She pushed across, holding on to Yasu and Mrs. Yamamoto, refusing to see anything except the hill, Hijiyama, the sanctuary.

Across the bridge, they collapsed on the riverbank, trying to regain strength. Yasu recognized two boys floating in the river wearing Rijo Middle School uniforms. He called out to them, but they moved serenely on toward the sea, both dead.

Yasu shouted Kenichi's name, and the names of his classmates.

"Here. Over here," a faint voice responded.

"Ken-chan," Chiyo breathed. She went over along the bank and knelt next to the boy. He wore a torn shirt and tattered underpants. The skin was peeled from his red face, swollen to twice the normal size. He was unrecognizable. But a name tag dangling from the shreds of his pocket said "Nishimura." He was a second-year student, Yasu said. Two others lay next to him, their skin bloated and a bluish white. They were dead.

"Nishimura-kun," Yasu said gently. "Are you all right?" There was no answer. "How did you get all the way over here?" Yasu prodded.

The boy's parched and puffed lips began to move. "They assigned us to Tsurumi—this morning." He had to stop after each utterance to gather enough strength to go on. "We were on the bridge when . . . we swam here." He lifted his head and tried to look around. "You see the others? Just three alive. I . . . huh? Any water?"

Yasu pulled out the canteen, almost empty. He poured the last drops through the boy's lips.

"Have you seen any first-year students?" Yasu asked.

The boy licked the mouth of the canteen, then pressed the steel against his face. "First year all on the Honkawa," he said. "More water."

"Nishimura Haruo!" A man appeared, unhurt. He seemed like a savior from the outside world.

"Haru-chan, is it you?" The man knelt by the boy.

"Papa?" He opened his eyes. "Did you bring us a strawberry ice? I promised these boys here . . . ice with strawberry syrup. From the store."

The man looked at the two dead boys, then back to his son. For a moment, he could not speak.

"I'm sorry, Haru-chan. No ice. But I have some water."

Haruo drank while they watched him. Afterwards the man handed the flask to the others. "I came in from Fuchu when I saw the big cloud," he said. "Do you know what happened?"

"Some kind of different bomb," said Yasu. "It burned us before there was any fire. And it's worse back there. We tried to get in, but we couldn't."

The man looked again toward the fire, then back at his mutilated son. He poured water on a bandage and pressed it against his son's face. "Your brother in there?" he asked Yasu.

"My sister," said Yasu. "And my best friend."

Chiyo gazed at the flames of the city, and tears splashed down her wet and sticky face. She was sweating and dizzy. The man gathered his boy in his arms, trying to find an unburned place on his body to hold him by.

"Come with me," he said to the others. "There's a first-aid station up on Hijiyama. I'll show you where it is."

Finally at the top, they saw that even here, this far from the bomb, the trees were stripped of their leaves. Soldiers were spreading out straw mats for the wounded to lie on. There was water. Chiyo soaked her face and peeled off the bandage. A soldier spread a soothing ointment on Yasu's back and on the face of the boy, Haruo, then gave some to Chiyo for her cheek.

Mr. Nishimura sat next to his son, rocking back and forth with his arms clutched around his knees, singing *Akatombo,* an old folk song about a man remembering chasing red fireflies as a child.

He stopped at the end of a refrain. "We'll stay here a while till you're rested," he said. "Then we'll go home to your mother."

It was dark again, as if night had come, though it was only afternoon. The sun shone at them through the black clouds like an angry, bloodshot eye.

They must have slept. It was twilight when she awoke. In the city below, the fires had died down, but short bursts flared up and scorched the sky, illuminating skeletons of buildings. Maybe Kenichi and the others had gotten out in time. Maybe they were safe out in Inokuchi or Ujina.

Chiyo looked around for Mr. Nishimura and his son, but they had already gone. Yasu lay with his head turned sideways on his mother's arm. A soldier came by and handed each of them a rice ball, sticky and turned sour from the heat. She and Mrs. Yamamoto ate theirs anyway, but Yasu awoke, looked at his, and threw up. Mrs. Yamamoto laid him back on the mat and bathed his face in water.

All night long Chiyo heard the voices of wounded students from the Girls' Commercial School. One voice, soothing and gentle, sounded like a teacher's. Sometimes they sang softly together.

At dawn, haunted by the vision of Yukiji's face disappearing into the flames, Chiyo fell into a restless sleep.

Chapter Eight

CHIYO AWOKE TO A SCORCHING DAY. Her head and cheek throbbed with pain. The smell of burned flesh invaded her nostrils. Skeleton trees haunted the landscape below, and the rivers moved sluggishly under the murky sun. Grandmother's Nakajima was a refuse heap. Her favorite temple, Jisenji, lay in ruins. Across the river was the Red Cross warehouse with its roof crushed, its walls bulging and the insides gutted. Next to it, the Industrial Promotions Hall had become crumbled plaster and gaping windows, its dome a crown of naked girders.

But the Aioi Bridge, buckled on one side as if some giant had tried to rip it to pieces, was still standing. She could even see people straggling across it. The fire was gone now, and she could go in and get Kenichi, take him home on her back if she had to. He would be hurt. Burned like that boy Haruo. But he was alive. Kenichi would not give up so quickly. Probably he was already safe in Inokuchi. They were all out there safe, only waiting for her to come.

To the north of Nakajima, the devastation of the city stretched endlessly. In Nobori-chō everyone's house was gone. Only the spires of Nagarekawa Church jutted at an angle toward the sky. Fukuya Department Store and the Chugoku Newspaper Building towered, lonely and ravished, above the rubble in downtown Hacchobori. Beyond them, gutted concrete bank buildings clustered along the Hondori shopping district.

She thought of Basho's haiku, written on his deathbed.

> Stricken ill on a journey,
> my dreams on withered fields
> are wandering still.

Was this the vision he had seen before he died?

The Yamamotos stirred beside her, but the girls from the commercial school were silent. Chiyo turned to look at them. Three students lay with their heads on the lap of their teacher, who was sitting only slightly slumped over, her hands placed protectively over them. All of them, even the teacher, were dead.

Chiyo envied them. Why had they died in the night and left her and Yasu and his mother still alive? The whole world destroyed, and yet she and the Yamamotos were left to witness the ugly end of it. As if the Goddess of Mercy had chosen only the pure ones to die and left the rest of them to wander endlessly, hopelessly searching across the face of the scorched earth, carrying with them the burden of their dreams. Yukiji burning under the house, his frail grandparents wandering off into the smoke and fire, the Kasamas crushed to death and burned. And by now the Ikeda grandchild gone too. Maybe everyone else in the neighborhood, even Mrs. Ikeda and her husband. He must have been right there at City Hall in the worst of it. What if she and the Yamamotos were the only ones left? Kyoko Ikeda would come home from the country to find her family gone.

Even here on the hill, so many had died in the night.

Soldiers were collecting bodies and building a funeral pyre.

Her bandage was stuck again to the side of her cheek. She got up, aching, and went to the barrel to soak her face and the bandage. Her cheek hurt terribly, but her feet ached even more. How could they get down the hill and across the bridge again?

Kenichi, right now, might be sitting by the river, burned all over, calling out for water and his mother.

Back at their sleeping spot, she saw Yasu sit up and feel his back, caked with blood and stuck to the bandage. "No, I don't want to soak it," he said. "Just leave it the way it is." His flu was gone. Shocked out of him.

More rice balls were passed out, this time even more sour than the last, but Yasu ate his. "We have to go back and look again," he said.

"You're hurt yourself," said his mother. "You go straight to Ujina and tell your grandparents we're alive. I'll look for Sachiko."

"Neither of you should go," Chiyo told her. "You don't have shoes to walk on."

Without a word, Yasu took the *zōri* from the dead commercial-school teacher, bowing to her and chanting a prayer to the Amidha Buddha, then fit them on his mother's feet.

They walked down the hill and through the smoke and exhausted sparks of fire. Everywhere was the stench of death. Among the smoldering ruins, they called out Kenichi's and Sachiko's names, turning over dead bodies so they could see the faces. Most of them were not recognizable. They had to look for other clues—metal identification tags, belts, underwear, shoes. And there were no streets. How would they find where Grandmother's house had been?

Old Mr. Takano, holding his glasses and looking puzzled, stood amidst the rubble at the site of the school. He saw Yasu first. "Oh! You here? You're all right? Lucky you're still alive."

"Lucky?" Yasu asked, peering up at Mr. Takano, his arms dangling hopelessly by his sides.

"Kenichi," Chiyo breathed. "Have you seen—?"

Mr. Takano shook his head. They stood in a silent circle, staring at what had been the school. "No," he said. "I was their teacher and I wasn't even with them when—" He said he'd been on the train coming in to Koi station when it happened. He hadn't been able to get to the school grounds until evening. Then he'd spent the night taking care of the ten or twelve boys he'd found alive. By morning, only one was left, and someone had taken him to a first-aid station near City Hall. The others were either dead or had been taken away by their parents.

"How could any parents get in here?" Chiyo asked. "We tried, but—"

"They came late at night," Mr. Takano said. "When the fires died down. Those parents walked all the way in from as far away as Kabe or Otake or —but they weren't injured themselves, you see."

The boys had been divided into teams, he said. Some of them in the classroom, waiting for their turn with the demolition crew, had been crushed under the building. A few had gotten out and run to the swimming pool, but many had been blinded and had drowned.

Others were standing on the Honkawa Bridge for the morning ceremonies, and when the bomb fell they dived with their teachers into
the river, singing the national anthem. Most of them had been
washed out to sea.

"And it seems a few more were already at work on the buildings.
That's what Yamanouchi Saburo said before we took him down to
City Hall."

Mr. Takano looked again at the rubble under his feet. "Around
here, I've found so many—" His voice broke, and he had to wait to
continue. "Just pieces, you know, and—" He pointed to a pile of
disconnected arms and legs, belts and lunch boxes. Chiyo searched
through the pile. Surely she would recognize Kenichi's lunch. But
all the boxes were burned black and the contents inside like charcoal.

In the distance, they heard the cry of a woman who had discovered her own son, already dead.

"Do you know anything about the First Municipal Girls' School?"
Mrs. Yamamoto asked.

"Oh, your daughter was one of those?" He couldn't bring himself to look at her, and his voice was unsteady when he spoke. "So
many just—carbonized. I can't imagine anybody—" He leaned
over again and began shifting through the debris.

"You'll have to look along both the Motoyasu and Honkawa riverbanks," he said without looking up. "I'll get word to you if I find
either of them."

They went to the Honkawa first. Along the banks were clusters
of middle-school boys. Dead. Yasu turned each of them over and,
if they were recognizable, pronounced their names. Chiyo and Mrs.
Yamamoto looked too, calling out the names of their children. No
one answered.

Chiyo, standing where she thought Kenichi had been the day she
brought his lunch, looked up toward the sun, imagining him on the
roof of a building, the airplane just behind him. Is that how it had
been? The flash and then Kenichi bursting apart in the light,
spreading out and falling, riding on sunbeams, an eyelash fluttering
down, a finger, then an elbow?

She sat on the ground, clutching her knees, unable to move.

He had been on the bridge, she told herself. He was a strong
swimmer. That other boy had swum up on the bank and dragged
two more with him. Kenichi could have done that. Or a rescue
boat had come and picked him up. And he was in a first-aid station
somewhere, resting and getting well.

Along the bank, a soldier was collecting bodies, piling them up. There was no one to say prayers for them, recite the sutras. She held her breath and moved in closer.

"Are you going to cremate them?"

"We're not allowed. It might attract another air raid." He showed her a collection of metal identification tags he had taken from the bodies. Kenichi's was not among them.

"I heard we have a similar bomb," said the soldier. "And it has been dropped on all the cities of the West Coast of America. Each of them has been destroyed." He spoke as if he thought the information would comfort her, but it did not. She was not interested in the West Coast of America.

They struggled back over the ruins to Takano-sensei. He told them to look for Kenichi and Sachiko at the first aid station at City Hall, and to check on Saburo Yamanouchi, the boy he had found alive the night before.

They walked along the west bank of the Motoyasu River, past the broken bridge Shinbashi to the Yorozuya Bridge, which was still standing. They called out again and again.

"Sachiko!"

"Kenichi!"

Their voices echoed across the wasteland. They crossed the bridge and went in toward City Hall. People lay everywhere outside the hulk of the building, all of them black and encrusted with blood.

"Anybody from First Municipal Girls' School?" Yasu called out. "Rijo Middle School?"

No one answered. He tried again. "Yamamoto Sachiko!" he called. "Hara Kenichi!" Still no answer. "Yamanouchi Saburo!"

A nurse pointed toward a motionless black form that was a few pallets away.

He was a piece of charcoal, his face almost obliterated.

"Yama-kun?" Yasu inquired, kneeling down.

"Ya-chan?" the boy said.

"Oh, Yama-kun, it's good to find you. Do you know what happened to the others?"

No answer.

"Does your mother know where you are?"

He didn't answer that question either. He had died, and Chiyo and Yasu sat motionless before him. Chiyo wept helplessly into her wet handkerchief. She had never met this boy, Saburo. Yasu was silent beside her.

"Am I the only one left of the whole school?" he asked her.

Chiyo looked at him and wept again.

Mrs. Yamamoto had been searching on the other side of the room. She came and stood next to them.

"We must find this boy's mother," Chiyo said desperately.

"Takano-sensei will tell her," said Yasu. "He'll know what to do."

Outside, they went back toward the river through what had once been Otemachi, then trudged along the east bank to look one last time for Sachiko before they parted.

"She couldn't be this far from where she was working, could she?" Mrs. Yamamoto asked.

"But maybe the river carried her here," Yasu said.

"Sachiko!"

"Sachiko, answer us!"

They called, one after the other, continuing the search among bodies.

Mrs. Yamamoto came upon a cluster of girls twelve or thirteen, all of them corpses clothed in shreds of uniforms like Sachiko's.

If only sixteen-year-old Sachiko had been at her regular job with the Army Communications Bureau over toward the East Parade Grounds —

"Sachiko!" Mrs. Yamamoto called. "Your mother's here. And your brother, Ya-chan. We came to take you home."

They wandered back and forth, among the bodies, calling.

"It's no use," Mrs. Yamamoto said. "If she's alive, she's already at her grandparents' in Ujina by now. We must go. I can't walk any farther."

They moved away from the river. Then Yasu saw a lifeless form, apart from the others. He waded into the river where the water was waist-deep, and crossed to the bank beyond. "Sachiko!" he shouted. They followed him, then knelt down beside a girl, almost naked and burned red, her breasts bleeding. She was staring up at the sky.

"Mama?" she asked quietly.

Her face was charred crisp and her eyes burned shut so that they couldn't recognize her. They could tell only by her breasts that she was female.

"Is it you, Sachiko?" Mrs. Yamamoto demanded. But the girl didn't answer.

"Tell us your name," Chiyo insisted.

"I'm blind," she said softly. "Is anybody else alive?"

They looked again at the cluster of young girls where they had been searching. Somehow this girl had been separated, but her arm was stretched out toward the others as if she had been trying to save them.

"It's worse here than anywhere," Yasu said. He stared out at the river and the bodies floating there, then leaned forward toward her face. "Sa-chan, is it you? I'm your brother, Yasu."

"Yes," she said weakly. "It's me."

They couldn't tell whether she had heard or understood.

"Look for her name tag," said Chiyo.

But there was only a small cloth around her waist and the thread of a shoulder strap from her chemise.

Mrs. Yamamoto tried again. "Sachi-chan, do you remember yesterday morning when your brother was sick with the flu?"

"Mama?" she said. Now it sounded more like Sachiko's voice.

"What is your brother's full name?" Mrs. Yamamoto insisted.

"Yamamoto Yasutaka," she answered. "Mama, I'm so thirsty."

They looked at each other and nodded, not knowing whether to feel relief or despair.

"Sa-chan," Mrs. Yamamoto said. "We found you." Tears streamed down her face.

Yasu took out the canteen and Mrs. Yamamoto held her up while he bathed her face and helped her drink.

"Where does it hurt the most?" Mrs. Yamamoto asked.

"It hurt all night, but I don't feel anything now, Mama."

Mrs. Yamamoto touched her handkerchief into the river and placed it over the girl's swollen brow. "Sachiko," she murmured again. "Sachiko." She sat hugging her own knees, rocking back and forth, reaching out and touching her daughter's shoulders and hands.

"How can we get her home?" she asked presently.

"I can do it," said Yasu. He lifted her up. "Am I hurting you?" he asked.

She shook her head. He placed her on his own wounded back. She was taller than he was, and her legs dangled almost to the ground.

"You can't do that. It will make your back worse," his mother said. "Give her to me."

In response, Yasu shifted her upward toward his raw shoulders. "You'll have to hold tight around my neck, Sa-chan," he said. "Otherwise you'll fall off."

He started south towards the streetcar tracks that would take them to his grandparents.

Mrs. Yamamoto hurried to follow him, then turned and bowed to Chiyo, not speaking.

Chiyo bowed back. "All my blessings go with you."

"I will pray that Kenichi is in Inokuchi," Mrs. Yamamoto breathed. She did not turn to wave again.

Chiyo stood alone on the riverbank, considering another search for Kenichi. Suddenly she realized that she had forgotten to look for Grandmother and Akiko. She was filled with anger at herself, and started north again toward Aioi Bridge, but after a few moments of stumbling over rubble, she knew that she no longer had the strength.

On the journey out of the city to Inokuchi she remembered only bridges burned and fallen into the river so that she had to shift directions to find a place to cross. The rails of the railroad bridge over the Tenma were twisted and the bridge itself so bent and slanted that she could not remember afterwards how she had managed to cross it.

Then the heavy concrete bridge at Koi and the streetcar filled with people. By some miracle it was still running. It had never stopped, someone told her. She pushed her way onto it. Hiroshi was standing at Inokuchi station, struck mute with horror when he first saw her, tattered and blood-caked. A moment later he was crying with relief.

"I've been waiting here all day," he said.

"And Kenichi, is he—?"

Hiroshi hugged her, took her by the hand and led her to the house. It was twilight. Dark forms, moaning, lay all over the garden and in the sitting room downstairs.

A young girl moved among them, giving them water. It was Yoko. She dropped the cup and hugged her mother around the legs, not speaking, not letting go. Yoko was eleven. Just one year older and she would have been working there in the center of the city, too.

"Is Kenichi here?" Chiyo asked. Yoko did not answer. Kazuko came and took her to the sitting room upstairs. Fusako was there. She and some others had been brought home by her father in one of the Toyokogyo boats all the way from Ujina across the edge of the Inland Sea.

In the twilight, Chiyo recognized two other forms. Grandmother and Akiko. They had been under the stairs, looking for Grandmother's forgotten storage box when the house collapsed, Akiko said, and they found their way out through a hole in the far wall.

"Mother just stood and looked at the ruins. She said it ought to save the demolition crew a lot of work." Akiko gave a short, bitter laugh. "Then we ran. We didn't stop until we got to Koi and found out the streetcar was running. We were the first ones to get to Inokuchi."

Everyone gathered around Chiyo, pouring out news.

"I couldn't recognize my own mother," Kazuko said. "Her face and ears and neck. All burnt. But Akiko. She was right there with Mother, and she wasn't burned at all."

Kazuko had laid them down, washed their injured feet and their other wounds with water and salt. Then the other refugees began to come. Kazuko and the neighbors had set up a first-aid station in the house and garden. No one had slept all night or through the next day.

"And people keep coming," Kazuko said. "They haven't stopped."

"Father's been here and gone again," Fusako told her. "He went to look for you and Kenichi."

"Where's Kenichi, Mama?" Yoko asked.

"He's not here?"

"You didn't find him then?" Kazuko asked. "We hoped—"

Chills went through Chiyo's body. She shook so uncontrollably that Kazuko got her a blanket and made her lie down.

"Husband will find him," she said. "He's searching everywhere for all of you right now."

Chiyo couldn't tell them how it was, how she'd searched herself, how no one else from the first year of Rijo Middle School had survived.

Dark, whispering shadows moved around her as she lay under the blanket. Wistful sounds. Movement in the flickering candlelight, and the voices moaning below. As if they were in a dream.

In the morning she would wake up and her neighborhood would be whole again. Kenichi would be there. She would cook his lunch and send him off to school.

Chapter Nine

THEY DID NOT FIND KENICHI IN THE days that followed. And there was no order or sequence, no sense of day or night. Isao came and went, searching everywhere in all the obvious places—the Red Cross Hospital, the temporary first-aid stations in City Hall, the shells of former grade schools, the basement of Fukuya Department Store, even the navy hospital on the island of Ninoshima, where so many had been taken that day and so many had died. There was no trace of Kenichi.

When Isao announced that another, similar bomb had been dropped on Nagasaki, none of them could give any attention to the news.

Fusako, Akiko, Kazuko, even Yoko, were sleeping in snatches and giving every waking moment to the wounded in the room and the garden below. They opened the old Ogawa medical clinic in the garden, and a nurse from the neighborhood worked with them around the clock. There were a few supplies—tinctures of iodine and a small amount of morphine, which they used only in extreme cases. But no one, not even the nurse, had any idea what to do. There had been no doctors in Inokuchi since their father died.

"Remember how much Father wanted me to be a doctor and carry on his practice?" Isao asked one night, gazing out beyond the *engawa* to the clinic where shadowy figures moved in the building and in the garden outside under the moonlight, endlessly tending the sick and dying. "It's no use," he said, "being an engineer at a time like this."

Kazuko worried about supplies. "Just if we had enough ointment to soothe the pain. Can't you get some from anywhere, Husband?"

But Isao's old associates had disappeared or were dead, and there were no new connections. Everything had turned inside out.

Grandmother was suffering from bouts of diarrhea and vomiting. Chiyo felt sharp pains on the side of her face and along her back and arm. The bandage covering her cheek was always sticking, and Fusako would come and soak it, daubing ointment on it. At times pain throbbed through her whole head, and she could not open her mouth to speak.

"Let's leave it open without a bandage for a while," Fusako said. "Maybe the air will heal it faster."

Chiyo thought of the others downstairs and in the garden, all receiving less attention, and dying without any of their family near them.

Again and again they summoned an old priest from the neighborhood, retired many years. He came, always leaning heavily on his cane, and recited the sutras over the ashes of cremated bodies piled high against the shore where they had played as children.

Grandmother went down to the garden a few hours every day to talk with the wounded. She sat beside them, listening to their stories. They began to call for her when they were dying. "Send that old woman here," they said. "I want to talk to her once more." In the night someone would wake her, and she would go down to the garden and sit, holding the dying person's hand, telling stories from *The Tale of Heike* and *The Tale of Genji*, sometimes reciting passages from the sutras, talking and listening until death came.

Chiyo's cheek began to heal and she insisted she was strong enough to go into Hiroshima to search. Isao reluctantly agreed to take her in the factory truck he'd been using to deliver food from the suburbs. No one was allowed in the city except for official business, but he had collected some Red Cross arm bands and he passed them out to people who needed to search for their relatives.

They started at dawn, speeding down the highway toward Koi Bridge.

"They've cleared the road enough for trucks to get through," Isao said. "And they've got the Sanyo Line running all the way into Hiroshima station now." He pointed north toward Yokogawa where a metal carcass with its paint burned off and its windows gone was moving cautiously along the tracks with an overload of passengers, winding its way through the desert.

Only the train and their truck were moving. A ghostly stillness hovered everywhere else. Landmarks were gone. Naked black trees and clusters of ravaged buildings stood in silence. But Chiyo could still remember the voices calling, pleading with her for help.

Isao slowed to search for the road. "They've cremated more of the bodies now," he said. "The smell isn't as—" Chiyo put her handkerchief over her face and Isao stopped talking.

Another bridge, wooden and unsteady, but passable. They lumbered across it. But at the Tenma Bridge, Chiyo had to get out and walk across. Then Isao turned north toward Aioi Bridge, which was still strong enough even for trucks. Chiyo was comforted when they crossed it, feeling a renewal of her unspoken belief that Kenichi was alive.

Once on the other side Chiyo felt suddenly weak from the shadeless heat and the stench. She had wanted to search along the bank of the Motoyasu, but she could not. "We'll do it later," Isao said. They drove on to City Hall to deliver the rice balls from the Inokuchi *Tonarigumi*. Offices had been set up inside the shell of the building and in tents outside the south wall.

A man with a bandaged head received the food. He looked exhausted.

"You'd better get some rest," Isao told him.

"Well, things are getting better. Food distribution is organizing. Trucks going in to each neighborhood. And somebody there seems to know how to get it delivered. At least we hope they do. We can't check too closely."

He told them about army platoons being sent in from outside to clear the streets and cremate the bodies.

"But there's so much else to do," he said, "and hardly any doctors or anyone left at City Hall. You knew the mayor had been killed, didn't you?"

Isao nodded.

"And your own wound?" Chiyo asked.

He smiled. "This happened just yesterday. Stumbling around in the rubble. I fell and hit my forehead. Nothing serious. I wasn't here when the bomb fell." He sounded apologetic. "Found your nephew yet?" he asked Isao.

"No. This is his mother, my younger sister. Hara Chiyo."

The man bowed to Chiyo but he could not bring himself to look at her. "Down there in the basement they're putting the bones and ashes in old newspapers and then writing the sex and approximate ages on the outside. Sometimes they even have those metal identification tags. But most of them were lost. Or they melted. Go down and have a look."

The crumbling walls smelled of burned metal and flesh.

Chiyo read the description on each of the bags which had been stacked in piles on the concrete floor.

"Male. Age twelve to thirteen."

On some was added the name of the school. Many were Rijo Middle School boys. Whoever cremated the bodies must have recognized the uniform.

Some of the names on the few metal ID tags were faintly familiar. But none bore the name of Kenichi Hara. Any one of the nameless bags could have contained Kenichi's remains. She could choose one, take it back to Inokuchi and hold a funeral for him. But she would never do that without proof. He could have suffered from amnesia and wandered off to some distant infirmary. She would search until she found him.

They went to the Honkawa Bridge, the one Takano-sensei said the boys had been standing on. A group of soldiers were there, clearing away rubble for a road. There were no more bodies, they said. All of them had been cremated and taken to City Hall.

They went to the foundation of Kenichi's school where Takano-sensei had been searching for his students, but he was no longer there. Instead, a group of fifteen- and sixteen-year-olds from Osaka had come as a rescue team with their teacher, a native of Hiroshima.

"Are there any of those metal identification tags?" Chiyo asked one of the boys. He seemed even younger than fifteen. Kenichi's age, maybe.

"Well, over here," the boy said, looking at her cautiously. "We've just been putting the tags in a pile while they're being cremated; then we put some ashes and bones in each bag. We don't have time to match the tags with the bones," he apologized.

He was taller and thinner than Kenichi. And undernourished. Everyone said there was less food in Osaka. Such a young boy. Surrounded by death. When she was his age, she had seen only one person die.

The boy pointed to two mounds of paper bags. "We've identified them the way they told us to at City Hall," he said, "and these here have names." He followed her toward the mounds. "But I don't remember that name, Hara Kenichi." He moved the bags around so she could see the writing. "Here's one with a tag melted so you can't read it."

She stared at it, trying to discern some clue from the vestige of one unmelted letter on the lump of shapeless metal. She could not.

"Then over there—" The boy pointed toward the demolition site, the place she had seen Kenichi on the roof that day.

"Those are bodies we just discovered under the rubble. Ready for cremation."

She hadn't noticed the mound before, and now suddenly the wind came, carrying with it the stench, knocking the breath out of her. Abruptly, she sat down on her heels, weak and gasping, readying herself to look at the pile of corpses.

"Stay here," Isao ordered. "I'll look."

The boy stood quietly next to her, not knowing what to say.

"Have you seen Takano-sensei?" she asked, still resting on her heels. "He was my son's teacher, and he was here the day after the bomb, trying to rescue everybody."

"Takano-sensei!" The boy's face brightened.

"You knew him?"

"Sensei!" He shouted to his own teacher. "This housewife here knows Takano-sensei!"

The teacher and a clutch of boys gathered around her.

"He was a year ahead of me at Hiroshima Higher Normal School," the teacher told her.

"Oh, then you must know my husband, too." She introduced herself, and they bowed to one another.

The teacher told her that Takano-sensei was still working when they arrived on August 9 and that they couldn't get him to leave, even to stop and take a rest. He had insisted that he must find everybody, because he was the only one left alive. He kept telling them that he should have been there with the others and died with them.

Finally, his wife had come with a hand cart and wheeled him back to Hatsukaichi. By that time, his hair was falling out and his skin an unhealthy color. "I don't think he could have walked even as far as the streetcar."

"If we had only known," Chiyo said. "My brother could have taken him in the truck."

Isao, his face rigid with control, returned from examining the pile of bodies.

"We're running out of fuel for cremating them," the teacher told him, "so the army's given us corrugated tin to put over them. Then eventually the heat takes over and burns them."

Chiyo looked again at the mound. Didn't everyone on earth at least deserve his own funeral?

"What kind of bomb was it, do you think?" the teacher asked.

Isao merely shook his head.

"Was it germs? Mr. Takano wasn't even here when the bomb fell, and yet he—"

"None of us know," Isao said, turning away from the mound and toward the river.

"No, I suppose not." The teacher nodded. "I'm taking these boys back to Osaka tomorrow. I know we haven't done enough, but I'm afraid we'll all catch this disease, and I'm responsible for them."

"You've done quite enough," Isao said. "And you're right about taking them back. You should leave as soon as you can. Another team will come. We very much appreciate what you've done for us."

They parted, bowing elaborately as they would have done for the emperor. Or for guests at a funeral.

Isao guided the truck along the cleared roads to Nobori-chō. She had given up all hope for the Kasamas, but Mrs. Ikeda had been off in the Danbara district behind Hijiyama that day, and everybody said the houses there, protected by the hill, had not burned.

They found Dr. Iwamura working at the ruins of the Fukuroma-chi Grade School infirmary, his wife and daughter helping him. He had not stopped since the bomb fell.

"You'll get sick like Takano-sensei if you don't rest," Chiyo warned him.

"But what can I do? Look at these people here, lying in their own feces. All we can do is bathe them and change their bandages just once before they die."

The floor was crammed with mutilated forms, suffering people barely alive. And still, he said, they kept coming. As soon as someone died and the body was removed, more wounded appeared. There was never enough room.

"But my cousin brought more supplies from Okayama. He's a doctor too. But we have no idea how to treat them. They're not ordinary burns, and we don't know why they're dying. Sometimes the sick ones get well and the healthy ones die."

"What happened to the younger Mrs. Ikeda?" Chiyo asked. "She brought her baby to you right after the bomb."

"Who? I don't— Oh. He died, I'm afraid. They were the first ones to come for treatment, but my clinic was burning and I grabbed my instruments and we ran down here. He was dead when we arrived; then so many others came that I lost track. The mother wandered off somewhere. I haven't seen anybody from your part of the neighborhood since. I'm sorry."

Chiyo bowed and turned away. "Ken-chan!" she cried out on impulse. "Hara Kenichi, can you hear me? Are you here?"

No one answered.

"If I had seen Kenichi, I'm sure I would have remembered," Dr. Iwamura assured her. "Your brother has been coming by and asking every day."

"He was wearing his uniform and carrying his lunch," she insisted.

Isao and the doctor looked at her, startled, their faces full of concern.

"I know," Dr. Iwamura said gently. "I'll tell you if I hear anything."

She followed Isao out of the infirmary, feeling foolish for what she had said. Three hundred and fifty boys in the first year of Rijo Middle School, all of them wearing uniforms, carrying their lunches, and the only survivor she knew of had died in the City Hall first-aid station the following morning. But still, some of those parents had found their sons. Takano-sensei had said so himself.

At Nobori-chō, Chiyo recognized the ruins of the Ikeda house, even the beam Yukiji had been under, and she saw that it had been moved.

"Then somebody must have found him," she said. "Somebody in the family is alive."

They left a message, writing in charcoal on the beam, telling the Ikedas they were staying at Inokuchi. Chiyo ached to see Mrs. Ikeda, but when she thought of Yukiji calling out from the flames, she dreaded it too.

The tiny Miyamoto house and stationery shop next to the Ikedas' had burned to the ground. And the only parts left of the Ishibashi mansion were the concrete foundation and the old stone lion which had once guarded the entrance. Its head was gone.

The Kasamas' house was a pile of ashes. No sign of life or movement there. And no relatives to search under the rubble and find their corpses. She had never given Mrs. Kasama the rice from Inokuchi. If only she had gone early that morning before the bomb— If only Mrs. Kasama could have had a bowl of white rice before—

"We must dig out their bones for them," she told Isao. "And give them a proper burial."

"They're buried under their own house," Isao said. "That's as good a burial as any."

Beyond the vacant lot on the other side of the Kasamas' were the remains of the greengrocer's shop. And across the street, the Tamioka house, the Yamamoto house, the Hara house, the Kakihara house. A crumbling wall remained erect on the Yamamotos' land. Only foundations remained on the others. Yet Chiyo and the Yamamotos had escaped. Surely some of the other neighbors were alive.

At the site of her own house, she left two messages, one under a stone in the garden and one on the charred remains of a telephone pole.

> Hara Kenichi—
> We are all alive and in Inokuchi with your Uncle Isao. Send word as soon as you can.
> Your mother

Isao had already left messages everywhere in Hiroshima—at the railway stations, at the entrance to Fukuya Department Store, on a board in front of the shell of the Geibi Bank Building.

"There's still a good chance he'll show up out at the navy hospital on Ninoshima," Isao said. "They keep bringing people out there, and they haven't identified everyone yet."

"Oh, yes. There's hope," she said. "There's still hope."

On the ground where her house had been, she recognized Kenichi's favorite science book lying on a piece of *tatami* matting, its back broken and its pages burned. A broken chopstick lay next to it. And one of her *zabuton* was ripped open, its stuffing pushing out, unburned and white.

They pushed away the debris, then lifted the movable *tatami* and pulled out the precious metal-lined box filled with emergency rice. Inside was only a mass of black kernels, stuck together like the contents of the lunch box she'd seen on the ground the day of the bomb.

"Let's take it with us," said Isao. "They say people don't even have cooking pots. Somebody will need it."

The pond in the garden was filled with mud that pillowed Shintaro's two prized golden carp. Both were dead.

But it was the sight of the old Russian bathtub that made her lose her remaining strength. Her father had bought it from among the army leftovers shipped back to Hiroshima at the end of the Russo-

Japanese War. He had installed it in their house as a wedding gift, and in the bomb it had blown clear from the second floor. They had not used it since the war began. Now it was split in half, its two sets of claws on either side dug deep into the soil. Hiroshi would never have a chance to splash in it.

Chiyo slept through the entire next day. The day after that, she wanted to go back and search again. Isao wouldn't let her. A rumor had sprung up that anyone who went into the city would die soon afterwards, and each day after Nagasaki, they were constantly on the alert for the next bomb.

"They won't do it to Hiroshima again," Isao said. "There's nothing left. But it could be somewhere close by. And anyway, people seem to think there's poison in the ashes. Or that it's contagious."

"But you go into the city every day," Chiyo protested.

"I never stay long, and I'm always careful," he said. "Besides, I wasn't there when it fell."

"If I'm going to die anyway, I want to spend my last hours searching for Kenichi."

He was angry. "You're not going to die. And we're doing everything possible to find Kenichi. You know that." He stalked out of the house.

It was pointless to argue with Isao when he made up his mind.

Chiyo decided to go out to Hatsukaichi to see Takano-sensei.

"You shouldn't," Kazuko reprimanded. "You're not healthy enough." But she saw that Chiyo was determined. "Take some of those peaches Husband's friend sent from Okayama," she said. "You know, they're the first food Mother's been interested in."

"We should keep them all for Grandmother."

"Just take a few," Kazuko said. "Husband can get more. You need a suitable gift for Kenichi's favorite teacher."

Chiyo had planned to take one of the family's hanging scrolls, but their only value was in trading for food. She took three of the peaches.

At Hatsukaichi, a suburb halfway to Miyajima, she found Takano-sensei still in bed, unable to throw off his lethargy. He had no appetite, his wife said, but their doctor had managed to visit him and had found a very low red corpuscle count. It was diagnosed as severe anemia, too risky to do a transfusion. Chiyo hardly recognized the former Takano-sensei.

"How is that boy, Yamanouchi Saburo, the one I sent you to see?" he asked weakly.

"He died a few moments after I found him. You didn't know?"

"I don't remember now. I only remember telling you to check on him."

For a time he lay staring at the ceiling, not speaking. "Go and visit Saburo's mother," he said at last. "You were the last one to see him alive."

She nodded in agreement, and then sat a while by his *futon,* telling him about the rescue team and what they had said about the teacher, Mr. Takano, and how much she and the other mothers appreciated what he had done for their boys.

He lay there, seeming to listen, grunting and nodding.

"*Oi!*" he called to his wife. "Listen, give Mrs. Hara the address of the Yamanouchi boy. You have it, don't you?"

He grew more detached, drifting away from her, and then fell asleep. Chiyo looked up at his wife, who had come and knelt on the other side of the *futon.* "I've tired him out," Chiyo said.

"No, it's all right. None of us can ever tell when he gets tired. Anyway, when he does, he just stops talking." Mrs. Takano sat with her hands clasped in her lap, gazing at his face.

Chiyo remembered the gift.

"Here, try these peaches," she said. "Such small, inadequate offerings. And hardly in season yet. But they are helping our grandmother, who was right in the middle of the bomb. She can't seem to eat anything else. Some people say they're the only food that helps."

She presented them wrapped in one of Kazuko's best *furoshiki.*

Mrs. Takano tried to thank her but instead covered her face with her kimono sleeve and began to weep. Chiyo stared at the peaches, wishing she had some word of comfort, but nothing occurred to her. These days it was the small things that made people cry. Three puny peaches. Before the war, nobody would even have picked them off the ground.

"Thank you," Mrs. Takano said at last.

"He's mostly just tired, you know," Chiyo said. "He'll get his strength back after he's rested more. I did, and now all I have is this scab on my face. And fresh food helps. We'll be getting more peaches from Okayama now that it's the season.

"And you know, we've been putting mashed potatoes on Grandmother's burns, and my face, too, and—" She looked again at Mr. Takano, asleep now. "Of course, he doesn't have any burns, does he?"

"No—" Mrs. Takano's voice broke again, not from sorrow, but anger. "He wasn't even *in* the city then, and afterwards he wouldn't come home. He just kept—" She swallowed hard, then changed the subject. "Yes. Fresh food. My uncle brought fresh vegetables from the country, and then we've been trying the moxa treatment, burning powder on his back. That helps a little."

They bowed vigorous goodbyes at the front *genkan*.

On the way home, Takano-sensei's voice kept echoing in her head. "Go and visit that boy's mother. You were the last one to see him alive."

The next morning, August heat still oppressive and with an urgent sense of time running out on her, she awoke determined to visit Yamanouchi Saburo's mother.

It was easy enough to get across the highway to the station platform, but after that, each moment of waiting at the platform, contemplating the rest of the journey in toward Hiroshima, drained more of her energy and nerve. When the streetcar came, only the memory of Takano-sensei's voice urged her on.

At Takasu, she thrust her way toward the exit, then saw that she was not in the peaceful, elegant suburb she remembered. Houses lurched to one side. An angry giant had ripped out the *shōji* from the upstairs windows. Broken glass and refuse lay strewn on the once-immaculate road. And she could see, through breaks in the hedges, that many houses had collapsed here, too.

Chiyo, following the map Mrs. Takano had drawn for her, turned down the alley and came upon the white plaster wall of a storehouse. Long black streaks were imprinted there, unevenly, as if rain had fallen. Black rain. It chilled Chiyo to remember the black rain that had covered her face and hands and to discover that the black sticky stuff had fallen here too, as far away as Takasu.

Finally she stood before the house, neat and serene in spite of its surroundings. The broken glass had been removed from the windows and replaced with newspapers, the *shōji* paper carefully mended, and the street in front swept clean. A beautiful bonsai pine stood in front. In the garden behind the hedge someone had swept away every fallen leaf.

A maid answered the door. It was that kind of household. Isao and Kazuko had had servants before the war, and there had been servants all through Chiyo's childhood. Now it seemed ludicrous.

"Is the wife of Yamanouchi in?" Chiyo asked, bowing low. But the maid merely looked at her, a little dumfounded.

"There is no such person in this household," she said.

The mother had died too?

Chiyo tried again. "Yamanouchi Saburo's mother? Does she live here?"

The maid stood immobile and stared at Chiyo. "He has already died!" she exclaimed. "You don't know that he died in the bomb? Who are you and where are you from?" She was not a young woman. Perhaps she had belonged to the household for a long time.

"He was a classmate of my son's," Chiyo said, pausing to see what effect her words had. "My son was also in the bomb."

The maid continued to stare at her.

"But so far we have not found any trace—"

The maid was suddenly sympathetic. "Your son was at the Rijo Middle School that day, too?"

"Yes," Chiyo said. "And I was sitting at Saburo's side in the hospital the moment he died. I have not been able to come before because I—"

"Come in, please," said the maid.

"Where is Saburo's mother?" Chiyo asked. "Did she die, too?"

The maid did not answer, but led her into a small room on the left side of the hallway, a Western-style room filled with overstuffed chairs and a low table. There was a musty air about it, as if it had always been used only for formal guests. She motioned for Chiyo to sit down, then pattered off down the hall. Was she summoning someone?

Eventually she reappeared, carrying a tray with a teapot, two cups and a plate of small sugar cakes made in the patterns of maple leaves and ocean waves, the kind Kazuko used to serve. She set the tray on the table and then stood at the door after she closed it, as if listening for footsteps. Finally she sat down on the sofa opposite and poured the tea.

"I am Saburo's mother," she said.

Chiyo stared at her, not touching the tea. "Then you are Mrs. Yamanouchi, are you not?"

"I am the maid, and Saburo was the heir of this household. It is the house of his uncle, Dr. Yamanouchi. When Saburo's father died— Well, it was a traffic accident, you see. Mr. and Mrs. Yamanouchi were in a taxi that crossed the railroad tracks in front of a train. Saburo was only two at that time, and I came here with him as his nurse."

She was staring at her lap as she spoke. "The doctor and Saburo's father were brothers, and Dr. Yamanouchi never married. So Saburo was the only heir of both households."

She paused, searching for some way to explain the whole affair.

"Of course, Mrs. Yamanouchi knew who Saburo's real mother was. She was barren herself, you see, and her husband needed an heir."

Had they really planned it all like that, Chiyo wondered, the wife knowing everything?

"Everyone close to the family thought he had been adopted from some distant relatives out in the country. And of course Dr. Yamanouchi does not know that I am Saburo's real mother. No one knew, in fact, after Saburo's father and Mrs. Yamanouchi died. Not even—" She struggled against a break in her voice. "Not even Saburo."

The woman's words echoed in Chiyo's head. "Not even Saburo."

To have a child and to be near him all the time and yet not to have him know that you were his mother! How could anyone manage that?

"I was going to tell him before he had to go into military service. Or at least by the time he was eighteen. But he was such a frail child and working so hard on that demolition crew. Besides, he was beginning to study for the exams to Tokyo University. I didn't want anything to disturb him before then."

The woman stared fiercely at her lap. "I have never told anyone but you," she whispered, "and I do not even know your name."

"I am Hara Chiyo," Chiyo said quickly. "And my son's name is Kenichi. Perhaps you know that Takano-sensei found Saburo and took him to the Red Cross Hospital. Right now, Mr. Takano is at home in Hatsukaichi, resting. I saw him yesterday, and he is still quite weak. He wanted to come and visit you himself."

"I am so grateful for what he did," Saburo's mother said. "He was Saburo's favorite teacher."

"Kenichi's too," said Chiyo.

"My name is Tanaka Yasuko," the woman told her. "And you saw my son in the hospital?"

"Oh, yes. But by the time we found your son, he was too weak to talk. We think he said 'Ya-chan.' Those were his last words. But we're not sure. He might have been gasping or sneezing. Or he might have been greeting Yasu, who was a close friend of Kenichi's and of course a classmate of your son's. He was with me when we found Saburo."

Tanaka-san said nothing, so Chiyo went on. "Saburo was very burned, I have to tell you. And very sick, but he died in just an instant. I don't think he suffered at the end. And on his face, there was a very serene smile." She didn't remember a serene smile, but it seemed an appropriate thing to say.

"Really?" said Tanaka-san, looking up. "Ya-chan? Did he say that? That's my nickname, too. From Yasuko. Saburo always called me Ya-chan. It sounded to me like *Ka-chan,* like calling me 'Mama.'" She beamed at Chiyo as if she had suddenly been released from prison into a field of sunlit daisies.

Chiyo began to cry, the tears coursing down her face as if a wall had broken inside her.

Yasuko Tanaka sat blissfully unconcerned. "Ya-chan!" she repeated. "He really said that? He said Ya-chan?" She bowed as far forward as her Western armchair would allow. *"Oku-sama,* honorable wife," she said. "I cannot find the words to express my gratitude."

She noticed Chiyo's moist face. "And your own son? You say you have not found him yet?"

"No, we have found nothing," Chiyo said. "No evidence that he died or that he's alive. Just—" She felt her face filling up with tears again. She did not want to cry in front of someone who did not know Kenichi, and she did not want to talk about him, even to this woman with whom she had formed a bond. "Just nothing," she finished.

"Oh, please drink some tea," Tanaka-san urged. "I'm afraid it's cold now. I'll get some more."

"No, don't," Chiyo said quickly, lifting the cup and drinking. It helped suppress the tears. "It's delicious tea, but I have to go now. Just tell me if you know of any other boys who survived, if there is someone I could ask, you know, someone who saw him that day, who knew whether he was in the classroom or outside."

"No," Saburo's mother replied. "There was no one I know of who survived. None of Saburo's close friends, certainly, and, except for a neighbor who brought Saburo's ashes, no one else has come to visit. I waited for Saburo to come home that day, you see, and when he didn't come, I went in to look for him the next morning. By the time I found him, it was too late. And they wouldn't let me take the body. They had to cremate him there, they said. So we had the funeral here after they brought the ashes. I haven't gone outside since. Except for shopping. Dr. Yamanouchi is gone most of the time, and I must see to this house. The doctor has always lived here with his mother, but she died a few days ago. From sorrow, I think. From having lost her only grandchild, you see. She was not injured by the bomb."

She wiped her eyes. "I can't leave this house," she whispered. "And I can't stay here either."

The afternoon grew darker. The shadows lengthened. Chiyo couldn't bear to remain.

"I will come again," she said. "Right now, I must go. Is there anything more I can tell you about Saburo-san?"

"No, it is enough," Tanaka-san said. "To know that he died serenely and with my name on his lips."

They bowed elaborately to one another at the gate and then bowed sporadically as they separated.

Chiyo had just turned the corner into the wide street beyond the hedges when the woman called out to her.

"Wait!" she shouted. "I don't have your address! And tell me your name! I have forgotten your name!"

Chiyo paused and reached into her handbag for her husband's name card, but of course she had none. They had been destroyed by the bomb along with her house.

It was unprecedented that they could have talked about matters so close, that this woman could have told her a secret she had never told anyone else, and yet that there had been no formal exchange of names. Chiyo hovered beside the hedge, which hid her from view, searching in her handbag for paper to write on. But she had none and she did not have enough strength to go back, not even to call out her name, and certainly not enough to comfort Tanaka-san in the coming months. She hurried along, bent over, to keep her head from protruding above the hedge.

"*Oku-sama,* honorable wife!" she heard Tanaka-san shout out once more.

Moments later Chiyo was at Takasu station, then on the streetcar bound for Inokuchi, hanging, breathless, on to the leather strap.

Chapter Ten

THE HEAD OF THE VILLAGE CAME AND told us this morning." Kazuko looked anxiously across the table at Isao. "He wants to use our radio. I told him it doesn't work well, but he says it's better than nothing, and he wants the whole village to be together when we hear. Do you have any idea at all what it's about?"

"No idea," Isao said. "But everybody in the city is talking about it."

Kazuko's lips quivered. "It's the invasion, isn't it? The American troops are going to invade us."

A dozen visions went through Chiyo's head. She and the others limping toward the hills beyond the railroad tracks, followed by giant American soldiers with spears at the end of their guns. They would want to rape Fusako and Akiko. Yoko, too. Maybe all of them.

"Probably not an invasion," Isao said wearily. "At the mayor's office they're saying it's another routine statement, asking us to keep our spirits up and work harder. Or maybe they're going to tell us about Nagasaki. They'll tell us that the details are still under investigation but that the damage seems to be light. That's the way they reported Hiroshima. Light damage." Isao pushed his hands inside his kimono sleeves. "The new mayor says he's estimated at least one hundred thousand died outright in Hiroshima and as many more are missing or have died since. If that's light damage, I wonder what the army considers heavy damage."

Isao, the taciturn one, was suddenly sharing the outside edge of his bitterness.

Grandmother set down her teacup. "Two hundred thousand? That's almost the whole population of the city!"

Isao nodded. "And maybe even more. There's no way to count."

The neighbors came limping, helping their wounded relatives and friends.

They knelt apprehensively on the *tatami,* staring at the radio.

Grandmother had declined the invitation to come down, saying she could just as well get the news later from her daughters. But when the strange, incomprehensible announcement sounded across the static like the voice of an apparition, using language that Chiyo had learned in school but had never in her life heard anyone speak, Grandmother appeared from upstairs and sat near Isao.

"It is the emperor speaking," she said.

"The emperor?"

They looked at each other and at Grandmother in stunned disbelief. No one even in Tokyo, let alone Hiroshima, and certainly no one in the tiny village of Inokuchi, had ever expected to hear the emperor speak. In the Western Paradise, perhaps. Not on this earth.

The high-pitched, unnatural voice lingered in the room long after the speech was over.

Chiyo could hardly follow the import of the message, but she knew, when the broadcast ended, that the war was over. They had been defeated, and the emperor himself had asked them to bear the unbearable.

The women, some who had come at midday from their field work, knelt with their faces buried in their arms and wept without making a sound. The men stood up and went outside, gathering in a tight knot on the veranda, muttering in disbelief.

"It isn't true," Chiyo heard one of them say. "It's a conspiracy. They've invaded the palace and got hold of the emperor and made him say that. He wouldn't do it of his own volition."

"I'm glad," Grandmother announced loudly. "I'm glad it's over. Who cares who wins or loses? Just end it. We've had enough."

A tear coursed down Kazuko's cheek and splashed on her hand.

Chiyo did not feel like crying. An ocean of relief welled up inside her. The war was over. What she had secretly prayed for since April. Shintaro could come home now and help them search for Kenichi.

How could an occupying army hurt them any more than they had already been hurt? An invading one, maybe. Not a conquering one. The war was over.

"Damnable army and navy," Isao muttered. "Leading us into this thing, then telling us all the time we were winning." He snapped the radio off, almost knocking it from the table, then sat down with his legs crossed, buried his face in his arms and wept.

Chiyo had never seen her brother cry.

For endless days, uncountable time, they sat like rocks in the garden of the famous Kyoto temple, Ryoanji. They were silent, motionless, in a wide expanse of eternity, not touching each other, not invading each other's thoughts.

The patients were gone from the room downstairs now, either dead or taken home by their relatives. Those who remained in the garden clinic were still calling for Grandmother. She was the weakest among them, but when they called for her she gathered her strength and went to them.

Fusako continued to bathe Grandmother's and Chiyo's faces in the Ringer's solution they had found among Father's supplies. Grandmother continued to insist that Fusako give her first attention to the patients in the clinic, and Fusako complied, managing somehow to take care of everyone. She began leaving the wounds without bandages for the air to heal. The treatment refreshed Chiyo, but it did not improve Grandmother, who had more wounds than Chiyo. Everyone dreaded the day Grandmother would ask to look in the mirror. Chiyo touched her own burn whenever she looked at Grandmother's face. It felt smaller and was lower on her cheek, but it pulled sideways and hurt when she spoke.

At least burns were something they had experienced before. It was the purple spots they worried about. Kazuko had seen them first when she was nursing victims in the garden. They appeared without warning on people's faces, on their necks and arms, even on their torsos. And inevitably, within a few days, people who had them died.

They searched themselves surreptitiously, with secret dread, checking their own skin, and afterwards looking shyly at each other's. Chiyo checked Hiroshi and Yoko every night, even though they had not been in the bomb, in case the spots were infectious.

The inevitable arrival of the occupying troops concerned them, too, and they waited with anticipation and dread, but so far there was no sign of any foreign presence. Isao predicted the soldiers would arrive toward the end of August, or maybe September, after the instruments of surrender were signed.

Chiyo continued her search for Kenichi. Now that the threat of air raids had ended, she put on the Red Cross badge and went into Hiroshima whenever she had the strength, making the rounds to the neighborhood, the infirmaries, the bulletin boards. Takano-sensei had given her the addresses of parents who had found their sons. She searched for one boy in Hakushima behind the castle, but none of the people living there in makeshift shacks had known the family.

She and Isao took the truck to check on a family living in a heavily damaged house in Midori-machi, south of Miyuki Bridge, an area which had not burned. The parents had found their son on the riverbank on August 6. He had been on the bridge with the others, had dived off, and then managed to swim ashore. But he had died at home on August 9 and there was no way to know whether Kenichi had been with him.

"As far as we know," the mother said quietly, "none of those boys are still alive. But I have heard that the Miura child died on the eleventh. You might go and see those parents. They live in Kure."

It was a long trip to Kure. They went just to satisfy Chiyo's dim hope that the boy might have mentioned Kenichi before he died. He had not. He had been sitting in the classroom when the bomb fell. But he had told his parents that one group of boys had already gone outside to work on the demolition crew. And so far no one had survived who could tell what had happened to them.

That night Chiyo awoke again from the nightmare of Kenichi on the roof disintegrating in the sun, the light piercing through him, then his eyelashes floating like butterflies, exploding on the ground and creating tiny bonfires all over the earth.

For days Chiyo did not have the strength to go back into Hiroshima. But Isao continued to go back and forth, delivering food, asking about Kenichi and missing neighbors, friends, co-workers. His energy seemed inexhaustible. Kazuko warned him repeatedly about doing too much and getting sick, but he replied that as long as his energy remained, he would use it.

They waited eagerly for him to come home each evening, bringing news.

He told them of the team of scientists who had come from Tokyo to investigate just after the bomb. They had concluded that the blast was produced by the power of splitting atoms, which meant that everyone had been burned by nuclear radiation rather than by fire.

"But what good does knowing that do?" Kazuko asked, exasperated. "Weeks have gone by. People are still dying and we don't know how to treat it yet."

Isao told them about the huge pumpkins growing in everybody's garden, including Chiyo's. "I didn't bring one home," he said. "Anything that unnatural-looking is bound to be dangerous.

"And I think somebody in the Ikeda family is alive. A person's been sleeping under their back shed and digging around trying to find things. I left a note."

"I hope Kyoko isn't there all alone," Chiyo said. "But if she is, she'll see the note. Any sign of the other neighbors?"

"No one there at all."

Chiyo offered a silent prayer to Kannon, the Goddess of Mercy, asking that the neighbors' spirits be protected from having to wander alone and homeless across devastated Hiroshima.

Isao gazed off at the Inland Sea.

"The bodies keep floating in all along the shore," he said. "Every day on any beach, someone finds another bloated body. They keep coming. They never stop. On and on." He shook his head.

Isao developed a high fever and diarrhea, the way so many others had. He couldn't keep anything on his stomach. They hovered around him, keeping constant watch, placing hot towels on his forehead, trying every treatment they had heard about. He couldn't eat the two mackerel Mr. Miguchi had brought him, freshly caught in the waters by his house, or the vegetables ripening in the garden, not even the peaches. Finally he was able to eat some o-kayu, soft rice with an egg. He fell into a deep slumber. A neighbor came and gave him moxa treatments, burning powder near the sore spots on his back. Gradually his strength began to come back. Kazuko refused to let him return to Hiroshima.

Grandmother was improving slightly, too.

"Chi-chan," she said one morning, "go and get the mirror."

Chiyo stared at her, not moving. "Why do you want to look in the mirror, Grandmother? Just look at me and you'll know how you look. We both have scars. I don't intend to look in the mirror again until I am healed. Maybe not even then."

Grandmother did not answer. She sat on a *zabuton,* her knees bent under her, her neat posterior resting on her heels.

"Get me the mirror," she repeated. "I want to see."

Chiyo went to the dressing table, lifted the cloth from the mirror that had been her mother's, and brought it to Grandmother. They stared into it, looking at each other, then back into the mirror, then at each other again.

Chiyo was not shocked by Grandmother's image. She had been looking at her every day since the bomb. But Chiyo's own face was something she could not comprehend. The scar had pulled her mouth into a permanent cynical smile, as if she were leering at herself and at the world. It was such an insignificant scar compared to the one that covered Grandmother's face. Yet it horrified her more.

"If that is you on the left, Chi-chan, then I must be the person on the right." Grandmother turned her head away. "Take the mirror back, Chi-chan, and thank you."

Chiyo obeyed. "We've gotten used to seeing each other," she said. "It will take a bit longer for us to get used to looking at ourselves."

"I do not believe I want to try," Grandmother said.

That night, alone in the upstairs sitting room, Chiyo heard whispering in the room where Grandmother and Akiko slept. She slid open the *fusuma.* "Is everything all right?"

Akiko and Fusako were sitting by Grandmother's bed, two Buddha sillhouettes against the moonlit sky. "It's Mother," Akiko said, her voice toneless, her emotions buried deep inside. "She was moaning but she says it's just a dream."

Grandmother was calm and impassive when she woke in the morning. It was impossible to tell how much physical pain she was enduring. If a wolf had been lurking inside her thin summer kimono, gnawing at her heart, she would not have told them.

She sat on a cushion in the upstairs sitting room, gazing at the Inland Sea through the open *shōji.* Later in the day, she had to lie down. They took her *futon* from the closet and laid it near the edge of the *tatami,* almost onto the *engawa* so she could feel the sea breeze.

"Let's wash our hair and get really clean," she said. "I haven't felt clean since the bomb fell."

Kazuko joined them and they set about, their spirits raised, scrubbing their hair with a tiny scrap of soap and then soaking it in barley husks.

Grandmother's hair fell out. Tufts of it came out with only gentle pulling. Grandmother, whose face was already burned and distorted, was suddenly without her precious hair, which she had meticulously dyed black for so many years.

That evening, Grandmother ate rice gruel, sitting formally, wearing the few remaining strands of her hair neatly arranged across her forehead.

Kazuko said it wasn't a sure sign. Many people at the infirmaries had lost hair and still seemed to be improving. The sure sign was the appearance of purple spots, and Grandmother had none of those.

In September, it rained incessantly, which was unusual for that time of year. Then, in the middle of the month, there was a furious storm and news of a flood in Hiroshima. It demolished the few straggly shacks, the newspaper said. Like the second knockout of a prizefighter who had just begun to struggle up from his knees. Now there were more Hiroshima victims, drowned because they were too weak to escape. In ordinary times, everybody from the suburbs would have gone in to Hiroshima to help. Now all they could manage was just to live through the day. And added to Chiyo's dreams of Kenichi was one of the flood coming and washing him out to sea.

Akiko received a reply to the telegram she had sent to her in-laws in Chiba. They were all right, they said. Her son, Koichi, was waiting for her to come back. And they expected word from her husband, Kikuo, in Indonesia. But Akiko did not have the energy yet to take the train up to Tokyo.

"Isn't it time Yoko-chan got ready for her entrance exams?" Grandmother asked one morning. "She'll finish elementary school in March."

It was an especially optimistic thing to say. But the day was an especially brilliant one, bright and cloudless, like the one on August 6. The sun was caressing Kazuko's persimmon tree, thrusting its rays at them through the leaves, and they could see the green fruit dangling there, waiting to ripen. The sky was an innocent blue.

Chiyo did not think there would ever be Girls' School again, or any other school. Or anything else civilized. And she did not want Yoko or Hiroshi to return to the ugly, charred world beyond Inokuchi.

But the sun was casting its midmorning brilliance on the *tatami*. The injured people were gone from the clinic now, transferred to the infirmary in town, and Kazuko spent her time nursing Grandmother and Isao. He had been up and walking for a few hours each day, and was puttering in the garden below. Grandmother, lying on her *futon,* was smiling. Suddenly Chiyo wanted desperately to go on living and have the world created again.

"Yes, time to think of school beginning in the fall," Kazuko said.

They decided to read Natsume Soseki's novel *Botchan,* written in the Meiji period just before the turn of the century, when Grandmother was a girl. Fusako, Akiko, and Yoko gathered around Grandmother and took turns reading out loud. Hiroshi came too and sat clutching his knees and listening.

"What is this word, Grandmother?" Fusako paused in the middle of a sentence and showed the book to her. "It must be a very old-fashioned Japanese character. I have never seen it before."

Grandmother rose from her pillow, rested her head on the palm of her hand, reached for her glasses, then read the whole sentence to them. She was especially animated, explaining how it had been in the days of the Emperor Meiji. She laughed and began to cough up blood. Everybody scurried around, laying her head back on her pillow, pressing hot towels to her forehead. Chiyo saw that purple spots had appeared on Grandmother's neck and shoulders. Maybe they had been there all along. If she had told them at least. Kazuko had heard that sometimes blood transfusions worked.

That night Grandmother began to vomit. She was dehydrated and they gave her water, but she couldn't keep it in her stomach.

"Sumimasen," she said each time she lay back in her bed. "Forgive me for causing you so much trouble."

At dawn, her lips curled and turned bright red; the rest of her face turned black.

She lay on her *futon,* chanting *Namu Amidha Butsu,* her hands clasped across her chest. She died at noon.

They chanted and prayed, gathered around her bed. Isao went for the old priest, who hobbled there on a cane, then stood, his frail bones hardly able to hold him up, reciting the sutras.

> Sooner or later,
> To me or my neighbor,
> On this day or the morrow . . .

In spite of his frailness, his voice was clear and strong, perhaps because of the stillness around him.

They laid Grandmother in the longest and widest drawer they had, one which Kazuko had taken from her *tansu.* It was all they had for a coffin, and together they struggled down to the shore, where Mr. Miguchi helped them dig a hole in the sand in a place looking out toward the sea, which Grandmother had stared at all during her last days. They piled on the driftwood and sticks from the pine trees. It seemed to take forever for her to burn. They stood silently, not touching each other while they watched. But Kazuko, who had not been near the bomb, leaned on Isao's arm, unable to stand alone. She had neglected to tie her *obi* properly, or to powder her face.

Yoko wept for days. The others could not cry. Chiyo could not even feel. She only envied the finality of Grandmother's death. Kenichi was still wandering somewhere, alive or dead in some ghost world, waiting for his mother to come and find him, dress his wounds or burn his bones and put them at last to rest.

But for Grandmother, at least, it was comforting to think of Basho's poem about the locusts singing in the fullness of life, unaware of their early death. Grandmother had died like that, surrounded by her children and grandchildren, laughing and reading to them from a book she loved.

Chapter Eleven

A T THE END OF SEPTEMBER ISAO AN-
nounced that he had regained his strength
and, in spite of Kazuko's objections, went cautiously back into the
city, assuring her that he would be careful.

When he returned in the afternoon, he spoke of the rivers restor-
ing themselves and people gathering grass, which appeared in the
most unlikely places, even along the railroad tracks. They were
cooking and eating that bitter-tasting food because of their will to
live. And the existence of the grass belied the rumor that nothing
would grow in Hiroshima again. More and more of the roads were
being cleared, and there was talk that the streetcars would soon be
operating from Koi all the way in to Tenma-chō even though people still had to get off and walk across the bridge. Next, Isao said,
they would be extending another line from Senda-machi to Ujina,
where the Yamamotos lived with her in-laws. In another month the
line would be running all the way to Nakajima.

And more shacks had begun to appear, some of them just boards
covering bombed-out caverns of basements and air raid shelters
where it seemed people couldn't possibly live, but smoke was coming out of them. Other people, though they were well enough to

move about, were living in the infirmary in the dark basement of Fukuya Department Store because they had no place else to go.

"Don't go back there again," Kazuko pleaded with Isao. "Let someone else take over now. The new mayor doesn't need as much help now, does he?"

Isao smiled and patted her arm. "I'm all right," he said. "Can't you see I'm well?"

She watched him anxiously, insisting that he eat at midday an extra bowl of *zōsui,* a rice porridge she mixed with vegetables from the garden. And more and more, he obeyed her commands, sitting quietly in the room by the garden and meditating.

Akiko's in-laws wrote, enclosing a letter from her husband, who was returning from Indonesia. He had written that he was expecting her to meet him in Tokyo.

More signs of her former liveliness appeared. She rose early, dressed, sat before the mirror experimenting with her sister's makeup, then settled herself on the veranda, carrying on an internal dialogue with her husband, whom she had not seen in two years. Chiyo envied her.

Isao managed to get Akiko a ticket. No express trains yet, and the local ones, crowded to the point of bulging, took seventeen hours. And there were no vendors at the stations selling food as they had in the old days. Kazuko cooked white rice and sacrificed the last pickled plum to make Akiko a *Hi no Maru bento*— rice spread out in a square lunch box with a sour red plum in the middle so that it looked like a Japanese flag. It had been the poorest, most frugal kind of lunch in the past. Now it was an unprecedented luxury.

For the rest of the journey, they gave Akiko *kanpan,* hardtack, which had recently been released from the huge store of military goods being distributed as quickly as possible. "Before the Occupation Forces come and confiscate it all," Isao explained.

Kanpan had been the mainstay of the Imperial Army. Although it was difficult to bite into and did not taste very good, it gave people the feeling of having eaten a whole meal.

"It will keep you alive until you get to Tokyo," said Kazuko.

Everyone wanted to ride into Hiroshima on the streetcar with Akiko. Eight weeks now since the bomb and the foreign troops had begun to arrive. Isao had seen some of them, even spoken once through an interpreter to a few who were visiting the mayor's office. They were not so bad, he said. Gentlemanly and restrained enough, and people were no longer afraid of them. In fact it was said that the only way to catch a glimpse of a real-life foreign soldier was to go to Hiroshima station and watch for one. It was the reason, Chiyo suspected, that the children were so eager to go into Hiroshima. Certainly no one had seen any soldiers in Inokuchi, and except for newspaper accounts of purges of people in high government and military positions, most people's lives hadn't been affected. The *Chugoku* newspaper explained that for the present the Occupation Forces would depend entirely on the existing local government.

On the streetcar, Isao acted as a guardian for the two children, holding his hands gently on their shoulders while they stood stiff, with their bodies pressed against the sides of the streetcar, struck dumb by the view of their world destroyed. Chiyo was heartened by the improvements. The streets had all been cleared. Wide alleys amidst the rubble created a strange, unearthly world. Smoke came from open fires near piles of bricks and lumber which Chiyo discovered, on closer look, were actually dwellings.

"Look at that!" Hiroshi pointed. At a distance were two khaki-colored jeeps lumbering at a purposeful pace, each carrying two tall foreign soldiers through the wide clearings as if they were sightseeing. They were relaxed, almost jovial, and without the stiff military bearing of Japanese soldiers. It was almost a relief finally to see them.

She saw a makeshift pole jutting up from the rubble, supporting laundry. "Look," she said. "People living like that, but they're still managing to get their clothes clean."

"Probably beating them against the rocks along the riverbanks," Kazuko said. "Such hard work."

They crossed Aioi Bridge and Chiyo looked out along the Honkawa toward the bridge where the Rijo Middle School boys had been standing. The river they had dived into was placid, calmly drifting toward the sea, covering the horrors that lay beneath its serenity.

"Though the whole country be torn, the mountains and rivers remain," Isao said, almost to himself, quoting from an old Chinese poem. She hadn't thought of it before. That ancient Chinese poem, written after some war or other. As if the poet had foreseen all this happening in some future, unknown place.

In the late afternoon sun, they stood on the naked train platform. There was a roof over only one small sitting area where people could keep out of the rain. Chiyo remembered the old express trains, the *Asakaze,* the Morning Wind, and the *Kamome,* the Seagull, starting south in Kyushu, arriving at Hiroshima late in the evening and in Tokyo the following morning. Chiyo had taken the *Asakaze* on her honeymoon with Shintaro, ensconced in the narrow upper berth all night with her limbs wound around his. That had been in 1930, the third year of Emperor Showa.

When the train lumbered to a halt, filled all the way to the vestibules with people, Isao rushed forward and climbed on.

"Akiko!" he called. "Here's a place to stand, and this man says he's getting off at Osaka."

At the rate the train was moving, Osaka was a good ten hours away.

"Remember. Write! The moment you arrive in Tokyo," Kazuko commanded. She scurried along after the train, waving until it gained speed and turned the bend. Her voice was unsteady. The departure had happened so quickly.

Another train steamed in, laden with passengers and carrying at the end three first-class cars which stopped in front of Chiyo and the others. Foreign soldiers flowed out and surrounded them, dwarfed them. The men were tall and rangy, wearing neat, clean, and carefully pressed khaki trousers and hats with visors. They were talking loudly to each other and laughing. Chiyo was paralyzed with fright, and she hugged Yoko and Hiroshi closely to her. But in a moment the soldiers were gone, clattering down the stairs, disappearing as quickly as the train.

For a time the family stood clustered together on the platform, unable either to say anything or to begin the journey back to Inokuchi.

Chiyo refused to give up her search for Kenichi. If she couldn't find him alive, then she wanted his bones to burn and settle to rest. The restrictions against entering the city had been lifted, and she could go without the Red Cross arm band whenever she felt strong enough. Sometimes Kazuko or Fusako went with her, and they returned again and again to Nobori-chō, looking for clues, looking to see if the notes were still there, looking for any sign of the neighbors. People in Nobori-chō were erecting small shacks or living in holes dug out under broken bricks and scorched lumber, but none of them were people she knew and none of them were on her street. There was still no sign of the Ikedas.

They searched through the infirmaries again, calling out Kenichi's name, looked at the lists of people and the death certificates. But the number of patients had dwindled now, and there was never any information.

She went again to see Takano-sensei. He was livelier and seemed to be improving.

"It's the peaches," his wife said. "My uncle brought us more from Okayama. I've mixed them with raw eggs and just poured them down his throat each time. His fever has gone, and the diarrhea, even the yellow look to his skin." She smiled at Chiyo. "I'm really beginning to think he's getting well. It's remarkable, isn't it? And it's all on account of your bringing those peaches the first time."

"My brother Isao has been sick, too," Chiyo said. "And I'm sure he's recovered for the same reason. Lots of fresh food and rest. That's the key." She did not mention that Grandmother had died in spite of the peaches.

When Chiyo said her farewell, bowing vigorously, she realized that she felt the same way about Takano-sensei as she did about Aioi Bridge. If he was still alive, then there was a glimmer of hope for Kenichi.

But her nightmares continued. Kenichi was always disintegrating and falling off the roof. Or sometimes Kenichi would be with her, watching Yukiji burn. He would turn and look at his mother, accusing. "Help him, Mama. Why don't you help him? Why are you leaving him there to die?"

In her daydreams, Kenichi was always deep in the country being nursed back to health. One day he would appear, smiling awkwardly. "Sorry if I caused you any worry. It's good to be home. Shall we go clam digging?"

Miraculous things did happen. Their neighbor, Mrs. Suzuki, whose two-year-old son had died in her arms on August 6, found her sister in an infirmary in the distant town of Kabe where she must have wandered, not knowing where she was going. It gave Chiyo new hope.

A few days later, some other neighbors found their teenage daughter lying in a shelter miles away from the dormitory of the munitions factory where she worked. No one understood how she had gotten there.

Chiyo thought the Yamamotos might have some new information, and when the streetcar began running all the way to Ujina, Chiyo decided to visit them.

She found them in a small, cramped house which they shared

with her in-laws. Mrs. Yamamoto was gradually selling all their possessions in exchange for food. Yasu had been very sick, she said, but was better now and was out standing in line for the canned goods distributed by the Occupation Army.

"And Sachiko?" Chiyo asked.

"You didn't know? Well, of course not, how could you?" Mrs. Yamamoto prepared Chiyo a cup of barley tea and served it with precise formality before she could bring herself to answer.

"She died before we got home," Mrs. Yamamoto said. "It was the day we parted. On August 7. We crossed the Miyuki Bridge, then stopped to rest on the riverbank. When Yasu picked her up again, he felt a kind of heaviness, and he asked a man nearby to push her higher up on his back.

"But the man told him to put her down again. He said there was no use carrying her anymore, that we should just get home ourselves." Mrs. Yamamoto could not meet Chiyo's gaze. Finally she looked up, her face brightening. "Anyway we managed to carry her here so we could have the funeral with her grandparents."

"I am so sorry," Chiyo whispered. "I was hoping— I've thought of you so often and been wanting to come and ask but—"

"I know," Mrs. Yamamoto said. "What can any of us do? We can hardly take care of our own families let alone— Any word at all about Kenichi?"

Yasu appeared, standing in the *genkan* the way he had done in the old days when he came to get Kenichi for school.

"Mrs. Hara!" He knelt before her, formally and elaborately, smiling wanly. "Have you heard—"

"No. I was hoping you might know something."

"Well, I did hear that our classmate Masa-kun is alive. Someone told me he's in an orphanage up on Hijiyama. But he wasn't at school with the others. I think he was waiting for the bus off in the outskirts somewhere. His parents were both working in the city, though, so I think they died. I'm going up there someday to find him."

"Did you get anything?" Mrs. Yamamoto asked him.

He nodded and took two cans from an old army rucksack. "More cherries."

"Have you gotten any of those?" Mrs. Yamamoto asked her. "It's our third distribution and always the same. We thought it might be corned beef or maybe tuna fish, but it's always cherries." She slapped her hand over her mouth, suppressing a laugh, reminding Chiyo of the days when they shared secret jokes, even when things were so terrible there was nothing to joke about. "Can you imagine? Canned cherries in some kind of juice? What on earth do these foreigners do with that?"

"How strange! We haven't gotten anything in Inokuchi like that yet."

"Well, at least they're good," Mrs. Yamamoto said. "A lot of sugar in the juice. And we've been eating wild grass. I find it up by the bridges when I go in to the black market. And everybody's mixing it with the American flour." She laughed again, behind the cover of her hand. "They call it Eba *dango*," she said. "Eba dumplings. I guess because people over in Eba discovered it first. It's not so bad, you know."

They hardly looked at each other when they bowed goodbye, fearing tears.

"You know, my in-laws are beginning to resent me," Mrs. Yamamoto whispered, coming out to the *genkan* with Chiyo and nodding toward the house. "We're draining them of all their possessions, trading everything for food. They wouldn't have the strength to do it themselves and I do it for them. But they don't understand. They just think I'm not getting good enough bargains." She shook her head. "I don't know what's to become of us," she breathed. "And sometimes I don't even care."

Chiyo, searching desperately for a way to comfort her, clutched Mrs. Yamamoto's hands. "Our husbands will be home soon," she said. "Then things will be better."

Two days later, Chiyo went up to Hijiyama Elementary School to look for Masa. But most of the children were primary school age or younger. Almost a hundred were living there and only four or five teachers to care for them.

"People keep finding them in the ruins, even now," one of the teachers said. She was a young woman, no more than twenty-three or twenty-four, but tired and unhealthy looking. As if she hadn't eaten or changed her clothes for weeks. All her attention was on the children.

"You must take care of yourself," Chiyo warned her.

"I came from outside," she said quickly. "I wasn't here when the bomb fell. I'm all right. But these children. Can you imagine they've managed to survive all this time, still looking for their parents?" She went on talking, grateful to find someone who would listen to her. "Sometimes an adult comes to get one of these children, says he's the father, and we have our doubts, but how can we be sure? Nobody has any documents to prove anything."

The teacher had heard of Masa. "He was here, I think, right after we set up the orphanage. But I haven't seen him for a while. You know, the older ones tend to wander off. We can't seem to keep them here."

Chiyo went to the island of Ninoshima, thinking she might at least find Masa. But only a few of the boys in the orphanage there were of middle-school age. None of those had been working on the demolition crews, and the man in charge was sure he had not seen either Kenichi or Masa. "Those boys from Rijo Middle School were so close to the hypocenter, you know. And people brought thousands of wounded because of the medical units here." He shook his head. "But all the military doctors had gone off to Hiroshima to help, so the ones rescued from the rivers and the fire were just lying here without water or food or anyone to treat them."

He looked at her apologetically. "I'm sorry," he said. "I'm afraid if your son did come here, then it's not likely—"

Chiyo began to hope that Kenichi had burned instantly, vaporized in the air the way she dreamed of him.

Middle of October now.

Hiroshi and Yoko began attending school in the neighborhood. Yoko sometimes brought her schoolmates home with her to play. But on other days she felt lonely, missing her classmates in Nobori-chō, especially Kyoko Ikeda.

Hiroshi plodded solemnly through his lessons, went to bed and got up and went to school and came home again and began on his new lessons. Nothing excited him. Nothing disturbed or surprised him. The expression on his face never changed. He did not speak of Kenichi.

Fusako went to a meeting of the remaining members of Hiroshima Girls' School. Only 35 of her 335 former classmates appeared. "I could hardly recognize any of them," Fusako said when she came home. "Some of them didn't have any hair."

They began to meet twice a week with their few remaining teachers in a primary school in Ushita.

Isao went on a small fishing boat to his old factory, Toyokogyo, where they planned to begin again their production of machinery and truck parts instead of the guns and ammunition the military had ordered them to make. The factory, far to the southeast, beyond Ujina, had not been destroyed by the bomb. Several government departments were establishing themselves in the building, including the Prefectural Office, which had formerly occupied an old two-story wooden structure built in Hiroshima during the Meiji Era. It had been instantly consumed by fire that day along with more than three-fourths of the employees.

Isao was healthier now. He seemed to thrive on working and on his association with the few government officials who were still alive.

He began to go once or twice a week, and one day, with just a hint of hope in his voice, he spoke of producing automobiles like the trial one they had made back in the thirties before the war with China, and before the army had requisitioned the factory.

Chiyo could not think of any other place to search for Kenichi.

More and more she thought of Shintaro. She dreamed often of his homecoming and awoke at dawn feeling very close to him, convinced absolutely that he was alive. She imagined how he would look getting off the ship, coming down the gangplank. Shiploads of people were coming home, soldiers and prisoners of war from Southeast Asia, but so far only civilians from China and the Russian-occupied areas in Manchuria.

She thought of herself and the children (in her daydreams Kenichi was always there too) standing on the dock, waiting for him. He would be thin, probably. Maybe injured. He might have lost an arm or a leg like Yukiji and would arrive in a wheelchair, rolling it quickly through the crowd. He would recognize them immediately, maybe catch sight of Hiroshi first and lift him onto his lap. Seeing his father would make Hiroshi laugh again.

Of course, it would take Shintaro a while to get used to Yoko, almost a young lady now. Even if he had received the photos, he wouldn't be prepared for how beautiful she had become. But there would be no distance between Shintaro and Kenichi. They would go on fishing trips again. And the whole family would take autumn walks, all of them searching in the hills for *matsutake*, the thick black mushrooms of fall.

She did not believe the cherry blossoms would ever come again to Hiroshima, but they would find some far up along the banks of the Ota River.

Three years now. How would it be between her and Shintaro? She had been so shy with him when they first married. Then those exquisite years before Kenichi was born, discovering how strong and tender he was. Every decision he made seemed right. Except the last one when he received the red draft card. She had wanted him to drink a bottle of soy sauce so that he would be too sick when he went for the physical exam. He was outraged that she would even suggest it. That night he had sat with his mouth set firm, holding up his rice bowl for her to fill again, then stood and walked out into the street, returning late at night. She pretended to be asleep. They lay beside one another in stony silence. The very idea that they would draft a forty-year-old man with three children and a wife to support and a job teaching the young. They needed teachers more than they needed soldiers. If the government couldn't see that, then Shintaro should take it upon himself to decide where he was important. He loved teaching and literature. He was always referring their lives to the ancient poetry collection, the *Manyoshu,* the Myriad Leaves, or the *Kokinshu,* the Imperial Collection of Old and New Poems. On the first night of their wedding trip, at the inn in Tokyo, he had gazed at her long black hair, spread out on the pillow, and quoted an ancient poem about a courtier who had been called to the capital. On his journey, every time he looked along the shore and saw the seaweed flowing, tangled through the rocks, he remembered his wife's hair and his wife's limbs tangled about him, and he discovered that although he thought himself strong, his sleeves were wet with tears.

Shintaro was like that in his tender, reflective moments, and it was worth all the uncompromising parts of him. Even the stubbornness that had made him go off to war.

She wanted to be in Nobori-chō, with the children, waiting for him to come home. If they built the house again, maybe Kenichi would come home, and they would all be there. She could indulge in her own ways, not as neat and precise or perfect as Kazuko's, but comfortable. She was growing weary of keeping up with Kazuko's standards, and she was tired of being the one displaced person who had not begun her life again.

"I wonder if I'd be eligible to apply for one of those houses the city has offered to build for people," she ventured to Isao one Sunday morning in late October when they were alone in the sitting room.

Isao looked at her, puzzled. "Those houses are for people who don't have any place to live, people holed up inside bomb shelters. Why would you want to go back into that desert when you could be here? This was our father's house, and grandfather's, and great-great-grandfather's, meant for a big family. You can all stay here the rest of your lives." His mouth was a hard, firm line. "I will

118

not allow you to go back there until your husband comes home, Chiyo."

She had hurt him. But there was no way to explain it. She sat, not knowing how to answer him.

"Aren't you comfortable here?" he asked.

"Of course I'm comfortable. I'll never be able to tell you how fortunate I feel, having an elder brother like you. If it weren't for you, none of us would be alive."

"You should have come to Inokuchi when I first asked you," he said. "When Hiroshi came. Before they put restrictions on the evacuation. Or at least when Yoko came. We could have enrolled Kenichi in school in Hatsukaichi the way I told you. If you'd done that—"

She looked at him and began to cry. The guilt so deep, suppressed so long, she could not put it into words. She sobbed without restraint, spilling out all the sorrow and anxiety of the past months—of searching and not knowing, of looking for purple spots, of watching Yukiji burn and Grandmother die and the boy in the infirmary and the people in the garden and the ones in Ninoshima and on the streets, all turning into corpses before her eyes. And watching the leftovers live in the charred, half-human, half-real world, and watching the innocence fade from the faces of her children.

And losing Kenichi. Yes, she had lost him. He was dead. He had been carbonized in the heat and fury of the bomb. Or his bones were buried under a pile of debris at the site of his classroom, or washed out to sea, or collected together on some anonymous funeral pyre, undistinguished from all the others, unsung, unpraised, unnoticed. Kenichi, her firstborn, her genius, the one with the truth of the solar system swirling in his head. Kenichi was dead.

She sat sobbing, weeping into the sleeve of her kimono, not caring what happened ever again in her life. Her son was gone and her husband was not there to share the sorrow with her. Maybe he would never come home. She would be alone to bring up the remaining children and provide for them without being a burden to anyone else. She loved Isao and his family, but she didn't want to live with them for the rest of her life. She wanted her own husband and children in her own house back in Nobori-chō, the house that had belonged to Shintaro's family for two hundred years until the bomb destroyed it.

Isao touched her shoulder. "There, now, I'm sorry, Chi-chan. I shouldn't have said that. It wasn't your fault. It's the way things are. None of us could help it. Maybe if he'd been in Hatsukaichi he'd have been assigned to the work crew anyway. And if he managed to get back here, he would have died like all those other boys, charred to a crisp and screaming in pain. I prefer to think that he disintegrated without a trace, that he didn't stay alive to feel the pain." He rubbed her back. "Cry, Chi-chan. As much as you want. You haven't cried at all."

He was using her childhood name, Chi-chan. Her husband had called her that sometimes after he heard the family using it. Isao never used it anymore. They weren't young enough or close enough. They had grown up. She cried even harder at the loss of her childhood and her parents and Grandmother and the innocent world. And who had gotten them into that terrible war? And why had Shintaro been made to go and fight in it? And why had all the twelve-year-olds been gathered in the center of the city to work in the scorching heat of the summer and then been rendered ugly ghosts by that unspeakable thing that dropped on them? How could any human on the face of the earth have considered using it on other human beings?

Her stomach ached, contracting and pushing up the sobs. She coughed, covering her face with her handkerchief, soaking it in tears.

Her sobbing had subsided and she drew it away. Was that blood? A big splotch of blood on her handkerchief?

Isao saw it, too, and they sat frozen, staring at it. Even if they called the doctor, it wouldn't matter. Grandmother had died within hours after coughing up blood.

"Lie down, Chi-chan. Try to go to sleep. And don't worry. It's just exhaustion from worrying and searching so much and crying so hard. I'll get someone from the infirmary right now."

Lying there in the same spot Grandmother had been, she felt a trickling from her nose and wiped it with her handkerchief. More blood. Her nose was bleeding. It was a simple nosebleed from crying too much. She hadn't been coughing up blood like Grandmother. She wasn't going to die. Isao was right.

Chapter Twelve

THE LAST OF THE PERSIMMONS WERE RIP-
ening on the trees. Hints of the November
chill were coming, and everyone was forecasting a bitter winter.

The clinic in their garden had been closed for some time, and
now the few patients remaining in the school infirmaries were being
sent to the Red Cross Hospital in Hiroshima.

The children were at school and Isao at work. Kazuko began
reordering the house, cleaning the room where Akiko and Grandmother had slept, nursing back to life the bushes and flowers outside which had been crushed by the wounded lying there. Chiyo
helped her, but did not share any enthusiasm for the task. It
seemed that everyone was back at work, carving out new lives
again. But nothing interested Chiyo except her dreams of Shintaro's
homecoming.

And the orphans.

She was haunted by their faces. So many of them, younger even
than Hiroshi, stood around Hiroshima station trying to shine shoes,
acting as pimps for their older sisters, stealing money, searching in
the trash cans for food. She remembered the young teacher at the
Hijiyama orphanage who had not slept or eaten, working relentlessly, never thinking about herself.

Chiyo trudged back to the top of Hijiyama to offer her services to the young teacher, Miss Hatanaka, who was overjoyed to see her again. They were still finding destitute orphans and gathering from the country leftover children whose parents had never come for them.

Chiyo's scar had healed. When she finally looked again in the mirror, she saw that it had pushed her mouth permanently askew into the cynical smile she feared. She had been hesitant about frightening the orphans, but they hadn't noticed. She worked one or two days a week at Hijiyama and at another orphanage that had opened in a bombed-out school building in the city, still hoping to find Kyoko or Masa.

Sometimes she would walk across Sakae Bridge to her old neighborhood, then stand at the foundation of her house trying to think of a way to rebuild it so that it would be ready for Shintaro. Grandmother had said that if he wasn't reported dead or missing, then he must be alive. Chiyo clung tenaciously to that thought, especially when visiting the site of their old house, cleaning up sections of it a bit at a time.

On a late Friday afternoon in November, chilled by the wind, she stacked old pieces of wood in a pile near the crumbled storehouse, trying to think how she could hire a carpenter to build a one-room shack like the others, and how she could pay the carpenter without telling Isao.

Gazing down the street toward the Ikeda house, she thought she saw movement there. Squatters living on the Ikeda land? She wouldn't allow that. Not until she knew for sure that the whole family was dead.

She hurried down the street, determined to evict whoever was there. If they had no place else to go, she would just tell them to move into the vacant lot next to where the Kasamas had lived.

But as she got closer, she saw some kind of structure, a straw mat spread across piled-up stones and bricks. Too low for anyone to stand up in. Whoever lived there would have to crawl in at night and just sleep.

"Hello!" she shouted. "Is anyone there?"

There was silence, then movement and whispers. "Who is it?" a voice called out sharply.

"I am Hara Chiyo, and I used to live in this neighborhood. I know the Ikeda family who own this property."

Two people emerged. The woman was wearing a threadbare spring kimono under a light *haori*, a half-coat. In the November wind her red, chapped hands stretched out from under her kimono sleeves, a chilblain on one arm, an angry red keloid scar on the other.

Chiyo shuddered, thinking how cold it would be clad in only that kimono and light coat. The girl was wearing a wool middy blouse and skirt from some girls' school or other, much too big for her, but warmer than her mother's clothing. Two outcasts like so many others.

"*Oku-sama?*" asked the woman. "Wife of Hara-sensei?"

So, it was someone who knew that her husband was a teacher.

"You don't recognize me, do you? And not Kyoko either. I appreciate your trying to preserve our land, but you see—"

"Mrs. Ikeda!" Chiyo exclaimed. She couldn't believe that she hadn't recognized them. Deep inside she had given them all up for dead. She bowed again and again, much too actively. It made her head ache. "I can't believe it!" she said. "You're here at last."

Mrs. Ikeda and Kyoko were bowing too. "Please come in!" Mrs. Ikeda said.

"But how can we—"

"Oh, it's not what you think!" She laughed. "We've dug a hole in here and we can sit quite comfortably. Sleep too."

They crawled in under the straw mat, then stepped down into an enclosure with a table in the center and another small hole under the table, fashioned as if it were a *kotatsu,* for warming their feet. There was enough space beyond for two people to sleep.

Now they were sitting around it with their feet underneath. Kyoko lit a candle.

"I can't believe it," Chiyo repeated. "You're both alive! And how long have you been here? I've left notes for you so often. And Kyoko, you found your mother." Chiyo gazed at her across the candlelight. She was much thinner than Yoko. A tight little wad of a girl, holding the pieces of herself together as if she might fall into a powder heap at any moment.

"Is Yoko-chan all right?" she asked.

Chiyo reached across the table and clutched Kyoko's arm, feeling the sharpness of her tiny bones. "She's fine. And she'll be ecstatic to see you." Still clasping Kyoko's arm, Chiyo looked around the cave. "How did you ever manage—?"

"We've only been here a few days," Mrs. Ikeda said. "But we borrowed a shovel from some people down on the streetcar line, and Kyoko and I dug the first day until we were exhausted. Then we found this old straw matting and—"

"But your husband?"

"He died," Mrs. Ikeda said abruptly. "Everyone's gone except Kyoko and me, my daughter-in-law, Haruko, and maybe my son Ichiro. He hasn't come home from the air force yet."

The vision of Yukiji in the flames invaded Chiyo's brain, and she drew in a sharp breath.

"Yukiji—" she began, not daring to look at Mrs. Ikeda. If only she and the Yamamotos had been stronger and quicker. Did Mrs. Ikeda know that they had tried to save him?

"He was cremated by the burning house," Mrs. Ikeda said. "We found his skull."

"I'm sorry." Chiyo bowed her head.

Mrs. Ikeda looked around the darkening room. "If we had a fire, we could make you some tea, but we haven't worked out a way yet to—"

"You've done all this yourselves?" Chiyo asked. "Just the two of you?"

Kyoko smiled triumphantly, reminding Chiyo of the carefree Kyoko of the past. "Our own house," she said.

"But winter's coming and you have no heat and there isn't any—"

"We're going to figure out something," Mrs. Ikeda said. "Other people are doing it."

"What about Yukiji's grandparents?" Chiyo asked.

"We haven't been able to find them. No bones under the house or— But they couldn't have gotten far. The fire broke out, and they couldn't walk fast, you know."

Chiyo lowered her eyes. "And your daughter-in-law, Haruko? You said—"

"Yes, she's alive." Mrs. Ikeda's face brightened slightly. "But her baby died. Maybe you know. She told me she saw you that day, and you wanted to help her, but she sent you off to see about Yukiji."

"We tried," Chiyo blurted out. "We couldn't. It was—the fire came and—"

"I know," said Mrs. Ikeda quickly. "I knew you tried, and I appreciate what you did for him."

"But we did nothing! We tried to lift the beam, but we couldn't pull him out. Then the fire came, and we just left him there." Chiyo covered her face with her hands. "Yasu ran into the flames to try one more time to pull him out, but we shouted for Yasu to come away." She gasped for breath. "I still see Yukiji and hear his voice in my dreams. I heard him calling after us when we were running away."

Mrs. Ikeda touched her shoulder. "I'm sorry he caused you so much trouble. I wish I could have done the same for Kenichi. He was down on the Honkawa Bridge with the others, wasn't he? Any news of him at all?"

"No news." Chiyo straightened her shoulders and took a deep breath. "Where is Haruko-san now?"

"Out at my husband's native place in Kabe, waiting for the new baby to come. There's a good doctor nearby, but he's so busy with the sick and injured he hardly has time to think of babies."

"And your husband?"

There was a long pause before Mrs. Ikeda answered. "I did find him," she finally said. "On the day after the bomb."

Chiyo held her breath.

"He was down by City Hall, stretched out on the ground. Stiff. Staring up at the dirty sky looking so—" She took a deep breath, searching around for the word. "So surprised. His clothes had all been blown off, but he didn't seem burned or injured. Until I turned him over and saw his back. It was— I don't know whether he died right away or whether—

"Anyway, I couldn't carry him. He was too heavy and taller than I am. And there wasn't anyplace to take him. So I cremated him. Lots of half-burned wood around. I just collected it and lit a fire under him. Everything burned quite rapidly, really. Except his bowels. It was his stomach, you know. His stomach wouldn't seem to burn. It took forever for his stomach—"

She looked up and stopped, seeing, through the twilight room, the horror on Chiyo's face.

"Well, then the soldiers came and they said, 'Oku-san, you can't cremate someone right here. We're the ones who are supposed to do that.'

"I said, 'I've already done it. It's too late to tell me that now.' I just picked up the bones and wrapped them in my *furoshiki* and started out toward my husband's native place in Kabe. I was still hoping that Yukiji and his grandparents would be out there. But, of course, what with that wheelchair and the parents not able to walk and—"

"Then did you go all the way to Kabe?" Chiyo said.

"Yes. I don't remember how I managed it. But Yukiji wasn't there, or his grandparents. So we had the funeral for my husband; then I walked back to Nobori-chō, still hoping, you see—and then —that's when I found Kyoko. She'd been sleeping all night in a corner of the air raid shelter. You know that shelter—just a hole in the ground with some metal over the top. It's a good thing no one was in it when the bomb fell. They'd have been burnt to a crisp."

Kyoko interrupted. "We were supposed to stay in the country until somebody came for us. But I kept worrying about Yukiji in his wheelchair. And another girl and I—well, we didn't believe what the teachers said about how everything would be all right and our parents would come for us. So we ran away together."

Kyoko had lost track of her friend by the time she arrived at Nobori-chō and at night had crawled into the air raid shelter.

"I didn't find anyone from our neighborhood. I was sure they were all dead."

The next morning, in the garden of their ruined house, she'd found a pumpkin, burned on the outside but cooked inside. "Delicious!" she said. "I was eating it when Mama came."

While they were still looking for Yukiji, Haruko arrived. She had also gone to Kabe, carrying the ashes of her baby. The two women had missed each other by only a few hours.

"You can imagine how glad we were to see each other," Mrs. Ikeda said. "We dug around in the foundation of the house until we found Yukiji. He—"

"Mama. Stop," Kyoko pleaded. "You're so tired. You mustn't tell those stories over and over again."

"You must come out to Inokuchi with me," Chiyo said. "You can't say here all winter without any heat. Our grandmother died in October. And Kazuko's sister, Akiko, just went back to Tokyo. You can stay in their room. Just until Ichiro comes home anyway."

"We're fine here," Mrs. Ikeda insisted. "We're going to manage."

Kyoko agreed. "It's more comfortable living here than being a burden on someone."

"But you wouldn't be a burden!" Chiyo said.

"Well," Mrs. Ikeda explained, "we were staying with my husband's brother and his family. We took Kyoko back to Kabe and stayed there the rest of August, then September, October—all the time waiting for Ichiro to come home. I did walk back in here again once, looking for the rice we'd stored under the floorboard, but it was all black. And I found your note.

"Then, just a few days ago, my brother-in-law said we would have to leave. He said Haruko could stay. At least until the baby is born or until Ichiro returns. He's my eldest, you know, and he's in line to inherit the family holdings. They need him on the farm. But they didn't want Kyoko and me even though we did everything we could to help. We're just too many mouths to feed. They don't have enough food even for themselves, they said, and—" Her voice broke.

Chiyo wanted to gather them up in her arms and take them off somewhere to sleep away their terrible memories and dreams.

"At least until Ichiro comes home, there are only two of us," Mrs. Ikeda said, wiping her eyes with the frayed sleeve of her kimono. "But if he doesn't come back, they may ask Haruko to leave, too. They won't want the baby if it's a girl. And if that happens, I don't know—"

How could it be, thought Chiyo. Kenichi gone, Grandmother dead, Shintaro's whereabouts unknown. And yet how much brighter her prospects were than Mrs. Ikeda's. The woman had suffered from every thinkable calamity. But the only sin she'd ever been guilty of was hoarding an extra measure of rice.

It couldn't be Christian sin that caused the evils, the way they had been taught at the Girls' School. It was Buddhist karma from a previous life. No one she knew in the present life had been sinful enough to bring this kind of calamity down upon the earth.

"Come back to Inokuchi with me just for tonight at least," Chiyo said. "At least for a nice dinner and a warm bath and a long talk about the old days. And so that Yoko and Kyoko can see each other again. Come. It's getting dark. In the morning we can decide what is best to do next."

Before they boarded the streetcar at Hiroshima station, Chiyo bought a few oysters at a black market stall with the money she had gotten pawning Shintaro's good *haori,* the half-coat he'd worn on special occasions. She couldn't bring guests to Kazuko's household unless they were accompanied by something to eat.

They arrived just a moment after Kazuko had gone out shopping herself, and Fusako and Yoko were bustling around in the kitchen.

"I've found the Ikedas!" she breathed.

Yoko led Mrs. Ikeda and Kyoko off to the *kotatsu* in the living room. Chiyo, busy in the kitchen, heard the conversation floating in, increasing in loudness. Finally, she heard laughter.

"I'll just run down to the market and get a few fresh vegetables," Chiyo said to Fusako, "before your mother comes home."

"It's all right, Aunt. We have enough," Fusako protested. But Chiyo was out the door. A new surge of energy strengthened her as she scuttled down the road, returning from the market only moments later carrying a fresh, plump cabbage. She cut some of it up for pickling, put on the rest to cook, and then went into the living room to check on her guests. She found them fast asleep, huddled together as they must have done those past months since August, taking comfort in one another. Yoko had brought them a blanket, tucked it around their shoulders, and then gone off to her room to let them sleep.

Chapter Thirteen

EVERYONE ENJOYED WATCHING THE
Ikedas take pleasure in ordinary comforts.
They loved the hot bath (their relatives had allowed them only a
begrudging dip in the lukewarm water late at night after everybody
else had finished). Kyoko was ecstatic over the dried persimmons.
They even expressed delight over a serving of sweet potatoes, the
one vegetable everyone else felt they had had enough of.

Mrs. Ikeda tried hard to be helpful without being in the way,
although she wasn't successful at either. Still, she seemed more
companionable than before, maybe because she didn't talk as much.
Most of the people she had gossiped about in the past were dead or
missing now, so there was nothing more to say about them. In the
upstairs room, she and Chiyo sat together for a long time, gazing at
the sea without speaking, each of them separately creating daydreams for the future or trying to eradicate the nightmares of the
past.

"What are they going to do?" Kazuko asked Chiyo after the
Ikedas had gone off to bed. "They can't go back and live in that
cave all alone."

"Well, her son Ichiro is coming home soon," Chiyo said. "Maybe they could just stay until he arrives. He'll help them build a house again."

"But we have no idea when he's coming, do we? They could be here all winter, and we hardly have enough food for the six of us. I don't know how we're going to manage as it is."

Chiyo felt ashamed. She and her children had doubled the burden on Isao. In 1943, after Shintaro was inducted into the army, she had received a monthly pension and there had been a small "on leave" stipend from Rijo Middle School. But now with the war ended, the Imperial Army defeated, and Rijo Middle School destroyed, there would be no income at all. If Shintaro didn't come home she couldn't go on living off her brother's largesse forever. And Shintaro's possessions and her own were dwindling away. She pawned them for food whenever she had a chance, not wanting to feel she was always on the receiving end. But even though Shintaro's *haori* had paid for the oysters and the cabbage, she knew she shouldn't have brought the Ikedas. And the oysters had been an extravagance.

Come spring, she and Isao could be dead. They were the ones who had walked through the shadow of that bomb, and at any moment they could die of the same dreadful disease that had taken Grandmother. Then how would Kazuko manage, alone, taking care of all the children?

"I'm sorry," she said. "I shouldn't have asked the Ikedas to come."

"Of course you should have," Isao countered. "We're on this earth to help our fellow man, not destroy each other. Isn't that what your Christian Girls' School taught you?" He knocked the ashes out of his pipe. "They taught you that, then they dropped the atomic bomb on us."

Chiyo sat for a while, tears forming on the rim of her eyes. Then she smiled at him. "Well, those particular gentle American teachers I had," she said. "I hardly think they were consulted about it."

He laughed at her, grabbed her hand and patted it, then was serious again. "It's going to be bad this winter. And the Wartime Protection Law that provided for treatment of war injuries ended in October, so a lot of people will be left out in the cold. They can't pay their own medical expenses." He sighed, his face suddenly drawn.

"There are so many like the Ikedas with nowhere to live, no energy to get a job, and no jobs anyway. Companies like mine, we're keeping our employees because we've got a new product, but a lot of businesses—" He waved his hands. "Completely destroyed. And the leftovers who survived don't have anyplace to go. The new jobs are going to people coming home from Korea and Manchuria. They're the ones who have the energy."

Isao stood up. "You didn't invite them to stay here through the winter, did you?" he asked.

"No, not exactly. I rather suggested it, though—"

He smiled again and nodded at her. "Let's just sleep on it. We'll think of something."

"That was a wonderful interlude!" Mrs. Ikeda said the next morning, putting down her chopsticks. "Kyoko and I must go home now. I'm worried about leaving our table there in case somebody finds it. We can't lock up corrugated steel sitting on top of a pile of bricks, you know. And there's looting all over the city. We found that table sitting in the rubble down the street. Actually, I think it belonged to the Kasamas." She looked as if she had just confessed her darkest sin. "But I suppose, since they don't need it, they wouldn't mind. . . ." Her voice trailed off.

"Anyway." She stood up purposefully. "Come on, Kyoko, we have work ahead of us."

"Perhaps," Chiyo said, looking hopefully at Kazuko and Isao, "they could come again for a bath and a good night's sleep once in a while."

"Of course!" Kazuko smiled pleasantly. "Of course!"

They stood at the door bowing to each other. Kazuko had found an old pot for them to use, the extra *futon* which Akiko had slept on, an old quilt, and a hibachi to cook on.

"Such precious gifts!" Mrs. Ikeda exclaimed. "I have never received any in my whole life as precious as these."

Chiyo and Yoko accompanied them to the train station.

"But what will you do for an income?" Chiyo asked Mrs. Ikeda.

"Oh. I'm going to be a clerk at City Hall. My husband's former boss, Mr. Yamada, is still alive. I met him by chance near the old Fukuya Department Store one day. Have you noticed the building's been requisitioned by the Occupation Forces? Huge khaki-colored giants moving in and out of it. They're Australian, you know."

"Really?" Chiyo said. She hadn't noticed. "But what about this job?"

"Well, Mr. Yamada said they need somebody to organize the City Hall files that were stored in the country during the war. He said

I'd listened to my husband all those years, so I probably know more about City Hall than anybody alive." She smiled. "And of course Nobori-chō Elementary School will be opening soon, so Kyoko's going to be busy too."

Chiyo stumbled back to Isao's, determined to find a way to live in her own house again. She had never worked at a job. But neither had Mrs. Ikeda, and even with her special connections at City Hall, she was no more skilled than Chiyo.

Through the winter, they continued to check themselves and each other for the purple spots, wondering how long it would be before they could consider themselves out of danger. Isao said the Occupation Forces had announced that radioactivity was completely harmless to anyone exposed a week or ten days after the explosion. No one was convinced. All around them were stories of people dying still, even those who had been healthy and active through the worst of it, even the ones who had entered Hiroshima weeks later. And there were stories, too, about people dying just from being in contact with the wounded and the dead. If that was true, then the whole family had been exposed one way or another. Kazuko, Akiko, Fusako, and Yoko, all working every day with the sick and wounded and dead. Even Hiroshi was not safe.

On the last week of the terrible year of Showa 20, the end of 1945, an American news service nominated the Hiroshima and Nagasaki bombings as one of the ten best stories of the year.

January was bitter cold, as had been predicted. Fuel was as hard to come by as food. They limited their baths to two a week. The army-issue *kanpan* rations were in smaller and less frequent portions. The servings of barley rice grew skimpier. Even the sweet potatoes and pumpkin from Kazuko's garden, which had once been bountiful, were in short supply.

For much of January Chiyo did not go into Hiroshima at all. But one night in February she could not sleep, worrying about the two Ikedas shivering together in their tiny cave.

The next morning she took the train straight into Hiroshima station and walked across Sakae Bridge over to Nobori-chō, with each step feeling a sense of dread for what she might find at the Ikedas.

When she arrived, she saw the foundation of the old house swept clean, all the lumber stacked in neat piles, and some kind of construction begun, a lean-to shack adjacent to their old cave. Had

Mrs. Ikeda been infused with some supernatural surge of energy? Or had she and Kyoko died and squatters finally taken over the land? There was a pounding noise, somebody hammering nails into the back of the shack.

"Hello?" she called. "Ikeda-san?"

"*Hai!*" A short, sturdy young man was grinning at her when he emerged from behind the shack. He came forward, offering his hand according to the American custom. She was not sure that she wanted to take it.

"*Hara-sensei no Oku-sama, deshyoo!* Teacher Hara's wife, is it?"

It was such a husky, hearty voice. It was Ichiro. Not at all like his brother, Yukiji. Ichiro had always been the vigorous one, the baseball player, the one whose voice you could hear singing the national anthem more loudly than the others. He'd been old enough to finish his education and join the air force as an officer, one of the first after the war with America began. There'd been a noisy farewell for him at the station, then the time he'd come home on leave when everybody suspected he was in the Kamikaze Corps. That was when he got his wife pregnant again, Mrs. Yamamoto had suggested.

"You're home!" Chiyo breathed. "You didn't die out there in a kamikaze plane." She placed her hand in his and the memory of his firm, strong grip lingered for a long time afterwards.

"I was a trainer," he said apologetically. "They wouldn't let me go on any raids because I had to train the younger boys."

Within a week, Ichiro had expanded the shack enough to make it livable for the whole family, including his wife and newborn son. "Not quite luxurious, you understand," he told Chiyo when she stopped by to offer congratulations. "That part will have to come later."

He had already collected his wife and month-old son from the relatives in Kabe, and Chiyo was delighted to see Haruko again and to greet the tiny baby.

"I told my uncle that I didn't want to inherit my ancestor's farm-land," Ichiro said proudly. "We can support ourselves."

His uncle had told him that his mother and sister had simply wandered off one day and couldn't be found no matter how hard they looked. But Haruko had hinted, when they were alone, that this was not true. They had indeed been asked to leave, taking with them only the clothes they were wearing. Clothes given to them by someone at City Hall who had removed them from the corpses.

"In the past, farmers at least offered up a little lunch when they sent their old parents off to die in the mountains. And my wife here tells me that they really weren't so desperately short of food. Can you imagine? They would have turned out my grandparents, too, if they hadn't died in the bomb."

But Mrs. Ikeda was no longer interested in her late husband's relatives. "Just look at this beautiful house!" she kept saying.

"Well, it's not exactly a house, Mother!" Ichiro countered.

"It's a palace to me. Especially after living in that cave."

Within a short time Ichiro was employed as a construction engineer at City Hall.

In April, the cherry trees bloomed in the outskirts of the city where people said nothing would grow for seventy-five years.

One bright and cloudless Sunday the Inokuchi household packed a picnic lunch and went in to see the miracle for themselves, walking up the road to the suburb of Ushita where Fusako had entered her first year at the Women's College, the Christian school Chiyo had attended, and which Yoko would enroll in soon. It had been an embarrassment during the war because of its American connections. Now it was the first school to begin again after the holocaust.

"I'll specialize in English, Aunt," Fusako said, posing for Isao's camera in front of the barracks classroom. "It's the wave of the future."

"How quickly the world changes," Chiyo commented dryly, remembering how Shintaro had wrapped up his English books and hidden them in the closet.

They crossed the Sakae Bridge to the old neighborhood and went first to invite the Ikedas to their picnic. Ichiro had made even more improvements. He'd left Kyoko and Mrs. Ikeda's cave intact as a storehouse, then set to work building a shack with two small rooms. The one for Kyoko and Mrs. Ikeda was a sitting room covered with their straw mat. The other was a smaller room in the back for Ichiro, his wife, and baby. The hard clay floor of the former kitchen remained, and he had managed to find the old drain and a battered metal box for the sink. There was no running water yet.

Chiyo remembered the Ikedas' grand, old sprawling house. But Mrs. Ikeda seemed more delighted with the tiny shack than she had ever been with the elegant house she had taken for granted.

At the site of the Hara house, Chiyo discovered that Shintaro's two cherry trees were alive and bravely thrusting up hints of blossoms.

The family decided to spread the picnic out on the foundation of the house. Chiyo had cleared off rubble during her weekly trips, but it still needed sweeping. Isao went to borrow a broom from a man standing outside a shack on the Kasamas' land.

"He says he's Colonel Kasama's grandnephew," said Mrs. Ikeda. "But he hasn't offered any proof, and he doesn't seem to know anything about the colonel's son. Every time I ask him questions, he's vague about the answer. Then he explains that he's always lived in Korea, and he doesn't know much about this side of the family. He just came back here because Colonel Kasama is the only relative he has, he said. I wish the son would come home and settle the whole matter."

Kazuko spread out her wide straw mat, and they sat there, facing the living cherry trees and the hint of green moss that had grown over the lumps of the toppled stone lantern and decorative rocks in the garden. Chiyo thought of her dancing lessons with Grandmother and the Noh drama *Yuya*—Taira Munemori's mistress, dancing for her lord under the cherry trees in spite of the sadness she felt over her mother's imminent death. Gaiety and lightness covering a leaden heart. Grandmother had taught her to practice that dance, holding the image in her mind of a broken heart encased in a box of burnished silver.

Isao looked thoughtfully at the garden. "Isn't there a Greek legend about rising again from the ashes?" he asked. "A phoenix that is reborn?"

Fusako smiled. "It's Egyptian, isn't it, Father? The phoenix burns itself in fire every five hundred years, then rises again from its own ashes. That's different from the Chinese legend."

"But Hiroshima was only three hundred years old," said Isao. "We didn't get our full term."

Chiyo thought she caught a glimpse of Hiroshi almost smiling at the bright, cloudless sky. He dropped his eyelids quickly when he caught her gazing at him and speared a rice ball with his chopsticks.

Their appetites were voracious. All of them could have eaten more. But for a brief moment Chiyo felt the illusion of plenty.

They cleared up more of the garden and, under the rubble, discovered the main *hashira*, the support pillar from the *tokonoma* where Chiyo had always hung Shintaro's calligraphy scrolls. It was charred and probably unusable, but it comforted her that some of it was left. Isao mentioned an old carpenter he knew who was skilled at setting new beams and pillars in place. But first they would have to find enough wood.

"We're all very impressed by what you've done, Ikeda-san," Isao said. "Maybe when my sister's husband comes home, you can advise him."

"If we could have something built by next spring so that Yoko doesn't have to go so far to school," Chiyo said.

"When your husband gets back, I'm sure he can do it as fast as I did," Ichiro said.

"I think I'd like to do it myself. Before he comes home," Chiyo said quietly, looking sideways at Isao.

"Hiroshi should finish grade school in Inokuchi," Isao said. "After that, if Rijo Middle School opens again—"

"Yes." Chiyo nodded to him. But she thought to herself that she would never, under any circumstances, stay in Inokuchi for two more years. Or Hiroshi either. He had already been there too long.

She wandered out toward the cherry tree.

"Shintaro," she said to it. "*Anata!* Beloved one. Come home. Do you hear me? I need you now. Don't make me wait any longer."

Part Three

Chapter Fourteen

CHIYO AND YOKO MOVED INTO THEIR new shack on a July morning in 1947. A dry wind blew dust around them in little swirls, whispering unpleasantries, depositing a layer of gray on the meager greenery in the garden. It seemed to Chiyo, while they carried in their few possessions, that things were not growing as well in Hiroshima as she had thought. Nor had Shintaro come home. Ships had been arriving steadily, unabated, carrying repatriates all through April, May, and June. Still there was no word from him.

The Hara dwelling had two small rooms and a kitchen, modeled after the Ikeda structure. But some of the boards Isao and the carpenter had collected were new and of even quality, giving the house a professional look. They had even found a tile maker in Iwakuni, and Chiyo's roof was the only real one in the neighborhood, a fact which rather embarrassed her.

The carpenter had used good supporting poles and crossbeams for the ceiling and had even grafted on to a stronger piece of wood the unburned part of the *hashira,* the support pillar which they had found on the day of the picnic. Now it formed her new *tokonoma,* the alcove at the entrance, where she could display *kakejiku,* hanging scrolls, as background to her flower arrangements. That one touch of the familiar delighted her. Nothing else in the tiny shack reminded her of those precious prewar days.

"The mosquitoes aren't as bad as they were last year," Mrs. Ikeda said when she called on them that evening. "You've never seen such a horde as we had then. Strange, isn't it, how the bomb hardly affected lesser creatures like those insects?"

Chiyo lay under the breezeless mosquito net, the buzzing sound around her endless. And in the still, dark air, she worried that she had made the wrong decision.

Isao had finally agreed about the house. But he had insisted that Hiroshi remain in Inokuchi at least until March, when he would finish elementary school. Hiroshi himself seemed not to care where he was or who he lived with. For the past two years, he had spoken his brother's name only once, and his father's not at all. Once, during the terrible winter of 1946, she had found him alone in the sitting room in Inokuchi, examining a picture of Shintaro in the old photograph album. "There he is, dressed in his uniform, ready to go off to war," she said. "Do you remember what he was wearing around his stomach? The *senninbari* cloth."

Hiroshi looked at her blankly.

"Well, if a woman gets a thousand people to each embroider a tiny knot in the *haramaki* cloth, the bellyband that every soldier takes to war, then it becomes a *senninbari*. And if he wears it always wrapped around his middle, then no enemy fire can ever harm him, because stitches have been sewn on that cloth by a thousand people who wish him well. That's what all of us did for our men before they went off to war. So, if your father still has that *haramaki*, he's safe."

Chiyo had actually thought the whole custom quite foolish and had sworn that even if Shintaro was called into service, she would never spend her time on anything so ridiculous. Yet, when the red draft card came, she went all over town collecting the embroidery, even from people she did not know. Yoko remembered the cloth vividly, having stood with her mother in front of Fukuya Department Store with all the others, asking for stitches from anyone passing by.

Hiroshi nodded solemnly but Chiyo suspected that he remembered nothing, not the day of his father's departure, not even his face. Shintaro had been gone five years, almost half of Hiroshi's life, and now the child's older brother had disappeared, too. Chiyo and Yoko had talked together about their memories of Kenichi, and in the darkness had hugged each other and wept. But silent Hiroshi would not share an inch of his interior with anyone. And the longer he remained in Inokuchi, she decided, the more distant he would become.

Chiyo lay awake in the new house, pondering the past and the future until just before dawn. In the morning, before Yoko was awake, she stepped outside to survey their barren, windswept surroundings, even more stark under the sunlight. But it was no longer a desert. Shacks were appearing everywhere, some belonging to people she had known before the war. At the Kasama site across the street stood a structure with corrugated sheet metal on one side, part of the former concrete wall on another, wooden boards nailed to posts on the last two sides. All of it had been erected by the man who claimed to be the Kasama grandnephew. He was living with a pretty woman he called his wife, and he made new additions almost daily—a veranda created from two sturdy posts supporting an old straw mat, a whole additional room made from a cardboard box. He had told Mrs. Ikeda he was planning to open a greengrocer's shop on the site of the old one as soon as he could grow enough vegetables. Earlier in the spring, he had discovered that the lot where they had grown squash during the war did not belong to anyone. He immediately set to work dividing up plots for each of the neighbors, offering to do the planting for them if they could pay for the labor. Now the beans and squash were growing well enough under the hot sun, their green leaves not at all daunted by the layer of dust, and the whole garden guarded by a scarecrow to protect it from birds during the day and thieves at night.

Chiyo looked at the random collection of shacks scattered on the street, letting her gaze rest on the house beyond the Yamamoto ruins where the Kakiharas, father and daughter, were living. He had come home from the navy to find his house destroyed and his wife missing without a trace. After weeks of searching, he had found his daughter, Fusako's age, in the Fukuya Department Store basement infirmary. He was so overjoyed that he set about immediately building a shack, then began selling whatever he could collect— household goods, clothing, furniture. Next he built a tiny lean-to amid the ruins of the Hondori shopping district, one of the first establishments to do business there again. The former neighbors were proud of him. But there were few former neighbors. Of the ten households in the *Tonarigumi,* there remained only four—the Ikedas, the Haras, the Kakiharas, and the Tamiokas, whose seven-year-old daughter had died at Fukuromachi Primary School and whose son, evacuated to the country, was still missing, apparently taken away by a man who claimed he was the boy's uncle.

The lot where the Yamamotos had lived remained forlorn and empty. A corner of the concrete wall to the back was still standing but crumbling, forming a jagged profile more pronounced each day as the wind eroded it and turned it to dust in the street. A terrible loneliness overwhelmed her whenever she saw it.

Chiyo swept the street in front of the house and watered it down, hoping to get rid of the haze of dust that kept invading their dwelling. Yoko was awake when she went back inside, and they sat for their first breakfast on the small chunk of *tatami* Kazuko had given them. It was already permeated with dust, but they pretended it was new and clean, and that it covered the whole expanse of their sitting room, which, at the moment, consisted of a series of rough boards.

It was the second day of Yoko's summer vacation.

"Let's go down to the Hondori shopping district," Chiyo said. "If we could find a few nails or hooks for the walls, and then we need a dishpan, and a small *tansu* chest if we can afford it."

Outside, stepping carefully over the cracks in the streets and the upended stones, Chiyo remembered the American cowboy movies she had seen with Shintaro, everyone stalking through frontier towns on wooden planks. But the buildings in those movies had always been lined up in neat rows. Here, scattered everywhere, were amazing hovels made of plywood boards, bamboo poles, rusty pieces of metal. Some of the cardboard boxes sagged from having been exposed to the spring rains.

The shops on the Hondori were a bit more substantial, most of them made of wooden boards pounded together—like Chiyo's house, but with space for show windows in the front (although no windowpanes had appeared yet). Some buildings were even two stories high, and of every shape and size, but all of them temporary. They were lined up neatly, facing the street, still rubble-strewn in places and torn up for sewer lines. A few shops were so rudely tacked together that the whole structure, like her neighbor's cardboard box, would surely not withstand the autumn floods.

The more substantial buildings had well-calligraphed signs or heavy *noren,* cloth curtains, hung out in front to advertise what was for sale. There was shaved ice with syrup, the kind the boy along the riverbank had asked for the day of the bomb, and another curtain announcing that a restaurant would open there soon. Chiyo could not imagine what they would sell for food.

142

Other shops, like Mr. Kakihara's, were small booths with boards nailed together on three sides and a roof to protect the proprietors and their goods from the sun and rain. Other people merely sat on the ground, displaying their wares on a cloth, old treasures like the ones Chiyo had once owned. Her collection at Inokuchi was dwindling away. And yet everywhere she turned Chiyo was mindful of how lucky she was to have two children still alive, to be living in a house with four solid walls, still in possession of a few treasures to sell for food, still anticipating a husband who, if the Goddess of Mercy willed it, would come home and take up his job again.

They found some nails, but nothing cheap enough to use for a dishpan. They took the streetcar to Hiroshima station to see the brisk black market trade. It was here that everything required money instead of the clothing and antiques acceptable on the Hondori. Some of the old Imperial Army *kanpan* hardtack was on sale, spirited away from government control by some illegal means. They sacrificed some money for that.

At another stand were goods from the foreign armies, especially American cigarettes and candy, nylon hosiery, canned asparagus, boxes of powder for making sweet cakes. She wondered who would buy such things, even if they had the money. Then she caught sight of a can of corned beef from Argentina, the kind her father used to buy and prized so much. Outrageously expensive, but if she'd had the money, she would have bought it just to share the nostalgia with Isao.

In front of the station, among the usual flock of scarred and ragged children, they found a battered aluminum pan for sale by an old man willing to part with it for twenty yen.

Each day Chiyo scanned the newspapers for announcements of ships coming home, especially the ones from China. She knew Shintaro would not desert her. He would overcome whatever difficulties there were and come home to her and the children.

It took all her energy planning how to make her supply of possessions stretch for food. She went every day to the black market while Yoko was doing summer homework with her classmates. She did not want her child to be exposed to the misery there.

Once she had seen a foreign soldier throw packages of candy and gum at a flock of orphans, who scrambled at his feet to pick them up. Sometimes she saw people emerging from a pile of rubble where a dwelling place probably existed somewhere beneath.

But most disturbing of all were the young women who stood for hours in front of the station, sometimes having conversations with the foreign soldiers, then walking away with them into the jumbled area of shacks. "Pan-pan" girls, Mrs. Ikeda called them, not the *baishōfu* who sold their laughter and good times to Japanese men but middle-class girls from good families. She could tell from the way they carried themselves when they walked. Some were not much older than Yoko.

When she passed the shacks, Chiyo could hear the laughter of foreign men floating out, hearty and booming. At least they did not seem cruel or dangerous, not even sinister. But very rough and uncultured.

One afternoon when Yoko was helping Chiyo carry home a small *tansu* chest she had bargained for, they encountered one of the foreign giants face-to-face—probably an Australian, Yoko said later, because of the insignia on his uniform. They had just stepped onto Sakae Bridge, and the man was standing there, towering above them, smiling down at Yoko. They couldn't turn around and go back, and there was no way around him, especially with the heavy chest between them. He didn't say anything, just smiled and held out a candy bar. They shrank back and shook their heads, but he took Yoko's hand and folded it over the candy bar.

They bowed and nodded politely, still holding on to the chest, then hurried to move past him on the bridge. But he reached out, took the chest, and lifted it high in the air onto his shoulder. Then he motioned to them that he would follow. There was nothing they could do. Chiyo did not want him to know where their house was, so they hurried ahead of him, almost running. When they arrived in their neighborhood, Chiyo stood firmly in the middle of the street in front of the Kasama nephew's house and pointed to the ground. "Thank you," she said. It was the only thing she knew how to say in English. "Thank you. Thank you."

He pointed to himself and then the chest and then the Kasamas' house, but she shook her head so vehemently that he finally shrugged his shoulders and started back toward the station. She and Yoko bowed to him, and he laughed and waved.

They stood in the middle of the street, continuing to bow, and watched him disappear before they picked up the chest and went inside, only breathing easily when they closed the door behind them.

"You must never, never go to the station alone," Chiyo told Yoko firmly. "Never!" Her heart was beating wildly.

They did not eat the candy bar. In spite of their ever-present hunger, especially for sweets, they could not bring themselves to eat it. Instead, it stayed in the kitchen, untouched, a thing of wonder to look at and show to Yoko's friends. Nobody could remember afterwards what had ever happened to it.

First week of August. Two years after the bomb. Chiyo and Yoko left their dwelling under the watchful eye of their new neighbor, Tetsuo Kasama, and went out to Inokuchi to prepare for Kenichi's and Grandmother's memorial services. They would hold a private ceremony at the house early on the morning of the sixth, then attend the city-wide service on the grounds of Jisenji, Grandmother's favorite temple, at the tip of Nakajima near the Honkawa Bridge. During *Obon,* the All Souls festival on August 15, Jisenji had always provided a service for *muenbotoke,* souls who had no relatives left on earth to pray for their repose. But now the priests had gathered unidentified bones there on the site of their destroyed temple so that people with missing relatives could pray for them. In Hiroshima it was now understood that *muenbotoke* included souls like Kenichi's, whose relatives were still on earth but who couldn't find their remains. And it was generally agreed that the *Obon* would always be on August 6 instead of the fifteenth.

In bed that night at Inokuchi, Chiyo dreamed of Kenichi, uniformed, head shaved and school cap in hand, wandering just on the edge of the misty fog that had banked up against the shore below the house. He was picking up rocks and clam shells, pocketing some and throwing the others away, chuckling to himself about some private joke.

In the morning, after the private services with the same frail priest who had presided over Grandmother's funeral, they sped toward Hiroshima on the road near the edge of the Inland Sea, riding in the Toyokogyo company car, Isao enjoying his race with the streetcar.

People crowded into the temple grounds. Flat, naked grounds where everyone had thrust incense sticks into the sand. A small fence, bedecked with Shinto prayer papers that fluttered in the sullen wind, surrounded a stark, wooden tower. It had messages of peace burned deep into it, heavy and dark, as if they had been made by a calligrapher's brush strokes. The remains of more than 3,700 victims had been collected and buried there, Isao said, none of them claimed by any family.

A few tentative plants clung to the edge of the fence, struggling to survive among the crowd that stood praying, pressing their hands together, whispering to one another, most of them woodenly stoic, some of them crying.

The heat, the unbearable humidity, and the herds of people distracted Chiyo from her thoughts of Kenichi. She was being pushed closer toward the memorial tower, pressed by the crowd. Isao had given her a stick of incense, and she lit it and placed it in the sand, then held her hands together and prayed. But the communion with Kenichi had already happened earlier in her dreams at dawn. It was not going to happen here. She pushed away from the press of bodies.

They climbed wordlessly back into the tiny sedan and traversed all the bridges again back to Inokuchi, where they sat on the veranda of the house, overlooking the sea, sitting where Grandmother had sat.

Isao did not go back to work that afternoon. Instead, he wandered down along the shore, picking up rocks and shells the way Kenichi had done in her dreams. It was most unusual for him.

Chapter Fifteen

THEY BEGAN THE FALL WITH FRESH EX-
pectations. Yoko was in her second term at
the Girls' School and had new friends but spent most of her time
with Kyoko Ikeda, who attended a different school. Hiroshi would
come to live with them in the spring. And surely by then Shintaro
would be home.

She was getting anxious. Already more than 200,000 had arrived in Maizuru alone, the newspaper said. Every day Chiyo
pored over the news of disembarking repatriates. Sometimes there
were photos of the arriving ships, taken at a distance, then at closer
range, with people hanging over the railings and waving, and finally at the point of disembarkation. Chiyo examined each of the
photos with minute care, searching for Shintaro's face among the
hordes of confused-looking people getting off the ships. The families had come home first, women and children returning from Manchuria and Korea, some after a lifetime there, many who had been
born abroad and never set foot on Japanese soil, all of them wearing
threadbare, ill-fitting clothing, clutching bundles and children, fear
and dread in their eyes.

The soldiers arrived next, hungry-looking and exhausted, wearing
Chinese and Russian uniforms. They didn't even look Japanese.

147

And none of the ones photographed was Shintaro.

Sometimes when it was announced in the paper that a trainload of returnees were coming to Hiroshima, Chiyo and Yoko would go to the station to meet them. But the emotions of the people greeting each other, and the disappointed faces of the others, including Yoko's, were more than she could bear.

One encouraging sign was Takano-sensei's recovery. She couldn't believe the change in him. He had been so wan and listless in the days just after the bomb, turning to look at her with luminous eyes, still daring to hope that at least one of his students had survived. Takano-sensei's own son had died for the emperor somewhere in the South Pacific. He had two daughters living but no other sons.

"Everybody's still sending us peaches," Mrs. Takano told her during one of her visits. "You know, your brother has sent boxes and boxes."

Chiyo had not expected him to live. Yet he was sitting at his desk, gazing at the garden, autumn air wafting in, stirring the red maple leaves on the ground.

"Well, I'm still alive," he said, smiling a little cynically. "All of the others died, you know. Not a single one of those three hundred and sixty boys survived. None of the teachers either. I've checked again and again. Some of them got home and saw their parents. But the last one died on August thirteenth." He stared at her. "Including Kenichi. Even though you couldn't find him. You do realize that, don't you, *Oku-sama?* No more false hopes. We must put this thing behind us."

Chiyo, on her knees beside him, bowed her head toward her lap. "You and Yasu Yamamoto are still alive," she said.

"But we don't count. We weren't there. I overslept, as you remember, and as punishment, it seems I have been condemned to go on living."

"And what if you had been with them that day?" she argued. "You would have died, too. What good would that have done? You are so precious to us all," she said, her voice husky. "You have been brave in such an extraordinary way, Takano-sensei, and we are all very grateful to you." She wanted to explain what it had meant to her all that time, knowing that he was in Hatsukaichi, fighting for his life. But he wasn't paying attention. He told her about a plan that was afoot to build a memorial for the 360 first-year boys who had died.

"It was so important what you said to him," Mrs. Takano whispered to her later as she was leaving.

"But he hardly heard me," Chiyo said.

"Oh, yes he did. I can tell. I've told him all those things my-self, but he's tired of listening to me. You see, he can't stop wish-ing he'd died instead of them."

She was a small woman and she seemed to have shrunk during that first year after the bomb, day after day trying to buoy up her husband's spirits.

The next time Chiyo visited, he had changed even more. He was up and around, supported by a cane, and he had taken charge of the movement to build the memorial and had collected essays, poetry, letters from the families. He hardly noticed her gift of autumn pears. Something more nourishing was sustaining him now.

"It's such a miracle," Mrs. Takano whispered to her. "He's even talking about going back to teach part-time."

With Takano-sensei's recovery she felt even more confident of Shintaro's return. But how would they manage until then? If Shintaro did not come home in the fall, there would be no ships until spring. She had begun to sell more of her inheritance, the china teacups, scrolls, and old kimonos that had been assigned her before their mother died. Isao did not like it.

"Borrow the money from me instead of selling them," he said. "Shintaro can pay it back when he's able."

"I can't borrow any more," she said. "We owe you too much already."

"Then at least give me first choice at buying. I'd rather keep your things in the family. Foreigners are buying up everything and taking it out of the country."

But Chiyo felt that selling her possessions to Isao was the same as borrowing money from him. She was already a financial burden, even more so because she was living separately. And he'd assumed Hiroshi's expenses and paid for Yoko's tuition. Now Yoko had out-grown her school uniform.

With the help of Fusako, who had promised not to tell, Chiyo spirited away Shintaro's grandfather's samurai sword, which she had stored in Inokuchi all during the war. She took it to the pawnshop of Ichiro Ikeda's friend, who promised to let her know if he had a buyer. With that amount of money, she thought she could last through the winter. If Shintaro wasn't home by spring, she would inquire about a job at City Hall.

She had never had a full-time job. The Girls' Normal School prepared her to teach, but the moment she graduated, she was caught up in all the preparations for marriage. Flower arranging, tea ceremony, cooking lessons.

She wondered how it would be, working at City Hall and fitting in all the household tasks at night and on Sundays. Mrs. Ikeda had managed it, but there were five people in her household. Besides, Isao didn't think it was respectable for a woman with young children to have a job.

And there was the other problem. Chiyo couldn't depend on her energy. Some days she awoke feeling she could accomplish anything. In October, when the fresh, cool breezes came, she had the wash hanging on the line before any of the neighbors, her shopping done, even time to give their tiny house a thorough cleaning. Then within a week, she would be laid low again, barely able to get up and prepare Yoko's breakfast.

"Don't tell your Uncle Isao," Chiyo pleaded when Yoko insisted that she stay in bed. "He would make us move back to Inokuchi. But I want to be here when your father comes home."

It wasn't just lack of food and energy that worried her. It was dealing each day with the changing rumors about who would die and who wouldn't. They were saying that people would die soon if they had been within 1,000 meters of the hypocenter near Aioi Bridge, the spot just below where the bomb had burst. If that was so, she and Isao and Akiko were all destined to die, leaving only Kazuko and maybe Shintaro to bring up the children.

There was no order to the deaths. People who had not been in the city at all had died because of exposure to their stricken relatives, who had gotten well. People with burn scars and keloids had survived, and people who hadn't seemed hurt at all were dying. She thought sometimes the scar on her cheek might save her. She had grown used to it now, although she shuddered to think how Shintaro would feel when he saw it. Maybe the scar was penance she had to pay for staying alive.

She managed through November without getting sick again, but early December was unusually cold, and the wind blew in through the cracks. There were no thoughts now of helping at the orphanage, not even of getting a job or guarding her energy. She could think only of getting food and fuel. Each evening, she and Yoko hovered over the *kotatsu,* allowing themselves just one of the burnt pieces of wood Yoko was always finding in the rubble.

After supper until time for the bath, Yoko did her homework and Chiyo wrote letters to Shintaro, one to his old army headquarters and one each to the ports of Maizuru, Moji, and Sasebo, where most of the repatriate ships were arriving.

> We're right here in the same place you left us, waiting for you to come home. Our house was destroyed, but we still have the old

tokonoma in this tiny new one, and Yoko and I are waiting for you. Hiroshi is out in Inokuchi finishing the school year. Kenichi is missing. Come home soon.

It was all she could manage to say about Kenichi, but she wrote the same paragraph over and over again, day after day, adding at the end new bits of information about the neighbors, about his job waiting at Rijo, about the children's progress in school.

Finally, every night, they struggled out in the cold to the neighborhood *sento,* the public bath. If they had their own *ofuro,* even the old Russian bathtub, they could go immediately to sleep afterwards, but as it was, they lost most of their body heat walking home in the cold air, rushing back to snuggle together underneath the quilts, and trying to fall asleep before the coals died out.

January was still ahead, the money from Shintaro's sword almost gone. And February would be even colder. But for the moment, the exhaustion had left her. She set out one sunny afternoon, determined to find something special for Yoko's supper.

Pushing through the black market stalls, she was tempted by a can of corn, made in America and bearing the picture of a green caveman wearing a garment of leaves.

"Are there really whole ears of corn inside?" she asked the man in a ragged army overcoat who was running the stall.

"No. Just the kernels," he said. "But they're very sweet. You should try it. Only three hundred and fifty yen."

It was an outrageous price. One-tenth the price of a house.

"Who can afford to pay that much?" she asked.

"Lots of people," he said. "The ones coming in from outside. They're making it rich, buying up everything and selling it for three times the price. The rest of us, we're just outcasts. Were you here when the bomb fell, *Oku-san?*"

Chiyo nodded.

"Well, better watch out. They'll cheat you blind if they can. Do you want that corn? It's very hard to get."

"No," she said. "I wouldn't spend that much money even if I had it."

He turned away from her. "Suit yourself."

She found a stall selling rice. Not the usual kind. It was from some foreign country, too. Long and short grains mixed together, and broken pieces. She had bought it before, and it jarred her sensibilities to eat it, but it was better than barley.

One more turn around, and she found a piece of *katsuobushi,* dried bonita fish to use for making soup. Two boys Hiroshi's age were carrying a bag of it, offering each piece for whatever price they could get. Probably it had been stolen, but she bought it anyway, thinking how ashamed old Colonel Kasama would be if he knew how quickly they had lost their discipline. There was no control or order. The man in the stall was right. The new people didn't care about the old residents. They just wanted money any way they could get it. Even cheating and stealing. Like the colored salt water Mrs. Ikeda had bought for soy sauce.

But there were other people like the Kasama nephew who gave their time and energy to helping the bomb victims. Whether he was really Colonel Kasama's nephew or not didn't make any difference now. He was part of their neighborhood, and a comfort to them all.

Chiyo had begun to feel a curious relief. She didn't have to worry any longer about what she said to people. She could complain about anything, especially the stupidity of the military for getting them into the terrible war. No one was watching them any longer or listening to every word they said. The Americans and Australians, who couldn't understand Japanese, barely paid attention to them.

She splurged and took the streetcar home, riding past the cabaret district in Nagarekawa, getting off at Kamiya-chō so she could have the pleasure of walking past the hulk of Nagarekawa Church, which towered above the rubble-strewn streets with its glass windows partly restored and its roof retiled. Reverend Tanimoto had been in the bomb, and yet he'd managed to begin restoration. He was even planning to go to America to raise money for orphans. Thinking of it gave her a new lift. It was a matter of will. If the Tanimotos and Ikedas could do it, so could she.

She was only a meter away from her house now, and as she got closer, she saw something sticking out of her mailbox. Letters were very rare. No one had the energy to write.

She paced herself, walking toward the front door, careful not to hurry or hope too much, dreading at the same time. Finally standing in front of the mailbox, she pulled out a strange-looking postcard, folded like a book with a return address on the back. It was two postcards sealed together. She tore the seal open and found inside a blank space on one side and something written on the other. It was in Shintaro's handwriting. Written with an unsharpened pencil, a bit shaky, but there was no question that it was his.

The Red Cross had sent it. He was alive.

She pushed her bundles into the tiny hallway and on into the living room, not wanting to stand outside with the world watching while she read it.

Greetings.

To wife Chiyo, eldest son Kenichi, daughter Yoko, youngest son Hiroshi —

I pray that you have survived the defeat of our nation and the bombing of Hiroshima. I am in Siberia in a labor camp for prisoners of war. It is cold here and we must work hard, but we have enough food to keep us alive. I am aching for the day I can come home.

You must reply on the attached postcard. Don't send anything else, not letters or packages. They cannot be delivered. Just tear off the postcard, write on it and send it back. I am anxious to hear from you.

Your ever faithful
husband and father
Hara Shintaro

He had heard about the bombing but not about Kenichi. None of their letters had reached him. And somehow he had gotten from northern China to Siberia. She had expected the Chinese to capture him. Instead, it was the Russians, and they had sent him to the coldest place on earth. But he was alive. And the proof was not secondhand. A letter in Shintaro's own handwriting, delivered through the mail, telling them exactly where he was.

She had known all along that he was alive and coming home. Her instincts had not betrayed her. They had been right to move into Hiroshima. If she had been in Inokuchi, it could have taken ages for the postman to deliver the letter. It might even have been returned to Siberia.

Shintaro home, sitting in their tiny shack house. None of them would ever be cold again. It could snow on them. They could be hungry. It was enough if he just sat there looking at her, wearing one of those strange Russian hats and coats. The smell of him. All the strange smells of foreign countries and distant worlds. Experiences she had never known. The sun shining on sheets of ice the way he'd described it in one of his first letters. Now he would tell her in person. He wouldn't mind her scar. He would hold her in his strong arms. She ached for him. Home with her and Yoko and Hiroshi. Huddled around the *kotatsu*. They wouldn't need charcoal anymore. Even if he were sitting on the other side of the room, she would be warm enough.

We are right here in Nobori-chō waiting for you to come home.

How many times had she written that? She picked up the pen and began to write it again on the card.

No. Everybody would want to write something. Yoko and Hiroshi. Isao and Kazuko. Fusako, who had always adored her Uncle Shintaro. The Ikedas. The principal at Rijo Middle School to assure him he still had his job. And the new greengrocer, the Kasama nephew, just to give him a sense of the neighborhood. She laughed to herself. They couldn't fit everybody onto the card. She thought of Shintaro's family out on the island. His sister-in-law, Sadako, would want to write on it. But it would take too long to reach her. Besides, she didn't like Sadako, and there were other people Shintaro would rather hear from.

She began reading the letter again, lingering over each character, letting his words seep into her mind. Not the meaning, just the feeling of them. She smelled the postcard. But it had no particular fragrance. Not like those earlier letters, the ones buried deep inside envelopes and carrying the essence and the perfume of the country he'd been in.

The postcard was pressed against her nostrils, covering her face when Yoko arrived home.

"Mama!"

Yoko lived in fear that her mother might go crazy at any moment. Just as Kyoko worried about Mrs. Ikeda.

"It's a postcard from your father," Chiyo breathed.

Yoko looked at the postcard, touched it, and finally read it, once to herself, once out loud. She hugged her mother and began to cry. Yoko had been carrying the doubt inside her all this time, Chiyo realized, but acting confident in front of her mother.

They called Inokuchi from the corner tobacco store. Yoko read the postcard to Hiroshi.

"We're coming out tonight so you can write on it," she told him. "Start planning what you're going to say and practice writing small. You won't get much space."

After supper, they sat around the table, drafting and redrafting their messages. Yoko had decided her mother could have four sentences, she and Hiroshi three, and everyone else two.

"Are you sure you want us to write on it?" Kazuko asked. "Don't you want the whole space for yourself?"

"No," Chiyo said. "I couldn't tell him everything anyway, so it's more pleasure for him to get messages from lots of people. He'll have a better idea of what he's coming home to."

She had been writing and rewriting her own message, and she read it to herself one more time.

> Overjoyed to hear from you after more than two years. Our house was destroyed in the bomb, but we have built a small shack on the same site and we are waiting eagerly for your return.

She paused, steeling herself for the usual message about Kenichi.

> Kenichi has been missing since the bomb and we are still searching.

That was enough. It prepared him for the worst without abandoning hope.

> Please come home soon. Let us know what port you are coming to so we can meet you. My thoughts are always with you.
>
> Your affectionate wife,
> Chiyo

Seven sentences instead of four. She crossed out "Please come home soon."

Yoko had been carefully crafting a picture of herself. Now she copied it painstakingly onto the card, then wrote her message.

> Here's how I look in my Hiroshima Girls' School uniform. Our school was the first to begin after the bomb. I passed the entrance exam with good marks and began six months ago in April. Come home before I grow out of my second uniform. I am 13.
>
> Respectfully and affectionately,
> Yoko

Next it was Hiroshi's turn. He showed his draft to everyone before he copied it into the upper left hand corner assigned to him.

> Dear Papa, I am in the sixth year of elementary school in Inokuchi, where I was evacuated to live at Uncle Isao's. Even though I am living here, I visit Mother and Yoko often and will protect them until your return. I am studying for exams at Rijo Middle School. I hope you will be my teacher.
>
> Your loving and respectful son,
> Hiroshi

"More space than anybody!" Yoko complained. She insisted he cut out the part about protecting them. "It isn't even true," she said.

"Never mind," Kazuko said. "You wrote five sentences yourself and used space for the picture. Anyway your father would rather hear from you two than from the neighbors."

Isao showed Hiroshi how to write very small and sideways in the corner, expanding into a pyramid shape.

Kazuko and Isao combined their short message.

> Wonderful to have news of you. We are awaiting your homecoming for the first postwar picnic on Miyajima.
>
> Isao and Kazuko

Fusako squeezed in directly underneath.

> Uncle, can you imagine I am in the second year at Hiroshima Women's College, studying English literature? Anxious to see you again.
>
> Your niece, Fusako

"Exactly two sentences!" she announced triumphantly.

"Well, but they're longer than Uncle Isao's," Hiroshi insisted.

Why did he always have to get the last word in? Kenichi had never been that way.

Early Monday, Chiyo took the postcard to Rijo for a message from the principal. Even more buildings had been added to the school grounds since the last visit. A group of boys were out in the field practicing soccer, playing with such energy. Probably none of them had been in the bomb. Yasu was not among them.

She went directly to the office of the new principal, who was pleased to see the card.

"Maybe he'll be home in time for the new term in April," he said. "We need your husband here to show us the old traditions and give us some continuity. He's the only one, you know. Mr. Takano has decided not to teach part-time."

He sat down and wrote immediately in the margin designated him.

> To Hara Shintaro, honorable teacher of Rijo Middle School. I have heard much about you and we are eager to have you home teaching at Rijo again.
>
> Nakamichi Jiro
> Principal

After supper, Chiyo and Yoko called on the Ikedas. Mrs. Ikeda sat down at the table, looked at the card for the second time, then broke into tears.

156

"So, he's finally coming home," she whispered, wiping her eyes. "He's alive and he's coming home." Joy and envy mixed together in her voice. She took Chiyo's pen and began to write without even asking anyone in the house what they wanted to say.

> What joy to hear from you! Eldest son, Ichiro, and his wife have a boy child, born in December 1945. Kyoko and Yoko are still best friends. We are stretching out our necks in anticipation of your homecoming.
>
> Your humble neighbor, Ikeda Sayo

Yoko watched, anxiously biting her lip. Mrs. Ikeda had written almost as much as Chiyo herself, but at least she had maneuvered it into a very small space.

"Can't I write just one word in the space underneath?" Kyoko asked. She had been sitting quietly next to her mother, occasionally whispering and giggling with Yoko.

"Of course you can!" Chiyo handed her the pen.

> *Banzai!* Hurrah!
> Kyoko

She wrote in tiny letters, almost illegible.

Ichiro's wife, Haruko, came into the room, carrying her sleeping child, Kunio, now two years old. She exclaimed over the postcard, turning it over and over to look at the address, the paper, the stamp. Kunio woke up and sat comfortably couched in her arm, staring up at them without a sound.

"That child hardly ever cries," said Chiyo. "Never complains about anything."

"I know," said Haruko. "Sometimes I wish he would cry or complain more. The way the other one did."

What had it been like for him, Chiyo wondered. Had he seen the flash of light clear through his mother's womb?

On the way home, Chiyo looked down the street toward the greengrocer's, then hesitated.

"Wouldn't Papa be glad to know the store is open again?" she asked Yoko.

Shintaro had loved the former store when he was a child, and it was special to everyone in the neighborhood to have the new store in the same place as the old one, even though the previous owners had died.

"I'd be honored to write a note," Mr. Kasama said. He wiped his hands on the new green apron a cousin in America had sent him.

To neighbor Hara. The shop where you used to buy Nappa cabbage is open for business again. I am saving something special to welcome you home.

Kasama Tetsuo, greengrocer

The card was complete, and there was even a small space left on the right margin where Shintaro could rest his thumb while he was reading it.

"It's a good thing everybody can write in Japanese," Yoko said. "If we had to write all this in English, it wouldn't fit."

Chiyo was surprised. "Really?"

"Well, Americans have to use a lot of letters for each word, but in Japanese it's usually just one character."

Chiyo gazed at the card. "Yes, there's certainly a lot of information here. Let's go straight to the post office and mail it. Then to celebrate, we can stop by an outdoor stall near the station for a special bowl of *udon* noodles."

Yoko danced ahead of her onto Sakae Bridge. "First noodles since way before the bomb," she said.

Chapter Sixteen

S HE THOUGHT IF SHE CLEANED THE HOUSE
and rearranged it, Shintaro would come home
on the first ship in the spring. She dusted the childhood collection
of folkcraft dolls that had been stored in Inokuchi and which she
would have sold by now if they had been worth anything. She had
made two of the dolls herself when she was a child.

She swept the straw mat she used as a *tatami,* humming the song
"Sakura" about cherry blossoms, practicing a dance Grandmother
had taught her to go with the song. She was rather pleased that she
still remembered as much as she did, and pleased, too, that her
energy had been restored. Maybe permanently. She was strong
enough to get a job, she decided. With an income she could make
the place even more comfortable for Shintaro.

She stood in the *genkan* wearing the old Western-style two-piece
suit she'd found in a trunk at Inokuchi. A bit tight around the
waist, but it had a purposeful look. And no wooden *geta* today. She
forced her feet into a pair of old patent leather pumps which had
probably belonged to Kazuko. They rubbed at the heel. No matter. It was only a short walk to the streetcar which would take her
straight to City Hall.

Mrs. Ikeda had been explaining about the big job ahead, collecting, copying, classifying the old city records they had found stored in the suburbs. She said the work was tedious sometimes, but she and the other clerks were right in the middle of plans for rebuilding the city and for laying out the Peace Park, which was to be in Nakajima, where Grandmother had lived and Kenichi had disappeared. Mayor Hamai was getting advice from everyone, and a lanky Australian was working with him on the master plan, always striding in and out of their makeshift building. Mrs. Ikeda and the other clerks enjoyed watching the hearty handshakes he forced onto the quiet bureaucrats, who weren't used to touching sweaty palms. They nudged each other quietly when he arrived. "Look! Here he comes again. Now watch Mr. Honda. He's wiping the palms of his hands on his pants, getting ready for the handshake!"

Chiyo practiced walking around the *genkan* in her pumps. It was a clear December day. New Year's almost upon them, and the future bright with promise. If she presented Isao with the accomplished fact of a job offer—

But she knew exactly what he would say. "Who's going to take care of the children while you're working?"

She smoothed her skirt, slammed her heels farther down in her pumps, then reached for the door. A shadow appeared on the other side, nervous, jangling the bell on a bicycle.

"*Oku-san, sokutatsu desu!* A special delivery letter for the honorable wife!"

She slid open the door to discover a young boy dressed in old army fatigues. He bowed, handed her the letter, then climbed back onto his bicycle, maneuvering it back into the street.

Standing outside under the sunlight, she examined the letter. Maybe Shintaro was already at the port of Maizuru and telling her when to come and meet him at Hiroshima station. No. Not his handwriting and the postmark was from Hatsukaichi. She turned it over. From the Takanos.

She tore open the envelope and found, inside, a funeral announcement. It was a stark, simple statement on stiff paper edged in black. Mr. Takano had entered into the Western Paradise, and the funeral would be held in a Buddhist Temple in Hatsukaichi, near where the Takanos lived.

A note from Mrs. Takano was enclosed.

> With deep gratitude, I will always remember your visits and the lovely gifts of peaches. I am convinced that his life was extended, if only for a brief period, by your presence and by those peaches.

Curiously, at that moment Chiyo didn't think of Takano-sensei but of Isao. He had been so encouraged by the recovery and believed so deeply in the peach cure. He was, in fact, obsessed with sending boxes of high-grade Okayama peaches to all the survivors he knew. It was the only thing he believed in. And now Takano-sensei was dead and so was Grandmother, and the miracle was gone.

Takano-sensei's voice reverberated in her mind.

"My that was good! Essence of Japanese spirit." He'd said it the day she took Kenichi his lunch and gave them all rice balls.

And right afterwards, Kenichi and Yasuo had gone back up on the roof and—

The terrible vision came again. She had trained herself never to look at the top of a building in the sun, never to think of that day or the time they found Takano-sensei searching through the rubble. But now it was too late. Kenichi shimmered before her in full force, breaking into a thousand pieces, scattering over the ground, shreds of scorched uniform and the contents of his lunch box spread out, burned black and uneaten, his identification tag glittering, its light piercing her eyeballs, blasting her head apart, ending with exhaustion and nausea. She went back inside, closed the door, took off the patent leather pumps, and sat on the edge of the *tatami* with her head buried in her knees. It had not happened to her for at least a year, but today she hadn't been able to control it.

Finally, she gathered enough strength to take off her two-piece suit and move her shaking, crumbling body back onto her sleeping mat.

"Mama!" Yoko was sitting next to her, puzzled, frightened, almost angry. "What are you doing in bed again?"

"Well," Chiyo said calmly "I think I ate something strange. Or maybe it's just a touch of the flu. Anyway, I've had a good sleep and I'm fine now." She started to get up.

"Oh, no!" Yoko insisted. "Stay there. I'll get supper."

At supper, Chiyo told Yoko about the funeral. "I have to go, of course, so maybe you could come out with me as far as Inokuchi—"

Yoko put down her chopsticks and began to sob. "I'm *coming!*" she choked, hiccuping back the sobs. "You are *not* going to leave me in Inokuchi."

"Of course, if you want to come, you're old enough." Chiyo had not expected such a strong reaction.

Yoko, swallowing back the tears, pursed her lips. "That's why you were in bed," she said accusingly. "It wasn't your stomach or the flu."

Chiyo took Yoko's hands in her own. "I didn't know you were old enough to remember him," she said. "I'm not sure you ever met him."

"I didn't meet him, but I knew he was out in Hatsukaichi eating peaches all the time and getting well. Now he isn't and he—" She began to sob again. "It's just— All the people who knew Kenichi —they're dead or they're dying."

The tears streamed down her face. Chiyo gathered her in her arms, rocking back and forth, smoothing her hair.

"We're still alive," Chiyo said. "And everyone in Inokuchi. And there's Yasu. And Mrs. Yamamoto and the Ikedas and your own father coming home soon. They remember him, too."

The Yamamotos were at the funeral. Chiyo gazed at Yasu's gaunt and stricken face through the haze of the service, the priest chanting sutras amidst a cloud of incense, the sound of bells, the *mokugyo*, the wooden drum, being clapped, the honorific posthumous name given to Mr. Takano's spirit.

Far toward the front of the vast room sat Mrs. Takano with her feet tucked under her in formal position. She held her swollen and bereaved face immobile, her head erect, staring straight ahead.

Outside, after the funeral, the dark figures of the mourners peppered the stark temple grounds. They stood alone and in clumps, mute silhouettes against the whitewashed walls. Some of the faces were vaguely familiar, but Chiyo's memory was not strong enough to span the chasm the bomb had created.

The Rijo school principal greeted her and introduced her to the new teachers who would be Shintaro's colleagues. One had been his classmate at the university.

"In spite of our sorrow over Takano-sensei's death, we're all very glad your husband's coming home soon," the man said.

"I still hope it will be in time for the spring term," said the principal.

Chiyo nodded and thanked him, wondering how long they would wait before they gave his job to somebody else. Then the Yamamotos came out of the temple and Chiyo excused herself. *"Ara!* Look here. Look at you," Chiyo exclaimed. The two women bowed frantically, dabbing their eyes with the ends of their kimono sleeves. Yasu was thin, but taller than she expected. At least the bomb had not stunted his growth. She had not seen them for at least two years.

"When are you coming back to Nobori-chō?" Chiyo asked.

Yoko was hanging on to her mother's hand, taking stealthy glances in Yasu's direction, hanging her head a little lower each time she looked at him.

"We don't know. We want to come, but my in-laws are getting older and sicker all the time. They need constant care, and we haven't heard from Husband since the end of the war."

Chiyo had helped Mrs. Yamamoto and her two children get settled when they first came from Manchuria in 1942, sent home by her engineer husband when he was inducted into the army. In those days it seemed that Captain Yamamoto had written twice as often as Shintaro.

"Oh, you're sure to hear soon," Chiyo assured her. "We just got a postcard sent through the Red Cross. With a reply card."

"We wanted you to write on it, too," Yoko said, "but there wasn't time." She bathed herself in Yasu's gaze for half a second, then returned her attention to the white pebbles below her feet.

"What did the stamp look like?" Yasu asked.

"Kind of Russian," said Yoko, still staring at the pebbles. "With a hammer and sickle."

"How is school, Ya-chan?" Chiyo asked. "I went there to see the principal, but I didn't see you."

"It's all right," he said without enthusiasm. "I'm the only one left, you know. I just wish—"

"He's studying for the entrance exams," Mrs. Yamamoto interrupted. "He's trying for Hiroshima University. He'd like to go to Waseda, but we can't afford it."

"He'll do well in any university," Chiyo said.

"Sometimes Kyoko and I stand on the foundation of your house and pretend you're still living there," Yoko said.

"Ikeda Kyoko?" Yasu asked. "Yukiji's little sister? The Ikedas are still there?" He looked at Chiyo, and the vision of Yukiji burning under the house rose dangerously between them.

"You didn't know?" Chiyo was surprised. "I thought I told—"

"Five of them are still left," Yoko interrupted. "Her mother and her eldest brother who built the house again, and—"

"Has Kyoko grown up as much as you have?" Yasu asked, regarding Yoko with the kind of awe people reserve for fragile teacups. For a moment Chiyo felt the presence of her daughter, Yoko, as a woman, not a child.

Yoko dropped her head quickly, only nodding in answer.

Mrs. Takano emerged from the temple. The crowd of black silhouettes had begun to fade, and the ones remaining hurried forward, propelled by their last chance to offer condolences before she was whisked away by the waiting black limousine.

Yasu stepped forward, apologizing for not coming to visit more often.

"Husband understood," Mrs. Takano said. "You were one of his favorite students, you know. Of all that he ever taught."

Yasu retreated into another formal bow, his face rigid.

Mrs. Takano reached out and clasped Chiyo's and Yasu's hands. "He was thinking of you both and of Kenichi at the very end, still remembering the day you brought the sushi, Mrs. Hara."

Chiyo bowed again, squeezing her eyes shut to keep the dreaded vision from appearing in her head. She thought fiercely about the day Shintaro would come home, imagining him on the gangplank of a huge ship. The other vision did not come. Nor did the tears. She straightened and smiled at Mrs. Takano. "I have thought of the same thing," she said, "so many times."

The New Year was almost upon them. Isao said he was going to receive a substantial bonus from the factory at Toyokogyo, and he could help her with expenses until Shintaro came home in the spring. Fusako would be almost self-supporting after graduating from college. She had applied for a scholarship at a university in Tokyo. Then she planned to study in America, an idea which distressed Kazuko but pleased Isao.

Chiyo postponed applying for the job at City Hall. At least until after the New Year. Or maybe until spring.

New Year's Day was warm and sunny. Kazuko had brought out the festival cushions for them to sit on, and set up the *byōbu*, the special New Year screens decorated with winter branches and white herons against a gold background. They had belonged to Grandmother. Neighbors came throughout the day to greet them and wish them a prosperous New Year. For that day, at least, the food seemed plentiful, their hunger assuaged, and the sea calm and blue, reflecting a brilliant, freshly laundered sky.

They took Hiroshi back with them to Nobori-chō for the rest of the holidays. The Yamamotos came for a visit, and Hiroshi and Yoko were ebullient. Hiroshi, his face solemnly deadpan, recited his whole collection of schoolboy riddles, some the same ones Kenichi had loved and all of them so outrageously banal that they laughed in spite of themselves.

Mrs. Yamamoto was pleased with the house, exclaiming over

every feature of construction, declaring that as soon as her mother-in-law got better and her husband came home, she would begin plans for rebuilding their own house.

Yasu ate without restraint, laughing at Hiroshi's jokes, stealing surreptitious glances at Yoko. Mrs. Ikeda and Kyoko joined them in the afternoon, and the youngsters went outside to play the special New Year's game of battledore and shuttlecock, leaving the three women inside to reminisce about old times.

"You've given us a wonderful day," Mrs. Yamamoto said at dusk as they were leaving. "It's quite a change from that dark old house in Ujina. Yasu hasn't laughed like that since the last time he was with Kenichi."

Shaken by the reference to Kenichi, Chiyo bowed excessively, seeing everyone out the front gate, not allowing herself to look at either the Ikedas or the Yamamotos. Yoko and Hiroshi had followed them into the street, but she ordered them back into the house.

"Please, just let us walk down to the streetcar stop with them," Yoko pleaded. "Kyoko is going."

"Please, please, please," echoed Hiroshi.

She released them. "Well, hurry up. Go along and catch up with them, then." She felt suddenly alone and frightened after they had gone. She slid the door shut, then sat down and stuck her feet under the *kotatsu,* catching the last warmth from the drying coals. She ate the last piece of *makizushi,* cold rice wrapped in seaweed and filled with tiny chopped orange carrots, green spinach, thin sheets of yellow omelet. Like the ones she had known as a child. She and Yoko had spent all day making them, and they were the first real sushi that either Yoko or Hiroshi could remember. She could not account for her cold fear or uneasiness about the future or her sudden harshness at the end of the pleasant day. It had to do with unpredictability. As if nothing she planned for the rest of her life would go the way she hoped. She had no control over any of it. Not her health or her moods or emotions. Perhaps not even her sanity.

The dishes were cleared and put away when Yoko and Hiroshi came back, their faces glowing from the walk. She sat them down at the *kotatsu* and dealt them out a hand of "100 poets"—the New Year game which required that they match the first part of a famous poem with the second half of it, printed on a separate card.

Hiroshi shouted gleefully, slapping his cards down on the table when he won a point, helping himself from the fresh plate of sushi she had decided to bring out instead of saving it for tomorrow. He was so seldom able to do what he wanted, especially when it came to eating.

He won handily, putting them both to shame. There was a time when Chiyo knew more about the 100 poets than her three children put together. Nowadays, she expected Yoko to win. But not Hiroshi.

Silent Hiroshi, her passive, beanbag lump of a boy, was laughing once again.

Chapter Seventeen

THE PLUM BLOSSOMS APPEARED EARLIER than usual that year and in profusion. Each spring since the bomb, they had rejoiced over the cherry blossoms. Even Shintaro's trees, damaged but struggling to exist, had sent out a few tenative pink blossoms that first spring. But the plum blossoms had slipped by unnoticed until now, when they burst out with such dazzling ferocity that no one could ignore them.

The family sat in the garden sitting room in Inokuchi on a February Sunday. Every now and then one of them stopped in mid-sentence or mid-stitch to gaze at the clump of plum trees. They could watch the seasons change in the garden. First the plum blossoms, then azaleas, then blooming cherry trees. In the fall were the feathery red maples, smaller than the leaves on Miyajima. After that, as a final note before winter, the blazing glory of the bright orange persimmons, hanging on leafless branches, miraculously suspended against the sky.

"Let's go out to Miyajima," Kazuko said suddenly.

"Go to Miyajima?" Chiyo's eyebrows raised above her needle. Hardly time for an excursion, she thought. The New Year just finished, and besides she would rather save Miyajima for when Shintaro came home.

"We haven't been out to Miyajima since just before the bomb fell," Kazuko continued. "We really should have a look at the old house, and see how the new renters are managing. And heaven knows these youngsters need to get away from their bleak surroundings just once and stop thinking about their exams."

Chiyo did not find the surroundings in Inokuchi bleak, but she did not say so.

"Wouldn't it be wonderful," Kazuko said, "to discover that Miyajima is still just the way it's always been, buildings and beach, everything the same?"

"Mama, it's not the same," said Fusako. "There's a girl at school from Miyajima and she says it's filled with foreign soldiers, and some of them get very drunk."

"Oh, we can ignore them," said Kazuko. "Disappear into a shop doorway if we see them coming. They're just people. They can't change the way Miyajima is to us, not the mountains and the sea and the old buildings in the back streets. Besides, we'll be spending most of our time in Sugi no Ura, looking at the old beach and the house."

"It's a lovely idea," Chiyo relented, "but won't it make us too sad?" Already she was struggling with the vision of Kenichi dancing in the waves and the memory of riding back to Hiroshima through the warm velvet night with Grandmother and Akiko. Of the four, only she and Akiko were still alive.

"Well, it might make us feel good," Fusako said. "All our memories are good ones."

"Let's go," said Yoko, slamming her book shut. "In March during spring vacation. Can I bring Kyoko?"

Chiyo stood outside on the ferry to Miyajima, holding her umbrella aloft, watching the rain melt into the sea. Kazuko and the others, each with a friend, were down below, drinking tea, disappointed by the rain. Chiyo didn't mind. Shintaro always said Miyajima was beautiful in the rain. Like the Moss Garden in Kyoto. When the sun was out, the world was flat, all one color and weight and with strong contrasts of dark shadows against the light, he said. In the rain subtleties were more apparent. Early in their marriage, she and Shintaro would wander all around Miyajima, noticing croaking frogs and tufts of green grass. He would quote from the old warrior ballad *Heike Monogatari*, because it was the Heike clan that had built the brilliant red shrine in the ninth century as a paradise on earth. Shintaro recited poetry from that time, too, *haiku* and *waka*. Sometimes he made up his own.

The high points of Chiyo's life were bound up in excursions to Miyajima. As a child with her parents and brother, as a teenager with Grandmother and Akiko and the Noh drama group, as a young bride with Shintaro, and after that the trips with their children, and with Isao and his family.

Her *omiai*, the arrangement for her marriage to Shintaro, had taken place on Miyajima in a small banquet room in one of the hotels. She first set eyes on him there, framed on either side by his parents. She had come dressed in her best kimono, accompanied by her parents and Isao, even Kazuko, who hadn't been married herself very long. But Chiyo hardly noticed anything except her own too-tight *obi* sash. And Shintaro. She barely had a chance to look at him. She knew he was watching her every move, but it was too great a risk to look up for fear their eyes would meet.

There had been that other candidate, favored by her mother and practical, down-to-earth Isao. The son of a sake dealer, a family with roots in Hiroshima as deep as the Ogawas. And money. Which is what had attracted her father in the beginning. Her mother liked the old Western-style house, situated on the back side of Hijiyama in Danbara, the social gatherings there, and the family ties with the old, important families in Hiroshima.

Chiyo had been willing to accept all that, but she did not like the man himself. Full, thick lips. Too self-indulgent. Self-centered and insensitive besides. He could hardly follow the conversation when someone else was talking. He was not a listener. And he was already getting fat. Her father and Kazuko thought so too, and said later that they had hoped Chiyo would reject him.

The second *omiai* was with Shintaro. Not as much money, and rather questionable family, claiming to be descended from samurai, but her father had discovered, upon investigation, that they were more likely pirates who had drifted onto an island in the Inland Sea and stayed there.

They had been *rōnin,* samurai who had lost their lord in battle, the Hara family claimed. In any case, they possessed the island, found the weather suitable for raising *mikan,* and named the place "Mikanjima," Orange Island. Different from "Miyajima," Shrine Island, the stronghold of the Ogawa family and a heritage which came, Chiyo's grandfather claimed, from dispossessed nobility connected to the imperial Heike clan that lived there in splendor in the eighth century.

The Haras had arrived on Mikanjima much later than that, but through the centuries they had held tenaciously to the land, always aligning themselves with the winning warlords, finally pledging fealty to the Lord Asano of Hiroshima when peace came in the 1600s. They cooperated enthusiastically with the new Meiji government in 1868. Shintaro's grandfather had been appointed postmaster by the Emperor Meiji, and that honor, too, had been handed down. Among the Hara family treasures was a letter from His Imperial Majesty, commending Grandfather Hara for the efficiency of his service and expressing surprise at the superior quality of the ink Grandfather had used when writing to the emperor with a fountain pen, a new invention he'd brought back from a trip to England in the 1880s. He had died before Shintaro was born, but both Shintaro's and Chiyo's fathers were Meiji gentlemen too, delighted by the wonders of the Western world, both travelers abroad, recipients of a gentleman's education. They had enjoyed each other's company during the brief period when they were both alive.

Shintaro had already become a teacher when Chiyo met him. There would be no hope of any luxury for her and her children, Isao had pointed out.

Chiyo didn't care. She'd rather have poetry than luxury, and she could see poetry in Shintaro's eyes. He was lean, a bit hungry-looking and rather fierce in his idealism. When she first saw him, she was afraid he might be too serious. But later, after the formal lunch when she was walking with him along the Maple Path, a bit separate from the others, both of them talking to each other in tight, half-finished sentences, she turned a moment to catch the expression on his face (she had just told him firmly that she thought women were every bit as rational and intelligent as men). She discovered that instead of walking beside her, he was hanging by his chin from the branch of a maple tree, his feet dangling lifelessly. He swung up and out to catch up with her again.

"Don't you see? It's hard enough walking along this path with such a dainty, angelic creature next to me, showing up my clumsiness and foolishness. But you're intelligent and rational too? I have to excel at *something*. Tell me, Miss Ogawa, can you leap up and hang yourself like this on the branch of a tree?"

And he did it again, right there in front of her, so high up that the sun obstructed her view of him.

"I am the fisherman," he shouted down at her. He was hanging by his arms now. "And you are the angel, wearing a feather robe, come down from heaven, and I have snatched the robe while you were off bathing in the sea, and I will not give it back unless you dance for me." He eased himself back down onto the path next to her, assuming his previous serious demeanor. He had just outlined the plot of the Noh drama *Hagoromo,* which was the very dance she had been practicing for a recital with Grandmother.

"I have heard from my father, who heard from your father, that you are a devotee of the Nishikawa school of traditional dance," he said, measuring his stride with hers. "I would be very honored to have the pleasure of seeing you dance, especially if you perform the *Hagoromo.*"

That was when she knew she would marry him. And later, to the distress of both their families, they decided they wanted to be on Miyajima for their honeymoon. It was considered bad luck to honeymoon on Miyajima because of the jealous goddess Itsuku-shima, who had consorted with the Lord Taira-no-Kiyomori of the Heike clan. He had boasted he could build her a bridge between two islands in the Inland Sea during the course of just one day. But by sunset, in spite of the feverish labor of his retainers, the job still wasn't finished. So he used an enormous fan to coerce the sun back into the middle of the sky until they could complete it. The goddess was displeased that he took onto himself powers not ordinarily extended to humans, and to show her disdain, turned herself into a snake when he came to claim his prize, a wedding night with her. Ever since then, it was said, Itsukushima has been jealous of honeymooners.

Chiyo and Shintaro finally gave in to family pressure and went to Tokyo for their honeymoon instead. But the goddess must have known that they wanted to go to Miyajima. Perhaps because she was still jealous, she was keeping Shintaro from coming home. There was no denying the power of Miyajima.

But Shintaro's island, Mikanjima, had been magic, too. In those early years just after she married Shintaro, even after Kenichi and Yoko were born, the harvesting had been like a festival. The *mikan,* bright mandarin oranges, hung lush and thick from the trees. The whole island seemed swathed in orange paint when they gazed at it from the ferry. The cedar trees stretched out on the beach below, the string of fishing boats dotting the shore, and the tiled roofs scattered through the trees, climbing upwards toward the temple at the top of the mountain.

And the days of picnicking after they had gathered the fruit, lying under the trees and the vivid autumn sky, Kenichi and his cousin, Yutaka, toddling through the grass, chortling, gnawing on the *mikan.* In those days everything about Shintaro was wonderful, even his family.

Then the funerals began, each one darker than the last, blotting out the bright, orange memories. Shintaro's father had died first, not long after Yoko was born. He'd passed on the inheritance to Shintaro's elder brother, Shinkichi. Chiyo's parents had died within a month of one another the following year. Shintaro's sweet and meek-faced mother had lingered on until just after Hiroshi was born. But her loving subservience had never applied to her daughter-in-law, Sadako, Shinkichi's wife.

"You never knew the other side," Sadako would murmur almost inaudibly to whoever would listen when someone mentioned the mother's devotion and sacrifice.

After the mother's funeral, the festive atmosphere of the harvests ended. So did Shinkichi's sense of playfulness and joy. Sadako had decided her husband was too weak and too generous.

Then Shinkichi died unexpectedly in 1943 while Shintaro was in China. There had been insinuations at the funeral, emotions smoldering near the surface, barely hidden conflicts over the inheritance. Afterwards Chiyo had vowed she would manage somehow to keep Shintaro free from the dark shadows on that island.

But after hearing about Shintaro's postcard, Sadako had written complaining she should have been the first to know. "I thought you would get in touch immediately inasmuch as your husband is a relative of ours even more closely related than your brother's family."

It was typical of Sadako, whom Chiyo had not seen since the funeral and who had sent no words of condolence for the loss of Kenichi. She was plotting, Chiyo knew, how to get Shintaro to take responsibility for the orange orchard, do all the work so that it could be inherited by her son, Yutaka.

It was drizzling when the ferry landed, and the passengers formed a line coming off the ferry under their umbrellas, black ones interspersed with a few pastel ones, a patched one, some in the pattern of army camouflage.

Once on land, they gazed up at the souvenir shops perched on the hill. Here, as Kazuko had predicted, the world was the same.

In the old days, if the weather was good, they walked from the ferry landing to their house in Sugi no Ura, Cedar Inlet. There had been one taxi on the island then, and now it seemed there were two or three. Kazuko, accustomed to her position as an Ogawa who commanded attention, hailed a taxi. But the driver regarded her aloofly and passed them by, his motor humming comfortably and the wet wheels sliding through the muddy streets to create a counterpoint melody, splattering mud on their feet and legs. He paused a few feet beyond them and opened his door in front of two khaki-clad SCAP military men with navy-blue raincoats and visors to protect their foreign faces from the rain. They did look very dignified, clean and well-dressed, Chiyo thought.

"Those are Americans," Fusako whispered after looking at them carefully. "I can't see the insignia, but one of them is a Negro, and there are hardly any black Australians in their army." She said it as if she were making an anthropology report to her college class.

Kazuko stood erect. "The very idea!" she exclaimed, taking her handkerchief out and wiping off the mud from her precious pair of nylon stockings. "We'll never get to Sugi no Ura walking in all this rain."

"We can't get there in one taxi anyway," said Fusako. "There are eight of us."

"The taxi could have taken two trips," Kazuko said, not ready to give up. "But maybe we can catch the old delivery truck that goes out once a day."

"There's the store right up ahead," Chiyo said. "Let's go and see."

Just then the mail truck moved in front of them, gaining speed.

"Hello, Mr. Mailman," Yoko shouted, running after it and waving her arms. "Remember us? The Ogawa family from Sugi no Ura? Do you have room to take us down there today?"

The truck had already passed them when it slowed down, then stopped, then backed up. "The family of Ogawa Shoichiro?" an old man with white hair shouted from the driver's seat. "Your grandfather was Ogawa Shoichiro?" Yoko nodded. When he saw Kazuko and Chiyo, he jumped out and greeted them, bowing vigorously, half laughing, maybe crying.

"I was afraid you were all dead," he said. "It's hard to get in touch with people." He looked down at his feet, fingering the cap he had taken off to greet them. "I asked them up at the house on the cove, and they knew that young Mr. Ogawa was alive, but they didn't know anything about the rest of you." His eyes were damp with tears.

Chiyo nodded and bowed. That familiar face from her childhood. "So good to see you again," she murmured, "healthy and vigorous as usual." He had grown old.

Kazuko was pleased. At least some part of the civilized world had been left for her to exchange amenities with. She bowed serenely, greeting the man with the elaborate and refined language Grandmother had used for formal occasions and recital times.

The mailman bowed, then looked up abruptly at the others surrounding Kazuko. "Oh, do you all want to come?" he said. "I'm afraid—"

It was clear that they could not all fit into the truck.

"There's room for three," Chiyo said. "You go with Fusako and her friend Yuri," she told Kazuko. "The rest of us can walk through the souvenir shops to the shrine. That's what Kyoko and Hideo want to see anyway, and we'll meet you there for lunch. At the far end. By the bridge."

Chiyo was glad of an excuse not to go to the cove. In another year she might be able to do it, but today she was afraid of the memories. Better to be with Kyoko and Hiroshi's friend Hideo, who had never seen the shrine at Miyajima. Back down past the ferry dock and the old inns that lined the street along the shore, then up the hill toward the souvenir shops, where, to their delight and surprise, they were surrounded by the aroma of the famous maple cakes cooking in leaf-shaped pans in some of the souvenir shops, the soft dough filled with hot bean paste. She had not expected the shopkeepers to be making those cakes again so soon after the war. Yoko and Kyoko commandeered a table in one of the open shops along the street, chattering in high excitement, and beckoning for Chiyo to join them. Hiroshi and Hideo ignored the girls, sitting aloofly at their own table, surreptitiously ordering an extra cake apiece and pouring themselves more tea.

Chiyo gave all her attention to the aroma and shape, the spongy outer crust of the warm brown cakes. One bite, with the steam escaping from the bean-paste interior, and the memory flooded back, so strong and powerful. That time when she was pregnant with Hiroshi almost twelve years ago. The China war had already begun, and she had craved the *momiji manjū* maple cakes so much that Shintaro had brought the whole family on a special trip just to eat them. It had been the last time. Hiroshi had never tasted them.

Chiyo gazed over the girls' heads at a counter where a row of *kokeshi* dolls were spread out, long, slender sticks of wood hand-painted with kimono-style patterns, and with round heads. Each face bore an individual expression of surprise or amusement or hope. She had never seen that kind of folk art in a shop in Miyajima before, not even in Hiroshima. *Kokeshi* dolls were traditionally made north of Tokyo, in the Tohoku region. Chiyo had a few in her own collection, but on Miyajima, people made *tsuchiningyō* dolls of clay. They were the kind she had collected as a child, some of them very old and handed down from her grandmother. The others she had made herself during summer vacations on the island. An older man, a friend of her father's, had given lessons in making clay dolls and pottery. And now, here in this souvenir shop, there were a few of those old-style clay dolls in among the new, fresh, and original wooden ones, which had a special vitality of their own.

She went over to the counter for a closer look. Their whimsical, shy smiles made her laugh. She clapped her hand over her mouth, noticing that everyone had turned to look at her. The shopkeeper was on the other side of the counter, trying to explain Miyajima's specialty wooden rice paddles to a clump of foreign soldiers who were staring with bewildered expressions at a showcase filled with them. He excused himself and came to see what Chiyo was laughing about.

"Who makes them?" Chiyo asked, pointing to them. "They have such lively expressions."

"I do," he said, smiling broadly. "I'm pleased that you noticed. Most people don't."

He was a small man, undistinguished-looking. But his smile warmed her. That and the knowledge that he had created those individual, bashful dolls and given each of them a special personality. He was lean and neat-looking, dressed in old army drabs much too large for him, a shirt tucked under a pair of baggy pants held up by a leather belt that was also too large. The end of it protruded beyond the buckle clasp and seemed to get in the way of his arms when he reached for things. He had forgotten the soldiers, and he was rearranging the line of dolls in clusters while he talked.

"I started making dolls when I was a boy, helping my father. I grew up in Naruko on the island of Sado. Then I was just taking over the business when I got drafted into the army. And when I came home from Siberia, I—"

"Siberia!" Chiyo interrupted him. "Were you in Siberia?"

He nodded. "Came home last summer, in fact."

"My husband's there. Hara Shintaro. Have you ever heard of him?"

He grinned again. The same broad smile, but with renewed interest and gentle sympathy. "Siberia is so big," he said, shaking his head. "Even if he'd been in the same camp, I wouldn't have known him unless he was sick. I was an orderly in the hospital, you see, and lucky to be always inside and warm. What is your husband's trade?"

"A teacher. Classical Japanese and Chinese literature. And some English."

"Oh, then, I'm sure he's doing inside work. Accounting or

keeping track of the commissary, maybe even interpreting if he's good at languages. Anyway, he'll be coming home soon. There wasn't any order to the way they were sending us back. They just told some of us to march down to Naborosk and get on a ship and some of us to stay behind."

"Well, we hope he'll be home in the spring. I'm bringing him right over here for *momiji manjū* cakes when he gets home. And to see these dolls," she added. "Why did you come here after the war instead of going back to Sado Island?"

"Not much of my family left up there," he said. "And this was my mother's native place. My uncle owned this store. I'm so busy here I hardly have time to make these dolls anymore, and the orders coming in so fast, especially from the foreign soldiers." He grinned again. "They like them a lot better than these rice paddles. None of the foreigners know what to do with them. They just want the dolls, and I can keep up with the carving all right, but I need someone to help me paint."

"I'll try it," Chiyo said quickly. She was surprised by her own words. "How many do you need?"

"Well, as many as you can paint. Have you ever done it before?" He reached under the counter, searching for the freshly carved pieces of wood and the round balls for heads.

"I used to make the *tsuchiningyō* clay dolls when I was a child and we painted their faces, too."

He stopped suddenly in the middle of counting out cylinders and looked up at her sharply, as if he were trying to recognize something about her.

"I am of the Hara family of Nobori-chō," she said. "Before I married, I was an Ogawa from Inokuchi, and our family has had a summer house in Sugi no Ura for several generations."

"Ah," he said. "So that's who you are." He bowed, folding himself over in a somewhat military stance. "I am Nakayama. My mother's maiden name was Sasaki, and her family has owned this shop for several generations."

"Of course! Of course!" Chiyo said. "I remember. It was your uncle who taught us how to make the clay dolls. Will you be selling any of those again? And how is your uncle?"

The expression on his face changed. "My uncle was in Hiroshima that day. And so was my wife," he added. "And my children."

"I am sorry," Chiyo breathed.

Nakayama had disappeared from view, kneeling and looking on the bottom shelf of the showcase for more cylinders. "How would this many be this time?" he asked, handing her a box of twenty pieces. "You could send the finished ones over with one of my shop girls who lives in Hiroshima. I'll give you her address. And I pay fifteen yen apiece for them. Not much money, but I have to sell them for thirty-five and I have to pay for the materials, too."

"I'll try," she said, smiling, reaching for the box and looking directly into his face. It was strange how he had grown in stature since the beginning of the conversation. He was not at all undistinguished. He wasn't handsome. Something was out of proportion. Cheekbones too high? No, it was the slightly receding chin, and his teeth protruding too far over his lower lip. But he had about him an air of suppressed hunger, some indefinable need that could be put off indefinitely but would eventually have to be satisfied. She recognized it because Shintaro was that way, too.

Chiyo thought of her secret dolls all the way to the shrine, all through the winding streets along the edge of the water past the stone lanterns, past the famous ancient red *torii*, past the stall where the white horse had always been kept (the one that miraculously turned white as soon as it was put there), past the center section of the shrine with the deck stretched out toward the sea, the place where the Heike aristocracy held their *Bunraku* dancing recitals more than a thousand years ago. In this shrine which they had created to be a heaven on earth.

She decided she would not tell anyone except Yoko about the dolls, and then only when they got home. They could paint them secretly. No one would ever have to know how she managed to make an income and to stay at home to take care of her family, too. Of course, it was a bit much to expect on fifteen yen apiece. But it was something at least.

The sun was out in full force when they met Kazuko and the others at the assigned place just beyond the bridge. They ate their *bentō,* the box lunches they had brought, in one corner of the *Senjogakuji,* the 1,000-mat temple on the hill. From there they could see the red *torii* below them, now basking under the sun.

Chapter Eighteen

Yoko was excited about the dolls. In the morning they laid out the wooden cylinders that were to form the bodies, then placed the heads above each one. Yoko started with the kimonos and Chiyo with the faces, each with a brush, each progressing toward the other.

"Look at this one, Mother. I've put tiny cherry blossoms on it. Doesn't it remind you of that old kimono Aunt Kazuko had? The one you said each of us wore to the shrine when we were three? All pink and red. So I suppose this one has to be a little girl."

Chiyo looked at Yoko's cylinder. Yes, that would be an interesting one. She took it and began to paint a face for it.

They worked slowly, taking great pains with each kimono and each face, wiping away their mistakes and starting again. By suppertime Yoko had painted three kimonos, one with cherry blossoms, another with tiny daisies around the hem, and one with faint wisps of plum blossoms. Chiyo had done seven faces, three of them for Yoko's dolls, and four kimonos. She could have done the faces more quickly, but she liked lingering over them, redoing the noses or eyebrows, or trying to get a sense of longing in their eyes. She kept thinking of people she had known and the way they looked at certain times in their lives.

"If we keep going at this pace, we won't even make enough money for the carfare out there to show him the first batch," Chiyo said. "Besides, you can't paint very often. You have to study. I can't let you sit up all night painting dolls and losing sleep."

"But it's so much fun," Yoko said. "I like it more than mathematics, geography, history. Any of that."

"I'm not going to let you paint any more dolls until you've promised me that you've finished every bit of your homework," Chiyo announced firmly.

Yoko sighed. "Anyhow, I can paint during the rest of spring vacation."

"But you have activities every day," said Chiyo. "Choir practice tomorrow morning, then your drama club meeting. And the volleyball team every day."

"Well, as soon as I come home," Yoko insisted.

When Yoko returned the next afternoon, the dolls were finished and lined up, their heads pinned to the bodies that matched them best. Chiyo had stopped creating new patterns, which made the work go faster, and in the end, in a rush of excitement, she finished everything.

"I was thinking we should take them out to Miyajima right now," she told Yoko, "just to see if Mr. Nakayama likes them."

She was sure he would. One demure doll with a purple iris kimono had long, sweeping lashes and a head that seemed slightly bowed. She had attached it at an angle.

Yoko was exploding with excitement. "If he likes them we can collect three hundred yen and more pieces of wood to paint. Then the next time he'll give us forty pieces of wood and we'll paint them even faster and we can make six hundred yen. And tonight we can stay in Inokuchi, since it's on the way." She set down her heavy schoolbag, then immediately devoured the mandarin orange sitting in the kitchen. "Let's go," she said. "I'm ready."

It was almost five-thirty and getting dark before they reached the island and began the long climb from the dock to the souvenir area. Mr. Nakayama was just closing his shop, pulling down the corrugated iron covers. Yoko shouted at him from a block away, embarrassing Chiyo with the shrillness of her voice. "Nakayama-san, we have brought the dolls!"

He nodded calmly (almost as if he had expected them), then opened the side door and waited for them.

He was pleased with the dolls. He didn't say much, but Chiyo could tell by the way he handled them, taking them one by one out of the box, examining their faces, their kimonos, turning them over to see the backs. He had the same feeling for them that she and Yoko did—almost as if they were people.

"Very elegant," he breathed. "Perhaps I will be able to ask fifty yen instead of thirty-five. I will give you fifteen yen apiece, as we agreed, for now. But if I sell them for more, I'll give you extra next time." He examined the lady with the iris kimono and the sweeping eyelashes again, then Yoko's red-and-pink-kimono child.

"These are especially fine," he said. "Make more of them. And the ones with daisies and *hagi* flowers, too. If you keep painting just a few kinds, you can do them faster and make more money, although I know from my own experience how interesting it is to experiment."

"Then we'll paint just those few for a while," Chiyo said. "My daughter, Yoko, did the cherry-blossom child, and I did the iris lady."

He looked at Yoko, then again at her doll. "Very talented," he told the doll, "especially for one so young."

Yoko blushed and lowered her head.

"And a very talented mother." He turned back to Chiyo. "Don't stop experimenting now and then," he warned her. "Remember, you are not a factory worker. You are an artist, and you must keep it interesting for yourself."

He sat them both down for tea and maple-leaf cakes. "I've discovered someone in Kyoto who can make these cylinders and balls for me on a lathe so I don't have to carve them anymore. I prefer making my own dolls, but I don't have time, so I'm lucky to find you."

He filled a box with forty cylinders and balls, then took money from the cash register and placed it in an envelope, smiled, and reached into his display case and pulled out a box of *momiji manjū*.

"You shouldn't," she said. "You gave us a box before."

"It's a token of my gratitude to you for appearing at the right moment to paint my dolls."

His smile and his face lingered in her head as they scurried down the street toward the dock. Yoko was ecstatic. "Of course we just *have* to go to Inokuchi now because we have *omiage* for them, this gift of maple cakes."

It was long after nightfall when they arrived at Isao's house, bursting with their news. Chiyo wasn't sure how Isao would take it, but she was determined to tell him anyway. Nothing he could ever say would keep her from painting the dolls.

Yoko stood in the hallway. *"Gomen kudasai!"* she shouted in her shrill schoolgirl voice.

They were met by the new maid, a young orphan who had appeared months earlier, almost starving, on Kazuko's doorstep. She bowed to them and gave them a formal invitation to enter. Not the usual warm greeting from Kazuko herself. The girl ushered them toward the large sitting room, but they had not followed her more than two steps before Chiyo realized something was seriously wrong. The door slid open to reveal Kazuko inside, the color in her cheeks too high, her face swollen, and her eyes red. Fusako was sitting in formal position next to her mother, rearranging and turning over a wet handkerchief which was spread across her lap.

Chiyo and Yoko kneeled on the *tatami,* quietly offered their greetings. Isao came in just then. Where was Hiroshi?

"What's happened?" Chiyo breathed.

Kazuko could not move her lips to speak.

"You don't know?" Isao asked. "We thought that's why you came."

"Hiroshi!" Chiyo cried out.

"No, no," Isao said. "He's all right. It's Younger Sister, Akiko."

"She is sick?"

"She is dead," said Isao.

Chiyo could not get any breath into her lungs. The room floated before her in a vague outline. They tried to explain. Akiko's husband, Kikuo, had been selected to work as an interpreter with the Occupation Forces, and the family was packing up to move from Chiba to a house in Tokyo, closer to SCAP Headquarters. On the day they were to leave, Akiko had suddenly become so weak that she could barely stand up, and she had a high fever besides.

The doctor diagnosed anemia and gave her shots of vitamin B_{12}. She told him she might be pregnant, and he said the exhaustion could have come from that. There was nothing to do but stay the night in their empty house and wait for the results of the tests. When they discovered in the morning that she was not seriously anemic and really was pregnant, they were relieved.

Akiko's fever subsided and, after that, things had gone smoothly. They had been living comfortably in their new house for a week, and Akiko seemed reasonably healthy until one morning when, cutting up cucumbers, she pricked her finger with a knife and began hemorrhaging. It was only a tiny cut, but she couldn't stop the bleeding. This time, the diagnosis was acute leukemia, not anemia. They started blood transfusions, but it was too late. She died at midnight. Her husband, son, and father-in-law were by her side.

Isao began quoting what Kikuo had said on the phone. "If only we'd gone right to another doctor when we first got to Tokyo. If only I'd asked more questions about the high fever. But she improved so much and we were so careful about her iron pills and vitamin B injections, and she got lots of rest and nourishing food."

They had talked about an abortion. Kikuo thought she wasn't strong enough to carry the baby. Besides, there were the rumors about deformed and retarded children being born to survivors of the bomb. But Akiko had wanted to take the chance. She wanted a daughter. And if not a daughter, then another son.

Chiyo remembered the day in Inokuchi when Akiko was packing for the trip to Tokyo and Kazuko had given her the child's kimono. "Bring another child into this world?" Akiko had said then. But now, it seemed, in spite of all the hardship and the devastation, Akiko had regained her faith in the future.

"I told Kikuo it didn't matter what they did," Isao was saying. "Acute leukemia. Even if they'd gotten the right diagnosis, they could only have prolonged her life a week or so."

"They should have let her live long enough to have the child," Kazuko burst out vehemently, lifting her red and swollen face to Chiyo. "If only they had allowed her that." She began to cry again, holding Fusako in her arms.

Nobody knew what she meant by "they" and nobody asked. The moon outside went under a cloud, and the room turned dark and cold, but no one moved. Hiroshi returned from his friend's house, came quietly into the room, went dutifully to his mother's side and sat next to her, taking her hand. She was touched by his attention to her, his urge to comfort her. Chiyo covered Hiroshi's hand with her own.

How could Kazuko and Akiko have brought such bad karma upon themselves from anything they had ever done in this or any previous life? They were so close to perfection and to Buddhahood in the present one.

Kazuko, Isao, and Fusako left the following evening on the *Asakaze,* the Morning Wind.

Chiyo and Yoko stayed in Inokuchi with Hiroshi until the Ogawas returned a week later, carrying ashes. Kikuo had kept most of the ashes and the important *nodobotoke,* the Adam's apple bone that looked like a sitting Buddha, for the main funeral up in Tokyo. But Kazuko wanted to have a simple ceremony in Akiko's honor, attended only by the immediate family and a distant aunt and cousin. She put the ashes together with Grandmother's in the family shrine that faced the garden and the sea.

There were no more members of the Nagatani family. Kazuko's father had died when Kazuko was a teenager. Then her brother, her mother next, and finally, Akiko. The younger brother had been killed early in the war on a lonely island in the Pacific before he had a chance to marry. There had been nothing left of him for the Imperial Navy to send home.

Chapter Nineteen

"HIRO-CHAN, ARE YOU COMING BACK to stay with us for the rest of spring vacation?" Chiyo asked. She and Yoko were packing up to leave Inokuchi after the funeral. "Yoko and I have a new job and you can share it with us if you like."

Hiroshi's lips twitched around the edges. "What kind of job?"

"It takes too long to explain. I'll have to tell you when we get back."

"Uncle said I could help him with a new kind of shortwave radio he's experimenting on. I'm going to become an engineer."

"That sounds exciting," said Chiyo. "Maybe you should stay here. It is so beautiful. You can play on the beach when you aren't studying and working with your uncle. And you have your friends here. In Nobori-chō, it's windy and dusty, and there is no scenery and no beach to walk along, and the house is small and uncomfortable."

"You and Yoko need me more than Uncle," he said matter-of-factly. "I will come with you."

Hiroshi liked the dolls. Of course, he didn't say so. Instead, he suggested it was more a man's job to be back with his Uncle Isao working on radios. But since his mother and sister didn't pay any attention to him, he stopped talking about Inokuchi and painted dolls.

They assigned him the hair. Chiyo did most of the faces and the kimonos with plum blossoms, irises, and the new design she had developed using the delicate violet *hagi* flowers Shintaro loved. Yoko did all the kimonos with cherry blossoms, most of the ones with daisies, and all of the children's faces.

Hiroshi followed along at the end and gave each doll a wig of black hair, encasing the round heads in crowns of respectability. After the first batch, Chiyo decided that Hiroshi should do the hair first. Then she could decide better what kind of faces to put on them. He made some of the hair parted at the forehead and swept down close to the eyes, some of it hanging just above the eyebrows in graceful bangs. Sometimes he painted it high so that the ears would show or so that it looked swept back into a Geisha-style knot, a *mage*.

He was very good. With hardly any instruction, he had found an artistic way of doing it just by looking at the ones his mother painted. None of them were like the traditional *kokeshi* model from the Tohoku region which Mr. Nakayama had given them for a guide. In fact, Hiroshi was creating designs nobody had ever seen before, and she couldn't understand where his inspiration came from. Or his speed. He was always so far ahead of the others that they let him experiment with new kimono patterns when he had no more hair to paint.

"I'm trying a solid color with just a few maple leaves around the bottom," Hiroshi said. "Wouldn't that be a good pattern for souvenirs for Miyajima? Maple leaves is what they're famous for."

He held it up for her to see. There was a faint tinge of orange paint spread evenly on the cylinder so that the wood grain showed through, a subtle line down the front to depict the kimono opening, and tiny brush strokes in yellow and orange for the maple leaves, one on each side and around the hem.

"You can give her a very sophisticated face, don't you think? See. Cherry blossoms for children like Yoko is painting. But maple leaves for mature women like you, Mama. That's the best time, isn't it, when you are wise and know everything?"

She put down her brush and hugged him, even though he was eleven now and would not ordinarily have allowed it.

"There is never a time in your whole life when you know everything, Hiro-chan. Not even at my age." She gave the doll back to Hiroshi. "Now finish it," she said. "Then wash off your brush and go outside. You both need some fresh air. You too, Yoko. I'll clean up."

They clattered out, leaving Chiyo with the silent, bashful dolls lying on the *tatami* staring up at her.

Working like this, all three of them, all day, they could finish forty dolls. And if Mr. Nakayama could sell them for a higher price and pay twenty-five apiece instead of the fifteen or twenty they were getting now, then they could— She put down her hands and folded them over her lap. It was no use figuring any kind of reliable income. Nakayama could never sell all the dolls for fifty yen. Only ten or fifteen out of the whole batch were good enough for that. And trying as hard as they could, working as fast as they were, they couldn't do any better. The only way to get them all perfect was to work even more slowly.

If Isao came and saw them working like this, he would make a fuss and insist that Hiroshi go back to Inokuchi immediately. And without enough income, she and Yoko might have to move back, too.

All she really needed was to hold out until Shintaro came home. If Kenichi were here, they could do it. He would paint another thirty dolls all by himself. Tall and lanky fifteen-year-old, grinning at all of them. Of course he would waste a few, creating outrageous designs and faces just to make them laugh. He would invite all his friends in to help. Maybe by now they would have created their own factory and set up a business, establishing his mother as chief designer.

But Kenichi was not here. And neither was Shintaro.

"Goddess of Mercy, just a little help," she breathed, "only enough strength to hold out through the rest of the spring."

She pushed the dolls away, tired of looking at their faces, talking to herself, mulling everything over.

Maybe if she just had a little nap while the children were—

She heard a faint whisper.

It was dark when she woke. Her head was spinning and her stomach queasy and uncomfortable. Where were the children?

"Yoko-chan!" She cried out in sudden panic.

"We're here, Mother. We made you some soup. Do you feel any better now?"

Chiyo rose weakly from her *futon* to see the shadows of her two children silhouetted against the *shōji* that had been closed against the cold front *genkan*. The streetlight outside accented their shadows. Like a play. Or was it a haiku poem someone had written? Two waif children left alone in the dark, tending to their tired, sick mother.

"Do you want the soup now?" Yoko called.

"No, I can't eat it yet." She lay back on her *futon* and fell into a deep sleep.

Shintaro was home. He stood at the doorway, smiling, a Russian fur cap on his head, vestiges of military leggings above his heavy soldier's boots. He sat on the *tatami* to remove them, postponing the pleasure of turning to embrace her. How had he gotten home without her knowing? Other people got telegrams from Maizuru.

"Shintaro! Shin-chan! *Anata!*" She shouted at him, waiting for him to turn around.

But when he turned, his face was a gaping black hole. She let go of her apron and screamed.

"Mama!" Yoko and Hiroshi were by her side. Shintaro was gone.

"It's all right," Chiyo said. "Just a nightmare."

"You have a fever," Yoko announced calmly. "You'd better not have any soup if you don't feel like it. Go to sleep, and if it isn't gone in the morning, I'll take you to the doctor."

"Dr. Iwamura," Chiyo said. "He'll come here if you ask him. He doesn't live so far away."

"He died, Mama, don't you remember?"

They were all dead. All except her. She would wake up in the morning and find that the Yamamotos had died. And Mrs. Ikeda. And Kyoko. One at a time. Each in his turn.

She turned her head on the pillow. "I'm all right. Just a little sleep and—"

She was outside, staring up on the roof at Kenichi, the sun surrounding him again in a halo and then breaking him into tiny little pieces, fingernails and eyelashes showering down. If she could pick everything up and put him back together. If she could just—but Kenichi slipped out of her hands, and he was climbing back up the ladder to the top of the roof again, and the sun—

Awake in the dark, she was perspiring. The house was silent. The children had gone to bed. She would have to stay awake all night to keep the dreams from coming again.

Toward dawn, she slept, deep and dreamless.

Days had gone by when she woke. Maybe years.

She sat bolt upright. It made her dizzy, her head throbbing and fuzzy. "What's the matter?" she asked, holding the sides of her head to muffle the pain. Yoko was there. And Kazuko and Fusako.

"Where's Hiro-chan?"

"He's out in Inokuchi," Kazuko said. "School started two days ago."

"How long have I been sick?"

"You've been running a temperature, Aunt," Fusako explained, "and the doctor said it was the flu. He said you have anemia, too, which is what made you susceptible. You have to get lots of rest and good food."

Anemia. That's what they had told Akiko.

"He's sure it's anemia?" she asked sharply.

"As soon as you're well again, the hospital's going to run a series of tests just to make sure, but they're quite certain it's anemia," Kazuko said. She gave Fusako an accusing look. "Really, Fu-chan, you don't have to—"

But Fusako, eager to explain, wasn't listening. "Yoko and I have been staying with you," she said. "Her school doesn't start till tomorrow, and I have a week yet before I go up to Tokyo. I got accepted at International Christian University, where the English instruction is so good."

"That's wonderful, Fu-chan," Chiyo said quietly, then lay her throbbing head back on the pillow. "You must be very busy getting ready."

"But I can stay another week and take care of you until you're well."

"Oh, Fu-chan, I'm perfectly well now."

Yoko, looking frail but relieved, had been wordlessly gazing at her mother's face. "Oh, Mama," she breathed, reaching out and hugging her. "You slept and slept and slept. Sometimes you woke up, but you never ate anything and then you went right back to sleep. You had such a *fever* and I was afraid we'd have to take you to the hospital."

"How long was it?" No one had answered her the first time she asked.

"Almost a week, Mama."

"Well, I can't understand it," Chiyo said. "I never get sick. Just a little tired sometimes."

She caught a glance between Kazuko and Fusako. But no one said anything. She thought of all the times she had been too sick or tired to do anything. Or frightened by things she couldn't explain. Nosebleeds. Visions swirling around in her head. Bad dreams. Exhaustion so heavy she couldn't get out of bed. It was a constant, steady decline.

Sitting up and holding Yoko close to her, Chiyo looked around the room. It was neat and extremely well ordered. Someone had been cleaning it. Kazuko, of course. So she had seen the dolls spread all over the sitting room floor. And if she knew about the dolls, had she told Isao?

Chiyo was dizzy again and lay back on the *futon*.

"You've been working too hard," Kazuko said. Her face was strained with worry.

"Fusako has been painting lots of dolls, Mama," Yoko whispered, leaning over to touch Chiyo's hand.

Why was she whispering? Wasn't it enough to wake up from being sick without having to guess every minute what was going on?

"Did you go out to Miyajima?" she asked Yoko.

"Oh, yes, Mama. Twice. And Mr. Nakayama kept giving us bigger boxes of wood so we could make even more dolls and more money. And he gave us maple cakes every time, too, and little notes for you, telling you to get well. Some of us stayed with you and painted while the others went out to take the dolls. We could have waited for the shop girl to bring them, but we were so anxious to keep working. And Fu-chan is so *good*, Mama! We think it's because of the dressmaking lessons she's been taking."

Well, so Kazuko apparently knew all about it. But would she know not to tell Isao?

"Look at this one, Mama. It's our prize." Yoko held out a slender box for Chiyo's approval. Usually they stacked all the dolls together in one box, but inside this private box, lovingly wrapped in tissue paper, was a demure, delicately smiling *kokeshi* doll resplendently attired in a lavish chrysanthemum-laden kimono, the flowers painted thickly, rich with myriads of colors all laid on top of a muted golden background. The pattern was like the famous *Kutani*-ware tea set that had been in Kazuko's family for generations.

"Aunt Kazuko painted it," Yoko said proudly. "We can't sell it because it is too beautiful. We haven't even shown it to Nakayama-san yet."

Chiyo suddenly felt small and helpless, lying there beneath the quilts that Kazuko had provided from their inexhaustible storehouse. She turned her wan and useless head toward Kazuko, forcing back the tears that were gathering in her thudding head.

How could she have doubted Kazuko, who moved easily and

effortlessly into whatever game they were playing, taking up the conversation without losing a thread, excelling at every task they assigned her, never commenting on anybody else's failures, always praising their successes. The shame she felt before Kazuko for messy housekeeping, for forgetfulness, for quarrels with her children, even for her own irritation with Kazuko's perfections—none of it was brought on by Kazuko herself. It all came from inside Chiyo. And now, as usual, Kazuko had joined them and excelled.

"Oh, Nē-san, Elder Sister, it is so beautiful! And all the while I thought you would be ashamed of us, painting dolls for souvenir shops on Miyajima. It's not exactly what the Ogawas are accustomed to doing."

"Well, you should see Husband," Kazuko said, smiling, not a little pleased. "He and Hiro-chan are out in Inokuchi painting samurai dolls with *chonmage*, their topknots. They're gluing extra pieces of round wood on the heads to make the knots. They've been carving long swords, too. And now, this morning, they were working on another shape to use for a sitting samurai—you know, like the famous sculpture of Minamoto Yoritomo." There was a triumphant glow on Kazuko's face. "They're bringing them in to show us as soon as they finish. You know, Husband usually works on Sunday, but they're so excited about those dolls that he called the office and said he wasn't coming. Can you imagine that?" She giggled, holding her hand before her mouth. "And when Mr. Nakayama saw them, he said he wanted lots more. He's got a big market for them with those American soldiers."

"Elder Brother, too?" Chiyo could hardly believe her ears. It was enough of a surprise to find out Kazuko had joined them. But Isao?

The April sunshine began flooding into the room, pushing into the corners that would have been dusty without the thorough cleaning Kazuko had given them.

"Hiroshi's enthusiasm was just infectious, you know," Kazuko went on. "Husband was shocked at first, of course. But then Yoko and Hiroshi began to show him the dolls, one by one. He just sat here and looked at the beautiful patterns you'd created. Hiro-chan told Husband it was his duty to go on working, especially when you were sick. So Husband started helping him. That's when they got the idea of making a samurai doll from driftwood."

Chiyo realized that her headache was gone and that she was hungry. "Let me stand up and comb my hair and wash my face," she said. "I want to try out my useless legs."

They watched her a little warily while she took her first steps toward the bathroom, and then afterwards gathered around her like a collection of pigeons, drinking tea and eating maple cakes, while she tasted the rice gruel Kazuka had made for her.

She felt like Urashima-Taro, the old man in the folktale who'd gone to the bottom of the sea on a turtle's back and stayed a hundred years in the twinkling of an eye without knowing it. She had been on a long and lonely journey and had come home again.

Part Four

Chapter Twenty

S PRING 1949. THE *GENKAN* WAS STACKED
with boxes of dolls brought in by the neigh-
bors. They had caught up on the backlog of orders from Nakayama
and now were supplying shops that had sprung up around the ruins
of the old Industrial Relations Hall that still stood on the banks of
the Motoyasu River, its walls crumbling and its steel girders gaping
against the sky. Nowadays, everyone referred to it as the Atomic
Dome, because it was the building closest to where the bomb had
dropped.

Nakayama had told them they could sell dolls to any shop they
wanted in Hiroshima, but he didn't want them selling to rival shops
on Miyajima.

At the moment, it seemed everybody in Hiroshima was painting
dolls, and Chiyo had the task of packaging and arranging for shipments. Isao had persuaded Toyokogyo to lend their truck twice a
week for deliveries, and they paid the driver out of their profits.
They were even beginning to ship dolls to shops in Kyoto and
Tokyo, and Chiyo had to keep track of that, too. She hardly had
time to paint dolls herself any longer. It was typical of Isao, building everything into something bigger and grander, destroying part

of its essence along the way. But they were beginning to make an adequate income.

This week she had 750 dolls waiting to be picked up by the truck. All of them packed the same way. She had done it with the help of Hiroshi, who had moved to Hiroshima with his mother and sister when he began his studies at Rijo Junior High School in early April. They were so busy with packaging that her own family had produced only twenty dolls. The neighbors had done the rest.

Out in Koi, Isao had found a bombed-out, unoccupied warehouse. The front had almost collapsed, but the back and sides were still standing, and he thought it could be shored up with new posts and the help of his carpenter friend. No one had located the owner, and Isao decided they could always pay back rent if he ever did appear. Meanwhile, he said, the packaging and collecting could be done there. Chiyo could do the accounts and write the letters at home and spend only a few hours at the warehouse preparing for the deliveries. But for the present, Chiyo was buried in mountains of boxes and tissue paper. And her smiling, petulant dolls were being created by someone else.

"*Gomen kudasai! Oku-sama!* Excuse me, honorable wife!" Morishita-san was already at the door. Chiyo liked him. He had been in some kind of airplane training during the war. A kamikaze, rumor had it. That day he'd been on the train coming home from Sasebo, had seen the mushroom cloud, and had entered the city to discover that his whole family—parents, a brother, two sisters, and a grandmother—had all been killed. He had found the bodies of everyone except the younger sister, a junior high student who, like Kenichi, had been working in the center of the city.

"Anything new?" she asked him, going out to the hallway and bowing from behind the mound of boxes.

He grinned at her and shook his head. "No, but that's quite a shipment you've got there today."

"Well, it's our first experiment with standardizing the packaging. What do you think?"

"I can't believe it. You're always ahead of everybody, thinking of something new."

"It's my brother." She shrugged. "He thinks of things. I follow orders."

"You made the first dolls, didn't you?" he asked gruffly, lifting a pile of boxes in his burly arms. She marveled at his strength. Those days after the bomb, he'd searched through the city for three weeks, expending even more energy than either Takano-sensei or Isao. Yet here he was, alive and strong, full of gruff enthusiasm and laughter. What made the difference? It wasn't timing or distance from the bomb. Or age. And karma didn't explain it. Nothing did. But it encouraged Chiyo to be in Morishita-san's bright and sunny presence, absorbing his energy.

"Well, everybody else is doing the painting these days," she said. "I hardly have time to manage the accounts, let alone all the rest of it."

"But every week you have more boxes," he said. "We'll be selling dolls to people on the moon before long."

"I know." Chiyo laughed. "We keep thinking the market will run out, but the orders are still coming in. And my niece, Fusako, up in Tokyo—she speaks good English and she's been around to American military bases and those PX stores they have. They placed orders, too, and now we can't keep them in stock up there."

"That's good," he said. "You know, I'm really proud to be part of this business. I wish I could do it full-time."

He climbed into his heavy truck and was off in a roar that unsettled all the shacks in the neighborhood, shrouding them in a thin film of black dust kicked up by his wheels.

She stood waving, enjoying the mild sensation he caused with his truck. Everyone in the neighborhood watched when he came to take their dolls. The younger Mrs. Ikeda painted at home, taking care of her four-year-old, who couldn't walk or talk well enough to attend nursery school. Kyoko helped if she finished her homework early enough. The greengrocer's wife, Mrs. Kasama, finished a doll or two a day while she was tending the store. Mrs. Tamioka painted some at home, but her eyes were going bad, and Nakayama had rejected them, but the shops by the Atomic Dome were willing to take them. "Those foreign soldiers hardly notice what they're buying," one of the shopkeepers said. "They're so anxious to get a souvenir."

Among the neighbors, the Kakihara daughter had the most skill. Her father couldn't afford to pay for cooking and flower-arranging lessons for her in preparation for a good marriage, so he decided, with characteristic optimism, that painting the dolls while she helped him in his shop was at least a good substitute for aesthetic training. With the extra money, she could pay for dressmaking lessons and have a real career in case she didn't find a husband. Everybody knew she had been in the bomb, and the whole neighborhood was painfully aware of how difficult it would be to find a husband willing to marry her. People were afraid the children would turn out like the Ikeda grandchild.

In the middle of May, when they moved into the warehouse the new business doubled production to 1,500 dolls a week. People had begun appearing on Chiyo's doorstep, asking for work they could take home. Desperate, destitute people. She was glad to give them some chance for an income, but they weren't skillful enough. She set up training classes in the newly repaired warehouse. Isao had a sign painted to hang out front. The Asahi Amalgamated Tool and Novelty Company, he named it. He envisioned a whole community of workers manufacturing products yet to be invented. And he appointed Chiyo president, which she knew was only symbolic, but it pleased her. She had not felt ill or lethargic for two months.

And things were always better in the spring. The neighborhood vegetable garden was beginning to produce. The rice had been planted in Inokuchi. And there was a tiny cooperative market blossoming in downtown Hiroshima where people came with anything they thought they could sell. The winter of 1949 had been especially hard. All the *kanpan* hardtack from the old Japanese army stores had been used up, and the delivery of Care packages and relief goods from America had slowed to a trickle. The Occupation was demanding increased productivity. Inflation was rampant and people had come home from overseas, ready to take up their old jobs again. But many of them were old and inefficient. The Americans had said they couldn't continue to provide handouts to shore up the whole Japanese economy. There were layoffs, then demonsrations and strikes, even violence. Earlier, everybody had complained about the tasteless American flour, but without it they had been much hungrier. Now, with the new vegetables maturing, they wouldn't need it as much.

Best of all, the ice was breaking up in the frozen ports of Russia. The ships bringing repatriates had dwindled to one or two in the fall and stopped altogether in the winter. But in early spring, ships had begun arriving from Shanghai. Now there was new pressure on Russia to send home the 400,000 Japanese prisoners still in Siberia. In 1947 and 1948, thousands of repatriates had come home, civilians, veterans, and ex-prisoners of war. Those who had no relatives to live with, nowhere else to go, had moved in to fill up the vacuum in Hiroshima.

Mrs. Yamamoto's husband had come home a year ago. A telegram in the night, and the next day he was at the port of Ujina. Chiyo had gone with the Yamamotos to meet him, always hoping that Shintaro might be there, too. Hundreds were thronging the docks, hugging or just looking at each other and weeping.

Captain Yamamoto emerged dazed and emaciated, with a Russian look about him, a precise mustache and a fur cap tied at the top to allow the warm Japanese air to caress his ears.

He stood speechless, staring at his family. "How tall you are!" he finally said to Yasu; then he hugged his wife and Yasu. "I've dreamt of this moment for a long time." He held Mrs. Yamamoto at arm's length and looked at her. He nodded to Chiyo, thanking her for neighborly favors, then began looking over everyone's heads.

"Sachiko!" he shouted, searching for his daughter, who had died the day of the bomb. Then he remembered, and he turned and hugged his wife and son once again. After that, the strength drained out of him and he lost interest in everything. And no, he had not heard of Shintaro Hara, which was not surprising, but disappointing all the same.

Now, a year later, he still had not looked for a job or made any move toward rebuilding the house in Nobori-chō. His parents were hoping he would take over their tofu business, which Mrs. Yamamoto and Yasu had been operating whenever soybeans were available. "At least until you find a suitable job as an engineer," his mother had told him. But he was not interested in that, either. So Mrs. Yamamoto continued to support the family, managing the paperwork and delivery for the company's last remaining tofu maker, who was old, about to retire, and teaching his skills to Yasu.

In late May, the Soviet Union announced they were sending home 95,000 prisoners of war, "to complete repatriation," they said. The Japanese and Americans were outraged. What happened to some 300,000 or so still unaccounted for, the journalists wanted to know. The Russians didn't answer, but Tass finally announced that the first of the spring ships bearing Japanese prisoners would leave Nakhodka for Maizuru within a month.

Late in June, after several ships had arrived, the newspapers began publishing passenger lists. A group of Japanese journalists had managed to board the ships, collect names, and wire them back to Japan. Not always accurate, because they weren't official lists and it was easy to miss people, but better than nothing. Everybody Chiyo knew was poring over lists for her. Each list was different according to each newspaper. It would be just like Shintaro, Chiyo thought, to be down in the hold when the reporters were going around asking.

One morning when she arrived early at the factory, she encountered Morishita-san, grinning at her, holding a newspaper in his hand. A word was circled in red ink. "Hara Shin," it said. No one had ever called him Shin before. Maybe part of his name had been obliterated when they sent the wire. And no town or region listed. Just "Hara Shin," stark among the other names. As if he had not wanted to talk to the reporters.

"There are lots of people named Hara Shin," Chiyo warned the children that evening. "There's no reason to believe that this particular one is your father."

"You'd better go up to Maizuru," Isao advised. "It's safer then sending a wire, and when you get there, you can talk to the officials and meet this particular Hara Shin even if he isn't Shintaro."

"Do you want me to go with you?" Kazuko asked.

Chiyo hesitated. If Shintaro didn't get off the ship she would want Kazuko to be there. But if he did, she didn't want anyone else around. Not even the children.

"I could come home ahead and the two of you could take a trip somewhere. Maybe Shintaro would like a few days in Kyoto getting reacquainted." She smiled knowingly.

It irritated Chiyo to have Kazuko always know what she was thinking.

"Thank you, *Nē-san,*" she said, "but I think I would rather do it alone."

"I understand," said Kazuko.

It was the first time Chiyo had ever taken a trip alone. She boarded a slow local train to Kyoto, then changed for an even slower one to Maizuru. It was crowded along the aisles, out in the vestibules, even in the toilets, with passengers standing crushed together. Chiyo had managed to get a seat by waiting two hours on the platform and then having enough luck for the train door to open in front of her when it came to a halt. Everybody behind had pushed her right onto the train and into a seat, where she sat alternately indulging in memories of Shintaro and gazing out the window. The rice fields were flooded with water, covering the tender new rice plants. Fields spread out on both sides of the train, reflecting the clean, pure sky and the mountains, stretching all the way to the Japan Sea. Here in the countryside, nothing had changed. The farmers had gone on planting rice and growing it. Of course the scars of the war were there, but they were buried deep inside the people. It was like the old Chinese poem which Isao had recited on the streetcar that day, *San ga Ari.* Mountains and Rivers. "Though the whole country be torn, the mountains and rivers remain." Isao had forgotten the rest of it, but Shintaro would be able to recite the whole poem, tell the political situation in China at the time it was written, list all the allusions to it by poets in the generations that followed.

He would be changed. Six years, and experiences she couldn't even imagine. He wouldn't be like Captain Yamamoto. She was sure of that. But there was the other fear. Rumors that the prisoners were being sent home brainwashed. Some had come home so enamored of the Communist system, standing at the stations in little groups, belting out the "Internationale" while their families waited to greet them.

"Of course Shintaro won't do that," Isao had assured her. "That's why he hasn't come home yet. They can't get him to say those socialist slogans."

"Well, if that's all he has to do to get home, I don't see why he doesn't just say it," Chiyo protested.

But she knew he was too honor-bound. Too much Confucian training. He believed in international brotherhood and the sanctity of the common worker, but he also believed in the emperor and tradition, and he didn't like showy, unreal demonstrations. And he didn't like being dishonest.

If he had refused to drink a bottle of soy sauce to keep himself out of the army, he certainly wasn't going to say anything he didn't believe to the Russians.

She stirred restlessly in her seat. A long trip, and she was hungry, but if she ate now, the food she had brought wouldn't last through the days of waiting in the dormitory with the other wives. No vendors in the aisles selling food the way they had during trips in her childhood. Or on the station platforms either. In the old days, hawkers shouted out the specialties of each region whenever the train paused at stations. Here there was only a young girl selling tea in crudely made crockery pots, pushing her cart through the crowded aisles. Everybody in Japan, it seemed, was going to Maizuru to meet the ships.

Chiyo bought the tea, then sat caressing the small, warm pot. Why not make teapots for Miyajima? The workers who didn't paint well could mold clay and fire kilns. And why not the old-style *tsuchiningyō*, the clay dolls she'd learned to make from Nakayama's uncle? Miyajima's traditional folkcraft should sell as well as *kokeshi*. Why hadn't she or Nakayama thought of that before? Maybe he couldn't get the clay.

She fell asleep.

When she awoke, passengers were gathering luggage and lining up before the exits. The loudspeaker was blaring. "Next stop is Maizuru. End of the line. First view of the homeland for the returning repatriates."

The word "Maizuru" hung on a plaque above the station platform. It was written in Chinese characters, in the Japanese syllabary, and in the Western alphabet. The characters were beautiful, Chiyo thought. "The dancing crane," they meant. The calligraphic strokes made the characters themselves look as if they were dancing.

Out in front of the station was every kind of conveyance. A horse-drawn wagon, open to the air, already crowded with people, but more were paying the driver and climbing on. Old *jinrikishas* pulled by skinny-legged men or men with bicycles, and one ancient car with a motor fueled by strange-smelling stuff, black fumes billowing from the back end. But behind the wheel was a stiff, neatly dressed chauffeur wearing white gloves.

Foreign soldiers with military police uniforms stood around the edge of the station, their faces immobile, not looking at anyone. Some were in jeeps in the background, watching the crowds emerge.

Chiyo pushed through the crowd toward the street, wondering if the open wagon was the only transportation. She followed a wave of other passengers and discovered a streetcar. People were clinging like insects to its exterior and filling the inside to the point of bursting. She pushed onto it, grabbed a leather strap covered with other hands, and found herself cheek to cheek with a woman who had already let go. "The force of the crowd is holding me up," she told Chiyo. "I don't need a strap."

"Is it always this crowded and frantic?" Chiyo asked.

"When ships are coming in, yes. This is my third trip from Kyoto, and it seems a little better this time. Last year, ships were coming in two or three a day. Then you couldn't even think of getting on the streetcar. You had to walk."

They reached the port at dusk and filed off the streetcar to a view of the fog moving in over the green hills that protected the bay. A beautiful place for Shintaro to come home to.

Chiyo had a better look at the thin, wiry woman who'd been talking to her. She was lively, at least sixty, and holding tightly on to a wicker basket with one hand and a young boy with the other.

"That island out in the middle of the bay," the woman said, "they call it Gate Island. Everybody watches it, waiting for the first glimpse of the ships. Then people start shouting, and they keep it up all the while the ship is coming closer. See, it docks way out there at the end of the pier, and the repatriates march into the reception center from there. You don't really get a chance to see them when they come off because the Americans won't let us any closer. Everybody has to go right inside that building, and we have to wait for three days before we really know who's on the ship."

"Three days?" Chiyo knew about the long wait, but she had at least expected to greet Shintaro as soon as he arrived. "That seems like forever."

The woman smiled knowingly. "Yes, everybody thinks that, but they have to go through a whole series of tests in there." She explained about the quarantine, customs inspections, medical treatments. "Then they get a hot Japanese bath. Just imagine how that must feel after all these years. But to tell you the truth, I'd as soon take my son off the ship, just the way he is, and take him home and give him the bath myself."

Chiyo laughed. "Well, from what I hear, they'll need several baths before they feel really comfortable again. But with two baths and all the tests how can it take three days?"

"They have to go through a line to get new clothing, toilet articles, railway tickets, and traveling expenses. And they can have free telegrams and barber services, and—I don't know what else. But it's those Americans asking them questions about the Soviet Union. That's what takes so long, you see."

The woman looked at Chiyo's discouraged face. "Don't worry. The time passes faster than you think, and anyway the last ship that came in, a woman next to me saw her husband and started waving. He shouted back, even at that distance. So sometimes you can recognize them right away.

"I've been here twice before," the woman said wistfully. "I came even though there wasn't any word. I was just sure he'd be home on the first ship, you see. And besides, Kyoto isn't far. But this time he's really coming. I found his name and address in the paper, and he'll be on the *Takasago Maru.*"

"That's the same ship my husband's supposed to be on."

"Really?" The woman nodded happily. "I have a big flag with his name on it," she said proudly. "Some of the other women had them last time and I think it's a good idea. He can see it from far away."

She bowed to Chiyo. "I am Tanaka Mie," she said, "and my grandson has already run ahead to save us a good space in the barracks. Come on, I'll take you over there."

Long, dark corridors inside, and rows upon rows of bunks, all filled with women and children, a spattering of fathers, uncles, grandparents. An old woman, apparently unable to walk, was being carried around by her son, quite feeble himself, maybe even simpleminded.

A mother and father with small children were sitting on one bunk, peeling *mikan,* mandarin oranges, and fighting over how to divide the sections. Some women were lying on their beds, listless, staring up at the ceiling. As if they had been living there for days. Chiyo wondered if she were the only recent arrival. But a whole line of people were in back of her, pushing into the barracks and looking for a bunk. Mrs. Tanaka whisked her over to a corner and pointed to a three-tiered structure.

"My grandson saved you one on the top," she said. "Mine is just below, and he has the one on the bottom. Of course, he may have to move in with me if it gets too crowded. I brought him along for company. I get so desolate waiting. I thought the little fellow would cheer me up."

Chiyo was usually delighted with the idea of the top bunk. But here she would have preferred being closer to the ground. Never mind. She nodded her thanks and climbed to the top, wondering if Mrs. Tanaka always chose some new person to initiate.

She awoke before dawn to the sound of creaking wooden floors and babies whimpering in slings fastened to their mothers' backs.

"Why don't you stay in an inn?" Isao had asked. "I've heard those government barracks are drafty and uncomfortable."

But Chiyo was glad she was here. More money to spend in Kyoto when Shintaro came, and besides, all through the snoring, creaking footsteps, the sniffling and whimpering of children, there was something in the air—hope so strong nobody dared show it too much. Like a rope cast out to sea with all of them holding on. Ships coming in, husbands coming home. It was infectious. Six long years. And some of the people in those barracks had been waiting even longer than that.

"Are you awake?" Mrs. Tanaka whispered up to her. "Fumihiko and I are going to the top of the hill. They say the ship's coming in at six. Just a short climb, and from up there we can see it come through that first channel to Gate Island."

Chiyo nodded, and without a word, rose and dressed. But as soon as they got out the door and saw the steep hill, Chiyo had second thoughts. Fumihiko, who was only eight, persuaded his grandmother to leave her flag behind.

Warm, soft breezes caressed them as they climbed. At last they stood high on the hill, with the sun serving up a pink dawn and the islands stretched out before them. They had the whole hill to themselves.

"Look!" shouted Fumihiko, pointing. Two nervous tugboats had shot out into the harbor from the dock. Smoke was pouring from their short, thick stacks, and a company of men stood in the bows talking excitedly, all looking toward the distant islands where the ships would be coming from. Then both boats disappeared from sight. Chiyo was getting cold. Fumihiko was shivering, too. These things always took a long time. Why hadn't Mrs. Tanaka told them to dress more warmly?

But the next instant, the *Takasago Maru* appeared, three or four times the size of the little tugboats accompanying it, and the decks crowded with clumps of people, all indistinguishable. As they came closer she could see a spot of white, maybe somebody's shirt. How excited Shintaro must be standing there, looking at the blue-green hills of his homeland. Would he be surprised to see her there? She cautioned herself against too much hope.

When the boat slid slowly and gloriously into the harbor, she forgot her warnings to herself. All along the shore, people were waving and shouting. A new group had discovered the hill and were climbing in a long line, pulling each other up. One old gentleman was wiping his brow and nodding affably.

"My son is on that boat," he told them when he reached the crest of the hill. "He's right there. See? Look." He pointed vaguely at the middle of the ship, insisting they all look where he was pointing. "You can't see his face, of course, but that's him jumping up and down, all right. I can tell. Just his style."

The ship was ready to dock at the end of the long breakwater pier.

"We'd better start down now," said Mrs. Tanaka. "They get off the ship out there, then march down that long breakwater so we can stand there and look at them. You have to shout out the names fast if you recognize anybody. They can't always hear you. That's why I brought the flag. Oh, dear, and we've left it in the dormitory. Fumihiko, will you go and fetch it fast and meet us at the pier?"

The boy nodded eagerly and ran ahead of them back down the hill, disappearing into the crowd. Chiyo was afraid he would never find his grandmother again.

"He'll hold up the flag," Mrs. Tanaka said. "It'll be easy to see him when we get over there."

They arrived at the edge of the pier, far in back of a crowd, all of them craning necks, peering around each other to get a glimpse. They stood just at the bend where the pier curved into the reception center and then disappeared.

Nothing happened. Fumihiko arrived with the flag and pushed in toward his grandmother. He knew exactly where she was even though she hadn't given him any directions.

Finally the men burst forth at the far end of the long, narrow pier. All in unison. All marching together, noisily stamping their feet, keeping time, singing the "Internationale." They formed a long, snakelike line, each man a vertebra. They were dressed alike. Good, sturdy, Russian-looking pants, shirts and caps, and blankets wrapped around their left shoulders, fastened with canteens at the right waist. All exactly the same. Except that some of them wore boots.

People were shouting at them. "Daddy, look over here! Look at us! We came to meet you!"

"Yasufumi, is that really you? I'm your mother. I'll be waiting at the station!"

The men ignored them, looking straight ahead, marching in time. Robots home from the Soviet Union.

Chiyo craned her neck, stood on tiptoes, waved her hands, then mustered her strength and shouted, almost screaming so her voice would be heard above the singing. "Hara Shintaro! Are you there? It's your wife, Chiyo. Meet me at the station." But her voice was drowned by the others and the singing. And all the soldiers were young. None of them Shintaro's age.

The serpentine line moved on and on.

"Tanaka Junichiro! Over here! Look at the flag!" Young Fumihiko was ripping his voice apart, screaming. "That's him over there, Granma! He looks just like his picture!"

"Where?" Mrs. Tanaka demanded. They looked in the direction Fumihiko was pointing, and one young man turned his head imperceptibly, just the flicker of an eyelid, the hint of a smile, before he became rigid again, marching on with the others. "That's him!" she said. "Over here, son. Here's your mother come to meet you!" She waved the flag. "Look! See your name? It's you, isn't it?"

But he had marched on.

"Welcome home, Toshio," a woman in front of Chiyo said quietly. She greeted a young man marching right by her, then broke through the line and ran along beside him on the pier, her prim, threadbare kimono flapping in the wind. She almost tripped, panting to keep up. His face lost its rigid expression for a moment, melted into tenderness. Then he caught the eye of a soldier next to him and suddenly reached out and struck her against the chest, pushing her back so that she almost lost her balance.

There was a stunned silence. People's voices caught in their throats. Even the chorus of the "Internationale" missed a beat, and the woman staggered back, leaning on the arm of the person next to her. "What can it be?" she murmured to no one in particular. "What have I done to make him act like this? He's my youngest and he's so changed."

Another woman took her arm. "It's all right," she said. "He'll be himself when you get him alone and away from the others."

The rest of the crowd stood rigid until the singing voices faded, swallowed up by the reception center as the men snaked inside. Now there was stillness. People began turning away from the pier. But Chiyo heard more footsteps on the wooden planks. A new group had emerged, almost unnoticed. Here were the older men, a few of them limping, limbs gone, emaciated faces and hollow eyes, some with the look of tortured animals, as if they'd been caged away from their compatriots. This was the group the Soviets couldn't indoctrinate. Sent home because they were useless, too old and weak to work. Soon it would be Shintaro's fiftieth birthday. He'd been forty-four when he went away.

Mrs. Tanaka had already pushed away from the crowd lining the pier. She stood behind Chiyo, clutching Fumihiko's hand. "Let's go," she said. But Chiyo didn't answer. Voices near her shouted out names, and a few of the men turned shyly, quietly, and waved back.

"*Anata!* Beloved one! I'm here. I'll be waiting for you." A woman, holding her hands over her mouth, whispered to the man passing her. He jerked his head as if a fly were buzzing in his ear; then his gaze met hers, full force, and he reached out to embrace her, but an American soldier, one of the escorts, shoved his arm between them and pushed the man gently along.

"No," the American said. "Meet her there." He pointed into the distance toward the railroad station. "No time now."

The woman moved back obediently, tears in her eyes.

Chiyo held her breath, waiting, trying to see every man's face, calling out Shintaro's name softly, afraid now of the American soldier. No one responded. She did not see Shintaro.

"That is all for today," an official announced over the loudspeaker. "After the third day, if the repatriates do not have any other problems, the families can meet their relatives at the railroad station. There is no further information."

Mrs. Tanaka had warned her. Still she couldn't believe it. Three days stretched before her. What was she going to do with all that time? She had not seen anyone who looked even remotely like Shintaro and yet she couldn't go home until she knew for sure.

"He's one of those Communists," Mrs. Tanaka said, crestfallen. She and Fumihiko were waiting for her farther down the road. "He hardly noticed us."

"Oh, but he did," said Chiyo. "Much more than any of the others. Didn't you see him smile?"

She looked at Chiyo. "You saw him smile, too? Then he really did smile? Fumihiko, did you see him smile?"

The child nodded, still clutching the flag, and Mrs. Tanaka hunched to the ground, her knees sticking up under her chin, and hugged Fumihiko. "It's all right. We can wait three days. We won't mind at all, will we?"

Chiyo watched the two of them wrapped in their cocoon of hope. She did not want to be with them any longer. Or with anyone.

Mrs. Tanaka stood up and looked sympathetically at Chiyo. "I know," she said, "you didn't see your husband in that big crowd, did you? But that's not unusual. I've seen it happen. It's easy to miss someone, especially with this crowd. Have you ever seen anything like that demonstration with the big, strong chorus and all? At first it was rather inspiring. The 'Internationale' is a beautiful song. But when they start treating their families that way— Well, the other times, it was so grand watching them get off the ship, even if none of them were related to me. They were so glad to be home and grateful for everything. Now, I don't know. I just hope—"

She sighed and shook her head. "Anyway, sometimes they post names outside here late in the afternoon, about four. It's not an accurate list, but the Relief Agency tries to tell us who's here. We can come back and look then. Now, Fumihiko and I are going into town to see if we can find him a flavored ice. Do you want to come?" She didn't wait for an answer. "And some of the women from last year— They're planning a little feast in the dormitory tonight, combining all the food we brought. You can join us. We have a wonderful time together. We're always writing letters to each other, you know."

There was a popular song—"Ganpeki no Haha," the harbor-gazing mama. Chiyo did not want to be one of them. Or a harbor-gazing wife.

She bowed. "Thank you, but I have a relative who lives in this area and I promised to visit her," she lied. "And thank you for that wonderful climb up the hill this morning. I'll always remember it."

She wandered off into town. Scruffy back streets and ragged children with ill-fitting clothes, runny noses, just like the other ragged ones all over Japan. Everybody said there was more to eat in remote country areas, but it was just as poverty-stricken here as anywhere else. There were shacks like the ones in Hiroshima, probably built by *hikiage,* the repatriates, who had no place else to go and no money to take them any farther than Maizuru.

Wandering along the shopping street, she discovered a tiny *noren* curtain on which was written *soba,* the characters for "buckwheat noodles," in elegant calligraphy. Captain Yamamoto had told Chiyo, in one of his rare moments of talkativeness, that the Relief Agency had tried in the beginning to give every returnee a hearty bowl of noodles, but now all they could manage was a cup of green tea and one roasted potato. Even so, it had tasted good, he said.

Inside the shop there were only three tables and no customers. The owner came to greet her with a warm cup of *mugi-cha,* barley tea. She ordered the noodles. Buckwheat had been scarce in Hiroshima. She couldn't remember eating any since long before Shintaro's departure.

When Chiyo's noodles arrived, she sat enjoying the fragrance and the steam on her face before she even began to eat them.

When she finished, satisfied and full of memories of Shintaro eating *soba,* it was still only one o'clock. Three hours before she could go and look at the list.

She took out the letter paper she had tucked in her handbag and began writing to Shintaro. If he wasn't on the ship, she could leave the letter for the next ship. And if he did come out of that reception center, three days from now, all whole and lively, she could give him the letter some other time, maybe on the tenth anniversary of his return.

To Shintaro.

Greetings from Maizuru.

Do you know that one of the women in the barracks says some men came home fat last year? Not emaciated and thin, as everyone expected, but really fat. They had malnutrition, too. And they looked more unhealthy than the thin ones.

It doesn't matter to me how you look when you get here. Fat or thin, mustached, wearing those bulky-looking Russian clothes and a fur hat. Singing the "Internationale" (although I hope you don't). I will cook for you and make you healthy again.

She rambled on with the letter, pouring out everything she could think of, telling him about the Asahi Amalgamated Tool and Novelty Company and how it had grown into a business so rapidly, especially after they moved into the new factory.

> And Hiroshi's doing well in his first year at Rijo even though he's working hard in our business, too. He moved back to Hiroshima this spring, and he's looking forward to having you come home and be one of his teachers.
>
> Yoko is in her third year at the Girls' School, and both schools have been reorganized according to the American system. Now, instead of having five years of middle school, they have six years of what they call junior and senior high school. They get an extra year before they enter the university. So Yoko will be in high school next year. Can you believe it? Of course, you'll be home in time for her graduation from junior high.

Still it was only three o'clock and Chiyo didn't want to go back to the barracks, even though her hand was getting sore. So she wrote once more about Kenichi just in case he hadn't heard before. It was easier to write about it this time. Then she told him again about rebuilding the house in Nobori-chō, about Mr. Takano's funeral, Captain Yamamoto, Mr. Nakayama, and the dolls. She did not tell him about Grandmother or Akiko or her own illnesses.

She was beginning on the story of how she had found the Ikedas when the proprietress interrupted her.

"We see a lot of people here waiting for their loved ones," the woman told her, pouring more tea and placing a tea cake before her. "It's your husband, isn't it?"

Chiyo nodded. She offered to pay for the cake, but the woman refused. "I have my husband here at home now," she said. "He was in the army, but he didn't die and he wasn't taken prisoner. I hope you'll be lucky soon, too."

"Thank you," Chiyo said, already feeling better.

By four-thirty she was back in front of the wall, looking for the list. There was no list. "No, we don't have it finished yet," an official told a group of them. "It's been impossible. The men are demonstrating in the middle of the reception center right now. And some of them won't tell us their names. They're demanding three sets of clothing apiece. They won't eat the food we've given them. Come back in the morning. Maybe we'll know something then."

Chiyo smiled wanly at Mrs. Tanaka, and they walked back to the barracks together, but Chiyo couldn't bear to go inside. Dark, hope-infested place. Hope turning sour.

"I have to send my brother a telegram," Chiyo said, and without even waiting for a response, she stumbled off down the streets where she had spent the afternoon, but she did not send a telegram. What was there to say? Instead, she returned to the *soba* shop, spent more of her precious money on another bowl of noodles, and sat avoiding the sympathetic glances of the proprietress while she listened to the woman's husband tell stories about the war and the returning ships. This time the noodles did not taste as delicious as they had before.

Chapter Twenty-one

IN THE MORNING, EVERYONE WAS BUS-
tling and chattering, full of anticipation,
streaming out of the barracks to go and look at the list. Chiyo
followed Mrs. Tanaka and Fumihiko, both of them bright and expectant. People crowded so thickly around the list it was impossible to see it, but Chiyo, pushed by pressure from behind, was up
front before she knew it.

"Here he is!" Mrs. Tanaka shouted. She was right beside Chiyo,
her nose only a centimeter away from the list, her rimless glasses
hanging askew. "Tanaka Junichiro. Kyoto. They've even got the
address correct."

Fumihiko was jumping up and down, clapping his hands.
"Uncle. Uncle," he shouted.

"Well, calm down. You can hardly remember him," she advised. "But anyway, you'll like him."

Chiyo was checking the Haras. Only two. HARA Kenzaburo.
HARA Masashi. No HARA Shin. She looked under the other read-
ings for Hara. None. She looked under other names that contained
the character for Hara like HARAGUCHI, HARAMOTO. None of
those people were named Shintaro or Shin. She tried names with

Hara as the second character. TAKIHARA, SHIMOHARA. No correspondence there, either. Maybe they had gotten the family names and the given names mixed up. She began looking under all the listings for names that began with Shin.

"Come along now," a woman in back of her said. "You've had long enough. Come back later and look again."

Chiyo pushed to the edge of the crowd, hugging herself and her disappointment.

"You didn't find it?" Mrs. Tanaka asked, following after her. "It's all right. It doesn't mean much. You know how they get mixed up. And they've had all that trouble in there, too. He'll be along with the rest of them. And if he isn't, then somebody will know him and they can tell you where he is. You brought his picture, didn't you? Then come on, we'll help you make a big sign. I found an old cardboard box stacked out behind the barracks."

She followed blindly after Mrs. Tanaka and Fumihiko, glad that somebody could think of something to do.

Fumihiko had brought his crayons and was delighted to have a chance to use them. The old box Mrs. Tanaka had found was soggy from a recent rain, but they cut off one side, then took the piece back into the barracks and pressed it flat on the floor. Chiyo and Mrs. Tanaka stood with their feet on each corner to keep it from curling while Fumihiko practiced his calligraphy on another sheet of paper. Should he write Hara Shin or Hara Shintaro, he wanted to know.

It was a problem. Would Shin Hara, if he wasn't Shintaro, stop and look at the sign? Maybe. But how about the real Shintaro, if he actually got off that boat? Wouldn't he think it was strange to find his wife holding a sign with a name on it that wasn't even his? Of course she could explain it later, but—

"Write Shintaro," she said.

He traced out the lines of each character, then filled them in with purple crayons. He wanted to edge them each with red for even more emphasis, but they wouldn't let him. "Purple for the whole thing," Mrs. Tanaka said. "She doesn't want her husband thinking some crazy person painted the sign." She laughed. "Or some Communist."

The characters were bold and firm when he finished. And huge. But there was extra space at the bottom even after they had affixed the photograph, so Fumihiko wrote Shintaro's name again in Roman letters.

"Maybe somebody who can't read Japanese will know where he is," Fumihiko explained, sitting back on his haunches to examine his work.

They stacked the sign with its face to the wall behind the steel girder of the bunk bed, then pushed the whole frame against it so they could keep it straight until the next day.

"I'll hold it for you when we're standing on the wharf tomorrow," Fumihiko offered.

"Oh, thanks, Fumi-chan, but you'll be busy with your own flag for your uncle. Besides, if my husband comes out of there, he'll think you're our youngest son, and he'll be confused enough with everything else around him."

She shared with them her last *mikan,* a mandarin orange she had brought from Hiroshima, and then a dried persimmon apiece from the box Kazuko had given her to use for treats for special people. Afterward she went back to look at the list again. Hardly anyone was standing there now, and she examined each of the 1,029 names, writing down anything that gave even the vaguest hint. No clues, unless of course this Masashi Hara—

She sat waiting her turn in the agency office.

"Just one more day, Mrs. Hara. And anyway, we're doing a second check. Half the people have refused to give their names, you know." The agency man was sympathetic but exhausted.

"We've had quite a time with these people. They haven't given us a minute's rest. Hardly anybody's slept all night, and more ships are coming in after this one." He leaned back in his chair. "Six million people coming home from Korea, Manchuria, China, Siberia. At least we're not the entry port for the ones coming from Southeast Asia. But I'm not sure I'll be alive to see the end of all this."

He shook himself back to Chiyo's problem. "Now, you do have a poster, you say? That helps. People always come up and tell the relatives what they know. Even if they don't, they'll remember the name and get in touch with you later. It's happened. They memorize each other's addresses, you know. It's not allowed to bring anything written out of Siberia."

He stood up and stretched his hands above his head, trying to stay awake. "And the name Hara Shin was listed in the newspaper, you say? Of course we could have missed recording his name. That's the most reasonable solution. But also, they could have told him to wait for the next ship. That happens a lot, and they're coming in one after the other right now."

"You mean I might have to wait another three days?"

He looked at her sternly. "There are four ships coming in a row from Nakhodka. You may have to wait six days. But the government has provided a clean, free place for you to stay." He gazed hopelessly at her crestfallen face. "Don't worry, now. He's sure to be home soon. Six days isn't much compared to the years you've been waiting, I'm sure. And if we find out anything, we'll put a notice for you on the bulletin board out there." He stood up, dismissing her, then nodded to the woman waiting behind her.

"Now. Next person."

Chiyo stumbled out of the office back onto the wharf. She could see the movement of shadows through the windows of the reception center. What were they doing down there? Nobody coming out until tomorrow, and then maybe six more days. Even living through today was intolerable.

She climbed back up the high hill to get a better glimpse of the ship steaming out of the harbor, back up to Nakhodka for another load.

On the third day, they announced they would let the men out late in the afternoon. Chiyo made five trips to the bulletin board. Nothing.

People waited in the dormitory, the men wearing white undershirts and knee-length underpants, smoking intermittently, holding their heads in their hands, lying on their beds. The women paced the floor, carrying their babies on their backs, jiggling them, speaking in soothing tones. The excitement of the first morning was gone. The feasting was over. Most of the food was gone.

Mrs. Tanaka sent Fumihiko down the hill to the reception center to get the news. He came back half an hour later. No, they weren't coming out today. Too many complications. Fumihiko repeated the stale information they had all been fed by the officials for days. People who wanted to meet their returning relatives would have to walk to Maizuru station. The men would march there together. Or be transported by sea. And everyone should start early. Before dawn. They were trying to get all the men out of the center before the next ship came in. Fumihiko stood importantly in the middle of the room and continued his announcements. People who registered for tickets could pick them up at the station. And they were giving out lunches. Two lunches for traveling a distance as far as Hiroshima. Four lunches for going all the way to Hokkaido. If accompanying families could prove their identity, they could get a free lunch too.

* * *

215

At the station, in the cold, hostile dawn, the young men stood with their blankets wrapped around their right shoulders down to left waist, their boots and Russian-style shirts all matching. They sang the "Internationale" again.

"It wouldn't bother me a bit if they never sang that song again," Mrs. Tanaka said. She was staring straight at her son, Junichiro, who was standing in the middle of the platform, linking his arms in scrum formation with his companions, belting out the song at the top of his lungs, enjoying the camaraderie so much that it seemed he would never want to go home to his mother.

Finally, they broke formation and filtered out among the people, some greeting their mothers and wives in spite of their companions, who tugged at their sleeves, admonishing them not to. The rumor was circulating that the men in scrum formation had promised to sign up at the Japan Communist Party headquarters before joining their families. One man was held rigid by a soldier on either side. He stared at his wife, trying to keep his face expressionless. She was crying.

"*Anata!*" she shouted. "Husband. Go with these men if you want to. Only come back to me. Or I'll follow behind and wait. Just talk to me."

"Wait here," he said softly. "I'll be back." His companions dragged him off. Then a child Yoko's age waved the Japanese flag in his face, dusting it across his eyes. He tried to wrench himself free of the men, but they held him tighter.

"Come home right now, Papa. We need you."

He turned his face away.

In another part of the station, a young man struggled against his family. They were pulling him and pushing from behind while he fought them, his canteen dangling and banging against his stomach. He was kicking so hard they finally picked him up and carried him off.

"This is for your own good," she heard one of them say. "You'll understand after you've been home a while."

Suddenly, Junichiro was standing in front of Mrs. Tanaka.

"*Ara!* Look at you! Look here!" She was much smaller and shorter than he was. Her tiny brown kimono, covered by a simple *haori*, her overjacket, blended into her son's khaki uniform. She buried her face into his chest and wept. He was a sunny, gentle-looking young man. How could he ever have been a soldier? He towered above his mother, healthy and strong, and a smile spread across his face, displaying his clean white teeth. Nobody was pulling him away, and he showed no evidence of malnutrition.

Fumihiko grabbed their legs and pushed between them. "Uncle! Remember me?"

Junichiro picked him up. "Of course I remember," he said. He exclaimed over the boy's height and size, then put him down and strode toward the train tracks. "Come on! Let's go home."

"Oh!" Mrs. Tanaka pulled on his sleeve. "You must meet my friend Mrs. Hara."

They bowed to each other. His smile was too wide and all-encompassing, as if he reacted to everything the same way.

"Did you happen to meet a man on the ship named Hara Shintaro?" she asked.

He puzzled a moment. "Well—I don't— You know it was impossible to pay attention to— More than a thousand people on that ship."

"Those other soldiers!" Chiyo blurted out. "Why aren't they trying to keep you away from your mother?"

He laughed. "Oh, that. I just told them I'd register at the party headquarters in Kyoto. I said my mother'd be coming, and what's the point of registering in Maizuru anyway? Those other people they were fighting over—they live here. And besides—" He beamed his sunny smile again, but lowered his voice just slightly. "I think they trust me. They're really convinced I'm a faithful party member, and I'll demonstrate with them when we get off the train in Kyoto. I just want to sit with my own mother on the train, I told them." He put his arm around her and held her close.

So that's how it was. He had compromised, probably said things he didn't believe. But it was easier for the young ones.

They all bowed again. "Visit us when you come through Kyoto," Mrs. Tanaka said. "We have a poor, humble house, but you are always welcome."

Everyone was scurrying off, pushing through the wicket, the loudspeaker blaring out. "Kyoto! Kyoto! Transfer point for all locations east and west." The men behind the Tanakas marched forward to the train platform like an invading army. Chiyo caught a last glimpse of Fumihiko waving to her before he climbed up the stairway and out of sight.

Where was the older group she'd seen on the pier? No doubt, they'd been marching at a slower pace, not wanting to encounter these noisy ones. Yukiji Ikeda had told her stories about the older men who'd been drafted near the end of the war, all of them holding a lower rank than the self-important, swaggering young officers who'd had military training in Japan.

And the stories from the taciturn Captain Yamamoto. Men trying to jump overboard on his ship coming home. One had succeeded. Bitter political battles, he said. People accusing each other of collaborating, of being traitors, of sacrificing the lives of their countrymen, of using each other and killing each other. And now with these men coming home a year later, the differences were even stronger.

The new group began to appear just on the edge of the departing ones. This time it was mostly husbands and wives, not parents and sons, and there were no agitators interfering, only weeping and embracing. Chiyo stood amidst this new ocean of people, holding her sign and photograph, staring at every man who didn't have a family surrounding him. Some of the men waited expectantly, but no one came to meet them. Others didn't seem to mind that no one was there. They went directly to the ticket windows, then to the train platforms. Some stood milling around the station, or went outside to soak up the air. Chiyo caught a glimpse of one man kneeling down to kiss the soil.

She concentrated on the expectant ones still looking for someone, finally gathering the courage to go up to each one and ask about Shintaro. They looked carefully at the picture, asked if she knew what part of Siberia he had been in, considered a while. In the end, no one knew him or had even heard his name.

Finally, no relatives were left in the station except Chiyo and the woman waiting for her husband to come back from party headquarters. It would be an hour before another train left for Kyoto. She had spoken to all the waiting men. She could not bear the idea of going back to the dormitory or to the *soba* shop either.

Two more men entered the station, neither paying attention to the other, both of them limping. Couldn't the authorities at least have provided these two lame ones with some transportation? But in fact there had been a bus. She had already seen the few old and tired men emerge from it, one on crutches, another in a stretcher being carried by two civilians, the rest limping or exhausted or very ill. These last two latecomers must have walked because they insisted on it.

The first was bloated, like the men she'd heard about, suffering from malnutrition. His face was pasty and lifeless. Chiyo held her sign up, but she did not ask him about Shintaro. She was concentrating on the last man, farther out, who— Yes, it was Shintaro. In spite of his limp, she could recognize his familiar walk, and he was the right height. As he came closer, she felt even surer. His profile and the cleft of his chin. He was thinner, and his army cap was strapped under his chin so she couldn't see the whole of his face. He was wearing an old khaki overcoat.

"Hara Shintaro! Over here!"

He turned his head and listened to her voice, but he didn't look at her and he didn't wave back. She ran up to him.

"Shintaro! I'm Chiyo, your wife."

He gazed right through her and beyond.

"What did you say?"

It wasn't Shintaro's voice. It didn't have his resonance. It had no expression at all.

"Hara Shintaro," she repeated. "From Hiroshima. You're a teacher at Rijo Middle School."

He looked startled. Didn't he recognize her?

"Oh, no," he said. "No, I am not." He started to walk away. But there was something. He acted as if he didn't know who he was. Amnesia? It was one of her worst fears.

She caught up and stood in front of him so he couldn't move away. She hoped with all her strength that he was not Shintaro. His soul had been lifted out of him.

"Then, did you know my husband, Hara Shintaro?" she asked. Maybe if she just kept repeating his name, he would recognize it. The lines of his cheek. If she could get him to smile, she would know. His glasses were much thicker than she remembered, and still he had not really looked at her, didn't want to see her.

"No." He turned away from her again.

"What prison camp were you in?" she insisted, moving in front of him once more. "And what is your name?" She decided that if he didn't know his own name, then— "You look so much like my husband, Hara Shintaro." Did he flinch at the words? He didn't answer her questions.

"Where is your family from? Are they from Hiroshima? Nobori-chō? Mikanjima? My husband was born there. Or Inokuchi? That's where my brother lives."

"I was born in Japan," he said tonelessly.

"But where? What part?"

"I worked in Port Arthur before the war."

So. He could remember his past.

"Then I was inducted into the army and sent up to Manchuria and the Soviets captured me. I've been in prison camp for such a long time."

There. That last sentence was like Shintaro's voice. As if he were on the edge of saying something sentimental and warm.

He was staring vacantly into the distance. Still he had not looked at her closely. His eyes were vague and uncertain. He was very uncomfortable with her presence.

She shivered.

"I have no family here in Japan," the man said. "I'm the only one left."

"Your wife?" she asked.

"I have no wife," he said abruptly. "It was nice to talk to you, *Oku-sama*. Now, I must go. I'm sure your husband will come home soon."

She watched him make his way toward the ticket window. He was not limping as much, but he walked haltingly, as if he wasn't sure where he was going. He collected the ticket, then started up to the train platform. From the back he looked even more like Shintaro. She also realized that she still did not know his name.

Quickly she purchased a platform pass at the window, then ran up the stairs. She was out of breath and panting when she arrived, and the man, standing alone near the track, looked at her, startled, then turned away.

"Excuse me, but what is your name?" she demanded when she arrived at his side. "If you are not Hara Shintaro, then I must know who you are. You walk the way my husband does. And you have the same voice. If you are Shintaro, you must come home with me. I will take care of you." Her voice was full of self-pity and she was on the edge of tears. She gasped to keep herself from crying. Who would want to come home to a woman who sounded the way she did?

He would not look at her.

"My name is Yamanaka Tadanori," he said with great dignity, bowing without raising his head to meet her eyes. "I regret that I have caused you so much anguish by resembling your husband. But now my train is coming, and I think it is best for you if you do not see me off."

"I am sorry to disturb you," she murmured, then turned and stumbled back down the stairs, walked through the empty station and out into the sunshine.

Surely this man was not Shintaro. There was only the coincidence of his height and the sound of his voice. And if he had amnesia, wouldn't he know it, wouldn't he want to follow up all the clues? But what if he was lame and sick, had lost all his energy and enthusiasm, and was ashamed to come home to them? He'd already created a new past for himself, making up that story about Port

Arthur. No, Shintaro wouldn't do that. He would never forsake her. He had told her so in every letter.

She took a streetcar back to the shopping district and wandered through the streets. She sat in a tiny shop, drinking tea. There had been a mix-up on the ships. The man in the agency said they switched people at the last minute. Besides, in a few days they would have the records straightened out.

She set down her cup resolutely. She would wire Isao to send her more money. Then she would stay in Maizuru for the next three ships.

Out on the street once more, she saw the man again. He hadn't taken the train after all. He was striding along with his hands in the pockets of his overcoat the way he had always done coming home from school. Early in their marriage she would come out on the street when he was due home in the afternoon just to watch him come down the block. Just to wave at him. She felt like that now.

"Hello, Husband. Home already?"

"I couldn't stay away," he always said. "I wanted to come home to you."

Maybe he was beginning to remember. There was a reason he hadn't taken the train.

She followed him. He stopped in front of a store offering Morinaga milk, shaved ice, and *anpan,* the bread with sweet red beans inside. He was having no trouble walking now. But he seemed vacant inside.

He went down into an area of stand-up bars, the former geisha houses, now become dance halls where a man could buy a girl's company. There were *pan-pan* girls standing around, brazenly shouting at the men. She continued to follow him, keeping her distance.

He stopped in front of one of the women, talked to her, then disappeared with her into the doorway of an inn. Chiyo almost ran through the entrance after him, then stopped. A newspaper headline loomed in her head. "Wife of former middle-school teacher grabs man away from streetwalker." She could wait it out, she decided.

Across the street from the bread store was a homely little shop that sold beer, salty snacks, and *oden* stew. Inside, she ordered tea and *senbei,* rice crackers. Five or six workmen sitting at a table stared at her. Let them stare. She found a table in the corner and sat sipping the tea and munching on the crackers, making herself as invisible as possible. The man would have to come out of the inn

eventually. All she wanted was some assurance that he wasn't Shintaro. If she could see his papers, some identification with his name
on it.

At dusk, he had still not emerged. She would have to walk back
to the barracks in the dark. And by now, the next ship would be
in. She wanted to be on hand if a list was posted.

"Excuse me," she finally told the proprietor. "I'm waiting for a
man to come out of that inn across the street. He's returned from
Siberia and I'm his sister. But he refused to come home with us
when we met him at the station today, so I've been assigned to
follow him. Would you mind watching for me to see if he comes
out, then notice where he goes while I send my family a telegram?
I'll be right back as soon as I can."

She was surprised at herself. and the man enjoyed the story.
"Went into that inn over there with one of the girls, huh? Well, I've
seen a lot of that in the past few years. I understand, *Oku-sama*. I'll
do what I can."

Down the street to wire Isao for the money. Then back at the tiny
shop again. Maybe twenty minutes had passed. "I've been watching
carefully, *Oku-san,* and nobody's come out yet."

"Well, he's been in there for four hours, now," she said. "Surely
he'll come out soon."

One of the men roared with laughter, but the proprietor turned
and stared him into silence.

Chiyo, whose money was almost gone, ordered a large portion of
oden, selecting a piece of the stewed chicken, an egg, the *konnyaku*
jelly made of devil's tongue. It was delicious. Shintaro had always
loved *oden*.

At eleven, she asked the proprietor if he would keep a careful eye
out. "I could be back first thing in the morning," she said.

"Why don't you just stay here?" he suggested. "You're living in
those barracks, aren't you, and it's a long walk back there. In the
dark, too. We have an extra *futon* to sleep on and I can put it there
in the room back of the bar. Nobody will disturb you, and you can
watch who goes in and out of that inn all night. I know you won't
sleep anyway."

She accepted gratefully, glad that she didn't have to return to the
questions of the watchful, anxious women in the barracks. And a
whole new group would have come by now to greet the next ship.
She had probably lost her bed even though she'd left her luggage on
it.

Chiyo lay all night under the old quilt the man had given her, her eyes fastened on the lantern at the doorway of the inn. She heard every voice and every footstep. Men and women entered all night, but only twice did anyone leave, and both times they were men in business suits, one very drunk and shouting.

In the morning, the proprietor's wife brought her a bowl of hot red *miso* soup and steaming rice, refusing to take any money in exchange.

"I've always lived in Maizuru," she said. "It was such a quiet little town when I was a child. Now it's like—well, I don't know anybody out on the street anymore. It's as if the world's turned inside out. All these people coming from everywhere. And the men—they'd rather be over there in the inn with those women than home with their families.

"Just enjoy this bowl of *miso* so you can face what's ahead of you today." She left Chiyo alone. It was comforting, sipping the warm, steaming soup while she stared at the doorway across the street. Someone had turned off the lantern at dawn. The harsh laughter and the sound of the blaring phonograph records had stopped.

She decided not to wait any longer. She would go across the street, find the owner or the madam, explain the situation, and ask to be taken to the man's room. Then she would insist that he show her written identification. If he could not, or if he admitted that he was Shintaro and he didn't want to come home to her, then that was fine. She just needed to know. She had managed this long without him. She could go on doing it.

A sudden downpour caught her in the middle of the street, and she realized she had left her umbrella somewhere, maybe in the tea shop yesterday afternoon. She arrived, dripping, at the inn.

Behind the desk was a woman, carefully coiffed, trussed up in a tight *obi*, her spotless underkimono meticulously arranged inside the outer one so that just a hint of pink showed around her neck. She listened sternly to Chiyo's story, averting her eyes and nodding, her lips pursed tight in her masklike face. She led Chiyo to the door of the room and slid it open, revealing two bodies lying side by side on the *tatami*. She left Chiyo standing there. The man was still asleep, but the woman was awake, and she sat up, startled and hostile. As if she were constantly on guard against air raids, police raids, attacks by thieves. She was not young, maybe as old as Chiyo herself. Tousled hair and shadows under her eyes. What kind of circumstances would bring a woman to this? If it had not been for Isao, and if there were no other way to support her children, could she have done it? But surely she would have found another way.

Even without Isao's support she would have thought of something. Making food and peddling it. Begging. But prostitution brought more money than anything else and maybe this woman had children to support.

Chiyo knelt in her most formal position at the entranceway. "I'm sorry to interrupt you like this. It's extremely rude of me, I know. But I'm trying to find out about that man there. I'm afraid he's my husband. He denied it when he got off the ship, you see, but I think maybe he's suffering from amnesia. Do you know his name?"

The woman laughed. "Well, I've never heard that one before." She leaned over on her elbow and Chiyo saw that she was at least dressed in some kind of satiny pink wrapper. Like the ones people wore in American movies. Probably a foreign soldier had given it to her.

The woman nudged her companion roughly on the shoulder, then shook him back and forth.

"Hey, you. What's your name?" She sounded like a policeman.

"Huh?" He had been sleeping with his face away from her, and he turned on his back, blinked his eyes and shook his head as if he were still coming out of a dream.

"What's your name?" she repeated.

"Kuwada Akinari." His response was automatic. As if he were speaking to a prison guard.

"See? He's not the one, is he?" She stared defiantly at Chiyo, consuming in one glance Chiyo's quiet respectability, her shyness and middle-aged dumpiness. Her prewar two-piece suit hung about her, shapeless and drab, smelling of wet wool. This woman probably wore bright red lipstick and shiny black shirts and sat on bar stools in a way that would reveal her thighs.

The man had still not acknowledged his surroundings. Suddenly Chiyo knelt beside him, grabbed him and shook him hard. "Shintaro! It's me, Chiyo. Your wife. I want you to come home. I don't care if you're sick. Or old or crippled. I will take care of you, feed you and nurse you back to health. And you can have your job back. The principal told me. Just say if you're really Shintaro. If you don't want to come home to me and the children, just tell me. You don't have to say why. And if you're not Shintaro, prove to me who you are. Show me some kind of identification."

She was still holding him hard by the shoulder, shaking him.

"Aargh!" he grunted, shaking himself free. "I am not your husband! Please go away and leave me alone!"

She sat gasping as if the breath had been knocked out of her. The woman was very still, waiting to see what Chiyo would do next.

In a flash, Chiyo had grabbed the man's chin, forced his mouth open and looked inside. Shintaro's teech had been perfect. He'd always managed to appear in every photograph with his polished white smile. But this man's mouth gave back a heavy, putrid odor of stale sake, half-digested onions and rancid oil. She turned her head away but not before she had gotten a full glimpse of the cavernous mouth and yellow teeth, many missing and some black and rotting.

No, not the teeth. He could have lost them in the hard Siberian winters, and all the more reason for him to be ashamed of himself. Before he could stop her, she was pulling down his cotton *yukata,* the sleeping kimono the inn provided. She yanked it from his left shoulder, holding firmly to the back of his neck, feeling below the right shoulder blade for the familiar brown mole she had reached for and touched so many times when they were making love. The mole was gone, too. Like his teeth. But was there an indentation? When she touched the place, she felt a shiver in his body.

"What happened to your mole?" she asked him.

"Get out," he said quietly. His eyes were vacant.

"Show me your identification first," she demanded. "Then I'll leave you. Show me something that says you're who you say you are."

He reached over and pulled out his wallet, then the army ID card, which he handed to her. The name Kuwada Akinari was written on it, and an old Tokyo address. She stared at the picture, then at him. Her energy was gone now, and she was disgusted with herself. She nodded and handed the ID back to him.

She knew now that he wasn't Shintaro, wasn't even the man she'd seen at the railroad station. She had wanted so much to find Shintaro that every man wearing a khaki overcoat looked like him. She was crazy. She had been in a frenzy. And now her face was red with anger and shame.

The woman reached over and held the man, trying to soothe him, moving her body closer to his.

"Hey, lover-boy, remember me, Hachiyo?" She put her mouth around his ear and licked it, then pulled his face towards hers, pushed him back down on the *futon* and slid herself on top of him.

Chiyo stood up. Nausea spread through her. Were they really going to make love right there before she even left the room?

She stumbled across the *tatami* to the hallway, slid the door closed behind her and stood shaking outside. She could hear breathing and grunting, and the noise followed her down the stairs to where the innkeeper sat. Chiyo bowed to her. "Thank you. I am sorry to have troubled you," she breathed.

She wandered around in the rain afterwards, dazed, maybe delirious, not minding that she was soaked to the skin. She couldn't believe what she had done.

There were three more ships. Chiyo waited for them all. She climbed the hill again and again. She stood with the poster bearing Shintaro's name and the photograph pasted onto it. She listened to the "Internationale" and watched the loud, rough performance of the men doing the Russian dances and shouting their slogans. She saw them ignoring their families and the young schoolchildren who had come bringing flowers to greet them.

Over and over again, she asked the returning men if they had heard of Hara Shintaro. None of them knew. No one knew.

Home in Hiroshima, she walked from the station. She had forgotten to send the telegram telling her arrival time. Yoko must have heard her footsteps, because she was waiting at the doorway.

"Papa?" Yoko inquired nervously.

Then she ran out and buried her head on her mother's shoulder. Hiroshi waited in the living room. He was like a piece of granite, listening to the story of the trip and the case of the missing Shin Hara. Chiyo did not mention the man at the station or the man in the brothel.

Yoko stood up quietly and took down the decorations, streamers hanging from the ceiling with family photographs pasted on them and a huge banner created by Hiroshi.

"Welcome home, Daddy," the banner said.

Chapter Twenty-two

WITHIN A WEEK, THERE APPEARED AT Chiyo's door a very purposeful woman. Hair tied in a bun and secured firmly to her neck. Properly fitting suit of good English wool. And no amenities in her greetings.

"I am the wife of Otsuka Haruo," she announced. "Former captain in the Imperial Manchurian Ninth Army. I understand your husband is still being detained in the Soviet Union." She didn't wait for an answer. "So is mine, and I've come up from Kyushu to help with the organization of the National Movement for Recovery of the Detained Compatriots. We have a large group down there. Now we need to organize here and elect a delegate for the national meeting in Tokyo. I was given to understand you are a very capable person, the president of your own company. We need people like you in our organization."

There wasn't much Chiyo could do but invite her in.

"Now, then," said Mrs. Otsuka, settling herself in front of Chiyo's living room table and pulling out printed materials, lists of names and addresses, photographs of people in Siberia who hadn't been heard from, newspaper clippings, envelopes with letterhead, "I'll explain about the Movement, then you can tell me what you know about people in Hiroshima."

"But I don't know anybody," protested Chiyo. "The only other prisoner of war I know is already home, and none of the women I met in Maizuru were from around here."

"Ah," said Mrs. Otsuka, "so you've been to Maizuru. That's how we got your name. From Mrs. Tanaka Mie of Kyoto, who is very active. She's met people in Maizuru from all over Japan."

"Yes, but Mrs. Tanaka's son is already home. Why would she need to belong to the Movement anymore?"

Mrs. Otsuka pushed her rimless glasses firmly back on the bridge of her nose. She had been peering over the top of them at her documents. "Mrs. Hara," she said, "you will finally come to realize that the Movement has turned into a lifelong commitment for most people. The fact that their loved ones have come home makes them all the more sympathetic towards those who are still waiting. Mrs. Tanaka, as I understand it, has met at least twenty ships, and has taken the trip to Maizuru three times."

Chiyo winced. Nothing less than a telegram directly from Shintaro or a letter in his own handwriting saying he couldn't get home by himself would ever lure her to Maizuru again.

"Of course, Mrs. Tanaka's perseverance finally paid off," continued Mrs. Otsuka. "And I am sure you will feel the same way when your husband comes home. Meanwhile, the Movement is at a crisis point and we need great dedication and energy from everyone. Let me quote to you from the Potsdam Declaration." She read in a ringing, official tone. "The Japanese army, after they are completely disarmed, shall be given the opportunity to return to their home country and lead peaceful and productive lives." She looked up at Chiyo to see what effect she was having.

"Now, then," she said, taking her glasses off and regarding Chiyo with a myopic gaze, "we in Japan have been in agreement with the Potsdam Declaration since the surrender, as you know. But the danger now is that if a clause to this effect—" she pointed to it with her glasses—"is not included in the prospective peace treaty, then neither the USSR nor China will have to feel legally bound to abide by this statement. The Americans and British, of course, have already sent their prisoners home." She put her glasses back on and looked firmly at Chiyo. "But the Russians and Chinese could keep our loved ones forever under the present circumstances. Even now, four years after the war has ended, many thousands of our compatriots have not returned. Unless we act quickly, we may lose everyone. Mrs. Tanaka, whose son has already returned, is helping us. Surely you, who still want your husband home, can do no less."

* * *

Within another week, Chiyo knew everyone in Hiroshima prefecture who had a relative still held prisoner in Siberia or China. It was like a groundswell. They came together in each other's houses and wrote letters to Diet members, to officials in the American Occupation Forces, to the International Red Cross, to any contacts people had in Russia and China. They collected petitions with long lists of signatures, taking turns standing in front of Fukuya Department Store or along the Hondori to collect even more names. Another group kept up a letter-writing campaign, pleading with the government, asking for financial support from every possible sympathizer. Chiyo and Mrs. Otsuka devised a series of sentences everybody could refer to so that each letter made the same request but sounded original.

Chiyo was pulled in three directions. The Movement, the growing success of Asahi Enterprises, and Hiroshi's push, beginning already in his first year of junior high, to pass the entrance exams to Tokyo University.

She gave her evenings to the Movement and to Yoko's and Hiroshi's studies. She spent her days at the new barnlike factory in Koi, giving training lessons, creating simple and clean designs the workers could imitate when they painted. She had convinced Nakayama-san to try out the clay *tsuchiningyō* dolls again, using his uncle's old kiln and molds. Isao thought the factory-finished wood cylinders and the clay molds should be manufactured to look as handmade as possible.

"But that's deceptive, isn't it?" Chiyo demanded.

"Well, it's successful. Orders are coming in from PX's and stores all over the country. And we're providing work for dozens of people who wouldn't have a livelihood otherwise."

She began to rely on Isao for advice in accounting and marketing, and on Nakayama for judging beauty and for the instinct of knowing what would sell. If the dolls satisfied him she could be confident about filling orders elsewhere.

But for now her heart was with the Movement. And with Hiroshi. It scared her sometimes that he was such an adult already, studying for the university with so much attention even though the exam was still four years away. All his ideas and instincts were right, and he never bumbled like ordinary children. But she worried about his single-mindedness and his overabundance of self-esteem.

Yoko, on the other hand, was never a worry, always eager and enthusiastic, sympathetic and sensitive. She was ready to try anything, not even noticing when she failed. "Oops!" she would say when the tea spilled, the rice bowl broke, the answer to the math problem was wrong. Then she would go right on with what she was doing. It was Yoko's help with the household tasks that made it possible for Chiyo to work full-time at the factory during the day and full-time for the Movement at night.

By the end of July, Chiyo had been elected delegate to represent Hiroshima at the Movement's national convention in Tokyo. They would focus on inhumane treatment of the prisoners and their over-long detention. Their plan was to protest and demonstrate loudly until the clause demanding return of all Japanese nationals was included in the peace treaty.

She left Yoko in charge of the house, and in early August, she and Mrs. Otsuka boarded the express night train, the *Asakaze*. The next morning they joined the hunger strike at Sojiji temple in Yokohama. Seventy elected delegates, representing families of the prisoners of war, sat for days spread out across the huge *tatami* in the main temple hall, knees bent with their legs tucked under them, hands folded on their laps, praying, bowing, chanting.

But still the official negotiators did not agree to their demands. They continued to fast, moving to Chidorigafuchi Park in Tokyo, where people set up tents and sat together through long, hot, sleepless nights, talking by candlelight, taking turns with the vigils. More people joined them, including returned ex-prisoners. Sympathetic Diet members and agency officials gave long speeches, and the protesters sat nights around a small campfire singing in low voices, the flames from their tiny charcoal fire lighting up their faces, bringing a sense of camaraderie and hope. They would not eat. They would starve if they did not achieve their goal. It was exhilarating, and she did not notice her hunger. There were housewives, young children, seventy-year-old grandfathers, even some who were grandchildren of men still in Siberia.

They sat waiting for some word from the negotiating committees, the men in their summer underwear, their shirts and trousers hanging on the long clotheslines surrounding the park encampment, the women fanning themselves against the flies and the heat, all of them talking interminably about the past and the war and their foolishness for believing in the military leaders. And their hardships and hunger.

The former prisoners of war sat gazing with hollow eyes at the fire, sometimes sharing memories. The hunger strike and the homeland stories were nothing compared to their stories from Siberia.

"In the good times," one of them said, "it was a tiny piece of sour black bread for lunch, and a handful of millet for lunch and dinner. In the bad times it was no breakfast at all, and for lunch and dinner combined a piece of bread that had to be divided among five men. We chose an engineer to do it, all of us watching like hawks. Then we divided the crumbs, too."

Another voice sounded. Chiyo could see only a profile against the moon. "My friend—he's dead now, rest his soul—he found a frozen potato lying in the snow when he was marching back from work. Took every milligram of energy to lean over and pick it up, but it looked so good he could hardly wait to get it into the coals of our *petchuka*, you know, the Manchurian-style stove. We all sat there, salivating, watching it roast, thinking of the roasted potatoes we'd eaten in Japan. But when it unfroze, we saw it was not a potato. It was horse shit. Frozen horse shit."

The women gasped.

"Did you eat it?" asked the six-year-old, wide-eyed. The man laughed gruffly and did not answer.

When the moon was high and the men thought the women had gone to sleep, Chiyo heard other stories, ones they would not tell the women. Stories about corpses lying frozen on the ground until there was a pile big enough to bury, about eating wild grass and dying from the stomach disorders, about frostbite and gangrene, about friends who had fallen in the snow on the way from work and had to be left there frozen because anybody who stopped to help them would freeze too.

During one long vigil, an ex-prisoner next to Chiyo thought he'd known Shintaro and described him accurately.

"You know, come to think of it," he said, "it was your husband who organized the cooking class. He and this man who'd been a cook on a passenger steamer thought of the idea. He gave lessons on Sundays. We'd vote on something like, say, *tendon,* rice with crisp shrimp on top. Then the cook would tell us every detail— how to choose good shrimp and fresh onions in the market, how to make the batter, how hot to make the oil, how to make a good dipping sauce. We'd take notes using pieces of steel to scratch with on a leather belt or soot from the stove to write on cloth. Then we'd have a question period and discussion, arguing about the best place to buy shrimp, and the regional styles of cooking it. Then each man would put away his own record, saying he would make it exactly that way when he returned to Japan."

Chiyo could see, even in the dark, the tears glistening as they coursed down the man's cheek.

"Every Sunday," he said. "Every Sunday we spent like that."

At dawn when everyone gathered for prayers and water-drinking, Chiyo caught sight of the unmistakable contour of Nakayama-san's back. She couldn't believe her eyes, which she didn't much trust, considering their unreliability in Maizuru. But there he was, the familiar shirt and old baggy pants with the too-long belt pushed all the way through the loops at the back.

"You here?" she exclaimed when he turned around and revealed his usual homely, open face. "Somebody in your family still in Siberia?"

He grinned, giving her the same look he gave her painted dolls. "No, nobody. It's just that all my old unit members proclaimed a reunion because of the vigil here. They said I had to come. No excuses allowed. What they really wanted was a chance to toss down a few cups of sake, which is what we've been doing for days now, and I'll tell you, I've had enough of that. So I volunteered to be the delegate."

He hitched up his trousers. That cumbersome belt wasn't even useful, she thought.

Suddenly there was a commotion throughout the camp, people shouting and waving flags. A man appeared on the platform used for announcements.

"We have won!" he shouted. "The government has listened to our pleas and finally agreed to amend their draft of the peace treaty! The clause demanding return of the prisoners will be included!"

A great cry went up from the hunger strikers, and a surge of excitement. Shintaro was surviving in his own way, defeating the Siberian winters, and now he was coming home. Everybody was coming home.

The loudspeaker reverberated, echoing and pounding back into her ears. People surged into the park singing and chanting, crushing each other, thousands of them packed into that tiny space. She was squashed against Nakayama-san so tightly that she could feel his ridiculous long belt cutting into her ribs.

They circled the row of hibachi with hot coals where the zōsui, the soft rice, was simmering. They linked arms and sang victory songs, then passed around the ritual bowls of soft rice, each of them taking two or three bites to break the fast. It tasted strange, and she felt weak for the first time.

Nakayama pulled her through the throng, out of the park, and down through narrow streets to a tiny shop very much like the one in Maizuru. The waiter let out a shout when he saw Nakayama, pounding him on the back. "I heard you were home," he said. He grabbed Nakayama by the shoulders and held him at arm's length.

"Home from Siberia. Not so much the worse for wear, either, from the looks of it. Well, sit down. What do you think of the old place? It was bombed out, you know, and the owner died, but I opened it up again when I came home." He nodded to Chiyo. "Remember?" he asked. "I met you right after your wedding. On your way home to your husband's native place."

"No," said Nakayama quickly. "My wife died in the bomb. I'm sorry. I thought you knew. This is Mrs. Hara. She's a business associate from Hiroshima. We're both delegates at the hunger strike in the park. It just ended, and I remembered your shop. I was hoping you'd be here."

The man bowed. *"Sumimasen,"* he said. "My deepest apologies."

Nakayama returned the bow. "I was also hoping that you had some of your famous *soba,"* he said, "those buckwheat noodles we always ate together."

The man grinned. "Well, it's hard to get it, but there's plenty for the likes of you."

"Thank you," Nakayama said, "But just one order. And two bowls of dipping sauce. Mrs. Hara here has been on a fast for a week. Her husband's still in Siberia." He looked sternly at Chiyo. "Only a few bites, now," he warned her. "It has to be gradual."

They were summertime noodles, nicely chilled and spread out on a bamboo screen, peppered with bits of shredded seaweed. All the summers of her childhood were in the taste, and she could see the enjoyment on Nakayama's face, too, as he twined them around his chopsticks, dipping them in the sauce, slurping them down his skinny throat, his Adam's apple bobbing.

Back at the tent, packing up her belongings, she was almost ready to leave when Mrs. Otsuka appeared, looking querulous and irritated.

"We searched all over," she said accusingly. "Whatever could have happened to you?"

But Chiyo didn't have to explain. Nakayama stepped between her and Mrs. Otsuka. "I've just found my cousin here after not seeing her for twenty-five years. We grew up together, you see, and I've been off in Manchuria all this time and then taken prisoner of war. We just had to go off and have a bowl of noodles together. In fact, Mrs. Hara mentioned you, and we looked around, but it was impossible to find anybody in that crowd. And now I've persuaded her to stay and have dinner with me and the rest of the relatives before she goes back to Hiroshima."

Mrs. Otsuka's rigid demeanor softened. "Cousins!" she exclaimed. "How wonderful for you, Mrs. Hara. And just at the moment of success."

"Anyway," she said, "I'm off to Fukuoka with the others. The work has only just begun, of course, but I am encouraged, aren't you?"

She grasped Chiyo's hand in a moment of ebullience, then bowed deeply to Nakayama and started off across the park, her heavy suitcase dragging down one shoulder as she walked lopsided, crablike, off the park grounds.

It was a moment before Chiyo realized that Mrs. Otsuka had left her, and she was in Tokyo with a man she didn't know very well.

"I'm sorry," he said. "Lying like that. I couldn't help myself. Your friend Mrs. Otsuka inspired it in me." He grinned again, then looked quickly away. "Actually, you know, I do have relatives here. My sister's down from Naruko with her husband and he wants to take me off into Asakusa on a drinking binge. The only way I can save myself from that is to insist on bringing you along. Then he'll have to bring my sister, too." He picked up her suitcase. "Just come and have dinner with us. They're staying in Shinjuku at the Sakura Inn, and you'll like my sister. She's been making *kokeshi* dolls all her life. And I can get you down to Tokyo station for the midnight train home. I might even ride back to Hiroshima with you."

Chiyo followed him out of the park.

Chapter Twenty-three

Of course I remember you. Every-body on the island knew the Ogawa children." Nakayama's sister, Midori, settled at the table in their room at the inn, poured out the remaining sake. "But I'm afraid I wouldn't have recognized you. I haven't been in Miyajima since I was a child."

They raised their cups to each other and drank, Nakayama and his brother-in-law all in one gulp, Midori and Chiyo sipping.

Midori's husband held out his cup for more sake. She searched around and found another bottle to pour from, filling his cup again. He drank that down, too, then began humming the strains of an old war song. "Remember that one?" he asked Nakayama. "We were marching south, down through Burma." He finished the song, clapping his hands, then shoved his cup toward his wife again.

"There's hardly any left," she said, pouring out more of it. He drank, muttering about the bunch of bumbling fools who'd led them into the war and defeat. After that, he succumbed to deep, snoring slumber.

"He thinks he could have saved the world if they'd just made him a general," Midori said, pushing him over onto the *futon*. But there was a softness in her gaze when she covered him with the quilt.

"You know," Midori said, "Younger Brother's been writing me letters about you. I thought you might be a little stuck up, being a member of the Ogawa family, but you're not at all like I imagined. And somehow I was hoping—well, Hide-chan hasn't talked about any woman except you since his wife died."

"*Nē-san!*" Nakayama's face turned beet red. "I've told you all about her husband. I remember writing you that. He is in Siberia, so of course we have a lot in common. And I wrote you that she has a good sense of design and color, can paint well, and has helped my business. That's all."

Midori giggled. "I'm sorry," she said. "But she's like one of the family. Like I've always known her."

"It's because you're both artists," Nakayama said. "My sister was the best doll painter in Naruko, Mrs. Hara. Everybody said so. But now she doesn't have time, being a farmer's wife." He stared at the prone form next to Midori. "He's a good man, though. You're lucky he came home from the war and that you're all alive."

Midori had fallen asleep, her head resting on her folded arms on the table. Chiyo and Nakayama pulled her gently onto the *futon* next to her husband and covered her with the rest of the quilt.

Nakayama looked at his watch and gasped. "Eleven-thirty! We've missed the train! We'll never get to the station in time."

Chiyo had given up the train long ago. "I can get the one in the morning. Nobody expects me home yet anyway. I said I'd send a wire."

He was sitting close to her, his homely face warm and gentle. "A whole week of fasting," he said, gazing at her with admiration, "and that terrible trip to Maizuru just before, and all the work with the Movement and Asahi Enterprises." He touched both her shoulders and held her at arm's length, examining her face. "You must be exhausted," he said. "We'd better say it's enough for tonight."

He smelled of fresh wood shavings. His clean white rumpled shirt, open at the throat, revealed the white flesh below his tanned and wrinkled neck. She held her back straight, not moving away from him, and agreed to being exhausted.

"But I'm not sleepy," she insisted.

"What happened to your wife?" she blurted out in the next instant. "And your children and your uncle and your cousin?"

"It's hard for me to talk about it," he said. "It brings back too much, you know."

She knew. She'd listened often enough when people spoke of it.

Just a stray remark could touch it off and bring back the memories full force. Once it started, there was no way to stop. You had to let the visions march out in front of you, play themselves out. Or talk. Expel it all by telling every detail until the devil was banished once more. Then some other reference would start it off again. Or the sight of a ruined building. Sometimes even the turn of someone's head, the motion of his hand. It was always there ready to flare up when someone touched a candle to it. She knew that about herself and everyone who'd been in the bomb. She didn't think Nakayama had it inside him, too. But of course he did. Kazuko and Fusako had it. Yoko and Hiroshi. Everyone who'd watched them die.

"I'm sorry," she said. "I shouldn't have asked you that."

He startled her, putting his arms completely around her, holding her close, brushing his eyes against her hair. Then he let her go again. "I'd like to get it out just once. It took me a long time to find out what happened and piece it all together."

His wife, Sumiko, had left their son, Hidenori, in Miyajima and taken her baby to the village of Otake southwest of Hiroshima to help their cousin Keiko care for sick relatives. After a few days, they sent Keiko's six-year-old son, Yuki, to Miyajima to stay with his grandparents, where it was cooler and the food supply better.

On August 6 it was Otake's turn to volunteer for the *tatemono sokai,* tearing down buildings to make a fire lane, the job Kenichi had been doing. Every family was responsible for sending one member. There were no exceptions. Sumiko volunteered to go in place of Keiko's sick mother-in-law.

"They were all marching, two abreast, from the railroad station," Nakayama said. "Keiko and Sumiko were each carrying their babies on their backs, and then—"

"I know about Otake," said Chiyo. "Every family from that village lost a member. Some of them two or three."

Nakayama nodded. "They were all there. Just by some stroke of fate. My cousin, my wife, the two babies, and even my uncle, Keiko's father. He found them just by chance not long after the bomb fell. And they all managed to get on a boat to Miyajima."

"So they survived that day?"

"Well, it seems Sumiko had just stepped into the shadow of a brick wall when the blast came. She thought that's what saved her, you see. But our baby—she was strapped to her mother's back and her face was burned crisp. She didn't cry at all, just stared up at her mother."

"But she was still alive?"

"Yes." Nakayama nodded. It was a while before he could continue.

"And the others?" Chiyo prodded.

"Keiko's baby died only a few seconds after the explosion. But she insisted on carrying the body onto the boat and home to Miyajima in her arms. Then my daughter died on the boat when they were halfway there. Keiko died after they landed at Miyajima while they were carrying her to the infirmary. It was just at dusk, my aunt said. And everybody's face was gray, both the living and the dead.

"I know all this because my aunt kept a record of it. Sometimes I think she did it for me because she thought no one in the family would be alive when I got home.

"Anyway, many ironies. My son, Hidenori, took the early ferry into Hiroshima the next morning. He knew his mother and aunt had gone in with the Otake Brigade. He left at dawn to find them, so nobody was awake to tell him that his mother had already come home.

"The ferry pilot remembered seeing my son boarding the ferry. He tried to keep the boy from going, but Hidenori insisted he knew exactly where to look. That was the last report anyone had of him. He never returned from Hiroshima."

Chiyo gasped. "Just like Kenichi!"

"Yes. Except that he was a bit younger. Just eleven and in his last year of elementary school."

Chiyo reached across the table and clutched Nakayama's hand.

Nakayama placed his hand on hers and continued. "My aunt brought everyone home the next day—my wife and the ashes of Keiko and the babies. Even though Sumiko hadn't been burned, she lost her hair a few days later. And she couldn't keep anything in her stomach. But she kept trying to get out of bed and go into Hiroshima—to look for Hidenori. Once she even got dressed and started down the hill to the dock, but she had to come back.

"Then Uncle died and my aunt fell into a lethargy. There were no more entries in her journal, and she couldn't seem to pay attention to Sumiko or Yuki, the neighbors said. Then she died too. Nobody knows why. She hadn't been in the bomb herself. Some people think she took her own life, but I don't believe she would desert Sumiko or her own grandchild.

"Anyway, Sumiko died a few days later, the neighbors said. Nobody could give me any more information than that. Not until one night last year when Yuki woke up in the middle of a bad dream.

"He was crying, and the whole story came out of him then.

238

After Aunt died, Sumiko got up and went to the door, but she fell. Yuki pulled her back into bed. She didn't move for a long time and he was afraid to leave her because he kept hoping she would wake up.

"Then finally when she did wake up, her face turned black. Right before his eyes. As if she were being burned from inside out, he said. Her lips were bright red and curled up, so that he couldn't recognize her any longer. He sat by her bed two whole days, afraid to leave her. And now he hates himself because he didn't go for help, but he was afraid, and he was only six. All he could do was stare at her. And after that, he carried the vision of her face in his head for three years. Until the night he woke up from the nightmare. Then he drew a picture of it. At least getting it down on paper got it out of his head for a while."

"Grandmother looked the same way when she died," Chiyo said.

Nakayama nodded, then, looking straight ahead, continued to talk.

"All the time I was in Siberia, watching my friends die, and trying to stay alive myself, I pledged that if I lived and got home to Sumiko and the children, I would watch every move they made, listen to every word they said, every complaint, every sniffle when they had a cold. I swore I would never let a flower bloom or the seasons change without savoring the moment. And I decided I would spend my life making my family happy and creating something small and beautiful like our dolls."

It seemed to Chiyo, sitting in the half darkness, that Nakayama's face had become a stone bodhisattva.

"But I forgot all that when I got home and found out. You see, the baby was born after I was sent to Manchuria. I only saw pictures of her. I never held her in my arms."

He shifted his gaze from the wall to his lap. "But Sumiko." He shook his head. "That death was the hardest. She was a beautiful woman." He looked insistently at Chiyo. As if he thought she wouldn't believe him. "She had the right to a graceful death.

"I kept seeing the picture that Yuki drew. Seeing it all the time in my dreams. Even now, I can't get it out of my mind sometimes."

Nakayama removed his hands from her grasp and wiped the perspiration from his face.

"Anyway, Yuki was the only relative left in Miyajima when I got home. The neighbors had been shifting him around from house to house and he didn't feel much wanted by anybody. We were very glad to see each other, I can tell you. He was eight by then, and we just set up housekeeping together. Then I started trying to find out what happened to Hidenori. I searched everywhere for him. I spent a whole year at it before I gave up."

"I know," Chiyo said. "Giving up was the hardest."

A tear coursed down his cheek, and she reached out and touched his moist face.

"I've brought Yuki up as my son," he said. "I didn't want to live anymore when I first came home. But then I got busy taking care of him. And I opened up the shop again. I knew that's what my uncle would have wanted me to do. And things were getting better until the night Yuki told me about his dream. Then I thought I'd just walk into the sea down below the big *torii*. It was midnight. I even had my shoes off, standing in the water, ankle deep. I heard it lapping up against the support poles under the shrine, and then I sensed the calm around me. It was unbelievably vast. Huge and powerful. As if the universe were humming. That's when I remembered the pledge I'd made in Siberia and thought of how brave Yuki'd been and how hard it would be for him alone. So I climbed out of the water and put my shoes back on. And in the autumn of that year, the maple leaves were such a deep red, wilder than I'd ever seen them. And the following spring you came."

He held her at arm's length, looking into her eyes. "You're one of the reasons I'm glad I'm here. I'm grateful for you and Yuki and the shop and the moments I can spare to make *kokeshi* dolls."

He let his hands slip from her shoulders. "I might have been an artist, you know, but I didn't get the training. So, I'm a doll maker, and that's good enough for me."

He touched her cheek once more. "I'm just glad I know you again as an adult. I liked you very much when you were a little girl. I still do." He smiled wistfully and stood up. "If we're going to catch the morning train, you'll need some sleep. I've kept you awake all night as it is."

He took two *futon* from the closet, spread them out on separate sides of the room, then collapsed onto one of them and fell into a sound sleep.

She lay on her own *futon,* on the other side of the room, and stared at the ceiling.

Sometime in the gray dawn, half asleep and half awake, she thought she heard her name whispered.

"Chiyo!"

Lingering close to her ear, restless. She turned and murmured. Was it at the other ear too?

"Chiyo!"

It was an insistent whisper.

She fell asleep, and it was brilliant sunshine when she awoke, the maid coming in to fold up the bedding and arrange their room for breakfast. Midori and her husband were bleary-eyed, looking at her puzzled, wondering why she was still there. But they were too polite to ask.

Chapter Twenty-four

At THE END OF OCTOBER, SHIPS CAME one after another. Chiyo and the children scanned every newspaper. Everyone in the neighborhood looked for Shintaro's name too, everyone in the factory, in Inokuchi, in the Movement, even Mrs. Tanaka in Kyoto.

In early November, two ships arrived in one day. No one knew when there would be another one.

Chiyo lay in bed filled with inertia. She had anemia, the doctor said. And kidney disorders. And she needed more vitamin B. She took shots. Mrs. Ikeda convinced her to go for tests to the American doctors at the Atomic Bomb Casualty Commission, which had opened a lab in Ujina.

"They're not giving treatment, you know," Isao said when he stopped by after his trip to Maizuru. "You're just a guinea pig for their experiments. If you're not dead, why aren't you? That's what they want to know."

"Isao! They were friendly and helpful. And they all wear immaculate white coats; the nurses, too."

Isao threw up his hands. "It's your body," he said. Then he sat down by her bed, berating her. "You can't be in charge of the whole world, you know. It's enough just to be mother to your children and president of Asahi Enterprises. Then you run off to Tokyo with that crazy Movement."

"But Isao—"

"I know it's important, but you've got to have a better sense of when to stop. And why don't we look into getting you a maid? At least someone to help with the housework."

"A maid!" There's hardly room in this shack for the three of us. Where would a maid even stand while she's doing the work?"

He looked around him, then sighed.

"So, what happened in Maizuru?" she asked.

Isao's shipping contacts had been investigating the whereabouts of Yamanaka Tadanori, the man she'd seen at the Maizuru station. They had unearthed a rumor about someone on the *Takasago Maru* jumping overboard, but no one could verify it. And there was no information at all about Shin Hara. No listing at the agency or in any other newspaper except the one in Hiroshima. A misprint, the bureaucrats in Maizuru had said.

In November, Isao had gone to Maizuru himself to demand an audience with the Occupation authorities.

"I made such a pest of myself those SCAP officers finally agreed to see me," he told Chiyo. "It was unprecedented, I think."

He sat thoughtfully puffing on his American cigarette. "Five military giants in that room wearing crisp uniforms. Not a wrinkle in them. And a hostile Japanese-American soldier was interpreting." He laughed. "I had the feeling that if I made the wrong move, they'd shoot straight from the hip, reach down to their hidden holsters and fire away from under the table, then call in somebody to sweep up the body."

"Isao!"

He smiled, satisfied with her reaction. "Anyway, they insisted they had no information about anyone jumping overboard or anyone named Shin Hara."

Chiyo sat up abruptly and began to brush her hair back from her face. "So, there's not much hope, is there? We'll never find out."

"I'm not finished yet," Isao said. "I hired a private detective and sent him to Tokyo to investigate all the listings for Yamanaka in the phone book, at police boxes, in temples, anywhere else he could think of."

"But what an endless task, and how expensive!"

"Well, the detective found a letter addressed to him from a woman who was apparently his daughter. She'd been sent home from Manchuria as a baby when her mother died. It seems her grandparents sold her to a geisha house and now she's some rich man's mistress. After the detective offered her some money, she promised to keep us informed."

"How amazing!" Chiyo said. "That man at the station told me his wife died in Manchuria. If he's not the same man, it's certainly a coincidence."

"Yes." Isao nodded.

"It would be a relief to know," Chiyo said.

"Well, I'm convinced that Shintaro had nothing to do with the newspaper misprint or any of the rest of it," Isao said. "He'll appear one of these days. After all, you did receive a letter from him."

"I want proof!" Chiyo exclaimed, slamming her brush down on her knee. Then she looked at Isao's concerned face and was ashamed of herself, knowing what he'd done for her sake. "Did anyone go to the inn or talk to that prostitute again?" she asked in a softer voice.

"Yes. I went with the detective. We checked the register and there was a Kuwada Akinari, but no one named Yamanaka. Then we saw the prostitute, and the detective tried to make her repeat everything the man had said, but she got irritated. She'd apparently been interrogated by the American Intelligence, too, and anyway, the only reason she remembered Kuwada is because of you." He smiled at Chiyo. "She thought you had a lot of nerve. I think she rather admired you."

Chiyo worked at home, writing up painting instructions, tracing out patterns on paper, outlines on the dolls' faces. It kept her from thinking about Shintaro or the man in Maizuru. Even though it sometimes reminded her of Nakayama.

She couldn't rid herself of the nightmares. The face of the man in the inn kept looming up and smothering her, his rancid black mouth opening and swallowing her.

Once, in a predawn dream, Shintaro was home, looking just as he always had, acting as if his absence had all been a joke. He'd stepped down the street for some tobacco and stayed talking a bit longer than usual. What was all the fuss about? Everything was the same. But he was looking out the door at Kenichi standing on the roof in front of the sun. Then the explosion came. Then Shintaro turned around to reveal his nightmare face with the gaping black hole.

Mornings after the nightmares she awoke exhausted but forced herself out of bed, determined not to be sick.

Other nights, when she couldn't sleep at all, she lay conjuring up memories of Shintaro, cataloging tender moments. But often Nakayama's face appeared instead, bringing the fragrance of fresh *hinoki* wood, the aroma of maple cakes, the memory of the night in Tokyo. And the long train ride home. They had sat squashed together in the aisles on a spread-out newspaper all the way to Nagoya before they were lucky enough to get seats.

His presence, always next to her, was calm and steady. Shintaro had been like that, but this was different. Nakayama had no cynicism. Shintaro could be enormously enthusiastic. And enormously depressed. He measured people and things against his ideals and found them wanting. But being with homely, down-to-earth Nakayama was like standing before the ancient wooden Buddha in the Byodoin Temple in Uji. Serene and solid. And behind its head the carved wooden angels wafted like flames toward heaven, changing right before one's eyes from body to spirit, bursting near the summit into pure ecstasy.

Nakayama Hideo. She had heard Midori say his personal name for the first time that night in the inn. It was a youthful, innocent name. Like his personality. Small things made him irrepressibly happy. Half an hour out of Tokyo, he'd seen the hawkers selling famous Yokohama *shūmai* on the platform. Steam dough wrapped around minced pork, garlic, onions and mushrooms. Nakayama had pushed through the crowd and thrown the windows open, shouted out that he wanted three boxes. No, four. He gave one to the young widow and her son on the seat near them. Then he took the chopsticks out of the second and third boxes, gave a pair to Chiyo, and insisted that they share each one consecutively.

"This way, it's double enjoyment," he said.

With the fourth box, Nakayama moved all up and down the aisle, in among the people standing, sitting on suitcases, lying down.

"Isn't that good? Is there anything better in the world?"

"Ah, *shūmai!*" he exclaimed, plummeting himself down next to her again. "I dreamed of it so often in Siberia. How many times we all thought of *shūmai.*"

The next moment he slapped his palm against his forehead.

"Higuchi-san, of course! He's the one who got us talking about *shūmai!* He was from Yokohama!"

Sitting on the floor, surrounded by the passengers he'd befriended, Nakayama told the story of Higuchi-san. Everyone in the barracks had been sick with raging fever from typhoid. Higuchi-san, the only one well enough, had gone outside alone for water.

"We always sent two people, because the well was a solid wall of ice. One man had to hold the other's feet to keep from slipping while he dipped in. The moment that water was lifted out of the hot springs into the Siberian air, it turned into ice."

The sick men had waited fifteen minutes for Higuchi-san, but he didn't return.

"So two of us managed to get outside. And we found him. Frozen solid. One of his hands was sticking straight up in the air."

They dragged him back into the barracks, laid him by the stove, covered him with blankets, breathed hot air on him, but it didn't help.

"In the morning, we found his other mitten stuck to the wall of ice. You see, when he tried to move his hand, it came out of the mitten and he lost his balance."

Nakayama clutched his knees up under his chin. Every passenger in the train car was listening to his story now.

"But the irony is that he could have saved himself if he'd come right back into the barracks. But no. He tried dipping in again. By that time his hand was frozen. He couldn't control it, so he poured the dipper of water all over himself."

The widow's son gasped. The other passengers were silent. Nakayama picked up the last piece of *shūmai*. "If only Higuchi-san could have eaten this before he died."

"Give it to him now," said the widow's son.

On the floor of the train, Nakayama and the other passengers bundled up newspapers to form a three-tiered imitation of the kind of rice-cake offerings people presented at temples to the spirits of their dead. Then they set the *shūmai* on top, pressed their hands together, and said a silent prayer for Higuchi-san.

Back in Hiroshima, Chiyo and Nakayama had studiously avoided each other. When he came to Hiroshima for training meetings, she managed to be elsewhere. She no longer took the choice allotment of dolls to him personally; she sent them with Nakayama's shop girl, who lived in Hiroshima.

Once during her bout with anemia, a box of Miyajima maple cakes had arrived. "Don't forget to think about designs for the clay dolls," he wrote. "But take care of yourself first. Don't get overly tired."

She tried not to think of him. But he appeared uninvited in her dreams, coming to her in the night and lying down beside her, wrapping his long leather belt about them both, locking them together, clinging to her, breathing on her and pressing into her. They would never stop. Shintaro would come home. "What's this?" he would say. "Who's the man with the belt?"

She awoke, filled with shame, and sat in the dark, thinking deliberately of Shintaro, of the times she had swum with him out to the double rock where Kenichi and the others had been that last day of innocence. She and Shintaro, just home from their honeymoon, had lain on the flat beach behind the burnished white rock, blue sea lapping up and spreading around them, the sky the same color, covering them like a blanket. Ships far out in the sea, their engines murmuring softly. Hidden behind the rock, they removed their bathing suits and dipped them in the salt sea and lay together naked, their arms entwined, merging with the sea and the earth, their bodies the same color as the sand. No one existed anywhere else in the world. She delighted in the memory, then suddenly realized that the man she lay with in her dreams was Nakayama, not Shintaro.

She stared at photographs of Shintaro, trying to fix his face in her mind. It horrified her to think of Nakayama lying in Shintaro's place on their secret beach.

"Mama! Make him stop. He's bothering us. We can't study."

Yoko's voice shot through her like a knife. They were in the sitting room, gathered around Yasu, who was tutoring them in math, especially Kyoko, preparing for her entrance exams to Hiroshima Girls' High School. Yoko, who had taken the exam at the junior high level, was not required to take it again.

"Hiroshi keeps asking us questions and slows us down."

"Oh, Kyoko doesn't have to worry." Hiroshi spit out the words. "She'll pass. It's only a dumb girls' school. I'm the one who has to support us."

"You're not supporting us," Yoko shouted. "Mama is." She smothered Hiroshi's voice in a *zabuton*.

"It's okay," Yasu said. "They can both learn it." He began his routine again, assigning each one the same problem, timing them, comparing their answers.

Chiyo threw off her covers and went out to the sitting room to help Hiroshi.

That night she had enough energy to make them all a bowl of *udon* noodles before Yasu took the long streetcar ride back to Ujina.

The next day she set about designing the maple-leaf pattern for the clay dolls, and the day after that, a simplified pattern with plum blossoms.

* * *

Six ships arrived in Maizuru the end of November. Chiyo felt as if she had spent her life holding her breath.

"Maybe you should go up to Maizuru again," Mrs. Ikeda suggested. "Just wait at the dock. Stand there and wish as hard as you can."

Chiyo merely nodded. Nothing could lure her to Maizuru again.

Four ships in early December. Then the terrible year of 1949 ended.

One ship in January, another in February.

"The big push will be in the spring," Mrs. Otsuka said. "They always send more in the spring."

Kyoko was losing her enthusiasm for her exams. There were days she didn't feel like studying with Yoko after school, days she couldn't take part in the gym classes. Sometimes she didn't feel like getting out of bed, Mrs. Ikeda said. She gave up her part in the school play. She stopped playing volleyball.

The doctors said Kyoko had a light case of anemia like Chiyo's. Nothing unusual. Everybody in Hiroshima had that.

"You always seem healthy," Chiyo said to Mrs. Ikeda, "and yet you walked all through the city."

"Well, I guess what saved me is that I was in Danbara behind the mountain."

"But that doesn't explain it," Chiyo insisted. "Mr. Takano was way out in the suburbs when—"

"No, that was different." Mrs. Ikeda said, folding her hands inside her apron. "You see, Mr. Takano stayed in the city for a week afterwards. But Kyoko and I went right back out to the country and—" She looked helplessly at Chiyo. "Do you realize how many times we've talked about this and tried to make sense out of it? Well, there isn't any sense. It's just—" Tears filled Mrs. Ikeda's eyes and she dabbed impatiently at them with her apron. "You know," she went on, "sometimes I think it's those keloid scars. If you're hurt externally it protects your innards some way."

Chiyo touched her own scar. It was like a tiny red worm crawling down the side of her cheek, just to the right of her mouth. She forgot about it most of the time except for moments when she looked in the mirror and considered what Shintaro would think when he first saw it.

What had Nakayama thought?

* * *

248

Kyoko took her exams on a biting, raw morning in March. She and Yoko hovered together in the living room over their books one last moment. They were on the verge of fifteen, like butterflies emerging from cocoons, their straight, bobbed hair sweeping down over their faces. But they were different from each other. Yoko was like a woodblock print by Sharaku. Strong, definite lines to her face and character. She made decisions quickly.

Kyoko did not make decisions. She blended in with her surroundings, changing shape and texture like gossamer to fit the moment. But her smile was constant. And ethereal. Once she had spread her hands out on the table, sitting next to Chiyo. There were transparent blue veins running through them, like the delicate, wiggling fish that swam through the waters near the edge of the shore on Miyajima.

Today, Kyoko turned her smile on Yoko, who was shooting rapid-fire questions at her. "It's all right, Yoko-chan, we've tried enough, and if I don't pass, we can still do things together. We don't have to be in the same school."

Mrs. Ikeda appeared in the entranceway, shivering from the biting wind. "They gave me the day off so I can go stand outside with the other mothers. Frankly, I don't know what good it does. But if everybody else's mother is there—"

"I'm going with you, Mrs. Ikeda." Yoko ran for her sweater. "It's vacation for me, so I can keep you company."

Chiyo, watching them depart, stared out down the street to the long line of mothers standing out on the school grounds, mutely waiting in the cold wind for their daughters to take the exam. What a terrible waste of time it was! And all that energy poured into algebraic and geometric formulas! What was the point of it for Kyoko? And what did mathematics and physics lead to anyway? It led to atomic bombs and death and destruction.

Four days later they waited in the sitting room while Kyoko and her mother went over to look at the list. Yoko was in the entranceway, peering out the door. Yasu and Hiroshi were playing with Mrs. Ikeda's four-year-old grandchild, Kunio, rolling him a rubber ball. He chortled gleefully, reaching out to catch it, usually missing and letting it roll past him into the *genkan,* where Yoko picked it up and threw it back. He had inherited Kyoko's sunshine smile, and he beamed at Yoko whenever he received the ball. He seldom cried. Everything that happened was instant joy for him. But still, at age five he could only say a few words.

"Here they come," shouted Yoko. "And she passed. They're both smiling!"

Everyone streamed out of the house into the street, circling Kyoko. Yasu threw his student cap up in the air and shouted, *"Banzai!"*

A thin blanket of wet snow covered the ground, and they stepped through it, back over to the school grounds to look at Kyoko's name for themselves.

People were standing in clumps, bowing and congratulating each other. Some were still searching through the lists, holding their faces rigid. Chiyo saw a girl and her mother scan the list, then watched them depart, feeling anguish herself for their disappointment.

Moving forward in line just behind the mother and daughter was a gaunt figure in an old khaki army overcoat, the kind the man at the railroad station in Maizuru had been wearing. And the man himself had the same stance. Chiyo shivered and pulled her shawl closer around her shoulders, breathing in cold air so deeply that it made her cough. The man turned abruptly and stared at her, holding her briefly in his gaze. She saw the same thinness around the cheeks, the same resemblance to Shintaro. He turned and moved quickly away. As if she had interrupted him before he finished scrutinizing the list. His pace quickened and he almost stumbled as he hurried out of the school gate into the darkening afternoon.

A moment later, Chiyo was caught up in Kyoko's triumph. Mrs. Ikeda invited them for tea at a new shop on the Hondori, and Chiyo, caressed by the warm fragrance of the tea and Kyoko's sweet smile, buried her anxieties. There were thousands of gaunt, hungry-looking men in Japan, all of them wearing old army overcoats. And somehow Kyoko's success seemed an omen of good things to come.

There were two ships in April.

"Now, they're beginning," said Mrs. Otsuka. They're finally going to bring every one of those three hundred thousand prisoners home."

In May, there were no ships.

"Last year, they didn't start to come until June," said Mrs. Otsuka.

In June war broke out between North and South Korea. It appeared there would be no ships until the conflict was over.

On August 6, 1950, the fifth anniversary of the disappearance of

Kenichi and the third month of the Korean War, the Occupation authorities strictly forbade public observances of any kind. The military police were everywhere, making sure there were no gatherings, demonstrations, protests. They maintained strict surveillance over every activity the Occupation thought even faintly left wing.

Some artists had published a new illustrated magazine called *Pikadon*, meaning a bright, shining flash of an explosion, the nickname people gave to the atomic bomb. Chiyo, charmed by the illustrations, poems and stories, had begun looking for a copy when the magazines were suddenly seized by the Occupation authorities. Further publication was prohibited.

Isao was outraged. He showed everyone his copy when the family gathered on August 6 for memorial services.

"There's nothing subversive here," he said, "just an account of what happened. Why can't those Americans allow the simple truth?"

Nobody answered him.

"They're not even calling it war in Korea," he continued. "It's a police action. In a few years, they'll have everybody thinking they didn't drop the bomb at all."

Chiyo sighed. "Well, it could have been worse. The Russians could have occupied us and sent us all to Siberia."

"I know," said Isao. "But all this bragging about the American way and its freedom of the press. A bit hollow, wouldn't you say?" He sat, cross-legged, in a pensive mood.

Chiyo realized that Isao was about to begin one of his polemic discussions and that eventually he would pull her into the argument.

"You know, Professor Saiga has written an inscription for the cenotaph they're building in the Peace Park. It says, 'Rest in peace, for we shall not repeat this evil.'"

He sat smoking, the family gathered around and listening to him. "People are already arguing about it. He says one of his colleagues suggested: 'Howl out from the bottom of your graves because apparently the error is going to be repeated and soon. Any day now in Korea.'" He laughed gruffly. "And another professor said to forget the inscriptions and demand a war criminal trial against the ones who dropped the bomb."

Isao ground out his cigarette. "Of course, the Americans won't like being included in the error. They'll just say, as they always do, that we brought it on ourselves."

"It will make a wonderful inscription," Chiyo said quietly. "It is the fault of all humanity. You know, the Americans didn't know how terrible the bomb would be. But now they know, they'll never drop another one. It's war that causes cruelty. Not people."

Isao stared at Chiyo as if she were a stranger.

"You really believe that, don't you, Chi-chan? After all that's happened to you. Kenichi obliterated from the earth without a trace. And your husband up there in Siberia freezing and starving."

She was too stunned to interrupt him.

"After all that!" He shook his head in disbelief.

"Of course I do. Look what people have accomplished! They invented the wheel and then carriages and automobiles. And writing systems almost simultaneously in China and Egypt and then literature. Think of the Mona Lisa and that beautiful, smiling Buddhist statue, the Kudara Kannon, created on different sides of the earth, but with the same spirit. And how about playing grass reeds and then symphonic music? Isn't that progress?"

"Yes," agreed Isao, "and so are bows and arrows, swords, gunpowder, bombs, airplanes to drop them, then this final sophistication with the power to blow up the world. That's progress, too."

Chiyo said nothing for a moment. But she couldn't be silent. He was so wrong. "But there aren't despotic emperors anymore who slash off people's heads just because the soup isn't hot enough. And look at the Americans. We were taught to believe they would kill all the men and rape the women if they won the war, but they didn't, did they?"

"No, but our own Japanese soldiers in Nanking did. And when they finished raping women, they buried people alive, hung them on telephone poles and roasted them from underneath, showered them with nitric acid. Did you know that?"

"Our soldiers?" Chiyo asked. "Our own Japanese soldiers? I can't believe that! It's not true."

"That's what a Chinese survivor testified in a law court in Tokyo," Isao said. "And given the fanatic zeal of our recent military leaders, I believe it. In fact, it's been reported that between 1931 and 1945 there were at least ten million Chinese killed by the Japanese. The Americans killed maybe only half a million in Hiroshima and Nagasaki. But they destroyed the first one hundred thousand in just a few seconds. That's a lot of progress in destructive power. And at least the Japanese military had to go through war criminal trials. Who's to keep the Americans from dropping another bomb? They don't seem to understand how much destruction they've already caused. Your favorite medical center, the ABCC, claims that only seventy-five thousand people died in Hiroshima, but we know, don't we, that they're not counting Kenichi and all the others who vaporized into thin air. The *Chugoku* newspaper has quite a different estimate." Isao searched around through the papers on his writing desk. "Here it is," he said, reading it out. "They've counted two hundred and sixty thousand who died outright; one hundred sixty-three thousand are missing or injured, sixty-three thousand houses destroyed, and thirty-two hundred acres damaged." He put down his paper and took off his glasses, regarding Chiyo. "That's pretty good for five minutes' worth of work."

Chiyo felt hopeless, wishing Isao would stop.

"Now, then," he continued, "those figures compare quite well with all the massacres of the past, don't they? Of course there weren't as many people living then. And you can argue that the Americans didn't know what they were doing and wouldn't have had the stomach to drop that bomb if they hadn't been so high in the air, but you must remember that they did drop another one three days later."

He looked at his desk again, searching through more papers. Chiyo suspected that he was in the midst of writing a letter to the editor and that he was trying out his theories on her.

"And there are the carefully premeditated Nazi horrors," he went on. "They were planned before a war even started. And the death toll was much greater there. Nine million people. It's hard to find any justification for that.

"Maybe you could say the rape of Nanking was done in a frenzy of wartime hatred, but why did it go on so long? Couldn't one of the officers have stopped and looked around and said, 'This is enough'?

"And I'm not forgetting the Soviets still using Japanese and German prisoners for slave labor. You could argue there's residual wartime hatred, but they're doing the same thing to their own countrymen who disagree with them. Doesn't it seem to you that the worst atrocities are in the recent past? And not necessarily because of war? They built the bomb because of a war, but they didn't stop making them when it ended. It's human cruelty and evil that causes war, my dear. Not the other way around."

Chiyo had run out of arguments.

"If there's a God," he continued, "he's uninterested and uncaring. He put us on this earth and allowed us a choice, so he has the right not to intervene, and we can't complain for what we brought on ourselves. Hiroshima and Nagasaki are such tiny incidents compared to what's in store for us next."

He lapsed into silence, and Hiroshi stared at him, nodding.

Kazuko looked at Isao, her face sorrowful, almost ready to object, but instead she wandered off into the kitchen.

"It's possible," Isao said, "that all this happened before. To an ancient and highly technical society long before the Shang Dynasty. Maybe they blew themselves up without a trace, and it took thousands of generations to get this far again. Only next time we won't have to go through it again. Next time will be the end. Or it already is."

"Stop," Chiyo said. "I don't want to hear any more."

"Uncle," Hiroshi asked, "do you think the world will blow up before I even pass my exams to Tokyo University?"

Isao regarded him thoughtfully. "No, probably not," he said. "Especially if you're hoping for a way to get out of taking those exams."

They smiled, but Chiyo's strength had drained out of her. And all her optimism. Even the shimmering view of the placid Inland Sea did not hearten her. She realized that Isao did not think Shintaro would ever come home.

Chapter Twenty-five

THE PXs IN TOKYO, YOKOHOMA, YOKO-
suka, and Sasebo had been increasing their
orders. At Iwakuni they were doubling each week. The neighbors
and their friends, the children on vacation, Fusako home from the
university, all painted furiously. Still, they couldn't keep up with
the orders. No one could understand why the whole Allied Occupation was so fascinated by the dolls, especially when the quality
was suffering from being produced at breakneck speed. But they
kept working, knowing the fad might die at any moment and leave
them with a huge supply of unsold dolls.

Chiyo had rearranged her office at the factory, expanding it so
that her two trainers, Keiko Kakihara and Miyo Maebara, could
each have a separate desk. Morishita-san's assistant, Honda-san,
was skilled at carpentry, and he moved out the old boards and crates
she'd used for her desk, then built new furniture.

During the summer even the young housewives, who usually
preferred working at home, came with their babies on their backs so
they could work in the cooler, airy atmosphere of the factory and
with the companionship of the other people. Often Chiyo and the
two trainers walked up and down the long tables Honda-san had

built for the workers. They showed people how to make fast brush strokes, mix colors, wipe off designs they were dissatisfied with. Sometimes Chiyo traced new outlines for them. But there were others working at home who needed help, too, and the trainers began scheduling home visits again.

The summer had whirled by like an assembly line of doll faces with everyone, even Kazuko, working seven days a week. Finally, in honor of the traditional *Obon* festival on August 15, Kazuko declared a holiday.

They sat in the room downstairs where it was cooler, having their first taste since the war of Kazuko's famous *chawan mushi*, cold custard cooked with mushrooms and spinach, bits of cooked chicken and tender bamboo shoots. Kazuko had even found a few tiny shrimp to spread through the cucumber salad, and there were Okayama peaches, the kind Isao's business associate had delivered every year since those days in August 1945.

The *shōji* were open, the cool ocean breezes floating in, all of them surrounding Grandfather's lacquer table, silently concentrating on the nostalgic taste.

A knock at the door surprised them. Nobody knocked. Delivery boys and neighbors pushed the door aside, jangling the bell and shouting, *"Gomen kudasai!"* A knock implied something foreboding. They looked up to see a tall shadow on the other side of the smoked glass door beyond the hallway. Maybe the slant of the sun made it seem taller.

They sat frozen. The shadow stood patiently, waiting to be noticed. It finally knocked again, freezing them even further into inactivity.

"Sumimasen ga, Fusako-san wa irasshyaimasu ka? Excuse me, but is Fusako-san there?" In very polite Japanese. Clearly the voice belonged to a male foreigner.

"Who is it?" Kazuko hissed at Fusako. "Where did you ever meet such a person?"

Fusako looked helpless. "I don't know, Mother. I can't imagine. Just only—well, maybe those men at the PX, you know, when my teacher, Miss Samuelson, and I went out to talk to them about buying dolls. Remember? In the spring, when I was home?"

"But how did he find out where you live? Did you tell him?"

"Of course not, Mother. Miss Samuelson did all the talking. I just smiled."

"Surely Samuelson-sensei would understand not to give him your address," Kazuko said.

Isao stood, his face rigid, containing his outrage. "So, if he understands Japanese I will tell him that my daughter is not at home to visitors from Iwakuni."

"Oh, Father, don't—" Fusako took a deep breath and held it in her lungs, clasping her fingers together.

His journey to the door was interminable. The late afternoon sun blotted out the details, but they could see the outline of a man in an American military uniform towering over Isao, bowing formally and correctly. A string of polite and feminine-sounding verb endings came out of him. Then, to everyone's shocked surprise, the man entered the front hallway, came toward the raised *tatami* platform, removed his shoes, and climbed into the sitting room. A foreign soldier was actually in their house, invited by Isao.

Hiroshi stood up, bowing to the foreigner as if he had been chosen by the emperor to represent Japan. "How do you do?" he said in the careful English he had learned in school. "How do you like the weather here?" He continued to recite the English phrases he had learned, not looking at the foreigner, but instead at some spot on the wall. He offered the *zabuton* Kazuko had laid out. "Would you please be seated?" Hiroshi queried.

The foreigner did not respond to him. Instead, he knelt on the *tatami* and bowed to each of them. *"Hajimemashite,"* he murmured politely. "This is my first time to meet you."

They returned his bows. Chiyo's heart was thumping. She saw that Fusako, engaged in a deep, profound bow, was observing every detail of his person.

The foreigner finally moved over to the cushion Hiroshi had offered him earlier. He pulled it closer to Fusako, then lowered himself onto it and, with unusual grace, tucked his astonishing long legs under him, assuming the formal position men use only for tea ceremonies or state occasions.

"Hello, Miss Ogawa," he said pleasantly in English. Chiyo understood the greeting, but she couldn't understand what he said next. She was enthralled by the flow of words that cascaded out of him, clicking and clucking. Hissing, too. His mouth moved around so much. Maybe foreigners were born with more energy to begin with. They used up so much of it talking.

Everyone looked toward Fusako, but she didn't translate for them. The language was too fast even for her, Chiyo decided, and the man must have realized it, too, because he suddenly began speaking Japanese. They listened intently, hardly understanding his extremely formal usage. And yet it was a marvel to hear this foreign person speaking their language.

He said that every time he went to Hiroshima on the streetcar, he wondered about the Miss Ogawa he had met at the PX. In fact he had asked everyone where the house of Ogawa was and had finally been told by one of the Japanese employees that if she was the daughter of Mr. Ogawa of the Toyokogyo Company, then his house was in Inokuchi beside the Inland Sea. "I have always admired this beautiful house by the sea," he said, "and finally today I had enough courage to stop and inquire about you."

He looked at each of them. They were silent, watching his mouth as he spoke. Chiyo had always believed that no outsider could be fluent in the language. Their teacher, Miss Samuelson, had taught in Hiroshima before the war and had been Chiyo's teacher as well as Akiko's and Fusako's. She had returned to Hiroshima to take up her duties again early in 1947, and they deeply admired her dedication and loyalty to old friends in spite of the war. But she could not speak Japanese well. Nor could any of the other American teachers at the Girls' School. All of them struggled courageously with it. Yet here was this young man using Japanese quite properly even though the form was stiff and archaic.

"Please excuse me for interrupting you in the enjoyment of your holiday," he said.

"*Dōzo, dōzo.*" Isao was being especially expansive. "Help yourself to these peaches here. They're from Okayama, which is famous for peaches. Fusako, explain that to him in English. And you! *Hora!*" He nodded toward Kazuko. "Go and bring him one of those glass dishes to eat his peaches from. And bring him some *chawan mushi* if there is any more."

Kazuko scurried out to the kitchen and was back again, kneeling down beside the foreigner and placing the *chawan mushi* on the table before him. She selected the juiciest-looking peach and peeled it, arranged it on the glass plate, accompanied by a tiny silver fork, then presented it to him, kneeling, one hand gingerly touching the *tatami*.

"Did you tell him about the Okayama peaches, Fusako? And explain what's in the *chawan mushi?*"

"I don't need to, Father. He can understand you."

"Tell him again. In English. To make sure."

"Do you know Okayama, which is the native place of this peach?" she asked the foreigner in Japanese.

He smiled at her and nodded. He was beaming. His face revealed so much. It was embarrassing that he didn't hide his feelings at all. "And this is *chawan mushi*," Fusako continued, enumerating on her fingers the ingredients included in it.

He listened to her with great attention. Pleasure showed in his face at everything they said, everything they gave him to eat. It made him seem so childlike and innocent. As if those Americans just let their children grow up with all their freedom and wonder intact. Hiroshi had been like that before the bomb.

"It is like a dream," the foreigner said. "Sitting here looking out on the Inland Sea, eating this delicious food. It is like being in heaven."

How Kenichi would have enjoyed this crazy foreigner. He would have imitated him for weeks afterwards, every nuance, every movement.

Isao smiled expansively and uttered a deep, guttural belly laugh. Chiyo had not heard one of those since long before the war. He was accepting an American cigarette, turning it over and looking at it with interest. "A Camel, is it? I have heard they are good." He was motioning again to Kazuko. "Remember the special sake? The kind we had for New Year's? Bring that."

Chiyo scurried out to the kitchen after Kazuko. It was getting serious, Isao offering his favorite sake.

"What is his name?" Chiyo whispered to Kazuko while they were heating the water for the sake. "Did you understand his name when he said it?"

"Bobbu. Something like that," said Kazuko. "Probably Fu-chan knows. Do you think he will like her too much, and come to visit her again? Oh, I hope not. I hope Fu-chan doesn't find him too fascinating and that he doesn't cause us lots of trouble and embarrassment. But he is interesting, don't you think? Have you noticed his face? How much it moves, and how often he changes expressions?"

"Exactly," said Chiyo. She and Kazuko always noticed the same things.

The water boiled, and they lifted the sake containers out of the pot, placing them on one of the family's most precious lacquer trays.

Back in the living room, Kazuko sat beside the foreigner, pouring his sake; Chiyo sat beside Isao, pouring his.

They had begun to talk about *kokeshi* dolls and how they were selling at such a fast rate.

"So many people out at the base send them home," the soldier said. "You see, we have put a rubber stamp at the base of each doll which says, 'Made by survivors of the atomic bomb.' That is why they are selling so well, I think."

Chiyo held the sake container in midair, forgetting to pour it into Isao's cup, staring at the foreigner. "Survivors of the atomic bomb?"

she repeated. "It is stamped on each doll?" Up until that moment, she had not addressed him directly.

He looked puzzled, not sure why she was asking him.

"My sister here is the president of Asahi Enterprises, which produces the dolls," Isao explained.

The foreigner looked at her again and nodded recognition. "Oh, yes, I've heard about you. According to Miss Samuelson, the American teacher, many *hibakusha* are able to have an income because of you."

"Not all of them are *hibakusha*," Chiyo said. "There are nonsurvivors, too. Just people who want to make dolls and who need work."

"Well, but the people buying them at the PX don't know that," he said, smiling comfortably. "After all, if that's what sells them, then it's good, isn't it?"

"We thought Americans were buying them because they are appealing," said Isao.

"Oh, of course they are. And an inexpensive souvenir and gift, too. But people also buy them because they want to help the *hibakusha*."

Chiyo was stunned. Her beloved *kokeshi* dolls serving as some kind of charity? It was the next step above begging. Blood was rushing to her face, and she felt hot. Charity from America, the country that had dropped the bomb. Better to give the whole thing up and work for City Hall.

His information had cast a pall over the gathering. Isao, who had been smoking the Camel with obvious pleasure, mashed it out abruptly. Fusako stared rigidly at her knees, her feet tucked primly beneath her. Yoko, from the beginning, had been gazing, awestruck, at the foreigner's face, his clothes, his hands, the way he held his chopsticks. Now she shifted her attention to her own dish of peaches. Hiroshi, disappointed that they were not carrying on the conversation in English, had gotten bored with everyone. But with this new twist, he was all attention again.

"Excuse my rudeness," said Isao, "but we would prefer not to have you stamp those dolls. The information is erroneous."

The foreigner seemed not to understand. Isao turned to Fusako, ready to ask her to translate, then thought better of it. "Please do not put that stamp on the dolls," he said bluntly in Japanese.

"But they might not sell. People like to know where they come from, who made them, how they were made."

"We have a stamp that says 'Made in Japan' in English," Isao explained patiently. "And our more expensive pieces are signed by the artist in Japanese. We could get the signatures in English, too, if you like. And we could write a description of how they were made. But you must eliminate that stamp."

"Isn't it your idea to help the victims of the bomb?"

"Our idea," said Isao, getting red in the face himself, "is to make something beautiful that people will buy because it is beautiful. That is our only criterion. If the customers don't think it is an excellent product and worth the price, we don't want them to buy it."

"Of course people think the dolls are beautiful, but certainly it doesn't hurt to give customers that extra incentive to buy. Isn't food more important than beauty?"

"It is not!" said Isao firmly, his face rigid and stern. Chiyo wondered if the foreigner knew how angry he was. Everybody in the family knew. "We want the person who buys to think only of excellence and craftsmanship, not sympathy."

The foreigner was still puzzled. Like a child offering his leftover cookie to someone who needed a bowl of rice.

"Please remove the stamp," Isao repeated, bowing his head. "*Onegaishimasu.*" He had retreated into precise formality.

"If you wish it, I will do what I can to change the situation," the soldier said simply. Then he pressed his hands on his knees and bowed to each of them. "I'm afraid I've intruded too long and taken too much of your time," he said. "*Honto ni gochisōsama deshita.* It was a marvelous repast. *Mata ome ni kakaritai to omoimasu.* I hope to feast my eyes on you again sometime." He stood up, still bowing, and backed out to the edge of the *tatami,* then across the *genkan* to the door.

They followed him outside, clustering around the gate, waving goodbye.

After he had gone, they sat in the living room, not knowing how to begin, how to explain what they felt.

"We must send someone to the PX to make sure they stop using that stamp," Isao finally said. "Until they quit, we can't be sure the enterprise is a stable one. Almost half of the factory's income is from that military base. So, if the sales drop, we'll have to switch to another project to keep those people employed."

Chiyo felt weak. She could not give up her dolls.

"I don't mean we'll stop making them," Isao said. "Of course there'll always be a demand for them in the tourist shops. And maybe the other PXs aren't using the stamp. But there are other souvenirs, too. How about rice paddles? That was Miyajima's *mei-butsu*, the special souvenir. Or place mats from dried rushes. Or maybe *suribachi*, those pestle and mortars for grinding sesame seeds. And rice bowls. Even American-style dishes. Surely there are some Americans who like to buy things because they're both practical and beautiful."

Later that evening Isao decided the best thing was to go out to Iwakuni for an interview with the manager of the PX. If everyone went, he said, then he could concentrate on talking, Fusako on interpreting, and the rest of them on watching the Americans' faces and analyzing the nuances. And to make a really strong impression, they should wear their best kimonos.

"But Hiroshi and I can wear our school uniforms, can't we?" Yoko asked. "We don't have any good kimonos."

Isao hesitated, looking at her eager face. "I was really thinking that only the adults would go."

"We're adults," Yoko insisted. "I'm fifteen. Hiroshi's thirteen."

"I thought four of us, looking very formal, would be just right. Six of us might scare them."

Disappointment spread across Yoko's face. Hiroshi sighed.

All right," Isao said. "We'll all go."

"And Miss Samuelson will have to go," Fusako said. "She knows the chaplain and she can help interpret. Besides, she'll say we want to taste those hamburgers she always raves about."

"Of course," said Isao. "We can't do it without her. But that makes seven people, so don't any of you talk unless I say so."

The tall soldier, "Bobbu," met them at the train station. First he shook hands with Miss Samuelson, who had chosen to wear her navy-blue wool serge with the perpetual white ruffled blouse. As usual, she towered over the rest of them. They stood behind her, Chiyo reveling in the woman's regal bearing, which, at one time, she had thought was the heritage of all Western women. But Miss Samuelson was not like other people. She never grew old and she had never been young. Even when she returned after the war she had not changed.

"Bobbu" could barely suppress his delight at seeing Fusako again. He bustled them off to a waiting military car, opening the door for Fusako to sit in the front seat, but Isao pushed his way in ahead of her and sat between them.

When they drove onto the base, through a heavily guarded gate,

Chiyo saw rows of huge houses, each surrounded by a green lawn. Blond children were racing back and forth on bicycles, tricycles, roller skates. There were no fences. There was no privacy. Everyone could see everyone else's house.

"Just look at that," whispered Kazuko. "Each house has its own separate park."

A smiling army chaplain and a big, beefy sergeant, the PX manager, were waiting at the entrance to the PX. They shook hands all around. The sergeant frightened Chiyo with his enormous hand and firm grasp.

Afterwards, they were ushered into the enormous dining hall Fusako had described to them after her first visit.

They sat in steel chairs at a huge wooden table. Chiyo's feet did not touch the floor, the table was uncomfortably high, and there was a strange antiseptic smell everywhere, like ammonia. The sergeant made a sweeping gesture around the table, and the waitress, a Japanese girl, brought the hamburger sandwiches and thick chocolate milk drinks. Hiroshi, absorbed in the food, forgot his promises to watch gestures and nuances.

Isao spoke to "Bobbu" in Japanese and asked him to interpret to the sergeant. On the train to Iwakuni they had agreed that Miss Samuelson and Fusako would listen carefully and insist on repeating anything that seemed inaccurate.

Isao explained that all the PX had to do was display the goods. If they weren't moving fast enough after a month-long trial period, someone from the factory would come and get them. The PX didn't have to be bothered with them anymore.

The sergeant laughed heartily. He told "Bobbu" to tell Isao that he would keep the dolls in the PX forever if they wanted. Nobody ever had to buy a doll again, he said, and he would still pay for them in advance.

"No!" insisted Isao. "Don't pay us until they are sold."

"But you've got to eat, don't you?" the sergeant asked, looking directly at Isao. "Huh? Eat? *Ku? Ku?*" He was making the motions of stuffing food into his mouth, saying the Japanese word for "eat" but using the verb to describe animals eating, not people.

"Bobbu" was uncomfortable. He kept trying to interrupt and explain, but no one was paying attention to him.

That beefy creature, acting like an animal himself and yet trying to describe them! Chiyo was afraid Isao might stand up, push his chair back, and walk right out of the strange white-walled lunchroom. They would have to follow him out, of course, leaving Fusako and Miss Samuelson to make the excuses, and she had only just bitten into the hamburger sandwich.

But to her surprise, Isao smiled with the benevolent condescension that only his own family understood. "Tell him that's the word we use for animals eating, Fu-chan," he said, ignoring "Bobbu's" interpreting services.

The sergeant gazed at Fusako with rapt attention, then held up two enormous fingers. "You got two verbs for that?" he asked incredulously.

"Actually, we have more than two," Fusako said primly. "One for animals, one for formal occasions, another for informal ones, and one for exalted people like the emperor."

The sergeant roared with laughter, pounding his fist on the table, which shook under the weight of it. "Well, that does take the cake."

They smiled uncomfortably at him and each other.

Eventually they agreed that the PX would keep a 15 percent commission and send payment through a military courier to the factory in Koi.

"Or I could drop it by your house," said "Bobbu" hopefully.

"Oh, no, we prefer separating social and business affairs," said Isao pleasantly. "You must come another time for a social visit." Chiyo knew Isao had no intention of ever inviting him anywhere near their house.

"Thank them for what they have done for us," Isao said, standing up and bowing. "And Fusako, would you tell him, once more, not to write anything on the dolls about who made them? It is very important to us."

The sergeant listened to "Bobbu," then shrugged and nodded.

"Okay, if that's the way you want it, we'll do it," he said. Then he stood directly, almost menacingly, in front of Isao. "In America, we shake hands after a business deal," he said. And once more he encased each of their hands in his enormous paw. "Bobbu" bowed to them, then accompanied them to the train, looking wistfully at Fusako when he waved goodbye.

For a while, they slackened their furious pace of doll making and experimented with other products. They made samples for a line of rice paddles and an offering of bowls by Hiroshima apprentices who'd been studying with Miyajima potters, using the traditional subtle purple glaze. They planned an experiment with place mats, using *suzuki* grass.

Meanwhile, Miss Samuelson took several trips to Iwakuni to meet the chaplain for lunch and to visit the PX afterwards. All of the dolls, she reported, bore only the stamp "Made in Japan."

Then contrary to what everyone had expected, the sales went up instead of down. It was only "Bobbu's" imagination that people were buying them out of charity.

And even more pleasing, from Isao's and Kazuko's point of view, was the news that "Bobbu" would be returning to America in the fall. He had stopped by the house one evening in September, laden with gifts. For Isao there was a whole carton of Camel cigarettes and two cans of corned beef. How had he found out that Isao liked it, they wondered. There were nylon stockings for Fusako, Kazuko, and Chiyo. There was chocolate for Yoko and Hiroshi. He was returning to civilian life, he said, and he gave them his address in Ohio in case any of them should ever go to America.

"He was looking right at Fu-chan when he said it," Kazuko told Chiyo, "and you can be certain that I'll make sure she never gets to Ohio."

Chapter Twenty-six

I N NOVEMBER CHIYO AND MRS. OTSUKA realized that only four ships had come from Nakhodka during 1950, the last one in April. There had been eighty-nine ships in 1947; ninety-six in 1948; forty-four in 1949. The members of the Movement drew up a new list of of prisoners still remaining in China and the Soviet Union. Again they sent the names to the Soviet Union together with petitions, letters, and requests. It had been five and a half years since the end of hostilities; the husbands still had not come home.

In December the United Nations adopted a resolution stating there must be a peaceful solution to the problem of the Japanese and German prisoners of war, but the Soviets absented themselves from the meeting. They had already refused to attend meetings of the Allied powers in Tokyo on the ground that the subject of prisoners of war in Russia was not suitable for discussion among the Council members.

"Maybe we'll be better off when the Occupation ends," said Mrs. Otsuka. "We won't have to worry about hostilities between Russia and America. We can negotiate directly."

"But surely they'll send the men home before the Occupation is over," Chiyo said. "Everyone in the world is watching. They'd be embarrassed not to. They'll come this spring. I feel it in my bones."

She waited for Mrs. Otsuka's usually confident, optimistic reply, but there was none.

They looked forward to the spring.

By April 1951 a year had passed since the last ship from Nakhodka. And there was little hope for the rest of the spring and summer. It seemed the Korean War would have to end before they could expect the ships again. The Soviets had continued to ignore their petitions as well as requests from the United Nations, the International Red Cross, the Allied Powers.

But at least the Occupation was allowing public ceremonies. The architect Kenzo Tange had been chosen to plan the Peace Park on Nakajima. Construction had begun for the Peace Memorial Museum and the stone cenotaph bearing Professor Saiga's inscription. A commemorative tower had already been erected in the place where Jisenji Temple had been.

Chiyo was crowding in toward the tower with Yoko and Hiroshi on August 6th when she saw the man again.

No overcoat this time. He was wearing a dark summer kimono of old prewar silk, something he could have found at an open-air market but of the style Shintaro might have inherited from his father. On the man's head was the most ridiculous and yet dignified felt bowler hat. Like the ones men wore in the Meiji Period in the 1880s. Her father had worn such a bowler, and Shintaro, because he admired it so much, had been awarded the hat in her father's will.

He moved away from them toward the chairs that had been set up outside for the ceremony. Chiyo pushed back through the crowd, trying to follow him.

"Mama, what is the matter?" Yoko asked anxiously.

Hiroshi ran up and took her by the arm. "I think we'd better go home now. You haven't been resting enough. Uncle Isao told you to be careful."

"That man!" she said. "I know I've seen him before." She almost told them she thought it was their father. But the next moment she felt ashamed of her craziness.

"We're going home!" Hiroshi announced firmly, and she meekly followed her two children onto the streetcar.

Yoko, looking bereft and sorrowful, insisted that her mother go right to bed. "Hiroshi's studying all the time, and I've joined too many clubs at school. We should take care of you better."

Yoko always thought everything was her fault.

"I'm not the least bit sick," Chiyo insisted. "I'm planning to go back to the river tonight and float a candle for Kenichi."

Instead she fell asleep and did not wake again until the middle of the night.

"You're a little crazy," she told herself. "It's getting so everybody in the world looks like Shintaro. If you met the Emperor face-to-face, you'd think he was Shintaro."

There was an American cowboy song that Fusako sang with her college friends. "Seven years of waiting. Ain't gonna wait no more."

"Imagine just seven years," Mrs. Otsuka had said. "Now, we Japanese, we wouldn't consider that any time at all. Twenty-five years is more like what we think is a long time to wait."

Well, she was wrong. Who would be alive in twenty-five years?

Just one postcard. To keep her from losing hope. Mrs. Otsuka had received three letters since the first one. A letter every year. It was easy for her to talk so cheerfully about waiting. She knew all about her husband and where he was.

At a convention in Hyogo prefecture in late August, more than three hundred delegates drew up a petition to the Soviet Union. They signed it in blood, pressing their signature seals into cuts they had made in their fingers, then stamping the paper.

Chiyo met Mrs. Hisako Oguchi, the delegate from Himeji, whose husband, like Shintaro, had been a middle-school teacher, drafted into the army at the same time and sent to the Ninth Army Headquarters in Manchuria. He had written regularly during the war, but afterwards she had received only one letter, like Shintaro's, from a prison camp in Siberia. She had sold the family treasures, then begun a small business cooking lunches for schoolchildren, but it had failed because she couldn't find a dependable supply of rice. During the terrible winter of 1949, her only daughter had died of pneumonia and malnutrition at the age of ten. Now Mrs. Oguchi was desperately searching for a way to support her eight-year-old son, who had never seen his father.

Back in Hiroshima, Chiyo sent Mrs. Oguchi sample dolls and instruction sheets, suggesting that she start a branch factory for Asahi Enterprises in the Himeji area.

Meanwhile, everyone in the Movement waited for a reply from the Soviet Union. People searched the Russian newspapers for a reaction. There was none. The Soviets refused to acknowledge they had even received a communication.

* * *

In the fall, the peace treaty was signed in San Francisco. Isao was in a state of elation. "Now we can get back to business. We'll sell our three-wheeled trucks all over Asia. And we'll never have an army again. It's written right into the treaty. We'll be like Switzerland."

He sat drinking sake, Chiyo and Kazuko on either side pouring for him. It was so rare to see Isao in a celebrative mood that Chiyo even enjoyed watching him get a little drunk.

"What's going to happen now that we don't have the Americans to help us get the prisoners home?" Chiyo asked.

"Oh, it's going to be better now," he said. "The Red Cross will help and the United Nations. You'll see."

During nights of insomnia, Chiyo would sit until dawn, thinking that if she could just bury one of them, if somebody could come to her and say, "Yes, I saw your son that day. He jumped from the bridge into the Honkawa with the other students, singing the national anthem," then she could face the uncertainty of Shintaro more easily. Or even if someone came and told her Shintaro had died, no matter how horribly. If he'd been the one who'd frozen to death out by the well or gotten his foot stuck in the snow and been left there to die, or been thrown into the river with the other frozen bodies. If someone could have brought back his *omamori*, the temple protective symbol she had given him when he went away, or the *senninbari*, the embroidered cloth with the thousand stitches.

Winter came, and it seemed to Chiyo that men in derby hats and khaki overcoats were everywhere, standing outside under the streetlight at night, wandering among black market stalls at the station, turning corners along the Hondori. But never close enough for her to see their features.

In the mornings, riding on the streetcar to the factory in Koi, she forgot about the overcoats and hats, too busy with thoughts of the expanding business. The factory had become the hub of community activity, a kind of haven. There were veterans, orphans, old men and women. Many were *hibakusha*, survivors of the bomb, whose health was so unpredictable they couldn't hold a regular job.

Everyone started work early and kept at it hard so that they could have a long lunchtime exchanging stories about their experiences in the war, about the bomb, about rumors. They told each other where the cheapest food was, where to find the best black market items. They talked about how to treat listlessness and anemia and how to cover up keloids.

Morishita-san had quit his other job and been employed as the foreman for some time. Now Honda-san was his full-time assistant. They did all the deliveries in a bargain secondhand truck Morishita-san had found that fall. And they were expanding their offerings of hand-carved rice paddles, teacups with the famous Miyajima blue glaze, place mats made from Suzuki grass.

There were enough competent doll painters now. It rarely happened that someone's work was so poor they couldn't sell it.

But there were exceptions. They worried about poor old Mr. Sato, whose face and hands were so covered with keloids that he could barely hold a brush. He had refused to work as a janitor or even with accounts, which is what he had done before the war. He wanted to paint, he said. He jabbed at the faces of the dolls, smearing the place where their eyes and mouths were supposed to be, then doggedly wiped off the face and tried again, sometimes working all day on just one doll. But one doll a day didn't make him enough to live on.

It was Hiroshi who had come up with a solution. "He really chooses colors well, Mama. He ought to be painting something so that it doesn't matter whether he gets the paint in exactly the right place." Hiroshi began collecting the rejected pieces of wood and clay which were imperfect for regular dolls. "Tell him to paint whatever he wants on these," he said. "Maybe he can make them look like something we haven't thought of."

Sure enough, there appeared lined up in the old man's tiny riverside shack the most amazing array of colored trinkets. Mr. Sato tended toward bright reds, oranges, and yellows with streaks of black and purple running through them, and sometimes surrounded by an azure blue. They had such fierce intensity Chiyo could hardly bear to look at them. She realized that he was creating images of August 6. As if they were the twisted shapes and distorted replicas of things that had burned, and all the more powerful because nobody could tell what they were, not even Mr. Sato.

Nakayama stopped by the factory late one afternoon when Chiyo was already home and immediately ordered a dozen of them, offering to pay in advance.

Morishita-san suggested they send some to the tourist shops foreign soldiers frequented down near the Atomic Dome.

"We'll just put them there and see what happens," he said.

Somehow the old man's creations launched a new school of art. As soon as the trinkets appeared in the souvenir shop, other people came in droves bringing wood carvings, paintings, poems, sculptures. The owner of the Atomic Dome Cafe announced that he would set up a special gallery for them.

In mid-December, the day of the opening exhibit, Chiyo watched everybody crowd into the shop with the most extraordinary objects, some beautiful but most of them garish and frightening.

Chiyo was amazed by the variety of submissions. She stood in front of a work that had been entered in the "sculpture" class. The artist had collected pieces of charred wood and roof tile melted by the blast into strange unearthly shapes and covered with bubbles like molten lava. He had arranged them around a replica of the now famous steps of the old Sumitomo Bank where a shadow had been cast by a person sitting there who had vaporized when the bomb exploded.

Tiny figures huddled amidst the wreckage as if shielding themselves from a strong wind. One figure was being blasted by the sun itself. It was the way Kenichi had—

She turned, afraid of her recurring vision, and almost bumped into the khaki overcoat.

"Chiyo!" the man whispered hoarsely. It was a soft, strangled sound, coming out from under the bowler hat, and she wasn't at all sure that she had heard him correctly. He was staring at her with fierce intensity. There were tears in his eyes, and he turned abruptly and went out the door. She followed him, walking in a dream state, as if destiny had called her.

He was hurrying ahead. Once he turned to see if she was still following. With the bowler hat bobbing up and down, he looked the way Shintaro had looked in the autumn of 1937, the year she married him. Except that this man was wearing the army coat. And the hair below his derby hat was gray. He was older. Shintaro's age, in fact. He was walking swiftly along the Hondori now, and she almost had to run to keep up with him. Couldn't he walk a little more slowly if he wanted her to follow? She ran, pigeon-toed, to keep her *zōri* from falling off.

That morning, in honor of the Atomic Dome Cafe exhibition, she had donned her kimono, the only one she hadn't sold, a dark, practical one of navy blue, suitable for all occasions and ages. She had worn it for the PX visit and on the day Shintaro went away, the day they took the last photograph of him. Was that the reason he had spoken to her? Because he recognized her for the first time? But surely he would have known. And he knew where they lived.

She caught up with him and touched his arm. "Shintaro?" she demanded. "Is it you?" He turned and looked at her. His eyes were the same. Warm and gentle, but crinkled around the edges. From age. Siberia had aged him. Born in 1899. He was only fifty-three. He had squinted too much to keep the snow and cold out of his eyes.

He took both her hands, then held them pressed inside his own. He was breathing heavily. "Follow me," he said abruptly, almost harshly. His voice was not the way she had remembered.

"How long have you been here?" she blurted out. "Why haven't you come before?"

"We can't talk here," he said. He let go of her hands and touched her cheek. "How did you get that scar?"

Now she knew it was Shintaro's voice.

"Shintaro," she breathed. "I've waited so long. Why didn't you come? I just can't believe— Come home with me," she demanded. "Don't you remember where we live? It's in the same place!"

He took her arm. "I couldn't come home," he said. "Follow me. I'll show you."

He kept ahead of her, threading his way through to the main street. She followed him onto the streetcar, where they stood, separated by the crowd. At Hiroshima station, she followed him off the streetcar to one of the shacks along the river, which he entered, motioning for her to follow. It was a small, neatly kept room built out over the river on stilts. There was even a window fashioned out of a piece of plastic. She looked around, then sat near the window, anger welling up in her. "You've been here all this time? So close to us? You've even built a house, and you didn't come?"

He knelt down on the *tatami* next to her, holding her face in his hands, gazing at her eyes, her lips, her scar, caressing her hair. "I've waited so long for this moment," he said. "If only I could tell you how—"

He embraced her, holding her face buried in his shoulder, and they wept, holding each other, rocking back and forth.

"Oh, Shintaro, you're home at last. I don't care how—"

"Where's Kenichi?" he asked gently, still holding her close.

She pulled away and stared at him. "Then you didn't hear? You didn't get the postcard we all wrote and you didn't see the letters stacked up and waiting for you in Maizuru?"

He shook his head.

"And why are you here instead of home?" she asked.

He looked around as if he'd forgotten where he was. "Oh," he said. "This place. It belongs to someone else. I haven't been here long." His eyes were vacant. As if a light behind them had gone out, and he wasn't with her any longer. He was in Siberia again. Or some other terrible place. It was the same hollow look he'd had in Maizuru. Then it was gone and he gave her his attention, his expression full of tenderness.

"Tell me about Kenichi," he said. "Then I'll explain. At least as much as I can."

He listened while she told him about Kenichi's school days and the work he had done tearing down houses, about her odyssey through Hiroshima that day searching for Kenichi, and then the day after that and the weeks and months following, hoping and searching endlessly, unable to think of anything else. "And dreaming," she said. "Dreaming that we'd found him, and dreaming that you were home again." She did not tell him about the nightmares.

His eyes were riveted to her face. One hand inside his overcoat was spread across his chest as if he were protecting his heart.

When she finished he stared out at the river. His shoulders were stiff and unbending, and he did not move. "I was afraid of that," he said. "You see, I've been following you, waiting for the right moment. I've seen Hiroshi and Yoko. I've stood outside the house and looked for you at night. At first I thought Hiroshi was Kenichi. He was so big. Then I realized when I saw Yoko—" Tears had appeared in his eyes again. "She is so very beautiful."

Chiyo nodded, fighting back her own tears. "You've missed so much of her childhood," she said. "And Hiroshi's. How could you—?" She was angry at him and impatient.

"I know." For a moment he could not speak. He folded his arms around his chest, pressing the sorrow inside himself. "You did all of that. Lived through the bomb and searched for Kenichi, took care of the two younger ones, even started a factory."

"You know that too?" She looked up, puzzled. "How could you know all that and not—" She began to cry again, pressing her eyes against her kimono sleeve. "What could possibly keep you away?" she shouted at him. "We've waited so long for you!" Then she saw his anguished face and turned away from him. "Isao helped with the factory," she said. "I couldn't have done it without him. But I wanted you here. We needed you and—"

"Don't say that again!" His voice exploded at her. "Give me a chance to tell you! Do you think it was easy for me? Do you know what we did to survive in Siberia? Do you have any idea how—?" He pounded his fist on his knee. "And then when I got home I couldn't even—" He was crying unabashedly now. He took her by the shoulders and shook her. "Our lives were endangered! Don't you understand that? Yours and mine and the children's! Do you think anything but that would have kept me away?"

He let her go. He was still sobbing, and she put her arms around him again. "I'm sorry," she said. "I know you wanted to be with us, that you couldn't help whatever it was, but it's been so—"

"Eight and a half years!" His voice resounded through the tiny shack. "Six years away and then two more at home so close I could have touched you!" His voice was harsh and angry.

"If I could have just had some hint," she said. "Anything to keep me believing that you were alive."

He touched her cheek, tracing his thumb across the scar. "From the bomb?" he asked.

She nodded. "But you recognized me anyway?"

"Of course," he said. "Of course." He gathered her in his arms again and kissed her cheek. "Do you think a scar could mar your beauty?"

She buried her face in his shoulders. "It doesn't matter where you were," she said. "You're home now. Let's go back to the house. Yoko and Hiroshi are waiting."

He settled himself cross-legged, pushing his hands deep into the pockets of his heavy coat. "I want to explain first," he said.

It was a long, confusing story. She couldn't hope to understand it the first time around. But there was a lifetime ahead, living again with Shintaro, listening to the stories of China, Manchuria, Siberia.

And yes, he'd been at the Maizuru railroad station. Dumfounded when he found her there. He'd waited until he was sure everyone had left the station, even stood on the deck of the ship when it first arrived until everyone had disembarked and the well-wishers had dispersed. He'd taken on the name of the other man, Yamanaka Tadanori, because they had told him that Yamanaka had no living relatives. He would be free to carry out instructions without interference from a family, they had said.

"But that wasn't true," Shintaro said. "There was a daughter who'd been sent home as a baby when her mother died. She'd been looking everywhere for her father, and she just happened to find my assumed name on a hotel register in Tokyo."

"So that was the same person! Isao hired a detective who talked to that woman."

"Yes." Shintaro nodded. "She deserved to know the truth. But I couldn't tell her. She'd wanted a father for so long that I just pretended to be him."

He was lost in thought.

"You were working for the Communists?" Chiyo asked. "You really defected and went over to the other side that time the land mine blew up?"

"Oh, so you heard about that!" He looked surprised.

"From Yukiji, who heard from your friend, Yamaguchi-san, who—" She sighed. "But I'll tell you all that later. You were really a deserter?"

"No," he said wearily. "The Japanese military intelligence recruited me because I know Chinese. It was prearranged that if the enemy attacked, I was to surrender immediately and join the other side. So I did. Acted like a deserter, got the information, and escaped into Manchuria. Then Russia declared war, came into our headquarters, captured us all, and put us on a train to Siberia. That was a bitter day. Still August and the freezing weather already coming." He shook his head. "And all that time I'd been thinking if I could just get to Manchuria, I was as good as home." He stood up and stared out the window. "Four more hard, cold years of it."

"But why were you carrying out their instructions when you finally did come home?" she prodded him. "And who's 'they'? You keep saying 'they' threatened you and asked you to do this and that. Do you mean the Soviets or the Communist party in Japan or—"

He stiffened. "Don't ask me too much," he said. "Don't expect me to trust anyone. Not even you. Not yet."

"But why did you follow their instructions?"

"Follow instructions?" he asked.

He had forgotten the point. Her husband, the prewar Shintaro, had never lost the thread of a conversation. But now he was eight years older, and the vacant stare had appeared again in his eyes.

"You said they wanted you to assume that other man's name so you would be free to carry out their instructions."

"Oh," he said. "Yes. Their instructions." It was taking great effort for him to concentrate.

"So I followed their instructions. Yes." He nodded. "I did it to get home early. They told me that if I would observe the way the socialist troops behaved when they disembarked, help keep the labor movement going—they said if I would do all that for a year, then I could come home early." He looked at her earnestly. "It seemed a good offer. You know, hardly anyone has come home from Siberia since. I'd still be there if—" He turned away and looked at the darkening sky. "Besides, I believed Japan would be better as a socialist state than a capitalist one. I'd seen what the Japanese troops did in China. I was disillusioned with imperialism and militarism—everything that got us into the war."

He sounded like the old Shintaro, the idealist, preaching to his students, explaining about loyalty and honor. But there was something else, an echo of the strident political language she'd heard in Maizuru.

"You mean you really—"

"No! I'm not a Communist!" he interrupted her. "I'm as disillusioned with them as I was with the Japanese army. I'm not even a socialist anymore. That's all in the past. They betrayed me, don't you see?"

He seemed to think that she knew everything, that she should understand.

"They told me that Yamanaka Tadanori had died. But I heard later that he'd been on the ship and had jumped overboard or maybe been pushed. Then I heard that the man who'd gone overboard was Shin Hara!"

He took his hands out of his pockets and rubbed them. "I was afraid you'd see that name in the newspaper and come to Maizuru to wait for me." He sighed. "And I was just as afraid that you wouldn't come. I didn't know whether you were alive. I'd heard about Hiroshima."

He wrapped his arms about his chest, rocking back and forth. "To see you at the station. And then I couldn't—" His voice broke again, and it was a time before he could speak again. "I couldn't even pick up the mail you'd sent. I touched the letters and smelled them, even held them in my hands. But I couldn't take the risk—"

"You were very convincing," she said wistfully. "I was sure it was you when I saw you, but you looked so terrible. You seemed lost, and you were undernourished and—and you denied me." She lifted her face to his. "Couldn't you have trusted me? Just given me some sign to save me from so much anguish? I wouldn't have told anybody."

"But there were so many spies," he whispered. "Spies everywhere. People watching other people, threatening to kill them and their wives and their children if they didn't—" He looked around the room as if he expected to find someone else there. "It was too much of a risk even with the station almost empty. That other man who was walking with me—the fat one. He was following me. I got immediately on a train to Tokyo so I wouldn't see you again."

"Then that wasn't you walking in the streets of Maizuru?" She took a deep breath. "Or in the brothel?"

He stared at her puzzled. "A brothel?" he repeated. "How

could—? You knew I wouldn't do anything like that, didn't you?"

"I saw a man wearing the same kind of overcoat, and I—so I followed him."

"You went inside the brothel and looked for me there? Really?" He laughed. Loud and robust guffaws like the ones in the old days. Then his face turned pale and he coughed. He turned away, covered his mouth with a handkerchief, and continued to cough. She put her head against his back, felt his ribs against her cheek, the movement of air in his lungs. "Are you all right? You're not sick, are you?"

"I'm fine," he said, wadding up his handkerchief and stuffing it into his pocket. The color had returned to his face now. "And what did they tell you in the brothel?"

"A woman in the hotel sent me to a room. A terrible-looking man was lying there with a prostitute, and I was so crazy I thought he was you. It was humiliating and—" She laughed. "Now it's funny, but it wasn't then."

He smiled. "I remember how persistent you are."

He told her about going up north to where the railroad strikes had been. "You remember that terrible murder, don't you? When they found the president of Japan National Railroads lying dead on the tracks? And then in the middle of July the train wreck when all those people were killed? And other things.

"You see, I was supposed to—" His hands were shaking and his face had become pale again. Gray. "I don't know who wrecked the train or committed the murder," he said, "but some of them thought it was a victory."

He grasped her shoulders again. "Death is not a victory!" he said. "Killing, for whatever purpose, does not bring victory." He let go of her. There was anguish in his face. "I did all that for a year. Then they said I must work another year or they could implicate me, have me put in prison for life. Or harm you and the children."

"Oh, Shintaro," she said. "Come home with me now. It's almost dark and Yoko and Hiroshi will be frantic. Can't you come now? Are they still following you?"

He did not move. "I must tell you the rest," he said. "You see, I escaped from the north that first winter and came down to Hiroshima. I was desperate to know how you were. I was standing in the school yard when you saw me." He shook his head. "So many close calls. But just seeing you was enough for me in those days. I was expecting to be home in a few months.

"Then I confirmed what I was afraid of—that Yamanaka Tadanori had been deliberately killed so I could take his place. That's when I began to plot for a way to have Yamanaka Tadanori disappear from the face of the earth." His smile was strange.

The sun had gone, leaving Shintaro in dark profile. She would know that profile anywhere in the world, she thought. She had known it at Maizuru, and she felt a surge of confidence, knowing that her instincts had not failed her.

He stood up. "Come on," he said. "I'll leave a note for Okura-san. This is his place. He's a junk dealer I befriended last summer."

"That was you last summer in the Peace Park wearing the summer kimono? Couldn't you have come to us then?" Chiyo asked.

"Oh. That was when I came down here to test my new identity, to see if anybody was still following me." He laughed. "I had to be sure my old contacts thought I'd really died. I came back here only a week ago, and I was trying to decide the proper moment to reveal myself when I saw you in your blue kimono."

He squeezed her hand, smiling triumphantly. "It's finally the end of the mythical Yamanaka Tadanori and his notorious career." His expression changed abruptly. "They won't be looking for me anymore. They've already gotten what they can out of me."

"Shintaro! Stop!" she said. "I don't understand any of it. Just come home."

She touched his cheek. "At least I had the children with me. But you—I can't imagine. What were you living on all that time? Did they pay you a salary?"

"Huh! Salary?" His voice was cynical. "Mostly I was selling junk. And up in Tokyo cooking shrimp dumplings on street corners. I wrote a lot, too. Some articles under another assumed name. Observations about postwar Japan. I enjoyed that part. Maybe I'll do it again."

He looked out at the river. "It's already dark," he said. "Go on ahead over Sakae Bridge. I'll write a note and follow. It'll give you some time to prepare the children."

Chapter Twenty-seven

SHE PAUSED IN THE MIDDLE OF SAKAE Bridge and stared at the lights reflected in the river. She had prayed so often to have him back in any condition whatsoever. Now he was here. And he wasn't crippled or blind as she had often feared. But his cough had frightened her. And he was trying to hide something. Explaining too much.

He had appeared so suddenly there wasn't time for the nervous anticipation she'd felt in Maizuru. Or the shyness. It was as if the intervening years had melted away. "So much to talk about," he'd said, smiling down at her when she left the shack. "Almost nine years to catch up on."

She entered her house a little cautiously, not sure how she was going to explain it.

"Mama!" Yoko screamed. "We called Uncle Isao! We were ready to call the police! Everybody's looking—"

"I'm sorry. I know you're worried," she interrupted. "But I have something important to tell you."

She took a deep breath, then settled herself in the *kotatsu*, ordering Yoko and Hiroshi to sit down across from her.

"Your father has returned," she said.

Hiroshi folded his hands on the table and cocked his head, his eyes questioning. Yoko held her breath, looking wary. "Mother, there haven't been any ships. How can you—?"

"I know it's strange," said Chiyo. "I'm very surprised myself, but I can't—and I don't understand it either. But he's here. He's come home, and he's suffered terribly. I don't think he's very well. We've got to work very hard to make him comfortable again."

She reached across the table and clasped their hands. "I'll have to admit I was beginning to lose hope," she said. "You see, there was a man in Maizuru—" She stopped. What was the use of trying to tell them?

"There's some connection with the Shin Hara whose name was in the paper, but it's not clear. Anyway, he couldn't come home to us right away. But for now it's enough to know that our dreams have come true."

She heard Shintaro sliding open the door behind her. Yoko looked up and gasped, then went over to the edge of the *tatami* to greet him. Hiroshi's eyes were searching his mother's face for some clue. He joined Yoko at the edge of the *tatami,* taking her hand as if to protect her. Chiyo watched. There was not a spark of recognition in Hiroshi's eyes.

"This is your father," Chiyo announced quietly.

It was Yoko who spoke first. "Papa?"

Hiroshi had turned to stone.

Finally he knelt before Shintaro in formal position, bowing his head. "Welcome home," he said, pronouncing the words carefully and precisely, as if he had learned them for a play.

Yoko stepped into the *genkan* and reached her arms inside the khaki overcoat, hugging her father around his waist, and began to cry. "Oh, Papa," she said. "Papa."

"You've become quite a young lady," he said. "I can't lift you up any longer and carry you around in my arms the way I used to." He looked warmly at Hiroshi, then reached out to shake his hand. "And you've grown up too. You're older than Kenichi was when I went away."

Yoko looked plaintively at her mother. "We don't have anything special for dinner."

"There's a *daikon* in the kitchen," Chiyo said. "Your father's favorite kind of radish."

In their tiny living room, he sat in the place she had dreamed he would be. He exclaimed over their *tokonoma* built out of the old *hinoki* wood, commented on all the changes and on the few familiar things that he recognized. He ate the bowl of rice and the *daikon* pickle, the smile of contentment from the old days spreading across his face.

He told Yoko and Hiroshi about China and the daisy fields, about the farmers planting rice the way they did in Inokuchi, about the long, cold winters in Siberia, the silver icicles, the frozen tundra, and how it had sometimes hurt even to breathe. He spoke of the warmth and wonder of the Siberian summer. He was the same Shintaro as the one in the letters he had written, and for a time Chiyo forgot about that other self he had revealed in the river shack.

"I'm tired," he said suddenly. "I think I'd better get some sleep."

She took him to the sleeping room she and Yoko had shared, then laid out the *futon*. For the time being, Yoko and Hiroshi would have to sleep in the living room.

When she returned, after clearing away the dishes and rearranging their beds, Shintaro was deep in slumber.

Yoko warmed to her father immediately. Not Hiroshi, who, in the days that followed, was obedient and polite, but always aloof. There was no pleasant bantering, no exchange of jokes, no looks of admiration as there had been between Shintaro and Kenichi.

Gradually, and rather tentatively, Hiroshi began asking him math questions. Shintaro seemed unsure of the answers at first, but because he stayed in the house most of the day, struggling with each new set of problems, he was ready for Hiroshi's study sessions each evening.

Afterwards, if the session was satisfactory, Shintaro spoke of the day he would return to teaching. Chiyo could stop working at the factory, he said, and become a housewife again.

"But there's time yet to see about that," Chiyo said. "You still need more rest and you have to get rid of that cough. Besides, you know, I rather like going to the factory."

He looked at her stiffly and she realized that he wasn't used to having her making decisions and telling him her preferences. "Anyway," she said, "the new term doesn't begin until April."

At night Chiyo and Shintaro lay together, as they had always done, holding each other close. Chiyo explored again the contours of his body, the mole on his back, the curve of his firm, high cheekbones, and the feel of his buttocks, which had once been very firm, and were now soft and a bit cushiony. Inevitably, by the time she had reached that far, he was asleep, and usually snoring. The first few nights he had been too tired, he said, too excited by each day's events. But on subsequent nights, when his attention wandered during her explicit advances, her concern and disappointment grew.

"Remember how it was with us before you went away?" she asked.

"I remember," he said. "It will be that way again. I just need a little more time."

She was not sure that she believed him.

In January, after the New Year holidays at Inokuchi, which had been especially festive, he made no move to see the principal at Rijo Junior High School and he was irritable when Chiyo mentioned the subject. He continued to stay at home, working on Hiroshi's math problems. Or reading Hiroshi's and Yoko's textbooks, often complaining that the young people nowadays did not have enough ethical and moral training.

He insisted that Hiroshi should study more classical Chinese and Japanese literature. "It's what will help you most in your life," he said. "Regardless of the profession you choose."

"But that's not what's going to be on the exam," Hiroshi said. "I can't spend my time on that. The exams have changed a lot since you were teaching, Father." He was polite but firm.

Shintaro closed the literature book and retired into the sleeping room.

Chiyo did not know what to say to either of them. After a moment she joined Shintaro and found him staring out the tiny window that looked onto the street.

"Aren't you going to be writing any more articles for the paper like the ones you were writing in Tokyo?" she asked.

"It doesn't seem important to me anymore," he said.

She did not want to nag him. Instead, because there was nothing else to say, she left him there and went to berate Hiroshi, whispering quietly.

"Can't you see that he's discouraged? Can't you treat him with a little more respect?"

"I'm trying, Mama." Hiroshi looked up at her, the hurt showing in his eyes. "What am I supposed to do? I have to study." And he bent his head toward his books again.

More and more if she came home early she found Shintaro in the sleeping room, peering out the tiny window, watching almost impatiently.

"Nobody's following you!" Hiroshi blurted out one afternoon

when he came home to find his father at his usual occupation.

Shintaro turned sharply and stared him down. "I hardly think you're the one to make a judgment on this matter," he said. Then he called Chiyo to come in from the kitchen. "What's happened to the education of our children?" he asked. "Is there no longer any respect for elders? Take this boy out of the room away from me."

"Hiroshi, how could you?" Chiyo said after they had gone into the other room.

"I'm sorry, Mama. I didn't really mean—it's just—he's always there, always doing the same thing and I—" Hiroshi put his hands before his face and began to cry. "I'm trying so hard, Mama. I'm really trying."

It would be even worse, Chiyo thought, if Shintaro heard his fourteen-year-old son crying. She hugged Hiroshi and held him close. "I know you are," she said. "We're all trying hard, and we've got to keep on trying. It's hardest for him, you know. We can't even begin to imagine what he's been through."

"Well, you've been through a lot, too, Mama. You've been through an atomic bomb!"

They heard Shintaro coughing, lightly at first, then more loudly, until it seemed to Chiyo that the coughing was shaking the whole house. She went back into the room and pressed her fingers on Shintaro's back, massaging him, but he moved away from her.

"It's all right," he said. His shoulders were hunched forward, his head bent almost to his knees. "Just bring me some water."

She called to Hiroshi to bring water, but by the time he arrived with it, Shintaro had stopped coughing. Chiyo helped him lie flat on the *futon,* pressing the covers around his neck. "You've got to see the doctor about your lungs," she told him.

"It's not serious," he told her. "It's just the cold this time of year."

In fact, the cough did subside, and she stopped nagging him. But at times he was angry for no particular reason. Small things bothered him. He did not like it when the meals were not on time, and he implied that if Chiyo were only home instead of working at the factory, the house would be in better condition, and as clean as he had remembered it.

She knew it would anger him even more if she pointed out that someone in the family had to make a living. And anyway, she did not intend to stop working with Asahi Enterprises even when he began teaching again.

* * *

There were other moments when he was overwhelmed with joy at being home again, at seeing people and places he remembered, especially the Ogawas in Inokuchi, the Ikedas, and the few other neighbors he had known. He loved walking across the old bridges that had survived the bomb, and he was delighted by the green-grocer's. Some days he spent the afternoon talking to Tetsuo Kasama and his customers about the old days and the old shop and the way the neighborhood had been before the war. He even helped out late in the day when the Kasamas had too many customers to handle.

He was deeply touched by the neighborhood gathering held during early January in honor of his homecoming, and especially glad to see Yasu again, realizing, Chiyo knew, that Kenichi would also have been that tall and that handsome and that intelligent. He loved watching Kyoko and Yoko's volleyball games, and even helped the teacher coach the class play. It was that experience, Chiyo decided, that would make him want to go back to teach at Rijo Junior High School. It was only a matter of time.

In February he came down with a severe case of the flu. They partitioned off one end of the sleeping room with a screen so that he could sleep without interruption. He coughed interminably and his temperature was very high. The doctor came for a house call and said it was an unusual virus, not very prevalent in Japan. "Your husband's been in Siberia, hasn't he? I've run into a few cases like this. Those men suffered from malnutrition for so long it's hard for them to build up their resistance to disease. We'd better take him into the hospital for a few days."

Every morning and night she was at the hospital cooking him *o-kayu,* soft rice with an egg. It was the only thing that didn't upset his stomach. She and Yoko and Hiroshi took turns staying overnight in his room to take care of him. The doctor was afraid of pneumonia.

He was home by the end of the month and getting stronger. One morning on a clear day, he was up early. "I'm going to see the principal," he said. "It's time to get on with things."

Late that afternoon when he hadn't come home, Chiyo went down to the tobacco store on the corner and called the school principal. "He was here," the principal said. "We had a good long talk. I told him to take plenty of time before he begins. I said I wasn't sure he would be ready by April. Then he coughed a lot and said he thought he should go home. I offered to call him a taxi, but he refused. He said he was fine, but he looked quite pale."

"How long ago was that?" Chiyo asked.

"Oh, at least three hours. And you say he isn't home yet?"

"No." Chiyo hung up the phone and hurried home.

Yoko suggested they take a taxi down to the school, then ride slowly along each road that led to their house.

"But he might have taken a taxi himself, or he might have stopped in at a bookstore," Hiroshi said. "He likes to do that sometimes."

"Or he might already be in the hospital," said Chiyo. "We'd better call there."

Hiroshi ran down the street to the tobacco store to use the phone. Shintaro wasn't in the hospital. They decided that Hiroshi should go to the greengrocer's and then to the station to see if his father's friend in the river shack knew where he was. Yoko would take a taxi and follow along the route to Rijo School. Chiyo would wait in the house.

She sat in the *kotatsu,* warming her hands under the blanket, holding herself stiff, not allowing herself to think of anything except how dirty the wall in front of her had become and how she would have to spend the day cleaning it sometime in the future when there was nothing else to do, nothing else to think about. Or worry about. Or hope for. Maybe if she were mending it would help. Hiroshi's socks. She stood up, then saw a shadow in front of the door, watched it open and watched Shintaro come inside. He came forward methodically, not looking at her, sitting on the *tatami* and taking off his shoes. She was struck by an intense sense of déjà vu. This had all happened before. But there was nothing strange about that. Shintaro had come home myriads of times and sat down on the *tatami* and leaned over to take off his shoes. She did not know why her voice was caught in her throat. She could not find the words to greet him and he had not yet spoken to her.

"You're all right?" she asked eventually. "I called the principal when you were so late and he said that you—"

He turned around and his face had a rosy glow. He looked almost too healthy.

"Thought I should walk a bit," he said. "Such a cold, crisp day. And I stopped at a few bookstores on the way home. Hope you didn't worry." He walked stiffly to the *kotatsu,* sat down, and pushed his feet wearily under the quilt. He was breathing heavily.

"You shouldn't have done so much in one day," she chided him softly. "Especially after the flu. Hiroshi and Yoko are both out looking for you."

He looked up sharply. "Really? You were that worried?"

She touched his hands and felt his forehead. "You have a fever again. I'll get you some tea and then you must go right to bed."

He was slumped over the table with his head on his arms when she came back from the kitchen.

"Drink this," she said.

He lifted his head and began to cough, pulling out his handkerchief and holding it in front of his face. There was blood on the handkerchief. Old blood and new blood. He stopped coughing. He was breathing heavily again and gasping. They both stared at the blood.

"I've washed all your handkerchiefs," she said. "I never saw that before."

He stuffed it in his pocket. "I throw them away if they have blood on them." He coughed again, breathing with great effort. As if a tiger were inside him rattling his rib cage.

"It's started again. It's consumption. I've had it since I was in Siberia. I thought it was cured. But it wasn't. I had to go back into the hospital. I didn't want you to see me until I was well."

"Shintaro," she said. "Oh, please don't—please get well. I just can't—" She stood up. "I'll make your bed up."

"The doctor didn't want to tell me that I still had it, but I knew that he knew. And I told him not to tell you. Not yet. I thought if I could just—"

She helped him undress. She gave him a cup of broth to drink. He was sleeping when Yoko and Hiroshi came back.

"He's very tired," she told them. "He overdid it. Got absorbed in the bookstores down on the Hondori."

He was better in the morning, smiling and contented to have her near him, bringing him rice gruel and fluffing up his pillows. She stopped going to the factory and stayed at home, listening to his stories.

"There are new drugs for that now," Isao advised. "They can cure it."

"He was in a hospital in Tokyo," Chiyo countered. "They thought he was well, but apparently he wasn't."

"We'll find somebody who can do something."

Isao persuaded a specialist in Osaka to come down for an examination.

"It's too late," the doctor said. "Too much of the lung has deteriorated. The best thing is to keep him comfortable."

286

Sometimes he woke her in the night and told her stories. "Don't worry about the spies," he said. "There weren't any spies. I just told you all that because I didn't want you to think I was sick. I'm sorry. I've worried you more this way."

"What part of this is true and what isn't?" she asked. But he wasn't listening to her.

It was like sitting near Yukiji's bed, not knowing which stories to believe and which ones were created out of delirium and ancient dreams and boyhood fantasies.

"But what about Shin Hara?" she asked. "And who jumped overboard?"

He looked at her sharply. "Jumped overboard? Did I tell you about that?"

He was snoring loudly.

In April, just before the cherry trees bloomed, he reached over in the middle of the night and shook her awake, then fell back onto his pillow. "Chi-chan!" he demanded. "When are we going out to the island? Isn't it time for the *mikan* harvest? And the daisies. When is Yoko going to make me a daisy chain?"

She sat up, lifted his head and put it on her lap. "As soon as you're feeling better we'll go."

He had closed his eyes, but she could not forget his gaze.

She sang to him. "Sakura. Sakura." The song about the cherry blossoms and the warmth of the spring to come. She told him about his cherry trees in the garden, and how they had blossomed every year, even the year after the bomb.

He did not respond.

In the morning Yoko and Hiroshi came and slid open the doors; Then they moved forward to kneel beside their father and their grieving mother.

Chapter Twenty-eight

THE DAYS THAT FOLLOWED SHINTARO'S death merged into a haze of furtive movements, whispers, voices, sentences begun and half finished. And tears. She couldn't stop crying. Whenever she spoke the tears drowned her with their intensity.

It had been a dark, cold winter, and through the rest of April, Chiyo seldom stirred from the house. Asahi Enterprises continued without her help. Hiroshi and Yoko managed the housework. Chiyo was not interested in wooden or clay dolls, in reading, in going shopping, even in eating. She could not sleep. She stared at old photographs of Shintaro. They had neglected to take any recent photographs, thinking they had the whole span of their lives to be together again. Now all that remained were the old photographs. She buried herself in memories of the days when their family was whole and the world around Shintaro and herself was filled with health and well-being, youth and laughter.

Shintaro's cherry trees bloomed ferociously, or so Yoko said. Chiyo refused to look at them. Her bones were cold and did not warm to the spring sun. She could hear Hiroshi's and Yoko's worried voices whispering from the other side of the *shōji*.

"If we could get her interested in something," Yoko said. "If we could just—"

Chiyo cooked their breakfast and cleaned the house. Gradually she began walking to the station for shopping. One day she stopped to visit Okura-san, the junk man, and sat where she had sat that day with Shintaro, listening to the man's stories about her husband. She wanted to know everything about his life in Siberia and Japan. She was haunted by the feeling that there was something someone could have done or said to make things turn out differently. She asked whether Okura-san had noticed Shintaro's illness. But the junk man had known Shintaro only for a short time. "You know, those of us who live as I do, we make friends fast, then lose track of people. We don't ask each other much. We just talk about where the best scrap iron is."

Chiyo pondered whether to make the trip to Tokyo to track down Yamanaka Tadanori's daughter. But she did not know what Shintaro had told the woman. And she did not want to reveal the real circumstances of Yamanaka's death.

She looked among his few possessions for an address book, a letter, notes to himself. A diary. There was nothing that could give her a link to the nine years he'd been away from her.

"At least you know where he is," Mrs. Otsuka said when she came to pay Chiyo a sympathy visit. "There are thousands of women in the Movement who've never received any word at all. Not a single letter."

"I know," Chiyo said. "I should feel fortunate, but I do not."

Chiyo began to go into the factory just to get away from the worried faces of Hiroshi and Yoko. She dusted her desk, cleaned out old files, talked to Keiko about the orders still coming in, unabated, from the PXs and tourist shops.

Everything was going so smoothly that Chiyo sometimes joined the factory workers at the long table and painted doll faces, which seemed more than anything else to temper the hard edge of her grief.

In August 1952, the cenotaph designed by Isamu Noguchi was unveiled in the Peace Park, a huge tunnel-shaped tomb in the style of a *haniwa* house, the kind made for the clay figures buried with emperors in ancient times.

After the mayor's speech, there was a ceremony dedicated to the unknown victims and enshrining the death certificates of the identified ones. Everyone pushed forward in a massive throng, pressing their faces inside the arch of the tomb to get a look at the names on the registries before they were buried. Chiyo, knowing Kenichi had no death certificate, stood at a distance in the plaza with Yoko and Hiroshi, gazing at the monument's vast shape, the arch slanting forward like the covered wagon she'd seen once years ago in an American cowboy movie in Tokyo on her honeymoon.

After the ceremony ended and the people moved away, the three of them went closer to see the registries and then look through to the other side of the cenotaph beyond the river where the Atomic Dome's framework stood vacant against the sky. Some people said the dome was dangerous, a hazard to children who played there. It could collapse at any moment and should be torn down, they said. But the mayor said it was strong enough and should stand there as a testament against war until some future time when it gave up of its own accord.

They read the inscription. "Sleep in peace; this grievous error will never again be committed." Isao's friend, Professor Saiga, had decided to write what he believed and ignore the comments of the others, let the controversy take its course. Now his solemn promise was engraved in stone, and it comforted Chiyo. Maybe Kenichi's death meant something to the rest of the world.

They wandered through the park, offering prayers to Kenichi's and Shintaro's souls, and at dusk floated candles for them from the new Peace Bridge that linked one side of Hiroshima with the other, along the line of the fire lane. The candle on Kenichi's paper boat remained unextinguished all the way out to the edge of the night, then disappeared from view.

The next day at the factory, Chiyo found Morishita-san looking at the new issue of the *Asahi Graphics*. In it was the first publication anywhere of photographs taken just after the bombing. Censorship had ended when the peace treaty was implemented, and now it was revealed that a Japanese news photographer had managed to get into the city and take a series of photographs right near the Aioi Bridge. One was of burned and naked people, taken just moments after the bomb fell. There were pictures of bridges and buildings destroyed, but the most terrible were the ones of people lying in the infirmaries, dehumanized pieces of charcoal.

Morishita-san, who had lost so much of his family, pressed the magazine shut and went outside to inspect the dahlias he had planted at the corner of the factory building.

Chiyo followed him. "I wish those pictures had never been published," she told him. "Why bring up those old memories now that people have them half buried?"

"But we can't forget," he said. "The rest of the world doesn't have any idea was it was like. The least we can do is get people to look at those pictures."

He gazed a while longer at his blossoming dahlias, then marched back into the factory, opened up the kiln, and inspected the result of his new glazes.

In the middle of August, Fusako, who was finishing her M.A. in English literature in Tokyo, became a member of the first group in Japan to be awarded a Fulbright Scholarship. She arrived home in a flurry of excitement, preparing to leave in September. Kazuko followed after her, shopping and helping to decide what to pack, tight-lipped and clenching her fists when she talked about it. She suggested to Fusako that, before going off to America, she should have at least one or two *omiai* with prospective husbands. "That way," she said, "you have something to look forward to when you come home."

Fusako would have none of it.

"She's got to marry by the time she's twenty-six," Kazuko complained to Chiyo. "She's twenty-five now. She should have married when she was twenty-three. You know how dangerous it is if she reaches twenty-seven or twenty-eight and still doesn't have a husband. She hardly has her pick of the cream now."

But compared to the adventure in America, Chiyo thought the problem was insignificant. "There will always be husbands for Fusako," Chiyo said. "All the bright young diplomats will want to marry her. She's beautiful and intelligent and will speak good English so that she can move in international circles."

Isao agreed. "She's going to be married the rest of her life, so let her enjoy a trip abroad. The rest of us never got to do that."

"You can come and visit, Mama."

"And where would we get the money for that? Nobody can afford a trip to America without a scholarship."

Kazuko and Isao came home from Tokyo bringing a series of photographs of Fusako standing at the ship's railing waving goodbye. Isao had caught the motion of her hand in each picture, the ship diminishing into the distance, Fusako's slender figure leaning out toward the shore until finally her face was no longer distinguishable from the others.

In the fall Morishita-san announced that the factory in Kyoto which had always supplied cylinders for their dolls was no longer in business. The man who made them had died and his son had gone into another line of work. He and Honda-san had their hands full keeping the orders filled for their new products. His Miyajima-style vases were selling especially well because of the purple-blue glaze he had developed. And Honda-san was occupied with producing high-quality wooden rice paddles. Even if they had another lathe, Morishita-san explained, they couldn't keep up with the painters, who couldn't keep up with the orders.

Chiyo decided she would have to offer higher wages to attract efficient factory workers. But she knew the painters would complain. Their own wages had not been raised for some time.

She consulted with Isao.

"You can't pay out all the profits in wages," he told her. "You have to keep some of it back for other expenses."

"I do," she said. "But the painters should get the rest of it. They're the ones doing the work that sells the product."

"There are expenses besides salaries," Isao said. "Deterioration of the building, rent we may have to pay someday. And the price of wood is going up. Maybe the painters will have to subtract the cost of making the cylinders from their own profits. That is if you can find someone who can make them in the first place. It's a special skill."

"You've got good artistic sense and high ideals," he said. "But I'm afraid that for business you need someone hard-hearted like me watching over you."

"Well," Chiyo said, picking up the leather briefcase he had given her when he appointed her president of the company she didn't really control, "I think I'll go home and think this over by myself."

At home alone, she wished desperately she could talk to Nakayama. He would know what to do. His father had operated a factory. But she hadn't talked to him since the train ride home from Tokyo. He had sent her a sympathy card and signed the guest book at the funeral. But she did not feel she could ask him for advice.

"We're at a crisis point," she said to Morishita-san and Keiko. "Let's call a meeting and ask the workers and shopkeepers what to do about prices and wages."

Chiyo chose a day when she knew Isao would be out of town. Morishita-san borrowed *zabuton* from a nearby temple, and they spread out a straw mat underneath them at the far end of the factory floor. Some of the women made tea and brought rice cakes. Even two American servicemen from the PX in Iwakuni came and milled around among the workers, bowing and trying out the few Japanese phrases they knew.

She saw Nakayama walk in and take a cushion at the back of the room.

The shopkeepers explained that they could sell twice as many dolls, that price was no consideration for the foreigner soldiers on leave from Korea.

They decided to raise the retail price to two hundred yen. Everyone began to agree to a big increase in pay for factory workers and a small one for painters, but no one was very satisfied with the solution, and nobody knew where they could find good wood-carvers.

"Excuse me," said Nakayama, standing up and addressing the whole assembly. "It's the painting that gives these dolls their folk-craft character, of course. We all know and appreciate that, but the shape is important, too, and nobody can paint unless there's something to paint on. I suggest you find an engineer, perhaps your brother, Mrs. Hara, who can design some conveyer-belt-style machinery. Then, with a good wage, you could have your pick of people who would want to operate the machinery. And you wouldn't need to hire more than one or two. Of course, it will cost more in the beginning, but the machinery should pay for itself soon and will bring bigger profits to everyone."

They were all enthusiastic. Except Chiyo, who was depressed by the idea of asking Isao for help.

Chiyo searched for Nakayama to congratulate him, then found him at the door ready to leave. He bowed to her. "I was extremely saddened by the news of your husband's untimely death," he said. "Having lost my own wife, I can feel the depths of your sorrow."

She murmured her thanks, returning the bow.

"Now I must go," he said. "I am shorthanded at the shop." He stepped outside and was gone.

She felt suddenly bereft. The meeting had been a success. Nakayama had given good advice. But she had not expected such distance and formality from him. And she valued his opinions as counterpoint to Isao's.

A week later, without warning, Isao arrived at the factory with a huge truck and began moving in equipment. It seemed he had designed it on weekends in Inokuchi, with Hiroshi helping, and had built it at Toyokogyo during evening hours.

Spread before her was a dazzling array. There was a machine that sawed the wood into the right length, one that shaped it with lathes into cylinders and balls of different sizes, another that polished the pieces and set them onto a conveyer belt, ready to be sorted. There was even a contraption that slapped the clay into plaster molds at a surprising speed. Isao stood proudly ordering people where to put it all. He'd brought an electrician to rewire the building for additional power.

"I think you should be able to produce two thousand cylinders a day instead of the eight hundred or so you used to turn out," he said. "If everything works the way I hope, we can supply even more equipment from the obsolete stuff we have out at Toyokogyo."

"Did you ask your brother secretly so you could surprise us?" Morishita-san asked her later.

"Not at all. He did this on his own without any consultation." She couldn't have felt more irritated with Isao. And yet he'd done exactly what they wanted without even being asked.

"We'd better have a ceremony inaugurating the new machinery," she said. "We'll call in a Shinto priest to bless it."

As she stood with the factory workers, watching the priest shake purifying water over the machinery, she knew absolutely that someday, if even for only brief moments, she would be able to enjoy simple pleasures again.

Chapter Twenty-nine

KYOKO AND YOKO GRADUATED FROM Hiroshima Girls' School in March 1953, the twenty-eighth year of the reign of the Emperor Showa. They gave up their blue serge high school uniforms forever and in April would become first-year students at the Women's College in Ushita. They would study English, and afterwards go abroad to school. Like Fusako. Or they would get a job using their English to promote international brotherhood, because Japan was going to be the Switzerland of Asia.

Chiyo and Mrs. Ikeda spent a whole day preparing a feast of broiled chicken and *makizushi*. They spread out thin sheets of seaweed, covered them with rice, then filled the middle section with long slices of cucumber and burdock, thin sheets of scrambled egg, cooked spinach, tiny red slices of pickled ginger. They rolled everything into long, black seaweed logs which they sliced into rounds and piled high on the two old family sushi plates that had been stored in Inokuchi, virtually the only items not bartered for food during the desperate times. It was the kind of sushi Chiyo had tried to imitate during the war, but this feast was a real one. And it was going to approach prewar abundance.

Everyone went to the ceremony, Kazuko and Isao, the Ikedas, Yasu and Mrs. Yamamoto. Afterwards, they gathered for the feast at the Ikeda house, which was larger than Chiyo's.

They sat around the table, laughing, telling school stories. Chiyo and Kazuko reminisced about their own days at the Girls' School. Isao shared memories Chiyo had never heard before.

The food kept disappearing, and Chiyo took serving plates to the kitchen. Kyoko, cutting the last roll of sushi, reached over to dip her knife into water and accidentally nicked her left wrist. She bled profusely. Water, towels, and ice cubes were of no avail. Yasu lifted Kyoko's arm high in the air, pinching hard against her wrist, but the moment he put it down, the bleeding began again.

Isao took Kyoko and her mother to the Red Cross Hospital in his car. The others followed on a streetcar, leaving behind the younger Mrs. Ikeda and her happy, hopelessly retarded young son, Kunio.

At the hospital, Kyoko's hemorrhaging finally stopped, and they gave her a blood transfusion. The doctors diagnosed a severe case of chronic leukemia.

"They were always telling us it was anemia," Mrs. Ikeda said, wringing her hands in the hall. "And she's been so healthy lately I thought she'd outgrown it."

"It's chronic, Mother. Not acute," Ichiro told her. "They say they can keep it arrested for years. Sometimes children get over it."

"She isn't a child anymore," Mrs. Ikeda said. "She's a young woman."

They took Kyoko to the Atomic Bomb Casualty Commission for another diagnosis, and it was the same. The doctors there said she should continue with the drug she'd been given at the Red Cross Hospital to provide temporary remission.

She stayed in bed during spring vacation, missing the trip to Kyoto she and Yoko planned.

In April, Kyoko wasn't well enough to attend the opening day ceremonies at the college. Yoko signed them both up for the same classes, brought Kyoko's homework to her every day, spent the late afternoons and the evenings studying with her.

By late April, Kyoko felt better and said she was ready to begin her college education. She and Yoko took the daily trip to college in a tiny three-wheeled taxi, a *bata-bata,* they called it, because it wavered through the potholed and muddy road. But it cost them only ninety yen, and they usually found other students along the way who were glad to ride and share the expense.

In May, when the azaleas were blossoming, the first-year students planned an excursion with their relatives and friends at Rakuraku-En, the Park of Enjoyment and Pleasure. Kyoko insisted, over her mother's objections, that she was well enough to go. They boarded the streetcar with baskets and bundles of food. A new group of students got on at each stop. They arrived at the park like an invading army, spreading out their straw mats under the trees on the hill so they could have a full view of the azaleas and the sea. They sang college songs, did folk dances, listened to one student who could play popular American music on a guitar and who taught them all to sing a song in English. Kyoko, sitting between Yoko and Yasu, sang at the top of her lungs. When the guitarist switched to Japanese music and began to play the "Old Coal Miner's Folk Dance," Kyoko clapped her hands vigorously to match the music beat, then stood up with the others to dance.

"Kyoko!" Mrs. Ikeda reprimanded. "You don't have to do everything everybody else does. Can't you just sit quietly and watch?"

But Kyoko had already been pulled into the circle. She danced the song through twice, finally collapsing, laughing, on the grass beside Yoko and Yasu.

It was late afternoon, the sun staring at them from just above the mountains, when they started down the hill. Kyoko stumbled on a rock. "Yoko-chan! I can't—" She spoke softly, but both Chiyo and Mrs. Ikeda heard her and turned to see her fall limply against Yasu's shoulder. Yoko caught her other arm, and Yasu lifted her up and carried her.

"I *told* you we shouldn't have come!" Mrs. Ikeda said harshly, turning to look at her daughter, who could no longer hear her. "I *told* you we should have gone home an hour ago."

Hiroshi ran down the hill to the entrance of the park and hailed a taxi. Not a three-wheeled one, but an expensive black limousine with a curtain in the back. He held the door open for Mrs. Ikeda, Kyoko, and Yasu, who entered swiftly and silently, telling the driver to go immediately to the Red Cross Hospital. Chiyo rushed forward, dumping all her money into Mrs. Ikeda's hand.

"It's all right," said the driver. "I can come by your house later and collect the money."

They sat in the corridor of the Red Cross Hospital, waiting until Kyoko's doctor finally appeared, his face serious and drawn.

"I'm afraid it might have become acute, but of course we're not sure yet," he said. "And no," he said in answer to Yoko's question, "it's not because of her getting overly tired. There's nothing anyone could have done to prevent it. Going on the excursion didn't matter much. And we're trying everything. There's still hope, you know. We're doing a blood transfusion, and we think we can get it into remission the way we did before. It's just— You'd better not go in to see her just now. Maybe tomorrow." He strode off down the corridor. "She has a bed in the A-bomb wing in ward B," he called back over his shoulder.

They took turns with the vigil, spelling each other through the day, each one waiting through the span of a night. Mrs. Ikeda refused to leave at all.

"It's no use tiring yourself like this," Chiyo told her. "We're all here and we'd let you know the minute anything changes. You've got to be sensible and get some rest."

She obeyed when she was too weak to argue, but there were times throughout the warm days of May and into the rainy season in June that they worried more about Mrs. Ikeda than about Kyoko, who had her good days and her bad ones.

Yasu seldom went home to Ujina. He alternated between the living rooms of the Ikedas and the Haras, snatching hours of sleep whenever he could, then sitting up all night in the corridors of the hospital or keeping vigil with Mrs. Ikeda in Kyoko's room, dashing off during the day to work on the physics project he needed to have finished by fall.

At the end of June, just when the rainy season was over, Kyoko was sitting up in her bed, laughing with her visitors and talking about going home.

"She's a miracle," the doctor said. "I think we've arrested it, maybe permanently."

Mrs. Ikeda began preparing Kyoko's room, which Ichiro had added to the gradually expanding Ikeda shack the summer before.

Yoko had been furiously folding paper cranes; *orizuru,* they were called. She and Kyoko and their classmates were making them in accordance with the old legend that a crane, a symbol of longevity and good fortune, could live a thousand years. "So if a person folds a thousand cranes, the person's wish is granted," Yoko explained. She and her classmates had already finished 782 of them, all colors and sizes, strung together in wreaths.

"We'd better go on folding anyway," one of the girls said. "Just in case."

"But if we fold them now when she's so much better, it's like a loss of faith," Yoko argued. "The Western Paradise has sent us a signal that she's going to get well."

Still, just to make sure, they kept the wreaths in Kyoko's room, and sometimes, surreptitiously, the classmates folded more.

Chiyo took the train to Himeji with Keiko Kakihara one morning to inspect the origami-style paper dolls Mrs. Oguchi and several of her friends had been making. They wanted Asahi Enterprises to distribute them nationally.

The dolls were beautiful and the arrangements so productive that Chiyo had to call Yoko to tell her they would stay an extra day and be home on the 10:00 P.M. train.

To her surprise, Yoko and Yasu were at the train the next evening to meet her.

"Why all this fuss?" Chiyo said. "It's only a short walk home."

"Kyoko's been asking for you," Yoko said. They went straight to the hospital.

Chiyo had not been to the hospital for almost a week, and she was shocked by the change. Kyoko's body was so thin that Chiyo could hardly make out where it was under the blanket. As if that part of her had already turned into spirit. Her hair was surprisingly thin, too, her brow fevered, her jawbones and the blue veins around her nostrils painfully visible. But Kyoko's eyes were burning, and her smile was stronger than it had ever been. She was beaming at Chiyo.

"Hara Kā-chan," she said. "Mama Hara, you came!" Kyoko had called her by that special name ever since the days after the bomb when they first came to visit in Inokuchi. Back then, Kyoko had been the strong one. Now her mother stood by the bed like the trunk of a cypress, gazing at Kyoko, not even looking at Chiyo for fear of missing something Kyoko said or did.

Mrs. Ikeda stood by Kyoko's bed all night. The rest of them walked back and forth by the light of a small paper lantern Kyoko's elder brother, Ichiro, had brought so that everyone could continue to fold paper cranes while they took turns standing next to Mrs. Ikeda in her silent vigil. The cranes filled the room from end to end, splashing out in brilliant colors and varied patterns.

"Come on. Keep it up. Keep going. Don't stop," Yoko said, handing out the origami, the colored paper, to everyone, even to Kunio, the Ikeda grandchild, who was now eight years old but fumbled with his portion of paper and folded it into wadded, crumpled bits. Yoko counted each of his efforts anyway, along with the others, adding them to the stringed wreaths she was making in between her own frantic folding.

Toward dawn, the doctor and two nurses, working frantically, gave her one more transfusion. The nurses, standing by her bed afterwards, folded several of the cranes themselves.

Kyoko died in the early morning when the sun's rays were pushing fingers of light into the room. It was the seventh of July, the day of the Tanabata Festival and exactly one month short of eight years after the day she had encountered the atomic bomb. They had just finished folding their 967th paper crane. Yoko was keeping count, and she was numb with pain and guilt for having stopped weeks earlier when there was still time, when they could have easily finished one thousand.

Mrs. Ikeda refused to move even after the orderlies came to wheel Kyoko's bed away. When they started to pull the sheet up over Kyoko's head, one of the nurses gently lifted Mrs. Ikeda's hand from Kyoko's brow and placed it on top of the other one, which Mrs. Ikeda was clutching against her own waist.

"Why her? Why her?" The question pounded into Chiyo's brain like a drumbeat. "Why her instead of us?" They straggled out into the hall and stood huddled together, staring off into space, waiting to collect the mountains of folded cranes and Kyoko's possessions.

"Why all of them instead of us middle-aged ladies?" Chiyo and Mrs. Ikeda and Mrs. Yamamoto, each of them wandering everywhere in the city that day, touching burning bodies, burning their feet and faces. "Why not us?" Three middle-aged ladies who'd been spared in order to bring up their remaining children.

Kyoko and Yukiji Ikeda and Kenichi Hara and Sachiko Yamamoto had hardly begun their lives. And Kyoko had been far out in the country when the bomb fell. And Takano-sensei hadn't even arrived in the city until midafternoon. And now they were dead like all the others.

And why Mrs. Ikeda? Like Chiyo, losing a husband and a son. And her parents besides. Wasn't that enough? Now Kyoko, too. And still looming ahead in the future, a grandchild growing up without the capacity to take care of himself. What terrible force could wreak that kind of vengeance on well-meaning, helpless, harmless Mrs. Ikeda?

And how could Kyoko die when the azaleas had been so brilliant that spring?

Chapter Thirty

ON A CLEAR BELL-LIKE MORNING IN November 1954 the radio announced the Soviet Union would begin again to send home prisoners.

Mrs. Otsuka called long distance from Kyushu, filled with enthusiasm about the Red Cross successes in negotiating. "They say it's going to be a massive repatriation, bigger even than the one in 1949. Everybody's really coming home this time. I just feel it!" She chattered on for a while, then stopped short, her thoughts turning to Chiyo.

"Someone on that ship will have known your husband," Mrs. Otsuka said. "That would be rather a comfort, wouldn't it? To talk to someone who has known him?"

"Well, it might," Chiyo said. "I don't know—"

Mrs. Oguchi wrote from Himeji, repeating hopeful stories and rumors that abounded everywhere about husbands coming home. Chiyo sympathized, but she did not want to hear the stories. She slipped away from the factory to a nearby Buddhist temple and prayed to Kannon that all the men be sent home soon. Then she could be done with the Movement forever.

At home she was faced with Hiroshi, studying as usual, and with

Yoko in her depression and torpor, unable still, after her father's and Kyoko's deaths, to give her full attention to her new college life.

When the passenger list was published for the ship arriving in Maizuru on December 1, Yoko found, printed clearly and unmistakably, the name of Haruo Otsuka.

Mrs. Otsuka arrived in Hiroshima on the way to Maizuru, barely able to contain the excitement that was packed into her small, reserved frame. Chiyo thought, looking at her from across the table, that she was like a young bride, her complexion soft and her face flushed.

She walked with Mrs. Otsuka to the station. Standing on the platform, waiting for the train to come in, she felt a jab of nostalgia for Maizuru and for the intense, hungry hope she had felt in those days.

Five days later a telegram came: "Husband arrived safely. Otsuka."

There was one more ship in March, but no news of Mr. Oguchi.

In April a letter came for Shintaro, written by a Kotaro Matsumoto in Kyushu.

Greetings to Hara Shintaro:

Now the plum blossoms have faded and the blooming cherry trees will soon march northward through Japan like an army. I think often of those days in Siberia and of the times we dreamed of our homecoming. I have finally returned after eleven years away.
Three of us from the old days were on the ship: Konoe, Shimizu, and I. We resolved to find you and the others for a reunion. Remembering your indomitable spirit and resourcefulness has been a constant comfort to me all these years.

We have chosen the seaside resort of Hikari at the Mirukai Inn for our reunion, and we plan two days of banqueting and reminiscing just at the end of the rainy season, the second week of July. Bring your wife and children so that we can meet them.

Deepest regards to you and your family.

In the Brotherhood. As always,

Matsumoto Kotaro

The next day a special-delivery letter arrived from Mrs. Oguchi, explaining that she had been invited to a reunion in Mirukai by a man who had known her husband.

It was the first inkling either of them had that their husbands had known each other.

* * *

The reunion was in a traditional Japanese inn, old and a bit shabby, but with a pristine purity, perched on a ridge away from the beach, the windows opening out to the gentle summer breeze and a view of the Inland Sea.

At the banquet on the first evening when they introduced themselves, Chiyo explained that her husband had died, and Mrs. Oguchi that hers had not returned. A wave of sympathy spread through the room.

During the dinner, they came one at a time, bringing their sake cups and bottles to greet the two women, pouring a toast to share, telling them what they remembered of their husbands. It seemed that Oguchi, Hara, and Matsumoto had formed a triumvirate of sorts to protect their unit.

"Right away, the Soviets recognized them as leaders," said Mr. Konoe, "and tried bribing them with extra food and comforts. Some men got bought off, you know, everybody so hungry and desperate to stay alive. But the only way they could get those three to cooperate was to keep the rations coming for everyone in the unit.

"There's a story about a captain who punished his own men when they didn't meet the quota, made them sit outside tied up against a wall all night. In the morning, half of them were dead." Mr. Konoe sat cross-legged, nodding as if he needed to convince even himself. "Our own countryman, you know.

"But your husband seemed to understand the Soviets better than the rest of us, Mrs. Hara. He managed to learn Russian very fast, you see, maybe because his Chinese was so good."

"He had a presence, Hara-sensei," Mr. Shimizu said. "He made us proud to be Japanese even though we'd been defeated."

Eventually the others excused themselves and went off to bed, leaving only Matsumoto-san with Chiyo and Mrs. Otsuka. He was a thick, heavy man of powerful build, at least five years younger than Shintaro, and he sat in a pensive mood, trying to analyze what could have happened to Mrs. Oguchi's husband.

"They knew the three of us were at the root of the trouble that time we refused to work. I'm sure they knew about the rations, too. We older men always took something out of our portions each day and saved it. And once we took a whole bag of rice from behind the guard's back."

Matsumoto-san was lost in thought. "But why only them?" he said finally. "They knew I was involved in all the conspiracies. Why didn't they take me too?"

"Take you where?" Mrs. Oguchi asked quietly. She was a small woman. All evening she had been sitting in formal position, her hands clasped across her lap, her kimono neatly tucked under her knees, quietly taking in the pearls of information she would later string together to make a coherent whole.

Matsumoto-san looked at her, startled. "Oh, of course," he said, "I didn't tell you the rest of the story."

He looked at both women, searching their faces.

"Before I go on," he said, "I want you both to know that it is because of their spirits that most of us here tonight are still alive. Not just because they thought of ways to keep us fed or ways to preserve our strength. But because of the way they lived. They never, never gave up. They never stopped hoping."

For a moment the three of them sat in silence.

"Thank you for telling us," Mrs. Oguchi said. "Now tell us the rest of the story."

Matsumoto-san nodded. "So, one day, just out of the blue, they announced that some men were returning to Japan. An old army truck came into camp with two Russian guards, and they took only your husbands and one German prisoner. That was all. It was a strange arrangement, of course, and we all wondered about it, but we were glad for them, and relieved that someone trustworthy would get in touch with our families.

"I should have known there was something funny about it. Usually, they sent back whole groups of men." He pressed out his cigarette, then went and stood at the window with his back to them.

"So, you see, if they took those two away because they knew who was in back of the strikes and hoarded food, then they would have taken me away too. But I was too outspoken about my politics. Your husbands were always warning me that it wasn't safe to talk too much, and it's a terrible irony that I'm here in this room talking to you and your husbands are not.

"In the end, I think, they saw that I was more useful to them in the camp, keeping the members of our unit alive. The three of us all working together—well, that was too much for them. But with the other two gone, then I couldn't steal as much food or make as many plans. They could control me better."

He came back and sat down.

"So we know now that Hara-sensei agreed to their arrangements." He looked up at Chiyo. "And he did it without losing his integrity. You see, he always supported more equality for workers and farmers and young soldiers in the army. He didn't believe in communism, but I suppose he was more of a socialist than the rest of us.

"Your husband was different," he said, turning to Mrs. Oguchi. "I don't think he could bring himself to agree. Even though I know he wanted desperately to go home. He couldn't make that promise and keep his integrity. And if he refused to do what they asked, well—who knows what could have happened to him?" Mr. Matsumoto lit another cigarette. "They were a wily bunch. And frightening."

Mrs. Oguchi stared at him with such intensity that he looked away. "If you think he was killed, tell me," she said. "The Movement has sent letters asking about him. But from what you say, they would have remembered him, wouldn't they? He's not somebody who just died in the snow walking back from work. And if they killed him, as you imply, they wouldn't admit it. But at least the people in the Movement could make a bigger fuss about it, try to make them admit something definite."

Matsumoto could not meet her gaze. "Yes," he said. "I think he died or that they killed him. It's been five years. And these days, you know, the men on every ship make lists of the ones still in Russia. His name hasn't been on any of the lists. I've checked."

Mrs. Oguchi bowed her head to her lap, nodding in appreciation. "Thank you," she said, "for telling me exactly what you think."

"But it's only my theory," he insisted. "They could have him languishing in solitary confinement where nobody would have a chance to see him. And the Soviets could reverse their policy any day and let him go. Maybe they've even forgotten why they put him there. We've all got to hope for that. At least until the final ship comes home."

She bowed deeply so that he wouldn't see her tears, thanking him again. "Now I would like to sit here a moment and look at the sea," she said. "I am sure both of you are very tired and would like to sleep."

Toward dawn Chiyo awoke to the sound of Mrs. Oguchi weeping endlessly and without restraint in the banquet room next door, pouring forth tears she must have suppressed for eleven years. Chiyo stared at the empty gray sea moving ceaselessly to its own rhythm and utterly indifferent to their pain.

On a morning in mid-September, examining plans with Morishita-san, Chiyo looked up to see Nakayama. An electric shock ran through her nervous system. It had been more than two years.

"We're doing fine," she answered him. "Our problem now is getting enough painters. The new factory workers are turning out cylinders and molds so fast. Now it's the painters who can't keep up."

"Oh?" he commented, distracted, searching around in his huge satchel. "Ah! Here they are! I brought my series of the Seven Happy Gods to show you." He began taking them from his bottomless bag. "Remember when I told you about them in Tokyo?" He looked up at her face. "Of course that was five years ago. You probably don't—"

"I remember," she said.

He lined up seven carved figures on the factory assembly table. They were breathtaking, all of them delicately carved in wood, the Indian Goddess of Mercy with long imperial robes stretched out beneath the huge *biwa* harp she held in her lap. And the Zen monk, his head thrown back, laughing, his hands clutching either side of his fat stomach, which was finished with a soft, flesh-colored varnish, the belly button carved tenderly and affectionately. Rokyo, the God of Intelligence, in the image of Mencius, had a bald head that stuck up above thick brows, extending into a column almost as long as the rest of his body. Chiyo picked up each figure in turn, caressing the high glaze and the shapes. There was the wise and whimsical Rice God with a huge bag on his back. And Vishamon, the temple guardian, who was usually angry and raging. But this one had a protective face, like a faithful watchdog, as lovable as the others.

"They are beautiful, Nakayama-san," she said. "It must have taken you forever to carve them and to get this special glaze effect. You must never sell them."

"They are for you," he said.

She held bald-headed Rokyo in midair, stunned by the generosity of his offer.

"No," she said gently. "You must keep them in your shop where many people can see them. It would be a waste if they were in my small, dark house."

"In your factory, then," he said. "Keep them here for the workers to look at. The hand-carved ones are impractical for mass production anyway. But I've made clay molds for you to try out. Maybe we could have a training class."

"They're wonderful!" Morishita-san said. "But how can we get that glossy effect on the clay? We haven't got the right glazes."

"I think I've found the right one," said Nakayama-san quickly. "I tried it out in my kiln." He pulled out a whole new series made in clay, not as refined but with shiny pink heads and stomachs that radiated warmth and joy. "See, it's two firings," he said, "a bisque one first. That gives the original clay a fleshlike quality. Then I used a transparent glaze for the second firing. I'd like to do a test in your kiln next week."

"It's exactly what we need," Morishita-san said. "A fresh change for the painters. They're getting tired of the old patterns, they'll enjoy these new faces, and they can learn to put the glaze on in just a few minutes. You're a genius, Nakayama-san; you really are. And how about a wood-carving class for these others? Well, but of course nobody can do these wooden ones except you."

He smiled and nodded. "I'm not sure I can do them again myself. It was a one-time project, I'm afraid."

He picked up his satchel and bowed to them both. "I must be going. But I'll be back next week to see if you want to go into production."

"You don't have to give us any time to think about it," said Chiyo. "We know right now, don't we, Morishita-san? We can set up the first training session for whenever you come. Say, Tuesday?"

"That's fine," he said. He started to go, then stopped and turned back. "Well, Mrs. Hara, glad to see you back in the factory and enjoying the presidency of the company once again."

She smiled and bowed in response, then watched him walk through the doorway, his figure silhouetted against the late afternoon sun, which cast his shadow back toward her. She could feel his intensity suppressed tightly inside his calm exterior. He turned to bow once more, and when he straightened, his face in the shadow, his upper body rigid, she could see that his knees were shaking.

Part Five

Chapter Thirty-one

OCTOBER 1956. THE THIRTY-FIRST YEAR of the reign of the Emperor Showa. Chiyo's niece, Fusako, knelt before the priest with her handsome groom and they drank from their red lacquer sake cups, exchanging vows.

Fusako looked like a doll in a glass case, wearing her traditional wig with the hair rolled out wide on the sides and high in the back to show the nape of her neck, the top covered with a white cloth to hide the mythical horns of jealousy which all women possess and which the groom must absolutely not see on his wedding day for fear of being frightened away. There was no way of telling what disappointments Fusako harbored behind her powdered and expressionless porcelain face. But there was something. Chiyo suspected it was "Bobbu" of Ohio, the American soldier of the early *kokeshi* doll days. Fusako had secretly written Chiyo about the trip to Ohio to visit him. But how strong or deep that friendship had been, no one knew. Fusako's lips were pressed together like a tiny rose, hiding the pain of wearing the heavy, tight wig that pressed against her temples. Chiyo remembered her own wedding headache lasting for two days. And the *obi,* her wide sash, wound so tightly around her waist that she could hardly breathe, let alone taste the elegant food being served at the banquet afterwards.

One thing was certain. This marriage was not what Fusako would have chosen for herself. Chiyo had seen Isao's letter, and she was angry at Fusako for acquiescing so easily.

"I'm glad you've had your studies abroad," Isao had written. "It will enhance our chances for finding you a good husband. But you must come home immediately and help us with the search."

"She wants to stay longer," Chiyo objected. "She hasn't finished her last year of graduate studies. What's the point of going over there and taking the scholarship unless she gets to finish?"

"We only promised her two years," Isao said. "If she stays another year, she'll be thirty, and Kazuko is already nearly out of her mind worrying. It won't be easy finding a *yoshi* willing to take on the family name. It's hard enough for a daughter at any age."

In the end, Fusako gave up her studies and came home to a series of *omiai* in expensive restaurants and tea houses, Fusako and each new prospect sizing each other up while the parents talked. Finally they found Toshio Okada, who was handsome enough, pleasant and affable. It seemed the best they could do. Men with a sense of mission or a creative plan for their lives didn't become *yoshi,* the adopted sons-in-law who gave up their own family names in order to continue the name bloodline of the wife's family. That was the path for those who wanted instant success. And money.

Chiyo had the uncomfortable feeling Isao planned to give Toshio a job at Asahi Enterprises, but the only suitable one was her own job.

Fusako and Toshio drained the sake from their lacquer wedding cups, pledging their vows to one another. The wedding guests flooded into the sunlight, milling around on the wide, barren castle grounds just outside the shrine, the photographer directing them onto special bleachers, photographing each group. First, the new couple, then the couple and their two sets of parents. Next, the couple with all their close relatives. Finally, the whole huge wedding party, including Fusako's foreign teachers and friends from the Atomic Bomb Casualty Commission.

The banquet room in the shrine was large enough for two hundred guests, all kneeling in formal style before the long, low tables arranged in a huge rectangle. The new couple sat at the place of honor in front of the *tokonoma* Kazuko had decorated with a family scroll and a flower arrangement. In descending order of importance, on either side, were their parents, then Toshio's college professor and his wife, who had acted as go-betweens, then the lesser relatives and other guests. The festival food came to each of them on a tray, so many delicacies that no one could eat them all in one sitting. Kazuko had arranged for boxes so that each guest could take the leftovers home. Chiyo shuddered to think how much money had been spent, wondering how she could possibly manage when Yoko's time came. Kazuko and Isao had invited everyone: Isao's business associates, the Inokuchi neighbors, Fusako's classmates and teachers, all of Toshio's friends and relatives, even the Ikedas, the Yamamotos, and the Kasamas. Everyone had come except the Ikeda grandchild and Captain Yamamoto, who rarely left the house.

Yoko and Yasu planned to throw rice at the new Mr. and Mrs. Ogawa when they emerged from the reception, ready for their honeymoon.

It was the first event Yoko had been enthusiastic about since Kyoko Ikeda's death. But Hiroshi was not especially pleased with his assignment. It was hard to get him to do anything these days now that he was in his second year at Tokyo University. He hadn't even wanted to come back for the wedding, but Isao had sent him train fare. And now that he was home, everybody fussed over him too much, praising him, exclaiming how smart he was. He was more surprised by the fuss than by his success at passing the exam. It wasn't pride exactly. Just that he thought the world had been created for him to succeed in. And at the moment, Isao was the only relative he would listen to. No one else was smart enough to give him any advice, but he had lots to offer his mother.

Today he sat fingering his camera during the wedding speeches —neighbors reminiscing about Fusako as a child, teachers and classmates remembering her during the war growing potatoes and squash on the school grounds, a college roommate telling about winning the scholarship. Fusako was the only one among them who'd fulfilled the dream of studying abroad.

An empty dream. Here she was home again with her studies interrupted so she could marry this ordinary young man. Chiyo had preserved Fusako's letters. They contained as many lively observations as Sei Shonagon's *Pillow Book* from the tenth century. Like that earlier diarist, Fusako had given detailed descriptions of everything American, listing things that were splendid, things that were strange, things that were awful. She wrote about her delight in communicating in English, about the difficulties and triumphs of studying anthropology, about her job as a teaching assistant in Japanese, her fascination with the linguistic side of anthropology. She told about the parties she attended—the food, the clothing, her dates with American students, the trip to rural Ohio to visit the parents of the ex-soldier, "Bobbu," the trip Chiyo had promised never to tell Kazuko about.

During the first part of the banquet, Chiyo watched Fusako suppressing her emotions and the pain of her wig. Before the speeches were finished, the bride changed into a less elaborate kimono and removed the wig to reveal her semiformal hairdo underneath. But the *obi* of her second kimono was still too tight for her to eat anything.

When the banquet and the speeches were finished and the guests were milling around, pouring each other toasts of sake, Chiyo helped Fusako change into her going-away Western clothes which brides wore nowadays. It was a simple beige suit and it made Fusako look herself again. The guests formed a line outside for the bride and groom to walk through. Yoko and Yasu moved behind each guest, passing out the rice and explaining how it was done at Western weddings.

"Waste all this good rice just throwing it onto the ground?" one of the older guests asked incredulously. "Don't these younger children remember what it was like during the war?" He poured his own handful into his pocket, explaining that he would take it home to eat for breakfast. But the rest of the guests obeyed, pelting the couple from all sides so that they had to shield their faces.

The couple's parents followed after the wedding taxi in a limousine. The rest of the guests walked the few blocks to the station for the final send-off. Chiyo strolled along listening to Mrs. Yamamoto, whose world had narrowed to a routine of managing the family's tofu factory and spending evenings at home with her disconsolate husband, who had not worked a day since coming home from Siberia.

Today, she was in high spirits, delighted to be away from the house and her husband. Her father-in-law had died the year before but her mother-in-law lingered on, infirm and in constant mourning, requiring even more attention than the captain. Mrs. Yamamoto did not complain, but Chiyo knew that she wanted desperately to be back again in Nobori-chō.

She paused a moment to look down the street to the place where her house had been. The only remaining wall had long since been torn down, and the greengrocer, Kasama-san, was planting vegetables there.

"Someday we'll come back," she said. "It won't be long before we start looking for a bride for Yasu, you know. He's already received job offers, one from a good engineering firm in Tokyo. But I think he wants to stay in Hiroshima. I've told him I wouldn't mind moving. There's a man who wants to buy the *tofu* business and Husband doesn't care where he is since he never goes out anyway. I should think Yasu would be glad of a chance to start a new life, but you know, since Kyoko died, he's never confided in me. Maybe he tells everything to Yoko-chan. Do you think? She's the only one left from his childhood."

They were crossing the bridge to the station now, and Mrs. Yamamoto stopped to look over the edge. "I always used to do this in the old days," she said. "But, of course, I've never felt the same about crossing bridges since the bomb. There's hardly a bridge in the city we didn't cross that day, is there?"

They began walking again. "I hope Yasu isn't a bother to you. He's over at your house so much."

"Actually, with my work at the factory, I haven't noticed either of them around much," Chiyo said. "Yoko's usually singing in the choir or directing the school play, or, you know, all those activities at the Women's College. And she'll be a senior next year. It doesn't seem possible, does it?"

When they entered the station, Chiyo caught a glimpse of Yoko and Yasu running up the stairs to the platform. She was shocked to see that they were holding hands. Acceptable behavior, maybe, if they were children. But Yasu was almost twenty-four.

The recognition of it paralyzed her. Had Mrs. Yamamoto known all along? Chiyo could not bring herself even to speak.

Everybody was crowded onto the platform, waving and shouting goodbye, Fusako and Toshio leaning out of the train window. They sang "God Be With You Till We Meet Again," Fusako's favorite hymn. Chiyo looked up as the train pulled out of the station to catch a final glimpse of Fusako's face against the closed train window, a puddle of tears, gazing back at her parents, aunt, and cousins, banished from their company. The sight of her tear-filled face hovered over the tracks even after the train had departed.

Chiyo turned to catch sight of Yoko and Yasu standing against one of the station columns, pressed close to one another by the crowd. They had hardly noticed the departing train.

The crowd dispersed, leaving the two of them still gazing at one another.

Mrs. Yamamoto didn't seem to notice. "Husband will be impossible to live with if I'm away a minute longer. Tell Yasu I've gone on ahead, and send him home, will you?" She disappeared with the others.

"Yoko!" Chiyo shouted. "The limousine's out front waiting to take us to Inokuchi. Yasu, your mother's already started home!"

They didn't hear her.

"Yoko!"

She averted her gaze from Yasu's. "You go on ahead, Mother. I'll come later on the streetcar. Yasu has something important to tell me."

Chiyo stumbled down the stairs and into the waiting limousine.

"You haven't noticed that before?" Isao asked as they sped down the highway. "It was quite obvious today. I've never seen anybody act like that except in a Kabuki drama. Yoko's only twenty, isn't she?"

"Almost twenty-one," Chiyo said.

"Well, she doesn't move or speak without checking that young man's reaction first. It's embarrassing. Who is he?"

"You don't know? He's the Yamamoto son. He was Kenichi's best friend. He and his mother and I searched all through Hiroshima that day, looking for Kenichi and his sister, Sachiko. He's been like a brother to Yoko."

"Brother!" Isao exclaimed.

They arrived at Inokuchi, dismissed the driver, and spread themselves out across the wide *tatami* room. Chiyo had been looking forward to a lengthy discussion of the wedding, Fusako's appearance, the conduct of the guests. Now all she could think of was Yoko.

Isao paced back and forth impatiently. "This young man walked all through the city with you that day and the next? And now he's in love with our Yoko? That will never do, you know. It would be a disaster. They could not have children. It would be one thing if Yoko had been in the city herself, but she was safe here in Inokuchi the whole time. We can't have her marry somebody like that with damaged genes. I don't care what kind of young man he is. We can't risk having her children turn out like the Ikeda grandchild. Anyway, it would eventually make her unhappy. Love is the fancy of the young. It doesn't last the way family does."

"*Anata!*" Kazuko exclaimed, her face vulnerable and wounded. "Do you really believe that?"

He smiled gently at her. "I grew to love you after we were married," he said. "I didn't have any romantic illusions beforehand. How could I? I hardly knew you."

It was onto this scene that Yoko arrived, followed by Yasu.

"Come in, Ya-chan," Yoko said. "Mother, Uncle, Aunt. Hiro-chan, are you here? We have something to tell you."

Chiyo stared at Yoko and Yasu, not believing her ears. This tiny, energetic child, now, at the age of twenty, had decided to marry. And as soon as possible, it seemed. Even before she graduated, if necessary.

Isao was a stone-faced *daimyō*, a feudal lord, his hands folded across his chest and his legs in a half-lotus position. "In our family," he said, "young people do not make decisions like this on their own. In our generation, parents made the decision and then consulted the children. Not the other way around. Both of you have seen too many American movies for your own good, and you are acting on impulse." He pressed his arms closer to his chest.

"Surely, Yoko-chan, you know that your mother and I, who must act in your father's absence, would not consider allowing you to marry the crown prince himself until after you have graduated from college. It is not suitable to marry before that, and considering your immature attitude toward the matter, I think it would be better for you to wait until you are twenty-five. You realize, don't you, that Fusako is twenty-nine? And you should realize, too, that the very afternoon of the marriage of our daughter is not an appropriate time for you to bring up the idea of another marriage." He turned away from her and gave his attention to Yasu.

"And as for you, Mr. Yamamoto, I am sure that if it were not for the unusual circumstances of the past war and the destruction of our native Hiroshima, causing the undermining of all our old traditions, you would prove a suitable husband for our Yoko. I understand you have done brilliantly in your studies at Hiroshima University and that you are considering joining a firm in Tokyo.

"However, because you are older, I would at least expect you to provide some restraint for Yoko. Surely you understand the proper procedure in such matters. Coming before the whole family at a time like this gives evidence that you may be unmindful of proper procedures in other matters as well."

Yoko and Yasu sat, heads bowed.

"Uncle is right," Hiroshi said. "You should have waited at least until you graduated before you asked."

"I do not think," Chiyo said icily, "that you have enough experience to discuss this matter. I would appreciate it if you would just keep quiet."

Hiroshi's face collapsed and Chiyo was sorry. Too late. Why did almost everything he did make her so angry? And why did she have to say such cruel things to him?

"You must be hungry," Isao said abruptly. "Kazuko was just setting out the festival food. Come and join us now, and we'll discuss this again in two years, after you've both graduated and settled into your lives. Until then, I think it would be preferable for you not to see each other."

"Uncle!" Yoko exclaimed. "We've just been at a banquet and—"

"Thank you for your kind invitation," Yasu interrupted, "but even without the previous banquet I would not be hungry now. And I must return to Ujina. Also, I would like you to know that we had no intention of marrying before we both graduate. Yoko has merely suggested that if I am accepted for a job in Tokyo, she would like to join me there as soon as possible, but at the very earliest that would not be before she graduates. However, we did want to inform you in advance that we have this plan. And because all of you are here together, I thought it an excellent time to discuss the future." He fingered a crease in the trousers of his new suit. "I thought you would be pleased," he said in a soft voice, not looking up. "Our families have known each other since before the war, and nowadays, more and more young people are making their own decisions in these matters."

He stood up. "Of course, I will gladly submit to your wishes and wait for two years before discussing the matter."

"Thank you, Uncle, for your kind advice," Yoko said with elaborate politeness, stepping off the *tatami* and bowing again.

"Where are you going?" Isao asked her.

"I will accompany Yasu back as far as Koi, then change streetcars and go home to Nobori-chō."

"Wait!" Isao said. "You may not—"

"Let her go," Kazuko said. "She's been embarrassed enough already."

Isao looked at Kazuko, angry, then, without protest, obeyed her. The four of them watched the shadows disappear from the other side of the door.

"You'll have to tell her that she can never marry him," Isao said to Chiyo. "Tonight."

Back at Nobori-chō, waiting for Yoko, Chiyo tried persuading Hiroshi to go to bed. "It's no good, both of us talking to her. I'd better do it alone. I know you want to help, and that you have our best interests at heart. I know I hurt you today by what I said, and I'm sorry. You've taken the place of your father and your older brother all these years, and you've succeeded more brilliantly than anyone could possibly have imagined. You're capable of doing anything, Hiro-chan, more so than Kenichi would have been. I really believe that, you know. You have more determination and discipline."

He looked at her, the hurt still showing in his face.

She sighed. "It was always easy for Ken-chan to get sidetracked, you know. Everything fascinated him. Remember the butterfly that time out in Inokuchi just after he'd entered middle school?"

Hiroshi nodded, smiling. "It came in through the window and landed on the corner of his book. None of us were even breathing. I remember that."

"Yes," Chiyo said. "Then he tiptoed out to the kitchen, got a glass jar to put over it, got Grandfather's old paint box, and painted it."

"And afterwards he took me outside with him to watch it fly away," Hiroshi said.

"But it was a time when we were so hungry none of us had any energy. So he was too tired afterwards to finish his homework. I scolded him, remember?"

"Yes, but it always seemed that you never meant it as much for him as for me."

"You know that isn't true, don't you?"

He didn't answer her. "Anyway, Ken-chan knew how to take advantage of opportunities, didn't he? Sometimes I just follow the plan I've made. Then I miss the most important thing. Kenichi knew butterflies like that come only once in a lifetime." He looked at her. "At least in his lifetime."

Chiyo had not hugged her tall, strapping eighteen-year-old for many years. She wanted to now, but she did not. How could she tell him how she felt? She had never been able to. She squeezed her eyes shut, pressing back tears, then looked at him again, her handsome son in his Tokyo University uniform.

"You do irritate me," she said when her voice had grown steady again. "Especially when you are being self-righteous. You needn't give advice, you know, unless you are asked to, and even then, you should be hesitant about giving it to someone older. Haven't I told you that before?"

"Well, you're giving me advice right now."

"I'm your mother. And I'm older."

He seemed ready to say something, but he didn't.

"But I adore you," she went on. "You must remember that. No matter what I say to you when I'm angry. I couldn't have survived these years without you. You and Yoko are more important to me than anything in the world."

The air was thick with unsaid things.

"Mother," Hiroshi finally said, "I just want to take care of you." He did not look at her. "That's all I want. I just want you to have a big, comfortable house by the sea like Uncle Isao's and not to work so hard and be able to do some of the things you like. I want to give that to you. I'd like to bring Papa back, but I can't, so all I can hope for is to make you more comfortable."

She gave up her restraint and hugged him, clinging to him. "I know," she said, "I know. And I am very proud of you."

They sat for a time, holding on to each other.

Finally she let him go. "Now, go to bed and leave me alone to talk to Yoko. You'll need to be around tomorrow to pick up the pieces."

He moved reluctantly toward the old sitting room where he slept, then turned to look at her again. "I was just going to say, out there at Uncle's before you interrupted me, that even after they wait two years, she'll have to marry him. She'll never be happy with anyone else, you know. Whether she has children or not."

Chiyo nodded. "Yes."

But it didn't matter what the rest of them thought. They had to do what Isao thought. He was the head of her husbandless family. And maybe Shintaro would have made the same decision. She didn't know.

She slept fitfully, waiting for Yoko, her head resting on her arms, her feet dangling down into the *kotatsu* hole. Sometimes she woke and looked at the clock, alarmed by how late it was, then fell into another slumber.

At midnight, she awoke with a sudden jerk and began pacing the floor. Had the two of them committed double suicide? She would have to wake up Hiroshi, then go to the police box and tell them her daughter was missing. They would launch a long, fruitless search in the river for the bodies. Like the Kabuki plays she'd seen with Grandmother. Star-crossed lovers found dead on the edge of the shore, at the bottom of the bridge, in the base of the volcano, embracing even in death. She searched for her shawl and was just going to waken Hiroshi when Yoko appeared, alone, her face as tragic as it had been when Kyoko died.

•

Chiyo burst into tears. "You're alive!" she said, kneeling on the *tatami* and covering her face with her hands.

"I'm sorry, Mama. We've been down in Nagarekawa in a place that stays open all night, eating *oden* and drinking tea. I knew you would worry, but we couldn't stop talking and arguing. Then Yasu had to catch the last streetcar. I told him to come and sleep in the living room, but he said he didn't want to embarrass you now that Uncle Isao has said we shouldn't see each other."

Yoko climbed up on the *tatami*. "I've been a terrible disappointment to you, Mama, and I'm sorry. I can't help it."

"I am shocked that my daughter, a member of the Hara and Ogawa families, would allow herself to be seen late at night in a bar with a young man. What were you thinking of?"

"Mama, I wasn't thinking of anything except what Yasu was saying, and about how Uncle Isao was acting. We didn't expect that reaction from him. I thought you'd always known I would marry Yasu. He's from a good family and you know his mother and—"

Yoko shook her head. Her face was tearstained.

"But Yasu says that Uncle Isao is worried about damaged genes and retarded children. It's true, isn't it? Yasu told me today that we shouldn't even ask."

Yoko's bright, dressy wedding kimono was wilted and bedraggled. Everybody must have noticed her sitting in that public place, wearing her expensive kimono. People would have recognized her and they would be talking. But why did it matter? What a foolish thing to think of at a time like this.

"Yasu says he doesn't have the right to marry me. He says I'll resent not having children and finally that I won't love him anymore. But that's not true, Mama. I don't care about not having children and I don't care about waiting two years. I'll wait for ten years. Twenty. Forever. I told him I would never stop loving him. Never, never, never."

She pulled herself toward the *kotatsu* and lay her head on a *zabuton*. Chiyo watched her beautiful, delicate daughter. She was like the flowers that blossomed all over Hiroshima after the bomb dropped, all the more exquisite because they shouldn't have been there at all. They should have stayed in Inokuchi. Then Yoko wouldn't have been close to Yasu or anyone else who'd been exposed to the bomb.

"Yasu said nobody wants to marry someone with a *kobu*, a wart, clinging to him." She looked up plaintively. "Mama, tell him it isn't true. Uncle Isao doesn't really think that, does he?"

Chiyo stood up and closed the *shōji* to the outside world, then came back and seated herself at the table across from Yoko.

"Your Uncle Isao did say that," she said gently. "He said that you are the daughter of two very important families. We are descended from samurai on both sides and this marriage could affect our descendants for generations to come. It is all right that your uncle and I are *hibakusha* because we will not have any more children.

"But for you—don't you see? Yasu could die at any time, and leave you alone. Or with children. You might have them even if you try to prevent it, and they might be retarded and you would have to bring them up alone."

"Mother!" Yoko stared at her through the shadows made by the electric light hanging from the ceiling. "You managed to bring us up without a husband. We were all right."

"But you are not retarded. You and Hiroshi are brilliant, beautiful children grown into adults. Warm and helpful. I couldn't have created Asahi Enterprises without you. Or survived. And don't you see? I want you to have what I didn't have. Yasu is a wonderful young man, but you cannot take the risk of marrying him."

"Then who will take the risk? No one loves him as much as I do."

Chiyo turned her face away from Yoko's. Maybe it would be all right, she told herself. Yasu might live to a ripe old age. After all she and Mrs. Yamamoto were still alive. And anyway a few years of happiness were better than none at all. And Yoko, by recent definitions, was a *hibakusha* herself, having cared for the injured in those days after the bomb. Except for Hiroshi they were all *hibakusha*.

But she didn't let go of the argument. "Look at the younger Mrs. Ikeda," she said, "always at home, always worried about her son. Like having a perpetual three-year-old at your side no matter how old he gets. And how could you work and take care of retarded children? The Ikedas have enough people in the family so somebody can stay home. But you wouldn't have anyone except me and Mrs. Yamamoto, and certainly you can't count on our being alive forever."

"Mama!" Yoko was almost shouting. Hiroshi was surely awake, sitting in the next room with his ear pressed up against the *shōji*. "I said we wouldn't have children. Our love is strong enough without them. I can get an abortion if I have to."

"You may think so now, but you have no idea how you'll feel when the time comes. You're not always in control of things like that, you know. And you realize, don't you, that Yasu walked all through the city that day? Every step of the way? It's a miracle he's alive at all."

"You aren't dead!" Yoko retorted. "Or Yasu's mother."

"We're miracles, too."

"You all went out to the suburbs the next day," Yoko argued, "and you had people to take care of you, and you're all very strong."

"Your Aunt Akiko had people to take care of her. And Mr. Takano was very strong. He was getting well. And then," she added more softly, "there was Kyoko."

Yoko fell back on the *tatami,* staring up at the ceiling. Chiyo could hear Hiroshi stirring from his bed behind her.

"If I cannot marry Yasu," Yoko said, "I will not marry anyone. There is no one in the world for me except Yasu. I cannot exist on this earth without him. And I cannot stop seeing him as Uncle Isao has requested me to do."

She rolled back and forth on her sides, sobbing and coughing. She was perspiring, and Chiyo went and got a wet towel and pressed it on Yoko's forehead, and sat, smoothing back her hair until she felt cooler.

Hiroshi came out of the next room and sat down beside them with his knees tucked under his chin, rocking himself back and forth, not touching either of them, not saying anything.

Chapter Thirty-two

CHIYO REMEMBERED NEITHER THE DECI-
sion to make the trip nor the trip itself. She
was simply standing in Nakayama's shop in Miyajima, observing
him while he knelt behind his glass case, the same position he had
been in when she first met him and saw his gracious *kokeshi* dancing
across the shelf above. Now his shelves were filled with her own
factory creations. And the shop was still populated with foreign
soldiers, but fewer than before. A sprinkling of Japanese tourists
sat at the familiar tables beyond the counter, sipping tea and eating
fresh maple cakes, their fragrance pervading the shop and the air
beyond in the streets outside.

Nakayama's nephew, Yuki, was filling the leaf-shaped irons with
dough and bean paste while he watched the people pass on the street
before him. He had grown so that, except for the unmistakable
Nakayama jawline, Chiyo would not have recognized him.

Nakayama reached for a trinket attached to a key ring, then
straightened up to discover that he was standing face-to-face with
Chiyo.

"Ah!" he gasped. "Uh! You here?"

"I came to ask your advice," Chiyo said. "You're the only person
who can help me decide."

He turned away from her toward the customer behind him. "Is this what you're looking for?" he asked. "It's the only one we have left."

The customer reached into his pocket, paid for the key ring and strode off.

Nakayama's face was serious, even frightened, when he turned back to her. Then he looked down at the counter. "Oh, here's another one of those key rings," he said, pulling it out of the case. His hands were trembling.

"You ought to go into key-ring production," he told her. "That's the best-selling item I've got this year. Use ceramics and wood. Even cloth and plastic's got possibilities. Start with the maple-leaf motif and—"

He was more relaxed now, the old companionship restored. As if she dropped by the shop every few days instead of every seven years.

"You never stop, do you?" she said. "There's always something new and exciting for you."

"Well," he said, "if I were Hiroshi and Yuki's age, I'd want to go into electronics. I envy Hiroshi. At the big university now, isn't he? I keep telling Yuki he ought to go into engineering, but he says he wants to keep making maple cakes and selling trinkets."

He looked at her, full force, for the first time. "What did you say you need? My advice? When you've got a brother like yours to ask? Why me?"

"That's exactly why," she said. "I don't always agree with my brother. Less and less as I get older."

They sat on a stretch of *tatami* at the edge of the garden in a restaurant high on the hill. During all the holidays she'd spent on Miyajima, she had never been in this particular inn. It was as if Nakayama had waved a wand and created it. The *shōji* surrounding the room on three sides had been pushed open so that they were sitting almost outside among the riot of red and orange maples. Not even a breeze was stirring, and each leaf hung motionless above them.

He had ordered *matsutake;* the aroma of it cooking mingled with the crisp air, bringing back memories of all the carefree autumns of her childhood, up and down the mountains searching for the elusive mushrooms that hid under trees, covered with dead leaves and pine needles.

In spite of her anguish over Yoko and Yasu and the constant emptiness she felt over the loss of Shintaro, Chiyo could not control her soaring ecstasy. It seemed that all the high moments of her life added up together could not touch this instant, now, with Nakayama, *matsutake* aroma floating over them, the shadows of the maples casting flickering patterns across his face and shoulders.

Sitting there before their splendid feast, she told him about finding Shintaro, about his illness and death, and about the trip with Mrs. Oguchi to Hikari. She described the wedding and her fears for Fusako's future. Finally she told him about Yoko and Yasu.

"And here you are," she said, "out on this beautiful island, contentedly running your shop. And your nephew perfectly contented, too, with what he's doing. I envy you."

"Well, it's true I couldn't ask for a better nephew. But I'm lonely. I envy you. Always surrounded by your family and friends. I don't enjoy Yuki's company as much as I do yours. As a matter of fact, I don't enjoy anybody's company as much as yours."

His face turned brilliant red. "Uh. Oh. Too much beer. I can feel it in my face."

He gave his attention to the contents of the steaming pan, dividing the last choice pieces of mushroom and beef between them.

"But I have often thought of the loneliness you feel at the loss of your husband," he said. "Even the close presence of your family and friends cannot make up for that."

She told him that Mrs. Oguchi had been advised to make a formal declaration of her husband's death by registering his name at the temple. "That way, she could receive a widow's pension," Chiyo said. "But she's refused. She says she'll never do it unless she knows for sure, not even after the last ship comes in."

Chiyo folded her hands together, leaning on the table. "At least, you see, I know that my husband is not starving or freezing to death in Siberia. At least his bones are buried here in Japan."

For a time they stared at the expanse of blue sea below them. "Thank you for your concern," she said at last, "but I didn't come to talk about my husband. I came to ask what you think about Yoko and Yasu."

"Yes, your daughter, Yoko," he said, smiling. "It's hard to believe she's ready to marry. But it seems they have a strong affection for each other, and they want to marry. Nothing else is as important as that, is it?"

She felt his warm gaze. For a moment, she forgot he was talking about Yoko and Yasu.

"You know," he said, "we Japanese make too much fuss about whether a marriage will produce perfect children. But you and I both know, having raised perfect children and then lost them, that the whole matter is risky no matter what we plan. Is it any worse to have an idiot child than to have a perfect one and then lose him? Or to have no children at all? Nobody can predict any of that. But you do know that those two really care about each other and make each other happy. At least they do now. That's rare in the world, isn't it? And they've been together all their lives. And suffered the same things. They each lost a brother and sister. And a mutual friend. It's like you and me with our lost spouses and lost children.

"Besides, maybe Yoko's next suitor would be a *hibakusha,* too, and he might hide the fact. You wouldn't even know. Yasu is a better risk."

"I can't imagine a better husband for her," said Chiyo.

"Exactly. Being happy is such an elusive thing. We catch it and if we hold on to it too long, it disappears. And sometimes we never find it at all, or we don't recognize it." He reached out and clutched her hand. "Tell her to take it now. The way it comes." He encased her hand in both of his, looking at her with such intensity that it almost frightened her. Then he let go and stared out across the red maples to the sea.

"Anyway, for what it is, that's my advice. I'm not sure you should take it. I know your brother's concerned about the family."

They sat, basking in the warmth and the view below until the sun, settling behind the Thousand-Mat Temple, began to cast a shadow across their table. The waitress came and knelt before them, presenting more tea and, to each, a small glass dish containing slices of the precious green Okayama melon, which, Chiyo knew, was outrageously expensive.

"A gift from the master of the inn," the waitress said, then left them alone again, closing the far *shōji* against the slight chill of the breeze.

Nakayama grinned sheepishly at Chiyo. "The owner's never seen me here with a woman before. He probably doesn't know what to make of it."

Chiyo poured his tea, and they savored each bite of the melon.

"I feel as if we have been floating on a cloud here at the gate of heaven," he said. "I don't want you to leave. Can you come back to my shop, then go for a stroll until dusk? I'll show you some workshops where people are carving all sorts of new objects and a kiln where they're trying out new glazes. I can put you on the last ferry."

She laughed, remembering the time in Tokyo when he tried to get her to stay and had succeeded.

Impulsively, she reached across the table and touched his cheek with the tips of her hands. "I'll never forget today," she said.

They wandered down the street, stopping to look at the workshops and the kiln, finally ending up at his shop. She examined the old statue of Ebisu he'd carved as a child, the chrysanthemum doll Kazuko had painted, and even, Chiyo was surprised to discover, the first iris doll she had painted for him nine years ago.

They walked down to the dock in the pink glow of dusk, watching the ferry slide alongside the pier.

"Take this box of *momiji manjū* back to Yoko," Nakayama said. "And this," he added, slipping a white envelope onto the top of the box, "is for you."

She waved at him from the railing of the ferry. "Thank you," she called. "For the advice and the wonderful afternoon."

When he had disappeared from view, she left the railing and went below to open the envelope. She found inside a haiku, written with a brush in the old calligraphic style. Nakayama's calligraphy. It was almost as distinguished as Shintaro's. Had he written it before, planning to give it to her someday? Or had he written it that very afternoon at the shop?

> *Tsuma dachi ni*
> *ou aki kaze no*
> *yukue, kana!*
>
> I would stand on tiptoes to follow after,
> But in the autumn wind, whither has she gone?

There was a double meaning. *Tsuma dachi* meant "standing on tiptoes," but *tsuma* also meant "spouse, wife, beloved one" and *dachi* had the meaning of "departing" as well as "standing." So the first line could read, "I would follow after my departing wife, my loved one." It would have been easy enough for Nakayama to write the word *tsuma* in Chinese characters so that their meaning was explicit. But he had chosen to use the Japanese *kana* syllabary, which expressed only the sound of the word and left the definition ambiguous.

She stared at the delicate white rice paper, the faint hint of a maple leaf imprinted in its background. There was another possible meaning. He might have been referring to his own departed wife who had died, expressing his intention to remain faithful to her even in death, maybe expressing his dismay that his memories of her were disappearing. But if that were the case he would have used the past tense, writing "departed" instead of "departing."

328

No, he intended that word *tsuma*, "my wife, my partner, my beloved one," to hover there, just hint, and then fade back into the more neutral "I would stand on tiptoes," which was standard phrasing in haiku and had allusions to the ancient *Manyoshu* poetry collection. Shintaro would know exactly which poem it alluded to. Would Nakayama know that, too?

Chiyo sat on the ferry, wrapped in a warm haze. It stayed with her all the way back on the streetcar from Miyajima-guchi as she stared out at the landscape that was fading into darkness, deep in thoughts of Nakayama and the lingering aroma of *matsutake*.

The conductor tapped her lightly on the shoulder. "We're at Koi station," he said. "End of the line. You'll have to transfer."

Chapter Thirty-three

F ORGET ABOUT WHAT UNCLE ISAO SAID," Chiyo exclaimed to Yoko when she returned from her college retreat a few days later. "We're not living in the sixteenth century and we don't need to spend our whole lives worrying about the continuation of our family line. Just marry him. All I ask is that you wait until you finish college and he's settled into his job."

Yoko stared at her mother, surprised.

"By that time, your Uncle Isao will have forgotten his objections to Yasu. If he remembers, we'll just smile and go ahead with the wedding."

Yoko still did not say anything.

"It's all right what you do. Have children or don't have them. Adopt them, even. I've been checking with my friends at ABCC, and they say it only affects the ones exposed inside their mother's wombs like the Ikeda grandchild. Nothing has happened to children born later, they said, even if both parents were exposed. Lots of normal children are being born nowadays. So it's not the problem Isao thought it was."

Yoko knelt down on the *tatami*, buried her face in her hands and burst into tears.

"Mama, Yasu is gone," she choked. "I haven't seen him since the wedding. I finally called his mother and she said he's in Tokyo having his job interview. He's gone off without even telling me goodbye."

"Sit down and tell me all about it," Chiyo said softly.

Yoko, drying her eyes, settled herself in the *kotatsu*.

"I visited Mrs. Yamamoto and told her I want to marry Yasu even though you and Uncle Isao said I couldn't. I told her everything, Mama. I shouldn't have, but I did. Anyway, I thought she should know the truth.

"And do you know what she said? She said you were right. I should marry someone healthier and richer and smarter than Yasu, she said.

"Nobody was on my side," Yoko choked. "And now you finally understand and it's too late."

Chiyo grasped her daughter's hands. "It's all right," she soothed. "He'll come back. I'll explain everything to Mrs. Yamamoto. She's just being hesitant, you know. I was out talking to Nakayama-san the other day and he made me see it's better for you two to marry."

"Nakayama-san!" Yoko exclaimed. "He's the one who convinced you? What does he know? He's not one of the family. I hope you haven't been telling my story to every acquaintance you meet."

Chiyo let go of Yoko abruptly. "Nakayama-san is not a passing acquaintance, Yoko! He's been associated with our business from the very beginning. He inspired those first dolls we made. Don't you remember that? And of course I haven't told your story to everyone. In fact, I would never have told Mrs. Yamamoto. That's something you chose to do. Nakayama is the only person I have told because I needed another opinion besides your Uncle Isao's."

Chiyo's words, edged with anger, surprised Yoko into silence.

"I'll go and see Mrs. Yamamoto myself," Chiyo promised.

Captain Yamamoto met Chiyo at the door and greeted her rather curtly. "If you've come about our son and your daughter," he said, "I want you to know I've already rejected the idea. I do not think our two families have enough in common."

"Now, Husband!" Mrs. Yamamoto said, coming out to the *genkan*, "Mrs. Hara has come all the way here from Nobori-chō. We don't even know yet what she wants to discuss, and I hardly think our decision about anything is as firm as all that."

She ushered them into the sitting room, then appeared carrying a tray of steaming tea. How did she get the water boiling so fast,

Chiyo wondered. Mrs. Yamamoto laid out the cups on the table over the *kotatsu* and signaled them to settle in under the warm blanket. It was already November.

Captain Yamamoto refused. "You ladies can discuss the matter all afternoon if you wish, but I want you to know that as head of this household, I have made my decision, and it is irrevocable. I am not the kind of person who changes his mind."

He retired into the room, where he spent his days reading and sleeping.

"I do want Yoko to marry Yasu," Chiyo began. "I think my brother Isao's objections had more to do with family traditions than with the effects of the bomb. He was upset by the way they made the announcement, you know, as if they thought the decision was all theirs."

"Yes, that's Yasu for you," said Mrs. Yamamoto. "He says whatever comes into his head without considering its effect on other people. You see," she said wryly, lowering her voice and pouring the tea, "there's a little touch of his father in him, hard as I've tried to eradicate it."

"But Yoko's the same way," said Chiyo. "At least it's more acceptable for a man to act that way."

She stared at the steaming tea, enjoying the fragrance. "Then Yasu didn't consult with you at all about marrying Yoko? Do you think they just decided the whole thing on the spur of the moment at Fusako's wedding?"

"No, he didn't tell me, but I did sense that they've been talking about it to each other. I couldn't help noticing how he looks at her. Even if Kyoko had lived, I think Yasu would have wanted to marry Yoko. I don't know why. I just feel it, somehow."

Mrs. Yamamoto poured Chiyo another cup of tea. "They're both very young, you know. They'll get over it. And anyway, it's dangerous for a girl like Yoko to take her chances marrying Yasu. He could make her extremely unhappy. We're all still in shock about Kyoko, after all." She caressed her warm teacup.

Kyoko Ikeda was never very far from Chiyo's thoughts, but now, suddenly, the image of Yukiji shouting out in the flames welled up before her eyes, and she knew Mrs. Yamamoto was thinking of him too, because she stood up briskly and picked up the teapot. "I'll just take some in to the captain," she said. "I know he's waiting to see if I'll bring it."

"I've been thinking about all this for quite a while," Chiyo said when Mrs. Yamamoto returned, "and I've decided I'm not going to worry anymore about that bomb. Yasu is a wonderful, wise, sensitive, intelligent, capable young man. Our lives have been richer because of him. And I cannot imagine a better husband for Yoko."

She looked up to see that tears were running down Mrs. Yamamoto's cheeks. Chiyo began to cry herself, and the two of them sat, remembering all they had shared over the years. She was pleased with the idea of having Mrs. Yamamoto for a relative.

"What are you two women wailing about?" Captain Yamamoto called from the next room. "I don't think this is a crying matter. Yasu can find lots of wives for himself whenever he decides he wants to look."

They did not answer him.

Mrs. Yamamoto lowered her voice. "I want them to be married, too," she said. "When the time comes. I just don't want any of you to be sorry later."

"Then let's tell Yasu we agree," Chiyo whispered. "After all, nobody's told him he can't marry Yoko. He's just assumed that. My brother is set against it, of course, but in time Isao's likely to forget what he said. He's like that, you know. So busy designing automobiles and machinery."

"I'll write Yasu tonight and tell him you came," Mrs. Yamamoto said. "I've already written about Yoko coming, but he hasn't answered yet."

"Well, you know what worries Yoko. She thinks Yasu might commit suicide. You don't think there's any danger of that, do you?"

Mrs. Yamamoto smiled slightly. "Oh, the romanticism of the young!" She shook her head. "No, I don't think so. You see, he hasn't really given her up yet. He's just trying to convince himself that he's doing the best thing for Yoko."

Chiyo set down her teacup. "Give me his address, and I'll write him, too. I know his feelings were hurt by my brother's cold reception. And certainly I didn't give him any support."

"But that's a problem." Mrs. Yamamoto sighed. "I've promised Yasu I wouldn't tell anyone where he is. Now, how am I going to get around that?

"I know," Mrs. Yamamoto said, suddenly cheerful. "I'll include your letter with my next one. And one from Yoko, too, if she wants. That way, I won't be betraying anyone."

"Wonderful," Chiyo said. "It should be more effective if he gets a letter from all three of us." She stood up. "I just know it's going to turn out all right."

She called pleasantly into the captain's room and said goodbye.

"Thanks for coming," he called back to her. "But just remember, no matter what you two ladies are plotting out there, it won't work."

Chiyo left the Yamamoto residence in high spirits. That evening, she and Yoko composed letters late into the night and sent a large special delivery envelope to Mrs. Yamamoto the next morning.

Three weeks went by. Mrs. Yamamoto finally called to say Yasu had answered the letters with a postcard. "He said he was fine and working hard. Nothing more. Really, I am irritated. And worried, too. If I just had the time and money I'd go up there on the train."

Chiyo stayed at the factory until late at night, experimenting with different kinds of glazes for the clay figures of the Seven Happy Gods. The flesh quality was perfect, but they hadn't been able to produce the same subtle shades for the clothing which Nakayama had used on his first set of clay dolls. And anyway she wanted some variety in the medley of colors appointed to each group of seven gods. She painted glazes and fired them during a period of two days, thinking of nothing else until she obtained just the right shade of creamy white tinged with blue for Mencius's robes and a subtle yellow for the rice god. By the end of the week, she had fired a batch and taken them to the shops along the Hondori and near the Atomic Dome. "These are special ones," she told them, "made by an anonymous artist. If you want to place an order, I'll need the money in advance." She sold three sets immediately, and two more shop owners expressed interest. She sent another set out to Nakayama, not making any comment or asking for a price.

The sale of the first three sets was enough for train fare for two people, and she took the money to Mrs. Yamamoto's house. "I know you'll feel like refusing, but you've got to find out what's on Yasu's mind. Two suicidal offspring on our hands, you know. I always worry about Keiko Kakihara whenever she's turned down after an *omiai*. She won't even let her father arrange them anymore. And remember that girl at the Women's College, graduated two years ahead of Yoko? I forget her name, but you heard about her, didn't you? She got turned down by only two candidates, then just disappeared. Nobody knows yet—"

"I know," Mrs. Yamamoto interrupted. "I'll take the money and go. But you've got to promise to let me pay you back."

"Later, then. If you insist. But do you think Yoko-chan should go with you?"

"No, I'd better go alone. Have her write another letter for me to take."

Chiyo and Yoko met Mrs. Yamamoto at the train when she came home a week later, her frail body and face drained. "He was just adamant," she said. "He insists it would destroy Yoko's life if he married her. He's put her out of his mind completely, he said. And that's that. End of discussion."

But while they were making their way through the station crowd, Mrs. Yamamoto turned and beamed at them. "Even so, I think he's weakening," she said. "There are signs. He has a nice dormitory room, for one thing. And he's working on some electrical project he's excited about. He's practically in charge of the whole thing. So you see he's not sitting around moping. He's too busy. No danger of suicide, certainly. And when he gets this project finished, which will be sometime in the spring, I'm sure he'll want to come home for a visit.

"Anyway," she said while they stood waiting for her taxi, "I left Yoko's letter right there on his desk. I knew he wouldn't read it while I was there. But now, you see, he'll be alone with it." She smiled triumphantly.

In mid-December, Yasu wrote his mother saying he would be home sometime in March. Yoko was ecstatic for a while, but since he had not answered her letter, she didn't know whether to write again or just be silent. She finally settled on a formal invitation to her graduation. He did not answer.

A few days later the newspaper announced the last ship from Nakhodka, arriving December 26, carrying 1,024 passengers. No more prisoners of war would be returning, the Soviets said. This was absolutely the last ship. Chiyo prayed for Mrs. Oguchi. When the names were published in the paper, she searched for Mr. Oguchi's name. Everyone in the Movement was watching for news of missing husbands, but Chiyo knew that if he were on the ship, Mrs. Oguchi would have heard long before the names were published.

"All the same, I'm going to Maizuru," Mrs. Oguchi wrote. "It's my last chance to find out what happened to him."

She called long distance after she returned to Himeji a few days later. "There are still twenty thousand who didn't come home," she told Chiyo. "And there is no information. Not a shred."

Chiyo could not think of any words to comfort her.

"The head of the agency promised not to give up," Mrs. Oguchi said. "But what's the use? It's all talk. I was hoping, at least, for a box with his bones. Quite a few of the women got those. The agency held a ceremony for them." Chiyo could detect a break in Mrs. Oguchi's voice.

"Come and visit us in Hiroshima," Chiyo said. "You can tell me about the trip, and I'll show you the new glazes I've developed. You might want to try them out."

"Yes," Mrs. Oguchi said and hung up. Chiyo knew that she had been praying for a box of bones that would set her free.

Isao had been elected mayor of Inokuchi. During the holidays, everyone from the village would be coming to pay him respects. Hiroshi was coming home with Fusako and Toshio, who'd been in Tokyo for training in electronics. Isao had established a new branch of Asahi Enterprises with a line of radios and tape recorders. Of course, Toshio would be president.

They removed from storage all the festival *zabuton* for guests to sit on and set up the folded screens that had been in Kazuko's family for generations—paintings of herons with golden feet standing against a background of pines laden with snow. Hiroshi, in his Tokyo University uniform, sat next to his uncle greeting the guests, bowing and nodding as if he were the samurai son in line to inherit the fief. Strung along on the other side of the room were Kazuko, Fusako, Toshio (looking chagrined for having his position usurped by Hiroshi), then Chiyo and Yoko. Yasu had not come home for the holidays and Yoko was subdued and listless, although no one noticed but Chiyo.

The guests came all day and paid tribute, bowing to Isao and his family. But in spite of the pleasure the neighbors showed at greeting brilliant and charming Hiroshi and beautiful Yoko, in spite of the honors they bestowed upon Isao, even in spite of the bright predictions they gave for 1957, the thirty-second year of the reign of Showa, Chiyo could not rid herself of the hollow void she felt inside her stomach and her heart for the anxieties of Yoko and the lonely, gnawing uncertainties that would face Mrs. Oguchi all the remaining days of her life.

A New Year's greeting from Nakayama was waiting for her when they returned home from Inokuchi. It was written on the same kind of paper he had used for the haiku.

> To Hara Chiyo.
>
> Greetings and felicitations on the occasion of the New Year from Nakayama Hideo.

> Your clay figurines were outstanding.
> I have sold them at a premium price.

An envelope containing two crisp 5,000-yen notes was enclosed. An outrageous price. She had been offered only half as much for the other sets, and she had not intended to sell them to Nakayama. She was irritated that he had sold them without asking her first.

She returned the money, enclosing it in a letter sent by special delivery.

> The dolls were intended as a gift. If you cannot buy them back, I will make you another set.

A letter came by return mail.

> I bought them back. Thank you. They are worth much more than the amount I sent, and the customer was reluctant to give them up, but I promised to sell him some later. You will see this set in my shop next time you come. When are you coming, by the way?

She sent him a brief note along with a New Year's greeting card.

> Thank you for buying them back. I put you to a lot of trouble, but I'm glad you did it.
> Yoko is graduating from the Women's College in March.
> Perhaps you could come to the ceremony?

She did not mention his invitation to Miyajima. She thought of him alone on the island in his shop. She would appear one day, unannounced. Take him completely by surprise. But not now. He was like her pearl necklace, hidden away under a collection of odds and ends stored in Inokuchi. She would come upon it someday, even search for it when the other things were taken care of.

Chapter Thirty-four

SPRING 1957. ALMOST TWELVE YEARS since the bomb, and Hiroshima was beginning to look like a modern city. New buildings were going up all around and there were fewer vacant lots filled with rubble. But the pitiful, ugly shacks remained along the rivers and on the land where the castle walls had once been.

Yoko, disconsolate and distant, put on the pale pink chiffon dress she would wear under her cap and gown at graduation. Yasu had not written, and it seemed that he was not coming.

Chiyo had suggested the pale pink to match the blush in Yoko's complexion, but today there was none. She looked exquisite anyway, her straight black hair falling to her shoulders in precise, even lengths. Other girls had permanents and bouffant hairstyles. Not Yoko. Her hair was the same as it had been when she was twelve and the simplicity of it was dazzling.

Hiroshi, home from Tokyo, ordered the taxi, and while they were riding to Ushita, Yoko projected her sunny smile. Not her real one. She was only practicing for the graduation ceremony.

Later, they sat proudly watching Yoko bow to the president, the blush returning to her cheeks, her shiny black hair sweeping forward and covering her face, falling back into place when she stood erect again and received her diploma.

Hiroshi was charming at the reception afterwards. He stood before the table laden with soft drinks and tiny sandwiches, and told jokes, holding his face rigid and serious. Wherever he went, a group of giggling girls followed after him like a swarm of bees. Chiyo had no idea he could be so successful with girls, and most of them two years older.

She tried to see him as they did. Brilliant, charming young man from Tokyo University. Was it the uniform that made him so appealing? Perhaps it was his sense of humor. He had always seemed humorless compared to Kenichi, but the girls didn't seem to think so. Nothing would ever stand in his way, Chiyo thought. He would have for himself whatever he wanted. But she couldn't understand what propelled him. He was only two years younger than Kenichi and Yasu. Yet he seemed to exist in a different generation. His future was laid before him like a shining jewel within his grasp. Not like Yoko, whose despair was covered by her bright smile as she moved among her friends.

And where was Nakayama? She had invited him to the graduation. But how could she expect him to be comfortable here, everybody wondering why he had come? It was a business relationship, after all.

There was a telegram waiting when they arrived home.

Congratulations on the day of your graduation.

Yasu

No other warm wishes. No excuses. No allusions to plans for the future. No promise to write.

"But he did remember I was graduating," Yoko said.

She changed her dress for a simpler one and went off with her friends to their favorite restaurant on the Hondori.

Hiroshi returned to Tokyo.

Yoko began her job at Toyokogyo, keeping personnel records, serving tea, sometimes writing English letters. It seemed almost an exciting time for her, earning her own money, attending movies and plays, eating dinner in restaurants with her girl friends, joining the company-sponsored activities—an English class, a bowling league, even weekends at the company *bessō,* the vacation villa in the mountains near Miyoshi. Isao was already suggesting candidates for an *omiai* for Yoko, but Chiyo put him off, pointing out that he had said she ought to be least twenty-five.

Yoko did not talk about Yasu. She did not send him letters. Once she went to Ujina to see Mrs. Yamamoto. But there was no news. Yasu had written polite, noncommittal letters to his mother. He had not mentioned coming home. He had not mentioned Yoko.

Toyokogyo declared a summer holiday in July. Three full days without work, and Yoko and her two friends decided on a trip to Tokyo. She had never been there before, she pointed out. Nowadays, high school girls went there on their school trip, but there had been no trips in Yoko's time.

They decided to stay in a small inn in the Tsukiji district near the Kabuki-za. "And I'm writing Fusako to ask if she can get us tickets to a performance. Remember how Grandmother used to talk about the Kabuki in Tokyo?" Yoko was like her former self, barely able to contain her excitement.

"Are you going to visit Yasu, too?" Chiyo asked gently.

"I hope so," she said, beaming a genuine smile. "We'll leave Thursday night on the *Asakaze* and I asked him if he could meet me Friday night or Saturday at Shibuya station. You know, in front of the statue of the dog?"

Chiyo knew what she was thinking about. All the romantic scenes from novels and movies of two lovers waiting patiently, and finally catching sight of each other in front of that statue. Chiyo herself had dreamed of a reunion like that with Shintaro.

Yoko giggled the way she had before Kyoko died and Yasu disappeared. "But of course," she added, turning serious again, "he might not come. He might not even answer my letter."

"It's three weeks yet," Chiyo said. "You'll hear." She hugged her daughter. "But be careful. And wise. Don't do anything rash. Promise me that."

Fusako wrote, saying she had managed to get the tickets. "I'll meet you at the train."

Three days later, there was a postcard from Yasu.

> Looking forward to your visit. Call my office when you arrive. 62-7892.
>
> Yasu

"He never wastes words, does he?" Chiyo commented. "For myself, I'd feel bad about wasting the paper. Look at all the extra space on this postcard."

At the station, the girls bustled with excitement, all of them dressed in stylish new two-piece suits their dressmakers had rushed

340

to finish in time. They arranged and rearranged their luggage, looked at their watches, stood nervously alert, ready to rush onto the train the moment it arrived. Yoko had saved half of her April, May, June, and July salary for the trip and was hoping for a summer bonus to pay for the rest of it.

Home alone that night, Chiyo counted up the months since she had seen Nakayama. October. And now it was July. Almost a year. The warm, ambiguous haiku had been swirling around in her head all that time. She decided that she needed more advice.

Customers were crowding the shop when Chiyo arrived. One man was leading a group who seemed to be buyers. "You see, it's all original work," he was telling them. "They've got *kokeshi* dolls because Mr. Nakayama is from the Tohoku region, but they're not traditional in this area. Here the local craft is *tsuchiningyō*, like those clay dolls there on the shelf. Production was revived after the war, and Mr. Nakayama's shop was the inspiration for all that, you see. Both these wooden dolls and the clay ones were handmade by *hibakusha,* survivors of the bomb. Now most of the work is done by machine at the factory, Asahi Enterprises, but a few artists still do them all by hand, mostly for Mr. Nakayama's shop. And the president of Asahi Enterprises is a woman. She's a *hibakusha* herself.

Chiyo recognized the man as the president of the Folkcraft Society. She had heard him make his opening speech at the convention in Hiroshima but she hadn't actually met him. Still, if he knew that much about the factory, he might say her name, or perhaps even recognize her. Morishita-san must have given him a tour.

She scurried over to a corner table, quietly ordered tea from one of the shop girls, then bent her face toward the steaming cup while she listened to the man. It wasn't just Americans who had to point out that the artists were *hibakusha.* It was everybody who didn't understand Hiroshima. As if past suffering made the art more salable. Or maybe nobody expected a survivor to be capable of making anything at all, let alone something beautiful.

A few moments later Nakayama-san emerged from his workshop. He selected certain pieces from the shelf, caressing and showing each one in turn. She was too far away to hear what they were saying, but she prayed that Nakayama would not introduce her to the men.

She saw that he was finally bowing to them at the door, then waving goodbye. He came over and stood at her table, brushing wood shavings off the front of his apron.

"An unexpected pleasure."

Chiyo looked up at him, his presence like the noonday sun.

"I see that I've come at a very busy time," she said.

"You've come at exactly the right time. As you can see, they're all gone now. The Folkcraft Convention is over. Did you have a lot of visitors at the factory?"

"To tell the truth, I didn't pay much attention. Morishita-san and Keiko set up our booth, and I was there only to hear the president's opening speech. Thank you for not introducing me just now. I was afraid you might."

He grinned. "I knew you wouldn't like it, his calling you a *hibakusha.*"

"Well, he must have gone to the factory Friday afternoon when I was busy getting Yoko packed. She's gone up to Tokyo to see Yasu."

He sat down opposite her. "Things seem to be working out for them. I can imagine how beautiful Yoko is. How can Yasu resist her? All his reserve will melt the moment he sees her." He reached out and rested his hands on hers. "I can understand Yasu's problem completely, you see." He searched her eyes. "Promise me that even if it turns out badly you won't put all the blame on yourself."

He didn't wait for her to answer. "I think I'll take the afternoon off," he said, standing up and bustling around the shop. He began counting up money in the cash register and putting it in the safe.

"In fact, let's all take a holiday," he announced to the shop girls and Yuki. "The convention's over, and we've all been working hard. Just close up the shop, will you? I'm going to take my business partner, Mrs. Hara here, on a fishing excursion with Jiro." He searched behind the counter for the sign.

CLOSED FOR THE DAY
OPEN AGAIN TOMORROW

Written in both Japanese and English.

He gently steered Chiyo outside, tacked the sign on the door, closed it, and waved back at the shop girls and Yuki, still standing behind the counter, bewildered, not sure yet what to make of the afternoon that had been given them.

"I haven't been fishing since I was a little girl," Chiyo said.

"All the more reason, then. I'll go down and tell Jiro while you get the lunches. There's a good *obentō* shop down the block. And I'll get the beer. See," he said, pointing, "it's that fishing boat at the dock next to the ferry." He turned and started off at a run.

* * *

When she arrived, breathless, with three lunches and a melon, he was standing on the prow, waving at her, crossing both arms above his head. Jiro was aft, sorting lines, and he looked up, smiling broadly, when she climbed aboard. He was a thickset man with a tanned face and deep furrows in his forehead, as if he were used to gazing across the horizon to the edge of the sky. "Welcome," he said. "Did Nakayama-san tell you I knew your father? He brought me into this world, in fact. Over there in Ono." He pointed across the sea to the mainland, then laughed. "Of course I don't remember any of that. But I remember your father."

She looked at him more closely. "Of course! I know you! You and your father always brought fresh oysters to our house in Sugi no Ura."

His smile revealed rows of even, white teeth, a gold one on the upper left. "Yes," he said. "That was me. I didn't think you would remember."

Jiro's boat skirted the island just beyond the edge of the beaches where the gentle waves broke into spray and lapped up against the sand. They passed Sugi no Ura and the beach where Kenichi had run, laughing, out to the waves that last Sunday afternoon before the bomb. They passed the two-pronged rock, the secret place where she and Isao played as children and where she had lain so many times in Shintaro's arms. It was clean and dazzling white, the narrow sandbar just appearing in the low tide. The old summer house, set back from the beach behind the trees, appeared small to her from that distance. It had seemed huge when she was a child.

Chiyo waved to a solitary figure on the shore, wondering if she knew him, then went aft, gazing at the speckled dots of islands that spread before her in the distance. All the way around to the back of Miyajima, the fishing boat cut a clean line through the blue salt water foaming white on the edges and rolling toward them, the sun and dancing waves washing clean her regrets and sorrows.

Nakayama came and sat beside her. "On a day like this, it's hard to believe there are any troubles in the world, don't you think?"

In response, she reached out and covered his hand, which rested on the side of the boat next to her.

"Well, your daughter, Yoko, is very brave to go and visit him," Nakayama said. "And wise, too."

Chiyo sighed. "Yasu's still worried about having children, I think. It's beyond his love for Yoko, you know. It's like being told the human race is going to end with him."

"Yes," Nakayama said. "These days, just being alive is a risk, isn't it? So it's a terrible responsibility bringing someone else into the world."

"I know," Chiyo said. "Sometimes I think the Ikeda grandchild is luckier than the rest of us, so beautiful and innocent. But who's going to take care of him when his parents die?"

Nakayama nodded and was silent, gazing out at the sea. "There's no solution," he said. "But there hardly is for anything." He glanced at her a moment, then turned away before speaking again. "It's been almost a year, hasn't it, since you came to see me after your niece's wedding?"

She smiled. "I seem to pick perfect days to visit. Autumn with the red maple leaves, and now this beautiful July day."

He laughed, holding tightly on to her hand now. "We're blessed, aren't we? Or maybe you have direct communication with the Western Paradise. You probably order them up. 'Give me six clouds today, a little two-minute shower to cool us off, and then a sun that sets at six-fifteen.' Is that how you do it?"

"Maybe. I don't reveal my magic without a lot of persuasion."

Jiro had slowed the motor and was steering the boat toward shore.

"Why do people think children are the most important part of a marriage?" Nakayama asked suddenly. "They're wonderful, but so are other things." He was looking toward the island. "Just think of what you and I have produced. Millions of beautiful dolls in all colors, shapes, and designs. We're becoming rather famous in folk-craft circles, you know."

Jiro dropped anchor in the cove of the Shrine of the Sacred Crow, the most remote, the most unvisited spot on the island. Chiyo had never been there in spite of all the boating trips of her childhood. Women were not supposed to visit the most sacred Shinto spots because it was said that a female presence had a contaminating influence on rites of purification.

They began collecting lunches and fishing rods.

"I can't go in there," Chiyo protested. "You know it's not allowed."

Nakayama, standing knee-deep in the water, reached up around her waist and pulled her down from the edge of the boat. "So, somebody has to test the gods," he said. "We can't go on trusting tradition forever."

They waded into shore, carrying fishing rods, lunches, and picnic mats on their heads.

Jiro set up two rods on the shore, baiting each with different lures. He drank a bottle of beer, waiting for bites. He ate most of his lunch. Then he grew restless.

"You know," he said, "I just have a hunch they're biting over in the next cove. I'd like to slip on over there and see what I can do. I'll come back in a couple of hours and pick you up."

In no time he had pulled himself into the boat and started the motor. It purred gently, then disappeared beyond the pine that jutted out at the edge of the cove.

Chiyo spread out the straw mats under the huge pine tree near the edge of the water. They ate the sushi in their lunch boxes, then the sticks of broiled chicken livers she had decided impulsively to add to the other delicacies. A fish jerked the pole Jiro had planted on the shore, and Nakayama went whooping out to the water, grabbed the line, pulling up a large white-bellied fish that flopped wildly along the sand until Nakayama finally caught it and whacked its head against a rock. He removed the hook, rebaited it, and placed the catch among leaves in the wicker basket in the shade.

"Now I know why I haven't come fishing since I was a child," she told Nakayama when he settled himself beside her again, dripping and smelling of fish, "It's because of taking out the hook and whacking them on the head. I can't do that."

He smiled, then pulled the straw mat, and her with it, out into the sun. They talked of their lives and their art, their successes and failures in carving, painting, modeling, firing. They were burnished by the sun, Chiyo wearing a wide-brimmed straw hat she had bought in the shop next to the fruit store. Nakayama was soaking up the full force of the sun, not noticing the perspiration dripping down his neck onto the collar of his open shirt and onto his hairy chest. She could feel his heart beating close to her and the sun pounding on her temples. She removed her hat, and he turned and looked at her. Such a homely, honest, vulnerable face, pockmarked, with a receding jaw, deep brown and wet under the sun. A peasant's face. How could it be that endearing? He was so close to her, she could no longer distinguish between him and the sun beating down on her temples. And on her groin.

He touched her shoulder. "We'd better take our swim while the sun is still on us."

"But I have no bathing suit," Chiyo said. "How can—"

Nakayama was off at a run. He tossed off his shirt, stepped out of his trousers, left his rubber sandals at the edge of the shore.

Chiyo removed her stockings, then her skirt and blouse, running quickly, jumping into the water before he could turn and see the chunkiness of her middle-aged body. The water was startlingly cold and refreshing. Joyful. She swam, all her energy concentrated on pushing herself over the gentle waves away from the shore toward Nakayama. The sky was spread over them like a tent. She was closer to him now, their heads bobbing up and down in the waves. He put his hands behind his head, and they floated there together.

He moved over toward the rocks, head down, his arms spread out; then he pushed himself up like a dolphin. "Dive down with your eyes open," he said. "Look at the fish." She took a deep breath and followed him under the ledge of the rock. She had always been afraid to open her eyes under water. Fish, striped, speckled, rainbow-tiered, sped past her, darting back and forth in a kaleidoscope of colors. A cluster of anemone, green and coral, their wild hair waving around the mouths, motioned to her, bending back and forth.

She began to surface for more air when a huge shadow darted out from the rocks, a swordlike projection pointing toward her. Nakayama came up underneath her, caught her around the waist, turned her over, and held her with his hands cupped under her chin, pulling her to shore so quickly and deftly that they were lying on the beach, clutching one another and gasping for breath.

"Don't know what that was," he breathed into her ear, "but I don't like the looks of it. It didn't like us much either, invading its home in this deserted, empty, sacred place." He pulled her closer, pressing against her. They were spread out on a hard, flat rock, waves of water covering them. He was on top of her, kissing her forehead, her eyes, and her lips.

She pushed her underpants down below her knees and kicked them into the sand so she could feel his hard, firm penis against the bare skin of her stomach. Then he was pushing gently into the firelike place between her legs. He removed her brassiere and kissed her breasts, pushing farther inside her. It hurt. She was fifty-one years old, and she had not made love for fourteen years. But she locked her legs and arms around him as they lay in that sacred, secret place where no one lived, and where no woman had ever been before. He came inside her like a warm explosion of light, and she responded again and again.

Had making love to Shintaro ever been like this? She could not remember. Nothing existed except her and Nakayama and the clear blue sky that covered them and their rock-bed cradle. The motors of the fishing boats hummed far out to sea. A plane flew overhead, and the waves sparkled beyond them in the waning sun.

346

"No dream I ever had of you," she said, breathing into the crook of his armpit, "has ever even begun to compare—"

"I know," he said. "It's the same with me."

They flattened themselves against the smooth rock. The pebbles spread out like a carpet of jewels below their feet.

Chapter Thirty-five

I T'S GOING TO BE ALL RIGHT, MAMA."
Yoko announced when she arrived home. "I
told him I would never be happy unless we married, that I'd never
marry anyone else, that he had no right to make the decision about
our future without me. I said I didn't care what my uncle
thought. What matters is that my mother agrees with me and
wants him in the family.

"And after all that, after he finally agreed, I told him you wanted
us to wait a couple of years."

"Actually, I said three years, didn't I? Until you're twenty-five.
If you wait that long and show your uncle how determined you are,
he really can't object."

Yoko sighed. "Well, anyway, I met Yasu on Saturday. We
walked all afternoon in the park around Meiji Shrine and up one side
of the Ginza and down the other. Then we had sushi and went to
an American movie in that huge, round *Gekijō,* the theater place,
you know, the round one you always see in pictures? It has all kinds
of restaurants, bars. Just amazing, Mama. There's even a theater
for Takarazuka dancing girls. And then he held my hand in the
movie. I couldn't think about anything except him." She gig-

gled. "You know, after the movie, we couldn't even remember what it was about."

This was a very different Yoko from the one who had gone up to Tokyo only three days before.

"It was wonderful, Mama. As if we'd never been apart. I'll wait forever to marry him. You know, it was good for us to be apart. It made us realize how much we miss each other."

For days, Chiyo basked in the warmth that emanated from Yoko and from her own memories of the Island of the Sacred Crow.

They decided, without consulting anyone, that they would rebuild the house. Chiyo hired an architect, a son of one of the factory workers just graduated and home from school in Tokyo, eager about his first job. He said he could build the new house right next to the old one, where they could go on living all through the construction period, then tear it down later if they wanted.

"Well, I think I could have found you a cheaper carpenter," Isao said when he saw the half-finished house. "But it looks good. I've been meaning to suggest doing it for quite a while now."

She knew he was hurt at not being consulted, but she was too busy with Asahi Enterprises to think much about it. Morishita-san had shown a whole series of buyers around the factory during the Folkcraft Convention and had taken a mountain of orders for both handmade and machine-made dolls. Now they were sending shipments to tourist shops in places Chiyo had never heard of. And she, Nakayama, Keiko, and Morishita-san were designing a line of kits with component parts: bodies, hair, glue, painting tools, and cloth for housewives who wanted to make their own dolls for gifts.

Chiyo discovered that all the increased activity required her presence on Miyajima almost every weekend, consulting with Nakayama. They had hit on the idea of an easier kind of kit for making dolls with pipe-cleaner bodies, papier-mâché heads and hair, then a collection of origami paper with instructions on how to fold the paper into kimono and accessories. The kits would appear in a variety of choices of patterns and styles so that each doll would be unique.

The idea delighted Chiyo. "So, nowadays, people can make dolls just for the fun of it without having to worry about the money," she told Nakayama. "But still I think Yoko and I had the most fun in the old days."

Nakayama laughed. "Probably seems more fun looking back on it than it was at the time."

Her weekly trips to Miyajima were crystal jewels, each one frozen in eternity.

"Mother, why do you go to Miyajima so often?" Yoko asked. "You never used to have to go. What are you doing out there?"

"Well, it's just that these new designs seem easier to create over there. You know how the air is in Miyajima. It's so clear and light, and Nakayama-san has a workshop upstairs with windows that look out over the Inland Sea."

Was there a shadow of suspicion on Yoko's face? Someday she would tell her daughter about Nakayama. But not yet. Not now. Wait until it was settled with her and Yasu.

When the new house in Nobori-chō was finished, Chiyo decided it was time to make repairs on the ancestral Ogawa home in Sugi no Ura. "It will be much more appealing to our renters," she explained to Isao, "and besides, we may be able to use it again ourselves someday. For weekends and summers. Especially now that you'll be a grandfather soon."

It struck her as ironic that after their starvation and exhaustion during the war, after the death and devastation at the end, and after the final defeat—that they could possibly afford repairs on the old Miyajima house, let alone have funds to rebuild the house in Nobori-chō. Suppose Shintaro were alive, had begun teaching again, and had insisted she give up working at Asahi Enterprises. They could never have afforded a new house on his salary. And she would never have experienced the delight of creating and designing the dolls. Or felt the power of knowing that she and all the others were capable of making their own living and their own decisions.

Nor would she have known Nakayama as she knew him now. She did not like to think about that. Or to compare Nakayama with Shintaro. What if there had never been a war and Kenichi had not disappeared and Shintaro had never gone away? What kind of person would she be now? Certainly she was more sure of herself, but she had lost Shintaro and Kenichi, and nothing could ever make up for that. It disturbed her deeply that the war she hated so much had caused this new affluence and confidence.

She consulted meticulously with Isao about every detail of the repairs on the summerhouse, suggesting that an extra *hanare,* an attached room, be added at the far end of the garden so that the Ogawa family could stay overnight if they chose to visit for the weekend. "Now that I'm designing so many of these new products with Mr. Nakayama," she said, "I'll need to be going out there a lot more myself."

But even after the new room was completed, Chiyo did not stay there. Nakayama's friend, the restaurant owner, managed a small inn nearby on the hill. Everyone there was sworn to secrecy. Chiyo would say goodbye at Nakayama's shop as if she were going to take the ferry home, then switch directions after a few blocks. Up the hill to the inn, where she would take a languid bath in the inn's large pool, always empty at that hour. Then a drowsy, quiet time on the wide sweep of the *tatami* near the open windows in the warm season; cozily ensconced near the *kotatsu* in winter.

When Nakayama arrived, he would place his cool hand on her forehead, caress her hair and her lips, embrace her lightly, then again and again with increasing intensity until they were undressing each other with delicious slowness, then entwined together. Afterwards, they entered the bath together, talking softly to each other through the steaming air. Back in their room, it seemed there was no division between the real world and her drowsy dreamworld which Nakayama entered so freely and with such ease.

The maid brought them evening meals on a tray, and they ate, then slept in one another's arms.

"I didn't think, at our age, we could perform such feats," he whispered to her. "It must be the Goddess Itsukushima. She's supposed to be jealous, but instead she's blessed us. Or maybe it's a trick, and we'll wake up someday and find out that it was all a dream."

He would rise at dawn and slip out of the inn in time to get back to his workshop before Yuki awoke. Chiyo would get up an hour later, pack up her belongings, then take an early ferry back to the mainland or a taxi down to Sugi no Ura to check on the house.

Sometimes, on the way home, she stopped in to see him again and they would go upstairs into the sunlit workshop for another session of carving wood, cutting and folding paper, pasting, and shaping. Chiyo was always carrying around in her head an array of memories of Nakayama's face mixed with bits of origami paper folded into shapes and wood carvings smeared with glue.

It was December. They had just finished a training session at a meeting hall near the shrine and were back in Nakayama's workshop, sorting out materials and ideas.

"Come on, let's stop all this indoor work for a while," Nakayama said. "Let's take that path up to the top of the mountain. It's a clear day and they're going to install an aerial tram up there soon. I want to get a good view of the sea before I have to share it with all the tourists."

Chiyo did not think she had the strength to follow the path all the way to the top. But finally, standing at the peak of the mountain after two hours of climbing, the brisk December wind blowing in her face, she felt she had the strength to do anything, that she would live forever, and in perfect health.

"Marry me," Nakayama said while they stood there on top of the world, the Inland Sea stretched below them, expansive and serene, an imperturbable blue. "Your children are grown. As soon as Yoko marries, can't you marry me? Your son is off in Tokyo and he'll be on his own soon."

She did not know why she was surprised. They had been together long enough now. But the idea took her breath away, and she could not speak.

He looked at her quizzically. "Wouldn't your husband want you to be happy here on earth without him? Surely he knows that we love each other. We've already committed ourselves, and there's no point anymore in our living separately. We need to be together."

She took his hand, then stared at the sea.

"It's your brother, isn't it? He wouldn't want you to marry an old shopkeeper like me—"

"Don't," she said. "Don't say that. Just let's try and see what we can do. After Yoko is married, then—"

"I can wait as long as I know you'll marry me. I do not want to spend the rest of my life alone here on this island. I want to share it with you."

All through the holidays that year, she did not see him. The whole family was home. Pregnant Fusako was there with her husband, Toshio, who would be finishing his electronics training in the spring. Fusako wanted the baby born in Hiroshima and was anxious to return. But Toshio seemed to enjoy Tokyo more and was already suggesting that he needed another year of training.

Hiroshi had been accepted into graduate school in nuclear physics at Tokyo University and had received a grant from Toshiba Electric Company to do research.

They were very proud of him, especially Isao. But Hiroshi was uncomfortable with his connection to a capitalist firm like Toshiba. When he first went to Tokyo, he had joined *Zengakuren*, a student movement that focused on peace issues and anti-A-bomb activity. He was filled with radical talk, especially about the new Security Treaty soon to be signed by the United States and Japan. Wasn't it ironic, he said, that the Americans had encouraged, in fact insisted on, the inclusion of Article Nine, renouncing war in the new Japanese Constitution? Now, with North Korea and the Soviet Union as enemies, they wanted Japan to arm to the teeth. The Americans were cunning, false, unreliable, he said. But the *Zengakuren* students were going to make sure Japan kept its ideals and its Peace Constitution. Isao agreed. They discussed it most of the vacation but argued when Hiroshi said he and his friends would prevent the signing of a revised treaty even if it meant they had to put their bodies on the line, demonstrate in front of the National Diet, snake-dance through Tokyo, form barricades against the police. They would never allow American negotiators to land on Japanese soil.

"That's really foolish, Hiro-kun," Isao said. "If you believe in peace, you can't use violence to get it."

"We're not creating the violence," he said. "We're just forcing them to confront us."

"This young generation." Isao shook his head. "I'm afraid you weren't old enough to understand the war around you. We all learned about violence in those days. We thought there'd been enough of it to last an eternity."

"But that's just what we're trying to prevent."

The gap between them grew wider.

Yasu came home, too, visiting them at their new house in Nobori-chō, sitting stiffly, uncomfortably, in the living room, talking politely to Chiyo. As if they hadn't known each other all their lives. As if they hadn't walked through the atom bomb and the shadow of death together.

"Ya-chan," she said. "I am pleased. I'll have three children in the family again instead of only two. I couldn't imagine a better son-in-law if I searched a thousand years."

He nodded warily, not certain yet whether she was friend or enemy. It seemed that, for the moment, there was no way to convince him.

On New Year's Day Yoko brought him to Inokuchi and presented him to Uncle Isao, bustling him into the room among all the other guests who had come as usual to pay homage to their mayor.

"He's working with electronics just like Toshio, Uncle," Yoko explained briefly. Isao nodded pleasantly, then turned his attention to another guest.

"He seems to have become quite a reliable young man," Isao commented later after Yasu had politely taken his leave.

Chiyo and Yoko smiled at one another. Maybe it was going to

work. But they'd better have the wedding soon. Chiyo decided not even to risk telling Hiroshi about the early plans. In matters of the heart, he seemed too much Isao's ally.

Mrs. Yamamoto, Yoko, and Chiyo all went to see Yasu and Hiroshi off to Tokyo at the station.

"Promise me you won't get yourself killed in one of those demonstrations," Chiyo said.

He smiled at her indulgently. "Yes, Mama. I'll be careful."

Then the train steamed into the station and they were gone.

Afterwards, Yoko and her two mothers sat up late into the night planning the wedding. Captain Yamamoto was not to be allowed into the secret either, they decided. Not until spring.

"Only women get to know," Yoko said. "We can trust Aunt Kazuko and Fusako, but not Uncle Isao." They smiled at each other, enjoying the subterfuge.

"Let's have the wedding in April," Yoko said. "When the cherry blossoms are out."

"That soon?" Chiyo asked.

"He's making a good salary now, Mama."

Mrs. Yamamoto nodded proudly.

It was cold. The middle of January. She could see her breath as she approached Miyajima on the ferry, the late afternoon sun slanting toward her.

When she reached Nakayama's store just before closing time, the sky had turned brilliant orange. She waited around the corner until she saw the two shop girls leaving, then continued to wait, hoping Yuki would come out too. But instead it was Nakayama himself who emerged and began pulling down the steel covers, closing the front of the shop. She had hoped to take him by surprise. But he did not even turn around when he spoke to her.

"I hoped you'd be here by tonight," he said. "I had a hunch somehow." Then he turned and smiled at her. "I told the girls they could come in late on Monday morning. Said I'd open up the shop. And Yuki's gone off to a friend's house on an island somewhere. We have the whole shop to ourselves."

He laughed. "I'm so glad to see you," he said. Then he was serious.

"Well, Yoko's wedding plans laid?"

She nodded. "In the spring."

The brilliant orange of the sky glared through Nakayama's windows in the workshop like the charcoal embers in her *kotatsu*. It bathed them both in a golden glow, a halo surrounding him when he encircled her in his arms, kissing her cheeks and her eyes and her forehead.

"We'll wait until six months after their wedding," she whispered. "By then Yoko will be settled into her marriage, and Hiroshi deep into graduate studies. Then I'll tell Isao."

They undressed each other, their bodies a rich and vibrant orange, warmed by the caresses of the waning sun.

Afterwards, they stretched out before the window, high above the other buildings, their love spent, languidly watching the lights on the shore of the mainland.

"You can stay, can't you?" he asked. "No one here in the morning. No one to disturb us all day."

"Well, I told Yoko I would spend the night on Miyajima, so she doesn't expect me back, and I haven't told Isao and Kazuko exactly when I would—" She turned to look at him and stopped talking, transfixed by his gaze.

Their bodies were indigo blue in the shadows. She shivered, and he reached for the quilt. They heard footsteps on the stairs, and turned to see a shadow appearing at the top of the stairwell toward the back of the room.

"You left your side door open," the voice was saying. "I rang the bell and pounded on the storefront, but I couldn't rouse you. Now I see why. I'm sorry to interrupt you, but I have a message for Mrs. Hara, whose son has been badly hurt in a demonstration in Tokyo."

Nakayama quickly swept their clothes under the quilt, clutched it around himself and reached for another to cover Chiyo. Then he switched on the light. She knew before she saw him that the voice belonged to Isao.

Chapter Thirty-six

Isao's voice jabbed again into the shocked silence. "I made you a sleeper reservation on the ten-thirty *Asakaze,*" he said. "If we catch the next ferry we can get there in time." He smashed out his cigarette in the ashtray at the edge of Nakayama's workbench. "I'll wait for you downstairs. Be there in five minutes." He disappeared into the stairwell, not even acknowledging Nakayama's presence.

They sat motionless, staring at the black hole which had swallowed up Isao.

"Hiroshi!" Chiyo finally breathed.

Nakayama pulled off his quilt and sorted out their clothes. She could not even remember telling him goodbye. Isao had already set off at a dead run when she emerged on the street.

"Students snaking through the traffic in front of the Diet Building," Isao said when they had settled on the ferry. "Somewhere around Toranomon. Hundreds of them. Traffic snarled. And the police out in force with their clubs."

"Did he—? He got hit with one of those clubs? I told him—"

"It wasn't a club. He fell in front of a car. Apparently the snake line broke hold, and the car's front wheels rolled over him. Crushed his ribs, broke bones in his elbow, his collarbone, one leg above the knee, and—" He took a deep breath. "Maybe a concussion."

Chiyo grabbed Isao's hand. "He's still alive, isn't he? Tell me the worst part first."

Isao withdrew his hand. "Yes, he's alive. He's at the University Medical Center. They don't know how serious it is yet."

They were the first ones off the ferry and Isao propelled her into a waiting taxi. His face was silhouetted against the window, chiseled out of rock and outlined by the moon that had risen above the Inland Sea. Chiyo did not speak. She did not want to explain about Nakayama.

"How will I get to the hospital?" she asked. "Do you know the address?"

He still had not looked at her. "I've arranged for Fusako to meet your train at Tokyo station," he said, pulling out his wallet. "Here's some money." He handed her two crisp 5,000-yen bills. He'd obviously been to the bank. She couldn't imagine what he'd gone through in the last few hours while she was out in Miyajima. He took care of everything when she needed him. He was always there, always dependable, and he was very disappointed in her right now.

"It was good of you . . ." Her voice trailed off. She was afraid she was going to cry, and she sat twisting her handkerchief. "My baggage," she said suddenly.

"Yoko is bringing it to the station." He turned and looked at her for the first time. "I have one berth reservation for you, and I can board the train and buy another ticket if you want me to go with you. Don't answer now. Tell me when we get to the station." He folded his arms in front of his chest and looked away from her again. "It took us hours to find you," he said. "We assumed you were at the summerhouse."

"I'm sorry." He was waiting for excuses or explanations. She had none. Instead, she was seized with a desire to compound his disappointment in her.

"Nakayama-san wants me to marry him," she said.

"I do not want to discuss your sexual transgressions at this time, Chiyo-san," he said firmly. "Mr. Nakayama's family is not the kind we Ogawas marry into. Frankly, I cannot even imagine the attraction."

"He's kind and gentle and honest. That's what the attraction is," Chiyo snapped.

"I consider the subject closed. I do not want to hear you mention his name again."

* * *

Yoko was standing on the platform, vulnerable and red-eyed, clutching Chiyo's old leather bag. She hugged her mother and burst into tears. Her display of emotion contrasted sharply with Isao's stern demeanor, and it comforted Chiyo immeasurably.

The mighty *Asakaze,* the Morning Wind, steamed in on the track, blowing Isao's overcoat collar up around his ears and covering the side of his face so that he seemed like a dark shadow, an ominous warning.

"I can go alone," Chiyo said to him. "You've already arranged everything, so if Fusako meets me at the station and gets me to the hospital, I'll be fine."

Isao nodded. "All right. But call Kazuko from the hospital after you get there."

"And I'll come as soon as I make arrangements at work," Yoko said.

Chiyo hugged her once more. "I know you'll take care of everything, but wait until I call before you come."

She bowed formally to Isao, thanked him with extreme politeness, and boarded the train.

She watched them waving, receding into the background. Yoko ran along the platform to the end, where she stood with her arms raised high in farewell. The track curved into a tunnel and shut her out of view.

Darkness around her and the humming train clomping its way rhythmically up to Tokyo. Chiyo stared at her upper-berth ticket and thought wistfully of the time in their childhood when she and Isao had been taken to Tokyo by their father. She was six and had insisted on the upper berth, then whispered all night to Isao in the middle berth while they listened to their father snoring in the one below. Had Isao remembered that when he reserved her ticket? Maybe it was just a coincidence.

Half an hour out of Hiroshima, the porters shooed the passengers out to the passageway while they converted the seats into beds. Afterwards, she climbed into her high sanctuary. But she could not sleep. There were images of Hiroshi, his face and body swathed in bandages, slits in the white gauze for his eyes and mouth. Why hadn't she felt his pain the moment of the accident? Mothers were supposed to have a telepathic sense when their children were in danger. But Chiyo hadn't been paying attention to her son.

She sat up abruptly, pushing the images out of her head, afraid of the other visions she dreaded—Yukiji in the flames or Kenichi bursting in the sun.

Finally she lay back, staring into the dark, trying to see the warm and tender face of Nakayama, but it would not come to her. She turned back and forth in her berth, slept fitfully, heard the conductor calling, "Osaka. The next station is Osaka." She pushed the blind open a crack and peered out at the station, listening to the train panting and gasping, letting off steam, accusing her. "It's your fault. You caused it. Behavior like yours brings down the vengeance of the heavens."

Sometime before dawn she must have slept. But she was awake and dressed, standing in the vestibule, when the train arrived in Tokyo.

Fusako, her face tight with anxiety, hurried Chiyo out to a taxi. "He's still unconscious," she said. "We don't know yet whether he can talk or recognize anyone."

A week sitting by his bed, hardly leaving the hospital. Fusako spelled her. Yoko arrived on Tuesday morning and Yasu came and sat with them evenings. "I didn't watch over him even though you asked me to," Yasu said, pressing his face into his hands. "I meant to talk to him, but I kept putting it off."

"He was already committed," Chiyo said. "Nobody could have convinced him otherwise. Not his uncle. Not even the Buddha."

In the lonely hours of the night, when Yoko was back at Fusako's apartment asleep, and Chiyo was the only person in the world awake, she sat watching over Hiroshi and giving thanks to the Goddess of Mercy for the family she had and for their being exactly the way they were, even Isao, whatever way he was, however different he was from her. He was always there and faithful in spite of her transgressions.

Most of all, she prayed that Hiroshi would get well. "If you can make him whole again, make him so that he thinks and talks, I'll give up Nakayama," she offered.

A few days later, Hiroshi regained consciousness, moved his free arm and wiggled his fingers. He did not speak, but then how could he, with his face wrapped in gauze? Every day she looked at his eyes through the narrow slits, and sometimes when they shone through, she was convinced that he recognized her, that his brain was still intact, and that once the bandages came off, he would be able to speak.

One more week and they removed the bandages. His face was an angry red, and there was a scar from the left of his mouth to his ear, making his mouth crooked. It was like Chiyo's scar, and it frightened her to see it. But his smile was unmistakable and deliberate.

The day after, he reached out his free arm and touched her. *"Kā-chan?"* he asked. "Mama?"

She leaned toward his bed and wept on his chest. He stroked her back. "Sorry," he breathed. "Caused you so much—" It was still hard for him to move his mouth.

"Hiro-chan," she said. "Never mind that now. Just get well."

They were home in another week, a long period of healing ahead of them. He was swathed in bandages and still had casts around his broken rib cage and collarbone, the broken arm above the elbow and the broken bone in his thigh. He could not walk or move his right arm, and he had trouble feeding himself with his left hand, but gradually he learned. He suffered from headaches that lasted sometimes for days, but the concussion was not as serious as they had thought. And he was beginning to read again. Everything he could find. Politics, physics, technology, even novels. But only for short spurts.

He screamed in the night when he had dreams. Sometimes he called out for Kenichi, and once he sat up in bed and told his mother, soberly, that his father had not died, that he was coming home again, and that he would walk through the door at any moment.

She did not go to the factory often. The kits she and Nakayama had designed were selling well, and in any case, it was the electronic and transistor side of Asahi Enterprises that was growing now. Fusako and Toshio were coming home in another month so that he could take up the presidency of Asahi Electronics. Fusako would have her first baby in Hiroshima after all.

There were letters from Nakayama.

> Heard that Hiroshi is improving. Keep up your spirits. I have been in deep anguish since you left me at the moment our life together seemed assured. But I pray constantly for his complete recovery and your return to Miyajima.

He wrote her a haiku about the sunset light shining in through his windows on Miyajima, and she read it and felt even deeper anguish herself. Almost three weeks in Tokyo, and a week at home now, and she had not called or talked to him once.

He wrote her almost every day.

> If I could see you or hear your voice. I wanted to call you in Tokyo, but I didn't know where to reach you, and I didn't feel I could ask your brother.

She ached for him, for just one moment away from Hiroshi's sickbed out in Miyajima in the workshop high above the sea with the windowpanes reflecting the sun. But she could not leave the bedside of her only son, who, even now, unless she kept her vigil and kept praying, was still not out of danger.

"At least tell Nakayama what's happening," she told herself. "At least you can get down to the tobacco store to call him." But she could not.

Finally, she wrote him a note.

> Thank you for your warm letter. Hiroshi is improving day by day, although he still has some bad nights. I think of you constantly.

She could not say more. She knew by then that she could not bear to hear his voice. Her guilt was too profound, her longing and self-doubt and anger at Isao too intense. The very idea. Telling her what kind of family the Ogawas don't marry into. She was fifty-six years old, and she would marry into whatever family she chose.

But she had promised Kannon, the Goddess of Mercy—

Nakayama called the tobacco store one afternoon while Hiroshi was asleep. The proprietor sent his daughter to get her.

"Chi-chan?" he whispered hoarsely. His voice didn't even sound like his. She recoiled slightly. She didn't want him to call her that. She didn't want anyone to call her that except her brother.

"Don't feel anything that happened is your fault," he said. "Promise me that. Just take care of Hiroshi and come back to me when you can."

"Yes," she said. "All right. How are you?"

"Well, it's lonely out here. I wish you could come. Or I'll come in and help you take care of Hiroshi if you like."

"No," she said. "Not yet. I'm not ready, but I'll tell you when I am. I miss you very much." She hung up, went home, and sat facing the wall, considering the bargain she had made with Kannon. A foolish, superstitious thought, a decision made in a moment of crisis. Even a human would forgive her that. Certainly the Champion of Mercy—

She did not stir until Hiroshi called her, asking for tea.

They postponed Yoko and Yasu's wedding until fall.

"October with the red maple leaves," Yoko said. "It's a better background than cherry blossoms."

Yoko spent her free time writing letters to Yasu and helping take care of Hiroshi, feeding him, emptying his bedpan, reading to him so he wouldn't get headaches.

In late spring, all his bandages came off, and his right arm and leg, which he couldn't yet move, were scrawny and scarred.

Improvement was more rapid now, but each step forward had its relapse. He began to walk, but still with the help of crutches, and hewas exhausted afterwards, morose over his limited physical powers. His face was filling out, and his speech, which seemed so garbled when he first came home from Tokyo, was clearer now, his thinking processes more precise. But sometimes, even six months later, he would say things no one could understand.

By August, he could hold chopsticks in his right hand again. Yasu came home early for the Obon holidays and spent most of his time at the Hara house. For three days, he and Yoko sat up late talking, meandered along the Hondori, settled themselves into their favorite teahouse for hours at a time, even went together to Miyajima. "Yasu's never seen the old summerhouse, you know." They had decided not to tell Isao about Yoko's plans until just before the engagement was announced.

On the day of the *obon,* the Yamamotos attended memorial services for his sister and grandparents; the Haras went to Inokuchi for their usual observances. It was the first time Hiroshi had been out of the house, and, after the services, there was cause for careful, muted celebration. Everyone began to think Hiroshi would be able to go back to school when the new term began in the spring.

Sitting there at the table, enjoying the festival food and the presence of her family, Chiyo at last felt some sense of peace, was able to forgive herself, and even able to forgive Isao. They had carefully skirted the subject of Nakayama. It would be a long time mending that rift. But at least Chiyo knew she would take a firm stand about Yasu and Yoko when the subject came up. These days Isao was deeply preoccupied with the new Matsuda Carol coupés he and a team were designing for Toyokogyo. And with his new grandchild.

He had named her Fumiko, choosing the Chinese character for "literature, art, and scholarship." Of course, he had hoped for a boy. But he was already planning a boy's name for the second child—Akio, using the character for "brightness and light." That way, he told them, the two names combined would spell *bunmei,* meaning "civilization."

"But what if the second child is a girl?" Kazuko demanded. "We can't call her Akiko, because that was my sister's name."

"The second one won't be a girl," Isao declared, his jaw set.

Chiyo and Kazuko caught each other's glances and smiled; then

Toshio offered a toast to Hiroshi's health and the renewed pursuit of his studies, and Hiroshi offered a toast to Toshio's and Fusako's next child, who would be a boy, and to Toshio's presidency of the electronics division of Asahi Enterprises. Isao offered a toast to Hiroshi's bright new future, and to Yoko's success as a working girl, "and eventually to your forthcoming marriage, eh?"

He drank the sake down while Yoko nodded and looked at her neatly folded knees. No one had announced the engagement to him yet.

"Well, Chi-chan and Yoko both deserve a toast for bringing Hiroshi back to health," Kazuko said. And they toasted that.

"And to my younger sister for remaining faithful to the memory of her deceased husband," Isao said. He didn't look at her when he drained his cup.

On the way home, in the taxi, Chiyo gazed longingly at the magic island of Miyajima, wondering how she could ever manage to go back there again and sit in the high room on the second story above the sea.

She and Nakayama had begun to write each other weekly letters, as if they were corresponding over a vast distance.

By the time Yasu left for Tokyo the next day, Chiyo and Yoko had already laid plans with Mrs. Yamamoto for the *yuinō,* the traditional presentation of the groom's betrothal money and exchange of gifts.

In late August, Hiroshi walked all the way to the Nobori-chō streetcar stop and back without crutches and declared afterwards that he didn't even feel tired from the exertion. He was sitting with his mother and sister on the veranda, facing the cherry trees Shintaro had planted so long ago. A few of their leaves had already turned yellow and fallen to the ground.

"You'll be able to attend my *yuinō* ceremony without crutches," Yoko said. They had not yet told him of Yoko's wedding plans, and they sat waiting for his reaction.

"Yes, well, that's good," he said matter-of-factly. "I'm going back inside now. It's enough for today."

Sometimes, when Hiroshi spoke, it startled Chiyo. His voice was like a talking machine. As if the accident had drained him of all enthusiasm.

They helped him stand and walk stiffly into the house.

"Then the first week of October, after the betrothal, we're going to have the wedding," Yoko said. "We're planning it that way so you'll be able to attend before you go back to school."

He didn't respond.

"What do you think?" she insisted.

"Sounds all right to me," he said.

"Well, aren't you surprised or shocked or happy or anything?"

He grinned. "I think I've always known you were marrying Yasu. Even before that time you made Uncle Isao so angry." He sat down heavily on his sleeping mat. "And of course I'm glad. But I'm not surprised because I've been listening to you plot that wedding all along. First in the hospital room, and then right here in the next room when you thought I was sleeping."

"Then you know we haven't told Uncle Isao!" Her face turned red and she giggled nervously. "Do you think he'll object?"

"No. He's let it go this far. He won't interfere now."

On the day of the *yuinō,* Hiroshi was up early, trying to walk without a limp.

Early in the afternoon, Fusako and Kazuko appeared at the door with Isao, out of breath from having escaped the crowd that always gathered when he parked his new Matsuda coupé with the bubble top.

"And yet he does insist on driving that thing," Kazuko said, rearranging her hairdo, blown apart by the drive. "I'm riding home with Fusako and Toshio when he comes to pick her up. And you, *Anata,*" she said to Isao, "just drive it home by yourself and don't tell me how fast you went."

They gathered in Chiyo's new living room overlooking the garden, wider than the old one but not as large as the prewar house had been. Later they went outside and sat on the *engawa,* waiting for the Yamamotos and the *nakōdo,* the couple they had chosen to act as go-betweens and presenters of the groom's *yuinō* offering to help with marriage expenses.

They watched Fusako as she guided her daughter, Fumiko, across the stepping-stones in the garden, helping her learn to walk.

Chiyo enjoyed the warm glow of familiarity, the spurts of talking and comfortable silences. The way it is when people have endured so much together for a lifetime. Nakayama would be comfortable in this group. But of course Isao—

She wished she had invited Nakayama to take the place of the bride's father instead of Isao. She smiled to herself, thinking of the outrage. It would destroy the *yuinō* ceremony, break up Yoko's engagement, rip the family asunder. And Kannon, to whom she had made her foolish promise, would make a cripple out of Hiroshi. Or kill him on the spot because she'd gone too far. Quite a price to pay for her defiance.

Isao's spirits were especially high. He was congratulating Hiroshi for his rapid recovery, Yoko for her engagement. He had raised no objections when they told him the day before. "It was sensible of you to wait until you're old enough. Twenty-five is a good age. Of course Fu-chan was even older, but we found her a good husband in the end anyway, didn't we? Eh?"

Fusako, returning from her garden walk, nodded politely, but without enthusiasm.

An uncomfortable silence followed, everyone thinking of Toshio, who really wasn't interested in Asahi Enterprises or his wife and her family or even his young daughter very much. The rumor was that he had collected several bar-girl companions in Tokyo, and he was sorry to have to leave them and come back to Hiroshima.

"Whatever could have happened to the Yamamotos?" Chiyo asked suddenly. "They should have been here half an hour ago, and they're hardly ever late to anything."

Yoko was beginning to look pinched and nervous.

"Toshio's not here yet either," Fusako pointed out.

They waited another half hour, their conversation growing desultory, their faces anxious. Hiroshi was pacing back and forth, hoping someone would notice that he wasn't limping, but everyone's attention was elsewhere.

When the doorbell rang, it was neither the Yamamotos nor Toshio but Yasu's chemistry professor and his wife, the *nakōdo* couple, Professor and Mrs. Haraguchi.

"We were supposed to meet at the Bus Center downtown," the professor said. "Exactly at one o'clock. We waited for the next three buses. Maybe there's been some mistake. They're not here?"

But they had hardly stepped into the sitting room when Mrs. Yamamoto appeared. "I met every train," she said, "Then it got late and I worried about the Haraguchis. I'm glad you came ahead," she said to them. "You see, on my way here, the girl from the tobacco shop came running down the street to say that I had a call from Tokyo." Mrs. Yamamoto was breathing heavily. She caught her breath and looked at the assemblage before her. "He's gone into the hospital," she announced. "He collapsed when he was getting on the train, apparently from stomach cramps."

They stared at her in stunned silence.

It was Hiroshi who finally helped her up onto the *tatami*. "He seems all right now," she said. "They've given him something for the pain, and—" She sat nervously pulling a thread at the edge of her kimono. "He said that under no circumstances does he want any of us to go up to Tokyo.

"Especially—" She looked sorrowfully at Yoko. "I'm so sorry, my dear. And I apologize to all the rest of you, causing you this terrible inconvenience, taking time out of your busy schedules."

"Never mind all that," said Chiyo. "What are we going to do about Yasu? Shouldn't somebody go?"

"Well, let's make the presentation, shall we, Haraguchi-sensei? In the old days when people did this, the groom didn't even come to the *yuinō* ceremony, just sent the representative." She smiled brave-ly at Professor Haraguchi. "As soon as we're finished, you know, I think I'll go up to Tokyo even though he's told me not to. If I run on down to the station and get a reservation on tonight's *Asa-kaze*—"

"I'll get you the ticket," Isao said. "I've got my car outside, and I'll do it while you're having the ceremony. I'm only acting in the absence of Yoko's father, so you can just as well present the gift to her mother." He disappeared out the door.

Mrs. Yamamoto and the Haraguchis knelt before the Haras in the wide *tatami* room, all of them mouthing polite phrases, bowing to one another, exactly according to protocol.

Isao returned with the ticket. Everyone knew how hard it was to get a ticket on the *Asakaze* at such short notice, and Mrs. Yamamoto thanked him profusely.

"I'm coming with you," Yoko said. "I don't need a seat. I can sit in the aisle."

Mrs. Yamamoto clasped Yoko's hands. "He doesn't even want me to come, you know. And he particularly asked that you not come. I'm sure you understand."

"Then take him this," she said, pulling off the locket from around her neck. "I was going to give it to him at the ceremony today."

After she had gone, Chiyo tried to finish the ceremony by serving the festival food, but no one had any appetite. Yoko only stared at the table until Hiroshi, usually the silent one, was moved to speak. "It's all right, *Nē-chan*. They told Yasu's mother it wasn't anything serious. And you'll hear tomorrow."

She smiled wanly, then looked at Isao.

"You told me not to marry him," she said. "Remember? You forbade me to see him again."

Chiyo held her breath, waiting for Isao's displeasure. Why did Yoko have to be that way? Why couldn't she let well enough alone?

"I remember, Yoko-chan," Isao said gently. "But I could see when you waited three years and then finally brought him at New Year's that you were set on it." He reached out and held her hands

366

in his. "You'll be all right," he said. "You're strong. And so is he."

He looked around the room. "So, where's Toshio?" he asked.

No one answered. Fumiko had fallen asleep in Fusako's arms.

"Well, I want to get this precious grandchild home before she catches cold in the night air. Tell Toshio we went on ahead, will you, Chi-chan?"

For two days there was no word.

"I didn't even think to ask what hospital he was in," Yoko said.

On the morning of the third day, Chiyo and Yoko left Hiroshi at home to wait for phone calls and took a streetcar out to the Yamamoto house in Ujina.

Captain Yamamoto, looking frail and confused, slid open the door. Yes, Yasu was fine, he told them. Just a short operation.

"An operation?" Yoko gasped.

"Now, don't you worry about it, young lady," the captain said. He stood in the *genkan,* acting like an armed guard. "He'll be back on his job in no time. Are you a special friend of his?"

He had no idea who Yoko was. He didn't remember Chiyo either.

"You know, we were neighbors," Chiyo suggested gently. "Our children grew up together, and—"

"Oh, yes, " he interrupted, nodding his head. Chiyo knew he still didn't remember. "Don't worry. I'll tell my wife you came." He started to close the door.

"Is there any way we can get in touch with her? Or with the hospital Yasu is staying in?" Chiyo insisted.

"Well, I don't know. I think she's staying with her cousin." He left the door and searched around in the room behind him.

"Here," he said, coming back to the door. "Try this address. That's the cousin, and she'll know which hospital it is." He thrust the paper at them. "I'm sorry I can't talk to you any longer, but I have an appointment."

They were back in the street again, holding only an address.

"An appointment," Yoko murmured. "Mrs. Yamamoto says he hasn't been out of the house in five years." They sent *sokutatsu,* special delivery letters. They waited two more days.

On the evening of the third day, Yoko said she wanted to go out to Inokuchi. "Maybe I'll stay there overnight," she said. "If I can help take care of Fumiko, I won't worry as much."

That night, Chiyo called a friend in Tokyo and asked her to check all the hospitals in the Tokyo station area for a patient named Yamamoto Yasu. The answer came late that evening. No one by that name had been found.

Home from work the next day, Chiyo found Isao and Hiroshi both spread out across the sitting room *tatami*, bent over tiny wires and colored cylinders.

"Any news?" Isao asked.

She shook her head.

"Well, surely somebody— In fact I'll try getting in touch with his office. He's at the Ministry of Technology, isn't he? We should have thought of that before."

"Of course!" Chiyo said. "It would have been easier than going to Captain Yamamoto."

"I'll do it first thing tomorrow," said Isao. He stood up and brushed the little pieces of wire and plastic from his trousers.

"By the way, do you know your son here is designing a new kind of transistor that's even smaller than anything on the market so far?" He gave Hiroshi a comradely slap on the back. "He got the idea while he was taking a bath in your new wooden *ofuro*."

Hiroshi, still engrossed in his wires, stopped to look up at her, his mouth set in a firm line. "I'm not going back to the university to study nuclear physics, Mother. When I'm well, I'll go up to Tokyo and take the same course Toshio took. Then maybe Uncle and I can get this into production. It's going to be very big, Mama."

She stood with her hands on her hips, looking at the chaos spread across her living room. "You mean," she said, "that before the accident you were a wild radical, and now you're a capitalist?"

He ignored the question. "I'm going to build us a big house in Hatsukaichi on the Inland Sea. There's good land out there."

"But Hiro-chan, we've got a house. We just built this one. Remember?"

"Don't you want to move away from here and all the old memories?" he asked.

"No," she said gently, "And I don't want a new house, either. But thank you for thinking of me. Right now, I'm just pleased you're well and you've found something you love to do." She knelt down and examined his tiny, intricate wires, some of them packed into a small case. How could anyone understand the confusion displayed there?

Isao stepped out into the *genkan*.

"I forgot to ask," Chiyo said. "How's Yoko doing out in Inokuchi? Is she feeling any better?"

"Yoko? In Inokuchi? Since when? We haven't seen her."

Isao stayed for supper. They called all of Yoko's classmates. At nine, they called the police.

"Of course she's gone off to Tokyo," Chiyo said. "And she didn't tell us because she knew we'd object. But what I can't understand is why she hasn't called since she got there. She's always been such a considerate child. And she knew how it felt when Mrs. Yamamoto didn't call. I can't imagine that she would have done that to us."

Isao stayed the night, all of them sleeping fitfully on the living room floor. They were awake at dawn, drinking tea. At seven, Yoko called from Tokyo. "I'm at Mrs. Yamamoto's cousin's," she said. "I took a taxi straight here, and everything's fine. Mrs. Yamamoto is going home tonight and I'll stay at least until he gets out of the hospital. They were doing a biopsy to check for tumors, and it's all right. It's not malignant. Will you meet her train in the morning?"

"Yoko-chan, we were worried sick. We've been up all night. Your Uncle Isao's been here, checking every hour with the police. How could you have done this to us?"

"Oh, Mama! You knew I was gone? I didn't think anyone would notice at least until this morning. You thought I was in Inokuchi and everybody out there thought I was home. That's the way I planned it."

In the morning, Mrs. Yamamoto stepped lightly off the train. "We're so lucky," she breathed. "Not cancer. I'm sorry about not writing. I was just—"

"It's all right," Chiyo said. "A little anxiety is worth it when things turn out. What hospital is he in?"

"They moved him to a government one in the Toranomon area near where he works. Someone in his office recommended it."

"And Yoko?" Chiyo asked. "Where's she been staying?"

"Well, at my cousin's, but her classmate lives even closer to the hospital, so she's going there. Don't worry. She's promised to write."

"You promised, too," Chiyo said to herself.

There were days of stepping over transistors and electric wires in the front living room. Chiyo hated them. They were ugly and sterile, especially compared to her vivid dolls.

By the end of the week, she had to admit there was a certain order and beauty to them.

Yoko wrote faithfully. Her classmate had a job at the National Diet Library and a small room very near Yasu's hospital in Torano-mon. Yoko spent every day at the hospital.

In another week she called and said Yasu was being released from the hospital and would stay in a friend's apartment nearby while he recuperated. Chiyo suspected that Yoko was staying with him there, but she did not ask.

"We're getting married as soon as he's well," Yoko said. "Maybe just up here in Tokyo, and not a big ceremony."

"No, Yoko-chan," Chiyo warned. "Don't do anything on impulse. Take a while to decide. Of course you can have a small wedding, but can't you wait until he's well enough to come to Hiroshima? What exactly is the matter with him, anyway? Why is it taking so long?"

"It's all right, Mama. He's making rapid progress, and I'll keep you informed."

There was silence for a while, but Chiyo didn't worry. She knew they were absorbed in each other and their plans. Another week went by before she realized she had heard nothing even from Mrs. Yamamoto. It was useless to go all the way to Ujina and find only Captain Yamamoto there. That would frustrate her even more than the transistor tubes rolling around the house.

Another telegram came.

We're coming home. Meet the *Hikari*. 7:00 P.M. Coach 9.

Yoko

Chiyo and Hiroshi watched the train appear on the bend of the tracks, pushing the last few yards into the station. Yoko was standing in the vestibule, painfully thin. And alone.

When she stepped off the train, they caught sight of Mrs. Yamamoto just behind her. Yoko turned and took one of her arms. The conductor had hold of the other arm. In Mrs. Yamamoto's hands was a wooden box, wrapped with a *furoshiki* cloth and tied to Mrs. Yamamoto's neck for support. It was the traditional way women carried boxes home from Maizuru, the way wives and mothers had received them from China and the Pacific all through the war, the kind of boxes that were stored everywhere in the temples and shrines of Hiroshima, all of them containing ashes and the Adam's apple bone that looked like the sitting Buddha.

"Stomach cancer," Mrs. Yamamoto breathed when she got closer to Chiyo. They bowed elaborately to one another again and again. "The doctors didn't find it the first time. Something wrong with the biopsy. It all happened so fast."

"But he was getting well," said Chiyo. "Yoko called and said he was out of the hospital."

In Yoko's face Chiyo saw both exquisite pain and an ethereal calm. So much living in less than one month. Her youth was gone.

"If Mrs. Yamamoto stays the night with us," Yoko said, "we can go out to Ujina in the morning and tell the captain."

Hiroshi stuffed suitcases and boxes into the trunk of a taxi. "You've got a lot of stuff here, Yoko-chan," he blurted out.

"Yasu's things," she said simply.

Mrs. Yamamoto, her head relentlessly erect, popped into the taxi seat, holding firmly to her box of ashes.

"I think I'd like to walk home with Mama across the Sakae Bridge," Yoko said.

Hiroshi nodded and climbed into the taxi next to Mrs. Yamamoto. "We'll meet you at the house, then."

The familiar trek home across the bridge, November wind biting at them as it came up from the river, which flowed expressionless, blending Yasu's soul with the rest—his classmates who'd gone before. Yasu was the last of them. Chiyo wondered if Kenichi was waiting for him in the dark night somewhere. Would they all be thirteen years old still? She hardly noticed that Yoko was talking.

"I just kept hoping he would get well. I thought if I prayed enough and thought about it enough, somehow he would just— I couldn't believe—I don't believe it now. But then near the end he was just, you know, so wasted away. Hardly anything left—"

Across the bridge and into the street now. Down the familiar road. Hiroshi had turned on the light in front of their house.

"I married him, Mama. Right after we found out he had cancer and that there wasn't any hope. By the time they found out, it was spread all over. He must have had so many stomachaches. But he never told anybody.

"Anyway, I told him I didn't care how long we had. Just whatever time it was, I wanted to be with him. So we went to a little shrine near his room, and the priest performed a ceremony for us. He didn't want to at first. He said our parents should be with us, but we explained we didn't have time. And besides, I'm pregnant, Mama. From the time he came home in August. I've known since September just before the *yuinō.*"

Chiyo managed to continue walking. Only a few more houses before they were home.

"After the priest married us," Yoko went on, "we went back to his room and his strength kept ebbing away. The two of us alone.

I only left him to go out and buy food. Of course he couldn't eat anything. And he didn't want me even to call his mother until it was almost too late. But it was all right. She had enough time to say goodbye. He'd been back in the hospital a couple of days by the time she got to Tokyo. Now I wish we hadn't gone back to the hospital. I wish we'd stayed there in that room where he was comfortable with everything familiar and—"

They arrived at the front door and Yoko lingered outside, composing herself before going inside to face the others. "It's hard knowing what Hiroshi's thinking, isn't it? Just that machine-smooth expression of his. I wish I were like that. Or maybe not. I don't know."

Yoko reached out to open the door, but still she hesitated, turning to look at her mother under the light above them. "I'm going to live with the Yamamotos, Mama. Since it's their grandchild I'm having. I'm in their family now."

Chiyo clasped her only daughter in her arms. Her own losses had been mostly gradual, scattered through leaf after leaf of hope and despair. Not this sudden devastation that forced Yoko to live her whole married life in one month. Then to have a child with no father to help, and to spend her days in the dark, depressing house in Ujina, caring for her sick, senile father-in-law, bringing up her child in the midst of it.

Arm in arm, they entered the house to greet Yoko's mother-in-law and to tell Hiroshi about his sister's new husband, who was already dead.

Chapter Thirty-seven

Hiroshima had changed into a bustling, nervous city crowded with people, buses, trams, and a whole army of taxis. There were the big limousines with curtains in the back and white-gloved chauffeurs, the kind people used when they wanted to make an impression. There were the medium-sized ones which middle-aged, conservative, and older people used. And there were the *kogata,* the "pocket-size editions," Isao called them. His company manufactured them. They resembled German Volkswagens, and they darted in and out of traffic like tiny, busy gnats, always hurrying, propelling some young businessman or a gaggle of college girls at breakneck speed through the yellow traffic lights at Kamiya-chō, where huge office buildings were rising up at an amazing rate almost overnight in the spot where, only a decade ago, the wide street had been a sea of mud every winter and every rainy season. Now the road was paved. Buses lined each side of the street, and in the dusk, huge neon signs twinkled down at people, dwarfed them as they hurried about doing their shopping.

Hardly a trace of the old Hiroshima was left. And yet down along the edges of the rivers the uneasy makeshift shacks still hovered as a testament to the suffering and poverty of the people living there. And in Motomachi, on the government land behind where the castle walls had been, and in front of the new castle built to replace the old destroyed one, people maintained their own shack community, formed organizations, put up self-constructed street-lights. Most of the residents there hadn't been able to get their health back. Many had spent years in and out of the Red Cross Hospital. Some of the women who had lost their husbands didn't have a way to make an income because they had to bring up their children. The old people had lost their claims to pensions because the companies they worked for had been destroyed, and the records too. The national government had given them very little atten-tion. But the city and prefectures and private citizens had helped to the point of exhausting available funds. And they had demanded unceasingly that the national Diet enact a *hibakusha* Medical Care Law, which was finally approved in 1957, issuing health cards so that people could get treatment. But it was not enough to help the ones with lower incomes who needed a living allowance and a decent place to live besides. In 1960 a Special Relief Law was passed for hardship cases, but the Japan Confederation of A-Bomb Survivors wanted compensation from the government, not relief.

Only the cities of Hiroshima and Nagasaki and their older citi-zens understood what it was. The rest of the people in Japan and in the world shied away from the *hibakusha,* saying that they com-plained too much. Many Americans who visited the Peace Museum said the Japanese started the war, so they deserved what they got. The Japanese from other cities said the *hibakusha* ought to think more constructively, get their energy back, and get to work again.

And the people in the shacks kept living on, poor and shabby still. But at least with some government recognition and assistance, they were not as hungry as before.

And in the midst of the growing affluence around them, in the midst of the test-ban treaties and the breaking of them and the unending acquisition by other nations of the weapons of annihila-tion, the *hibakusha* kept on trying to explain the danger and the horror of it. There were conferences, peace missions, research projects, books, articles, poetry, and music. And every year on August 6, the mayor stood up and gave warning to the world that nuclear weapons led not to winning or losing, but to suicide.

Often it seemed that no one was listening.

Even the people in Hiroshima bustled about, working and con-suming. Their city had grown to giant proportions, the population exceeding 400,000 now, more than it had been before the war.

On the Hondori, beautiful and expensive specialty shops had opened, selling kimonos, *obi* sashes, *geta,* perfume and cosmetics. There were dressmakers for made-to-order Western clothes. Young women, especially *hibakusha* with disfigured faces who could not hope to marry, had taken lessons and started their own businesses. Yoko and Chiyo had put in an order with one of Keiko Kakihara's friends for a wedding going-away suit, and it had been completed on the day Yasu died. Yoko said she could wear it to work after the baby was born.

On a side street along the Hondori, Hiroshi discovered a shop that made ice cream in different flavors. Not just vanilla, but chocolate, strawberry, and almond. He brought some home for Yoko. "It's good for mothers-to-be," he said. Later the shop developed special Japanese green-tea ice cream, which Yoko liked best. All the flavors were richer and creamier even than the kind Chiyo had tasted as a child.

But most of all it was Fukuya Department Store that gave Chiyo a sense of the universe expanding. She enjoyed shopping there as long as she avoided going downstairs, which reminded her of those days in 1945 when she had searched for Kenichi in the dark basement filled with the wounded and dying.

Nowadays Fukuya was more than the elegant department store it had aspired to be in the innocent thirties. On every floor was a dazzling array—cosmetics from France, leather from Italy, glassware and furniture from Scandinavia, fancy name brands from America. And a host of cheaper Japanese-made goods that seemed just as good.

Chiyo was always searching in Fukuya for baby clothes.

Yoko wanted to be with her own mother during the pregnancy and for at least six months afterwards. Then she and the baby would move to Ujina.

She seldom spoke, rustling quietly about the house, her lips pursed, as if she were holding the memory of Yasu inside herself, not wanting to share him with anyone. She cooked, cleaned, spoke cheerfully when spoken to, helped Hiroshi with his projects, served him tea. Chiyo spent more time than usual at the factory to get away from Yoko's relentless pleasantries.

In April the baby was born. A beautiful, healthy boy. They named him Yasuhiro, using the Chinese character from the first part of Yasu's name, meaning "easy, lighthearted, and fair." The last part was the "hiro" of Hiroshi and Hiroshima, meaning "wide, expansive and broad." Captain Yamamoto was so overjoyed by the baby's presence that he regained some of his former vigor. He had been almost comatose after Yasu's death.

At the end of the month, Hiroshi went off to Tokyo carrying a bag full of electronics books, tiny transistors, and radio parts. Two weeks later, as Chiyo was preparing a box of new samples of clay dolls to take out to Miyajima, a phone call came from the administrator of the electronics school. Everyone was very impressed with Hiroshi's work, the man said, and excited about its practical applications.

"But he's working too hard and not taking care of himself," he added. "We've told him he should be home where his mother can watch over him and feed him properly until he's completely recovered. It's only a matter of a month or so, you see. So he won't miss out on his studies. We can give him the assignments by mail."

The man waited for an answer from Chiyo. She knew he expected her to be pleased and to respond positively, but she could not.

"I'm sending him home tomorrow night on the *Hikari,*" he finally said. "Your son says you live close to the station. I hope such short notice doesn't inconvenience you."

"No," she said softly. "Thank you for calling." She hung up, feeling the burden of disappointment. And guilt. It was retribution for forgetting her promise to the Goddess of Mercy.

She searched for a place to store the box. Too late to go to Miyajima today anyway, and Hiroshi coming home tomorrow. She had not written Nakayama since Yoko's return from Tokyo. Too much to say, and she wanted to wait until she could surprise him in person.

Chiyo and her two grown children spent the rest of the spring together, Yoko still doggedly cheerful and Hiroshi's transistors crawling around the house like tiny bugs, a wire sticking out of each end of their bodies. Hiroshi tried to keep the sitting room free of his paraphernalia, and Chiyo understood how hard it was. Yet the more considerate he and Yoko were, the more they irritated her. Only the baby, Yasuhiro, was a joy. She often held him in her arms, singing him to sleep after Yoko had fed him.

"I'm going out to Miyajima," she announced briefly to Hiroshi one morning when Yoko had gone off to show the baby to the Yamamotos. "I may stay overnight, so you can have the whole house to yourself."

"Really?" Hiroshi marked the place in his book before looking up. "Going out to see how the tenants are getting along? I thought that was Aunt Kazuko's job. You really do too much, Mother. You're always taking on everybody's else's jobs. And you've been so busy taking care of me. I want you to rest more."

She wanted to scream at him. Instead, she smiled. "Don't worry about me," she said. "I enjoy going out there. And anyway, I want to see what kind of dolls Nakayama-san is making and selling these days."

Hiroshi was sorting through his bent wires. "After I get the transistor factory started, I'll build my own house in Hatsukaichi. Then you can come and live with me, and I'll take care of you. I know what you sacrificed for me and Yoko-chan. Besides, I'm your only son, and it's my responsibility."

She sighed, stepped down into her shoes again, put her hands on the door, then turned to him.

"Nobody," she said, her voice calm, "is ever going to take care of me."

The sunlight danced on the water on the way to Miyajima.

The ferry moved in toward the pier, and the crowd burst out onto the dock. She separated from the others, sunlight still following her through the winding streets toward that familiar place, her spirits rising even higher with each step until she reached the shop, the windows there above her facing out toward the sea.

Nakayama was not inside. Nor Yuki. A stout middle-aged woman was behind the counter. The usual gaggle of tourists were gathered at tables drinking tea and eating cakes.

Yuki came out from behind the curtain that covered the door of the stairway into the workshop room.

"Mrs. Hara!" he exclaimed. "You here? Uncle will be so glad. He's just gone out, but he'll be back soon. Sit down and have some tea and a cake. I've got a new one I want you to try. It's got marzipan inside instead of bean paste."

She smiled at him. "You look fine," she said, sitting down. "Healthy and strong. The air over here is so good. I'm going to bring my daughter for a visit. It will brighten her spirits."

Yuki bowed formally. "We heard about her husband's tragic death," he said. "We are so sorry."

The mention of it made Chiyo want to cry, but the woman distracted her, coming from behind the counter and bringing tea.

"You are a friend of Mr. Nakayama?" she asked.

"And this is Suzuki-san," Yuki said to Chiyo. "She's replaced

Michiko. Remember her?" His face turned a brilliant red. "I'm going to marry her," he added.

"Yuki! That sweet, quiet girl? How wonderful! My warmest congratulations! *Omedeto!*" She stood up from her chair and bowed to him, giving him all the polite wishes for the future, all the formal phrases.

He laughed with delight, scrubbing the top of her table, which didn't need cleaning. "She quit working here about six months ago so she could take tea ceremony and flower arranging lessons, and—" He smiled even more broadly. "And cooking! She doesn't want to take lessons from me. She's going to create her own special dishes. I've already sent you an invitation. It's on June fifteenth."

"Here on Miyajima?"

He nodded. "It's supposed to be bad luck to get married here or have a honeymoon, but we're not superstitious."

"Me neither," she said. "I'll be there. Nothing could keep me away."

Mrs. Suzuki looked from Yuki's face to Chiyo's, trying to discern their real relationship. A customer came and Yuki excused himself.

"I'll just get you some more tea," Mrs. Suzuki said, picking up the teapot.

"Well, why don't I finish this pot first?" Chiyo said.

Mrs. Suzuki tightened her grip on the teapot. "You know, Mr. Nakayama really needed help, what with Yuki off visiting his girl-friend all the time. He couldn't manage alone. I shudder to think what might have happened to him if I hadn't come along. Really. Now what did you say your name was?"

"I am Hara Chiyo," she said a bit stiffly. Yuki had just introduced them. Mrs. Suzuki's memory was apparently very short.

She drew back abruptly, and her face tightened into a stiff smile. "Oh," she said. "Mr. Nakayama has spoken of you." She put the teapot on the table and sat down. "But less and less lately. In fact, just the other day he mentioned he was sure you had forgotten all about Miyajima."

Although Yuki was very busy at the counter, Mrs. Suzuki remained seated. "I think you should know before Mr. Nakayama comes back that I will become his wife within a few weeks," she continued. "We plan to be quietly married soon after Yuki's wedding and before the tourist trade gets too heavy this summer. Both of us lost our mates during the war, you see, and we both come from shopkeeping families. I was born on this island, and I understand all about managing this kind of shop."

Yuki finished with the customers and returned with an almond cake. He scanned their faces.

"I'll go and get Uncle," he said abruptly. "I think I know where he is."

Customers crowded into the store, but Mrs. Suzuki paid no attention.

"Won't you have some of this tea?" Chiyo asked her. "This is unexpected news for me, and I would like to hear more about it."

Mrs. Suzuki turned and saw the customers. "Excuse me a moment. I'll tell you more if you like when I'm free."

Chiyo watched Mrs. Suzuki behind the counter. She was a very large woman. Fat, actually. And taller than Nakayama. What could have moved him even to consider marrying a woman like that? And it wasn't just her appearance. Commandeering. Stern. Without any humor or joy. Standing there smiling at the customers, she looked as if she already owned the store. Nakayama probably did need a reliable manager. Certainly neither she nor Nakayama nor even Yuki was interested in sales and financing. Maybe he had made the best choice. It was practical. What could Chiyo do for him? She couldn't even promise to marry him. Not until Hiroshi was settled.

If Nakayama walked through the door, it would be unbearable to sit and listen to him explain. "I don't think I'll wait," she told Mrs. Suzuki on her way out. "Just tell Mr. Nakayama I left these dolls and that he has my best wishes."

The woman nodded, smiled triumphantly over the top of her customer's head. Chiyo was out in the sunlit street again, but it was no longer warm or bright. She was sorry now that she had left so abruptly. It was exactly what Mrs. Suzuki wanted her to do. Why hadn't she understood that?

She stood uncertainly in the street. It wouldn't do to walk back into the shop now. She wandered aimlessly, pausing at another shop two blocks away, finally going inside and ordering more tea. She knew that she had to see Nakayama. Today. The old inn where she used to stay? If she went there and waited, maybe sent one of the maids with a message to be delivered only to Nakayama? Too suggestive. He might not feel that way about her anymore.

She stood up and paid for the tea, then wandered closer to the ferry. At least if she checked the departure time again, then walked back up to the shopping area, then maybe —

Down at the dock, she saw people lining up for the next ferry, which left in twenty minutes. Without knowing why, she bought a ticket. "I can use it later," she told herself. Then she joined the line waiting for the ferry. "I won't get on the gangplank," she thought. But the crowd was pushing her forward.

A moment before she had to make the final decision, she saw Nakayama. Their eyes met, and the same old electric shock spread through her.

She stepped out of line and went to him, searching his face for some sign. He stood rigid like a stone Buddha. Then his face broke into a wide smile. He lifted his arms to hug her, thought better of it, let them fall back down by his side.

"You haven't gotten any older," she ventured, trying to smile, but the tears welled up behind her eyes. He took her hands in his and held them, gazing at her without speaking. Everyone was staring at them. They all knew who he was and who she was. The shock waves would reverberate around the island and back to Inokuchi and Hiroshima for months. Still they stood clasping hands and staring at each other.

"You're not going on the ferry, are you?" he finally said. "Your ticket's good on the next ferry. And the next one, and the next. Come on."

He commandeered the island's taxi and in no time they were at the inn, high on the hill where, so long ago, they had eaten the autumn feast of *matsutake*.

Today, he ordered *chawan mushi,* the soft egg custard containing chicken, spinach, bamboo shoots. He took her hands in his. "I had almost forgotten how beautiful you are," he said.

She withdrew her hands. "I am not beautiful. I have a scar and a crooked smile. And what about this Mrs. Suzuki?"

He grinned, then laughed with embarrassment. "I'm sorry I wasn't in the shop when you came. It would have saved a lot of misunderstanding."

He leaned forward, cupping his chin in his hands. "You know, I didn't promise her anything. Really. All I said—and it was once, late at night, when she was helping me with the inventory—I just said that I'd been waiting a long time for someone, and I was about to give up. She must have made some assumptions from that."

He was looking at her gently, as if he were afraid she would break if he breathed too heavily. "I don't know what Mrs. Suzuki told you, but Yuki said he thought he overheard something about a wedding being planned. I had no idea her assumptions had gone so far."

"It's not too late, then?" Chiyo asked. "There's still hope? Hiroshi went up to Tokyo in April, but they sent him home again because he wasn't healthy enough. He's going back soon, though. And Yoko intends to live with the Yamamotos starting in August. I don't much like the idea. That dark house. But she's made up her mind, and I've told her she can come home whenever she wants."

He sat quietly, waiting for her to go on.

"What I'd hoped to do," she said, "after Hiroshi's gone back to school and Yoko's settled in, is to announce that I'm going out to Miyajima to live."

She waited for a reaction. But he merely smiled at her.

"You see, Hiroshi's going to take an engineering course, then come back and get this transistor factory started that he's so excited about. After that I suppose we'll have to start helping him look for a wife. But even if he doesn't get married right away, he doesn't need his mother living with him anymore. He can take care of himself. Do you know he invented some kind of new transistor for radios? He says he wants to build a big house and live with me in Hatsukaichi."

She reached over and touched him on the cheek, and he caught her fingers and held them there.

"I've asked too much of you," she said. "It isn't fair for you to wait any longer. I know that if we marry before Hiroshi's found a wife, my brother will say I'm damaging his chances for a good marriage."

She withdrew her hands. "But I couldn't bear it if you married that woman. I can't even bear the thought of it."

His smile was even wider now. "Here, Chi-chan. Look. The *chawan mushi* is here."

The young waitress knelt before them with the tray, placing the steaming dishes precisely, not even looking at their faces. Then she was kneeling on the other side of the door, closing it behind her so gently there was no sound.

Nakayama touched Chiyo's chin and turned her head toward his. "I know what you've been through this past year," he said. "I wanted to be with you and comfort you, but there wasn't any way I could get near you. I just—I felt so helpless, and I—"

"I know. I couldn't call you. I couldn't even write. I did something— It's haunted me. You see, I promised the Goddess of Mercy that I would give you up if I could have Hiroshi back alive and whole. I was so frightened then. And guilty about it afterwards because I knew I couldn't give you up. Every time something else terrible happened, I thought it was retribution. And it's only seeing you again that makes me not afraid anymore."

"Kannon is a compassionate goddess," he said. "Not vindictive. Promise me you won't think of it again."

She nodded, relieved that she had finally told him.

"I'll take care of Mrs. Suzuki," he said. "Of course it will be hard for her, especially if she's told everyone else on the island. But I've made no promises. I'll tell her I'm sorry about the misunderstanding. Then let's marry as soon as we can. Do you know it's been twelve years since that time up in Tokyo? And I want you here. Living with me on the island. Or I'll even move to Hiroshima if you like."

"No," Chiyo said. "Miyajima is better for both of us. Your workshop is here. And I'll marry you now. I won't wait for Hiroshi to find a wife."

"Just come to Miyajima this summer. That's enough for now. I can wait as long as you're near me and working with me." He smiled again. "Anyway, I've told Yuki about you and me, so we don't have to be so secretive anymore. And he'll be off in his own house with his new bride. We'll have the whole shop to ourselves."

"I'd rather marry you right away," she said. "I don't want to risk losing you to that woman. We can have a civil ceremony in Hiroshima and go off to Tokyo for a trip, visit that park where we had the hunger strike, and go to that place for noodles. Remember? And we can ride to Osaka on the Shinkansen, the new rapid express. Then I'll tell my brother. After the job's been done."

"No," Nakayama said. "We'll tell him first. I'll ask for your hand."

She shook her head. "I'd better warn him. He's pretty terrible when he's outraged. There's no point in subjecting yourself to that. If Isao is really opposed, then I'll just disassociate myself from my family and marry you anyway."

"Well, if you think that's how it's going to be, let's wait at least until after Hiroshi gets engaged. That way, your brother can't blame you for anything."

He looked at her intently, his face very serious. "Do you really want to go through with this? It's a rather serious step, giving up your family."

"I'm sure," she said. "And all right. We'll wait for Hiroshi. Then even if Isao disowns me, I won't care."

They wandered down the hill and through the shrine, gazing at the placid blue sea laid out before them. Nakayama called Yuki and told him to lock up.

At dusk they strolled along on the path above the Thousand-Mat Temple toward their favorite inn. The innkeeper greeted them as if he had been doing nothing but wait for their return for the whole year and a half of their absence.

"Your old room just happens to be available," he said proudly, "and this evening, it being a week night, there is no one in the large men's bath. I will make sure that no one enters until you have finished."

The sunset blazed through the steaming wide windows of the pale rose tile room as they soaked, steaming in the hot water until the sun had set behind the hills of the mainland.

They emerged, whispering to each other, warm and drowsy, toweled each other off, and wrapped themselves in the warm quilt *tanzen* kimono the inn provided for the cool evenings of late spring.

All night long, even in their sleep, they held each other close.

Chapter Thirty-eight

I THINK I'LL MOVE OUT TO MIYAJIMA," Chiyo announced to Kazuko and Isao. "The air is purer out there, and we don't need to rent it out anymore, you know. The old tenants have left, and if I'm living there you can come out and stay whenever you like. The way we used to before the war."

"Seems like a good idea," Kazuko said, looking up from the baby afghan she was crocheting. "You seem to have become very attached to Miyajima these past few years."

"What about the house in Nobori-chō?" Isao asked.

"I'll rent it out. Unless Hiroshi wants to live there. He's coming home from Tokyo next spring and of course I won't be moving until then."

Isao gave her a stern, questioning look, and Chiyo turned away, not wanting to look too closely into his eyes.

"Well, go ahead with it if you want," he finally said. "We might as well have someplace to relax in our old age."

By the time Hiroshi arrived home the following spring, engineering degree in hand, Chiyo had rented the Nobori-chō house to a young American couple, English teachers in the Girls' School. Hiroshi would be allowed to stay in his own room on the far side of the house. "Of course I'll want you to spend weekends out on Miyajima," she told him.

"I don't know how much time I'll have for that," he said, looking resentful. He had told everyone not to bother taking the long trip to Tokyo for his graduation ceremony. "I just want to get to work on these transistors."

She felt his disappointment. His mother would not be there in the house, as she had always been, to take care of him, serve him tea, listen to his complaints. Especially, he would not have anyone to complain to when he began setting up the new factory. Chiyo knew there would be frustration ahead establishing procedures under his cousin-in-law, Toshio Ogawa, president of the Asahi Enterprises Electronics Division.

Hiroshi finally decided on an apartment, and Chiyo went with him to look. He chose a brand-new one, just built in the area out toward Ogonzan Park, not far from the Toyokogyo factory and fairly close to Ujina, where Yoko lived with the Yamamotos. They selected some furniture from the house in Nobori-chō. After everything was in order, he decided to have a small housewarming party, inviting old friends from his high school and from Tokyo University.

"I'll cook festival-style food," Chiyo offered. "We'll make it like New Year's time, with everybody dropping in whenever they want.

"And if it's all right with you, I think I'll invite Nakayama-san, too. And his nephew, Yuki and Yuki's wife."

"Well, Mother, it's an awfully small place, but I suppose——"

When Nakayama heard about the housewarming, he set to work sanding down and preparing a slice of wood cut from the old Itsukushima Shrine *torii* recently taken down. According to Shinto law, the *torii* had to be replaced every twenty years. Pieces of the old, massive supporting posts were then sold to the highest bidders. Nakayama had found an especially beautiful slice of it, and he stayed up late in his workshop, polishing and waxing it, affixing the table legs.

Hiroshi's tiny apartment was crowded with people when Chiyo and Nakayama arrived. There was hardly room to stand, let alone get near the festival food Chiyo had prepared there the day before. Nakayama and Isao were crushed up against one another. They nodded affably and talked impersonally about politics. If only Isao could forget that dark night on Miyajima.

Now they were talking about *Zengakuren,* the radical student movement Hiroshi had belonged to. Chiyo was surprised to discover that both men were in support of it. "We need a radical side to shock us out of our complacency," Isao said.

"But they're too much," Hiroshi interrupted. "Too violent. You can't do politics that way. You always said so yourself, Uncle."

"Well, you can't give in to American demands all the time either. I'm glad you were snaking up there in Tokyo even though you did get your head bashed in." He gave Hiroshi a fatherly pat on the shoulder.

"And don't you dare ever do it again," Chiyo told him.

"I'm too old for that now," he said. "In fact, Uncle, I'd just as soon you didn't mention it to any of the workers in the factory. Or even at Toyokogyo, for that matter."

Isao chuckled. "So, the conservative young businessman is ready to amass himself a fortune, American style."

"I haven't given up my ideals," Hiroshi protested. "I've just gotten more practical."

Isao smiled. "You're all right, Hiroshi. We're proud of you the way you are."

Chiyo, watching them, realized that Hiroshi would always be more Isao's son than hers. Even after the long struggle to get him back to Nobori-chō, their work together in the early days of the factory, their combined efforts to get him into Tokyo University. Even after this last long bout with his illness. Hiroshi's heart belonged to Isao and his world. And it was all right. It didn't matter anymore.

Yoko arrived with her mother-in-law and son, Yasuhiro, a one-year-old who toddled expectantly into the room, then submitted happily to everyone's exclamations about his growing so fast, his sunny nature, his resemblance to Yoko.

"He is such a happy child," Chiyo said, cuddling Yasuhiro in her arms. "Nothing ever upsets him." She thought of the Ikeda grandchild, who had also accepted the world with such placid cheerfulness, and she was suddenly gripped by fear. Had Yoko and Mrs. Yamamoto thought of that? Chiyo looked at Yoko, the proud mother, whose face had lost its thin, parched look. Now she was smiling, even giggling at Hiroshi's jokes. Chiyo pressed the nagging fear out of her mind.

Mrs. Yamamoto announced that she had hired a new manager for the tofu factory. Now she could retire, stay home and take care of her grandchild. Yoko was planning to go back to her job at Tokokogyo.

Yuki and the others arrived, guiding the huge, polished table up onto the *tatami*, steadying themselves as they came. They put the table down, deftly removed the food from the smaller table, stood it up sideways against the wall, then rearranged the food on top of the larger one. They were almost out the door before Hiroshi recognized Yuki.

"Stay!" he shouted. "Stay and have some of this food my mother cooked. You can't go now!"

They came back reluctantly, a little sheepishly. Yuki introduced his bride to everyone, then explained how hard his uncle had worked on the table.

"That's enough, Yuki," Nakayama commanded. "Everybody with a connection to Miyajima should have one of those tables. And certainly young Mr. Hara here has more connections than most. I still have his original samurai doll out at my shop."

Hiroshi, always embarrassed by references to his folkcraft beginnings, ignored Nakayama's remark and exclaimed over the quality of polish on the table. But Nakayama wasn't ready to let the subject go. "You helped him with that samurai doll, didn't you, Mr. Ogawa?" he asked Isao. "I've been told it should be designated a national treasure. People at the Folkcraft Museum in Kurashiki want to buy it from me, but I've refused to sell it at least until I could check with you or Hara-san."

"Really? That tiny piece of wood Hiroshi and I carved fourteen years ago? They want to put it in a Folkcraft Museum?" He threw his head back and laughed. Whenever Isao really laughed (which was a rare event), one had a sense that the world was in order and full of joy.

It was Nakayama who had made her brother laugh like that.

But Nakayama wasn't laughing. "I know it seems unbelievable, but they're serious. And the museum would also like your original chrysanthemum doll, Mrs. Ogawa, the one painted like a *Kutani-ware* teacup."

Kazuko nodded slightly in recognition, tilting her head in his direction, wearing on her face the quizzical look which signified: "Me? You're troubling yourself to talk about unimportant, trifling me?"

"How much is the museum offering?" Isao asked.

Nakayama grinned broadly. "Only fifty-thousand yen apiece. I think it's possible to hold out for more, though. You see, even though I hate to give them up, I think they should be in the museum. More people would be able to see them."

Chiyo was stunned. Nakayama had not told even her the news.

Isao shrugged. "They're your dolls," he told Nakayama. "We sold them to you quite a while ago, as I remember. At one hundred yen apiece. And anyway, you're the one who inspired the work."

Chiyo could hardly contain her delight at hearing her own sentiments expressed by Isao.

"No," Nakayama said, "I'd rather act as your agent. I'll take a fifteen percent commission on whatever the final sale is. That is, if you want me to go ahead with it."

"But, really, Nakayama-san, wouldn't you rather just keep them in your shop?" Kazuko asked. "They've been there all this time. You'll miss them, won't you?"

"It's ohkay," Yuki said, pronouncing the word in imitation of the American GIs. "I've already photographed them for display at the shop. And I'll write underneath: 'Original home of Kurashiki Folkcraft Museum Treasures.'" He smiled, rather proud of himself.

"Well, maybe you should keep the dolls and sell the photograph to the museum," Isao said. "Fifteen percent. That's hardly compensation for fifty-thousand yen, which would pay a month's salary for this new engineer here."

Hiroshi was embarrassed, but Isao didn't notice. He dug his hands into his pockets, thinking. "I'll agree to having you send them to the museum on one condition," he said, addressing Nakayama. "That you take back the value in stock in the new division of our company. We could use the capital, of course, so we'll just issue you stock. How's that?"

"It's a deal," Nakayama said. He bowed, then shook Isao's hand Western style.

Chiyo began to think maybe Isao wouldn't mind when she announced her intention to marry.

"Then it's settled," said Isao, pouring out sake all around. "This makes a Renaissance man out of Hiroshi—master craftsman, electronic genius, industry executive, writer. You know, he's just published an article in an electronics magazine about the application of small transistors. It might even get translated into English." He lifted his cup to Hiroshi.

"Let's toast the dolls, too," Hiroshi said, lifting his sake cup. "We wouldn't have started the electronics industry if we hadn't had the dolls first."

They shouted *"kampai!"* in unison, then drank.

In the fall, they began looking for a wife for Hiroshi. Isao and Kazuko volunteered to help with the *omiai*.

The first one was held at an old *bessō*, a summer residence near Saijo which had been turned into a special restaurant. The girl's parents made the arrangements, and both families came for a carefully planned *kaiseki ryori,* the tea-ceremony meal. They gathered first in a special ceremonial teahouse designed especially for that purpose. It was dusk. An excellent time for watching the fiery red of the sunset while enjoying the tranquility of the tea ceremony. The prospective bride did the serving in order to demonstrate her skill at the ancient art, and Chiyo knew that her parents, uncles, and aunts, even her two sisters and young brother, were all watching the Haras and Ogawas to see whether they participated in the ceremony with the proper finesse, the right amount of small talk. They were also watching to see whether the color of the *obi* sashes the women wore were properly attuned to the patterns of their kimonos. Chiyo noticed that the mother and daughters had chosen their own attire according to correct, traditional standards. But there was no evidence of the aesthetic flair that Kazuko, Fusako, and Yoko were gifted with.

After dark, the group (fifteen of them in all), retired from the teahouse to the *kaiseki ryori* banquet in a wide room where the full moon illuminated the carefully trimmed shapes in the garden. It was late September and the sliding doors opened wide onto the garden, providing just enough bracing chill air to give them a feeling of alertness and exhilaration.

Chiyo had never attended an event as carefully orchestrated as this, even before the war at the height of her family's influence. But before the evening was over, even before the last taste of the delicately seasoned dishes, each portion carefully arranged on a plate that matched its texture and color, Chiyo felt that Hiroshi would be rejected. He was a rising young executive. He had been unusually charming that evening, and so had Yoko. The Hara and Ogawa families were descended from a long line of samurai. And Isao's presentation of himself and his family had been flawless. She couldn't imagine why, but she was certain it would happen.

The rejection came by letter a few days later.

"Do you suppose they rejected Hiroshi because his mother is rather strange?" Chiyo asked Kazuko. "Maybe they think I'm too unconventional, letting my son live alone in an apartment, not taking care of him enough."

If she was a hindrance to his chances now, what would happen when she announced her plan to marry Nakayama?

"Of course not!" said Kazuko staunchly. "Isao says it's because of money. They want money already earned. Not potential. They want it firmly settled that their daughter will enter the kind of society that connects them with the president of Hiroshima University, the president of Toyokogyo and Mitsubishi, maybe even Prime Minister Ikeda himself. Apparently they thought Isao's connections were stronger than they really are."

They stared glumly at the garden. "Why did they accept the offer of an arrangement in the first place?" Chiyo asked. "They could have found out about the connections before they met us. Do you suppose someone said afterwards that Hiroshi's a *hibakusha?* You know if that kind of rumor starts, there's nothing anybody can do. They say even a signed affidavit by a dozen lawyers won't help once somebody implies that. He'll never get a wife then."

"No," said Kazuko. "If there are rumors, we would have heard them by now. It's just outright snobbishness if you ask me. And I really don't think Hiroshi cares. But ask him."

"Well, I didn't like that girl," Hiroshi said later. "Too careful. Too much like a china doll. She was very unnatural. If she hadn't rejected me, I would have rejected her. I imagine they'll have a hard time finding her a husband."

It occurred to Chiyo that she couldn't remember much about the girl. She could only remember the family and the atmosphere they had so painstakingly created. The girl's skill with the tea ceremony was commendable, and the gracefulness of her wrists when she set the cups down. But what did her face look like? And what had she said?

The *omiai* with the second girl was almost two months later at Zakuro, the Restaurant Pomegranate, which featured folkcrafted pottery dishes from famous areas like Mashiko and Bizen and old-fashioned country-style culinary arts. It was a much cozier gathering than the earlier one. Only Isao, Kazuko, and Chiyo were present on Hiroshi's side. Yoko, Fusako, and Toshio had not been invited, and the girl came only with her parents. She was a graduate of Hiroshima Women's College, Chiyo and Yoko's school, and that credential alone was enough to endear her to Chiyo. But there were other qualities, too. She was the slightest bit rounder and plumper than photographs of the models in women's fashion magazines, and indications of the girl's warmth and good nature kept appearing even though it seemed her parents would have preferred the girl's sense of humor to be more suppressed than it was.

Her father had reached forward to pour Isao some sake, just barely missed the cup in his nervousness, and spilled some on the table. Everyone elaborately pretended it hadn't happened. But Chiyo caught a glimpse of the loving and understanding smile she gave her father.

And Chiyo discovered that the girl loved Miyajima, had visited there many times, knew Nakayama's shop, even remembered the two dolls which would soon be in the Kurashiki Museum collection. She also knew about the folkcraft section of Asahi Enterprises because her aunt, whose feet had been so injured by the bomb that she couldn't walk, had spent most of the rest of her life painting dolls. Chiyo had known her well and only last year had attended her funeral.

"That's why you look familiar," Chiyo said. "You used to come for your aunt in a taxi sometimes."

They sat in the room at Zakuro, the steam from the *mizutaki* stew warming their faces, drawing them together in a huddle against the chill of the November air. Chiyo knew she could be comfortable with this family whose past was similar to hers, who lacked pretensions, who enjoyed simple and humorous things. The girl's father had been an accountant in an executive firm. During the war, he'd been a quartermaster's sergeant, taking care of diminishing supplies and armaments in Odawara, where the army had dug themselves in for the final defense of the homeland. The girl's mother had been in Hiroshima, just like Chiyo, had wandered all through it, and had tenaciously survived afterwards. But her daughter, like Hiroshi, had been out in the country with relatives at least five kilometers away.

Chiyo was euphoric at the end of the evening when the families bowed away from each other out on the street.

"Why don't we all go down to The Willow?" Kazuko suggested after the other family had gone.

"Well, what do you think, Hiroshi?" Chiyo asked when they'd settled themselves in a booth and ordered coffee.

He was hesitant. "What do you think?"

"Marvelous," said Chiyo. "She's just the girl for you. Considerate, friendly, not too pretentious, intelligent, lots of fun, and rather sexy, don't you think?"

Hiroshi stared at her incredulously. Neither Isao nor Kazuko seemed offended, but Hiroshi clearly was.

"Well, isn't that a consideration?" she persisted. "If it isn't, it should be."

"Mother!" he exclaimed. Then he turned to hear his uncle's impressions.

"I don't know," said Isao. "She seems nice enough all right, but not unusual. She certainly isn't dazzling in any way. But she's solid. She'll give you good support and be comforting. Did you notice those wide hips? Easy childbearing."

"I'm not getting married just to have children," Hiroshi complained. "I'm not so interested in children anyway. One or two later maybe. Certainly no more and maybe none at all."

"Of course you'll want children!" Isao exclaimed. "How could you have thought otherwise?"

"I mean it's not my first concern," he said. "What about you, Aunt? What do you think?"

"Well, all right, I guess. Certainly she's all those important things your mother and Husband said. But not enough flair. Not enough sense of what's appropriate at the right moment. For a young man like you who is going to move in so many different circles, influence people, travel everywhere, have an effect on the direction the country takes, even—well, I don't know."

She thought a moment, then looked at Chiyo. "Of course you noticed the kimono, didn't you? Entirely the wrong color, and I can't imagine her mother allowing her to wear a pattern like that. Those big peonies. All wrong for her."

"That's true," Chiyo said, "but certainly a much less serious problem than being too rigid or nervous or snobbish. We can show her what's proper to wear. It's not really an indication of character or even artistic awareness, I think. Just that she hasn't concentrated on it. She's been more interested in her studies. She majored in English, didn't she? Which certainly ought to help Hiroshi with his international contacts. And did you notice how excited she looked when she was talking about her graduation thesis? She's the kind of girl who can get interested in things easily, which is certainly the best asset a person can have in international circles."

"But that's just the trouble," said Hiroshi. "I don't want a wife who's off talking with some women's club about English literature all the time. I want someone who is going to make the house look nice and be concerned about whether I have all my buttons sewn on my shirts."

"Really, Hiroshi, you must have discovered by this time—you're twenty-seven years old, aren't you?—that a person who doesn't have any interests of her own is extremely dull to live with. You wouldn't care at all about her if she just followed you around like a slave. You'd lose interest immediately. How do you think your Aunt Kazuko has kept Uncle Isao interested all these years? Certainly it wasn't because she obeyed him every time he issued a command."

392

"Hmph," said Isao. "That's an irrational theory if I ever heard one. In my opinion, obedient women are extremely charming!" He glowered at Chiyo, then laughed. "Come on, Hiroshi," he said. "What do you think about her?"

"Well, I don't think so," he said, glumly pushing away his coffee cup. "I guess I've got my heart set on someone more beautiful."

Chiyo sighed. "If only middle age could give a little insight to these young ones," she said. "And that girl liked you, too. The family will be so disappointed. Think about it a little more before you decide, will you? I did so have my hopes up for a companionable daughter-in-law like that. And I liked her parents, too. Not that I'll be living very near you."

"Well, you may someday, Mother," Hiroshi said. "You can't live out on that island forever."

Chiyo ignored him and stood up. "What's next?" she asked. "Is there anyone else waiting in the wings?"

"Yes," said Isao. "We've got one more. Girl of very good family from Yamaguchi Prefecture. They're coming in next week, and we'll have another meeting at Zakuro. Is next Wednesday all right with everyone? Let's keep it to just the five of us."

Hiroshi chose the last candidate. She was a neat, precise china doll very much like the one who had rejected him earlier. But she was smaller, a shade more beautiful, and impeccable in appearance and action. Every hair was in place, and she did not seem to move without first considering what effect she would have on everyone watching her. She had worn a pale pastel kimono with just a hint of delicate daisies bordering the hem and a few luminous petals showing at her knees when she sat with her legs folded neatly under her light, almost weightless posterior. The nape of her neck curved gracefully forward from under the collar, which was a navy blue, shading into light green pastel. Her silhouette reminded Chiyo of the old folktale about the white crane who transformed herself into a woman so that she could marry the country bumpkin who had saved her and mended her broken wing.

Her name was Sueko. When she spoke, people had to lean forward to hear what she was saying, her voice was so delicate. It seemed strange, Chiyo thought later, that she couldn't remember the mother and father. They seemed to fade into the background in the presence of their luminous daughter.

For several months all the women—Chiyo, Kazuko, Yoko, and Fusako—were busy helping the new couple choose furnishings for the house in Nobori-chō. Hiroshi had decided they would live there until the new house was built in Hatsukaichi, where Isao had helped them buy land.

Everything went well. And yet the more Chiyo saw of Sueko, the more she felt the cold, standoffish nature of the girl and the distance between them. Still, Chiyo had to admit, she probably was the best choice for Hiroshi, the rising young executive. He had chosen the job at Toyokogyo because of the benefits and prestige instead of the more challenging one working as chief engineer with Toshio at Asahi Enterprises. He had promised his uncle he would advise Toshio on the side and continue inventing the factory machinery that would get the transistors into production.

"I can't say I blame him," Isao said. "It's the same thing I wanted when I was his age. Family businesses are a sideline, after all. And I'm looking forward to having him with us at Toyokogyo working on those new automobiles. That's where the real excitement is. Toshio can handle Asahi Enterprises."

The wedding was planned for late spring, and before it took place, Chiyo decided to tell Isao and Kazuko about her own wedding plans. "I'll just go and feel him out," she told Nakayama one Sunday morning at the end of January. "Then you can come later and make the formal request. I'm sure it's going to be all right now that Hiroshi's marriage plans are settled."

She took the ferry over that afternoon.

She hadn't yet seen Fusako's second child, a girl born just after the New Year. Isao, not admitting his disappointment, had named her Myoko, using another pronunciation for the Chinese character that spelled "civilization" when teamed with Fumiko's name. Chiyo held the baby, admiring her tiny, wizened face, which, so far, didn't resemble either of her parents. Then Fusako and Toshio piled both daughters into their tiny Matsuda Carol and took them to Onomichi, where they could show off the new baby to Toshio's parents. Chiyo, Kazuko, and Isao settled into the *kotatsu,* looking at pictures of their grandchildren, then searching back through photograph albums and memories of the past.

They were looking at an old photograph of Miyajima when Chiyo told them that she and Nakayama planned to be married in the fall. "Just when the maple leaves turn," she said. "It's my favorite time." She had wanted to lead up to it gradually, hint at her affection for Nakayama, tell them again (as she had so often before) how excited she was about his creative and artistic sense, how fresh and renewed she felt when she was with him, how, now that the children were settled into their lives, she felt she could start a new life of her own. Instead, she told them straight out.

"I thought you'd given that up," Isao said.

"Well, I found that I couldn't."

"What's this couldn't? Do you think I've given in to every passing temptation in my life? It's family that's important. We don't give up our families just because of some sexual attraction."

"I'm not planning to give up my family," Chiyo said. "Why would I have to give up Yoko and Hiroshi just because I'm going to marry? I've brought those two up into adulthood, haven't I? They're independent now. Yoko belongs to another family. And I'm not going to marry until after Hiroshi is settled in Nobori-chō. They can all bring their children out to Miyajima to visit me. It's an ideal arrangement."

"Do you intend to live in our beach house with that shopkeeper? Are you going to marry him and then live with him on Ogawa family property?"

"Well, not if you don't want me to. We can both live—"

"In the upstairs room where I found you that night?"

"What night?" asked Kazuko, puzzled.

Isao ignored her. "You'd spend the rest of your days in that tiny, squalid place as a shopkeeper's wife? A member of the Ogawa family who grew up in this household and who married into another samurai family, and now you're going to become a shopkeeper's wife? I can't believe it. You're not some teenager, you know. You're already beyond retirement age. In fact, before this unpleasant subject came up, I was planning to discuss your retirement from the presidency of the folkcraft section. It's time Toshio took over the whole company. He'll never be able to prove himself unless he's in charge of the whole operation."

"Just a year ago, out at Hiroshi's, you promised you wouldn't do that," Chiyo said. "You told me Toshio isn't even interested in folkcraft. He's hardly interested in electronics."

"Morishita-san can go on being general manager. Things won't change that much."

She stared at Isao. "Let me get this straight," she said. "What you want me to do is not to marry Nakayama-san and not be president anymore either? And both my children are grown and busy with their own lives. What am I to do with the rest of my life?"

"Well, relax," Isao said. "You've worked hard enough, haven't you? Accomplished quite a lot, especially for a woman. You've had an impressive career."

"And I intend to go on having an impressive career," she said. "You can't believe what Nakayama-san and I have in the works, ready to go into production. A brand-new line of—" But she stopped. Why let Isao in on their plans?

"*Ni-chan*," she said, "beloved elder brother. You are older than I am. You're more intelligent. You've accomplished more. You've worked unstintingly taking care of all of us to the point that no one believed you could even stay alive. Yet, you're not retired, are you? You're past sixty. You're still working full-time at Toyoko-gyo, still making all the important decisions for Asahi Enterprises and setting up the new factory. You're still mayor of Inokuchi and working hard on the Hiroshima-Inokuchi merger. You're even involved with all the problems of the land reclamation."

Kazuko, sitting across from the two of them, moved her eyes from face to face, not knowing what to do or say. No one had asked her opinion about Nakayama.

"Now what do you think would happen," Chiyo went on, "if someone came along and told you to stop all those activities, to give them up because it was time for you to get some well-deserved rest? How would you feel about that? And wouldn't Inokuchi and the factory and Asahi Enterprises suffer without you, even though everybody decided you're too old to do any work?"

"Well, I'll have to relinquish all those things eventually. That's why I'm anxious to get Toshio going on them."

"Why not now? Why don't you give them all up tomorrow and sit in the living room and let Kazuko bring you tea while you read the morning paper all day? Wouldn't that be relaxing for you?"

He looked at her, exasperated. Then he grinned. "All right. You win. I'm always thinking how busy you've been rebuilding your house, bringing up children, and then having a full-time job too. Most women would be glad of a chance not to have to keep working. But if you want to do it, then fine. We'll just have Toshio be president of the electronics side. He can wait."

"Let him be president of everything now," she said. "I don't mind being vice-president or whatever anybody wants to call me. As long as I can go on doing what I'm doing. Designing new things, and overseeing the quality of the production."

"Seems reasonable enough," breathed Kazuko.

"And go on working with Nakayama," Chiyo added. "And marry him."

"Well, have your affair with him," Isao said. "I've thought maybe you were doing that, anyway."

"Husband!" Kazuko exclaimed. She was hurt that neither of them had confided in her.

"Have the affair," Isao repeated. "But just don't live with him openly, and don't marry him. That's all I ask."

"It's too much to ask," said Chiyo.

"What is this?" Kazuko insisted. "Why haven't you told me, Husband? Or at least you, Chi-chan!"

"I was going to tell you," Chiyo told her apologetically. "I was just waiting for the right moment."

She turned back to Isao.

"I'm sorry if you're disappointed," she said, "but I'm going to marry him whether you like it or not. What possible difference can it make to anyone now?"

"It makes a difference to me whether you marry him," Isao said. "We Ogawas don't do that sort of thing. Especially at your age."

"I really can't believe you're saying all this. Who cares anymore about scandals and appearances and kinds of families? It's a miracle that any of us are alive. Especially the two of us. We've survived my Kenichi and Grandmother and Akiko and—the neighbors and Kyoko and Yasu and Mr. Takano and—" She broke off. "Suppose you and Nakayama-san and I were the only people left on earth? Would you still be saying he doesn't belong to the right kind of family?"

The tears were gathering and she could no longer speak. She went out on the veranda and sat daubing her eyes. Kazuko came and sat next to her, not speaking, not touching her.

Isao stayed in the room. She heard him press out his cigarette, stand up, light another one, pace the floor. Then he came out on the veranda. "Marry him, then," he said. "But if you do, you are no longer a member of this family."

Kazuko gasped. "Anata!" she shouted. But Isao ignored her.

"If you marry him, don't step over this threshold again, Chi-chan. "Think about what you are doing, and what this is doing to your family. Think about how Hiroshi and Yoko are going to feel."

She stood up. "I was prepared for this," she said. "I had hoped for your understanding, but I expected this of you. It's your choice, Brother, if you want to disown me. It's your loss. Not mine. And we'll be perfectly happy living in the workshop over his store. I don't want the beach house."

She started for the door. "Wait, Chiyo. Wait." Isao took a few steps toward her. "I mean it about disowning you. But if you insist on marrying him, take the beach house. The rest of them can go out and visit if they want. At least it won't degrade the family to crawl up through those souvenir shops in the middle of Miyajima to see you."

She stared at him, rigid with anger. It was making her dizzy and light-headed. "That is fine with me," she said. "Now if you'll excuse me, I'll go."

Kazuko was weeping, and Chiyo felt the contest of wills behind her as she struggled with the sliding door to let herself out. She had never left the Ogawa household this way before. Someone was always there, standing in the hall to see her off. Today she was alone.

"Go on, then!" Isao shouted.

After she managed to get the door open, Kazuko appeared, her face streaked with tears.

"I will be at your wedding if you want me there. I will be at the beach house whenever you want me to bring the grandchildren. Or I will come without them. Whenever you ask me to come."

Pressing back the tears, Chiyo buried her face in Kazuko's shoulder. They stood together in the hallway of the house where Chiyo had been born, where Kenichi had been born, where her wedding reception had been held, where almost everything important in her life had happened. Except for this last thing. This liaison with Nakayama. That had happened in Miyajima, which was where she would spend the rest of her life.

Outside, under the sun where all the world was watching, she and Kazuko bowed formally to one another just as they had done during all the leave-takings on the countless Sundays of their lives.

Chapter Thirty-nine

A T CITY HALL ON A WEDNESDAY AFTER-
noon in mid-October, Chiyo and Nakayama
affixed their signatures to the marriage papers. They dipped the
tips of their ivory-carved *han* seals into vermilion paste, pressing
hard against the papers so that each corner contained their names,
vivid red Chinese characters enclosed in circles, stamped so close to
one another that they almost touched. An uninterested city clerk
processed their papers, treating them as if they were applying for a
fishing license or a permit to build a house.

They went back to Miyajima to the house along the shore that
Chiyo had supervised in all its phases of remodeling with just this
purpose in mind. They warmed sake, the special *Tokkyūshu* top
grade. Their first toast was a silent one, made with their eyes when
they touched together the tiny porcelain cups that had belonged to
Nakayama's uncle.

They poured more sake for another toast.

"*Kampai* to this moment achieved in spite of all the years," she
said. "And the lovely moments we've had while waiting."

Nakayama laughed and poured another cup. "And here's to wash
away the superstitions about the jealous goddess, Itsukushima, cast-

ing spells on us. And to Kannon, the Goddess of Mercy, for listening to your prayers without exacting your promises."

They touched their cups once more, and the sake flowed down Chiyo's throat, smooth as velvet.

At dawn, they rose and walked on the beach, arm in arm, and Chiyo pointed out the old white rocks that beckoned just beyond reach in the sea. "The first warm day of summer, we'll swim out there and lie and listen to the seagulls and the murmur of the boats," she told him.

The October days stretched before them like endless summer, tranquil and serene as the Inland Sea, disturbed only now and then by a faint and rustling breeze.

They spent their days at the shop, waiting on customers and working on new items to be created by Asahi Enterprises. Chiyo and Yuki's wife, Michiko, divided the duties of Nakayama's former employee, Mrs. Suzuki. On the two or three days when Chiyo went in to work at the factory in Koi, Michiko took her turn in the shop.

"But I may not have a job for long," Chiyo said. "If Isao makes Toshio president."

"Don't worry." Nakayama grinned at her. "Remember that stock he gave me in exchange for selling the dolls? Well, I've been buying up more shares lately, and with your stock and Morishita-san's and the shares the other workers have, I'm sure we've got controlling interest. So we can buy your brother out and have our own company. Name it—well, what shall we name it?"

"Nakayama Dolls, Incorporated," she said. *"Nakayama Ningyo."*

"We make lots of things besides dolls. And why Nakayama?"

"But it's the dolls we love the most, isn't it? And now my name is Nakayama, too."

They discovered that Isao and Toshio weren't surprised or even interested when the employees of the Asahi Folkcraft separated themselves from the mother company. It was a fairly uncomplicated legal procedure. And Chiyo continued her routine, creating with Nakayama, planning production with Morishita-san and the trainers.

Gradually the world beyond Miyajima became less appealing to her. "Someday soon," she said, "I think Morishita-san should become president."

Meanwhile, she was satisfied with the portion of the world that came to her doorstep. Yoko was the first to visit, bringing the boy, Yasuhiro, exploring the house with him, showing him the window in the kitchen which brought in bright sunlight so that it was a warm place to work in, contrasting sharply to the dark hole that was the kitchen at the Yamamotos'. It was an innovation of Chiyo's architect, the same person who had done her house in Nobori-chō.

Chiyo had left the upstairs the way it had always been—two large eight-mat rooms with sliding *shōji* that opened to a small veranda and a view of the sea. All the old things were there, the brocade tablecloth on the lacquered table and the picture of the young emperor just after his inauguration. In his mid-twenties then. And the photograph of General Nogi as a guest of Chiyo's grandfather. There were pictures of Chiyo and Isao as children and one of their father, whom Yoko could barely remember.

When they came downstairs again and settled at the table across from Nakayama, Yoko fixed her eyes on her lap, not quite sure what to say or how to react. But Yasuhiro held out his arms to Nakayama, and Yoko was forced to surrender him. He sat contentedly in the crook of Nakayama's arm.

Chiyo, watching the child, was sure that he would not turn out like the Ikeda grandchild. He reminded her of Kenichi as a baby.

"I remember when you were a little girl, Mrs. Yamamoto," Nakayama said. "You were only twelve or thirteen that day you shouted at me, running up from the ferry." He cupped his hands over his mouth in imitation of her. "We brought the dolls! We brought the dolls!" He laughed, remembering. "The whole neighborhood heard you. I think your mother and I were both a bit embarrassed. Do you remember?"

"I remember," Yoko said. "And I remember the first day we met you. When we took our first excursion to Miyajima after the end of the war. And after that, when we painted so furiously. That was when I first began to hope we would survive. Before that, you know, I wasn't so sure."

"Really, Yoko-chan?" Chiyo was surprised. "I always thought, in those days, that you never doubted. I doubted myself, but you were the one who made me want to go on."

Yoko gave Nakayama one of her special smiles when she left that day. Chiyo went with her in the taxi to catch the ferry. "I'm glad for you, Mother, really I am," Yoko breathed while they stood waiting for the ferry. "Almost jealous. You've had two wonderful husbands in your life, haven't you?" She bowed, took Yasuhiro from Chiyo's arms, and started up the gangplank.

"And who's to know what's in store for you, Yoko-chan?" Chiyo said, following her onto the ferry to help her find a seat. "There's a whole life ahead with strange and wonderful things. I know it doesn't seem that way now, but it will. You'll see."

She hugged Yasuhiro once more, then turned to go. "Anyway, come often and next time stay overnight the way we used to when you were a child."

Yoko nodded. "I'm never going back to Inokuchi again," she said. "As long as Uncle disowns you, I'll disown him."

"No, don't do that to your uncle. You have the only boy child in the family. Don't deny your uncle the pleasure of seeing him. He deserves it, you know. This quarrel is ours, not yours. We'll resolve it eventually. Meanwhile, promise me you'll treat him well."

Kazuko was their next guest, and after her first visit she came regularly, never mentioning Isao. Sometimes she brought Fusako, sometimes the grandchildren. Once, when Isao was off on a business trip, all the Ogawas came together, even Toshio, bringing Yoko and Yasuhiro and Mrs. Yamamoto too.

It seemed to Chiyo that they enjoyed Miyajima better than they ever had, walking along the shore through the languorous autumn and on into November. But once, when Kazuko came alone, Chiyo could tell by her expression that she had argued with Isao, probably about celebrating the New Year at Inokuchi. Chiyo had been away from Inokuchi at New Year's only once in her life, the year she was first married and had gone with Shintaro to visit his relatives. She missed the comfort of Isao's presence, presiding over family dinners. But it did not bother her as much as it bothered Kazuko. Chiyo enjoyed her separate world in Miyajima, just herself and her husband, sometimes Yuki and his wife, and the loyal part of the family who had chosen to defy Isao.

But it bothered her that Hiroshi remained aloof.

A month after Hiroshi's wedding in Yamaguchi prefecture, Chiyo had paid him and Sueko a formal visit at Nobori-chō, examined the wedding gifts, exclaimed over Sueko's genius at interior decorating (she would have suffocated living in the house herself—too many knickknacks). It was then, when Sueko was in the kitchen getting tea, that she told him matter-of-factly about her and Nakayama's intention to register their marriage in City Hall and to live in Miyajima on one side of the beach house. The other side, she explained, would be reserved for members of the family when they came to visit.

"What does Uncle say?" Hiroshi had asked.

"He says that if I marry Nakayama-san, he will disown me."

Sueko returned from the kitchen, Chiyo drank the tea politely, and before Hiroshi had a chance to express any opinion (she knew perfectly well that without a father or husband to take orders from, she was supposed to ask her son's permission in all matters), she took her leave.

Hiroshi did not get in touch with her. In October, she wrote him that the registration at City Hall had been completed and that he and Sueko should come and visit soon. Sueko had never seen the Miyajima house, she reminded him.

He did not write back. She wrote again, telling him she was anxious to have them visit. They did not yet have a phone installed, but he could call Nakayama's shop. She gave him the phone number. There was no answer.

Finally, in the middle of December, Kazuko came bearing a small letter, carefully written in precise calligraphy.

"He can't even acknowledge I have my own address?" Chiyo asked, fingering the letter. "He has to send it to you to bring to me?"

"I didn't get it directly either," Kazuko said. "He gave it to Isao to give to me."

The letter, painfully formal, sounded as if Hiroshi had tried to find a model in a book that gave samples of what to write on certain occasions. But there was no book anywhere that told a son what to write to a mother who had married beneath her.

> Greetings. And thank you for your letter and postcard. I am sorry I was unable to respond sooner, but perhaps you've heard through Aunt Kazuko that I have been working on developing a rotary engine, so I have no time to think of anything else but that. However, I do plan to see the family during the New Year holidays. We must go to Yamaguchi for New Year's Day, but Uncle Isao has been kind enough to invite us for January 2nd on our way home from Yamaguchi. Thank you for writing me.
>
> Your son,
> Hiroshi

"Well, what does all this mean?" Chiyo exploded, throwing the letter onto the table. "Is he refusing to come and visit or is he asking me to ask him once more? Is he going to pretend that I didn't get married at all and that Nakayama doesn't exist?"

Nakayama was outside on the beach with Kazuko's grandchildren, and Chiyo was glad of the chance to complain as loudly as she wished.

"Maybe Hiroshi's going to disown me too. Is there a precedent for that?"

"I think he's just busy with his work," Kazuko said. "He doesn't realize how this letter comes across. I'll get them out here to visit. I've invited them to stay overnight when they come on January second, so I'll bring them out on the third."

"No, don't do that," Chiyo said. "It would just make Isao angry. And if Hiroshi doesn't want to come on his own, then I don't want him to come."

Chiyo and Nakayama spent New Year's Day at Yuki's house, Chiyo exclaiming over Michiko's skill in creating traditional New Year's dishes.

Yuki smiled proudly at his wife. It pleased him, he said, that his own family had been extended to include both a wife and a mother, even a stepsister and brother. He added, rather shyly, that they were hoping for children soon and that they wanted their own child to be as handsome and healthy as Yasuhiro was.

"Well, there's plenty of time yet for children," Chiyo said. "You know, my Hiroshi didn't even consider marriage for the longest time, but now he's in a big hurry for everything at once. I hear he's already started building his house, and he's probably wishing for twins because that way he can get the children produced faster, and—"

But the jokes caught in her throat. Maybe she would never see Hiroshi again. It occurred to her that if he disapproved of the marriage, it wasn't because of Isao's reasons. It was because he wanted his mother to come and live with his family so he could show the world he was taking care of her. He wanted her living with them, doing all the grandmotherly things, making wise and funny comments the way grandmothers did on the new TV serials.

"Come on, *Kā-chan*, Little Mama," Yuki said to her, "We're going outside for a walk to the shrine, maybe even climb up to the Thousand-Mat Temple. It's a beautiful clear day."

Chiyo took his arm. "I had no idea how wonderful it is to celebrate the New Year on Miyajima."

On the third of January, the family arrived in two taxis, and Chiyo held her breath, watching to see who would emerge. First Kazuko, carrying Myoko. Then Fusako and Fumiko. Then Yoko.

Where was Yasuhiro? And who was in the next taxi? Yasuhiro emerged from it, running up to Nakayama, asking to be lifted into his arms. After that, Hiroshi's long leg, covered by the trousers of a charcoal-gray business suit. Then the whole of him, tall and self-possessed. Already he looked like a diplomat, his dark tie containing just a few flecks of red to offset the gray. He had never gone through a shy, awkward age. Now he was a mature, handsome young man escorting his female relatives on an outing. Bemused and serene, he helped Sueko out of the car, then paid off both taxi drivers.

"Greetings of the New Year, Mother. How good to see you and how very nice you look."

He bowed politely to Nakayama, who welcomed him into the sitting room amid a flurry of exclamations, greetings, New Year's wishes, boxes of gifts. Special New Year's sake, and Kazuko's *omochi,* New Year's rice cakes, which they made in Inokuchi every year when the neighbors gathered to pound rice in the Ogawa's huge mortar. Three or four people to turn the glutinous mass of rice, one to pound with the big hammer, all in rhythm, carefully choreographed so no one would miss a beat and have his fingers smashed by the hammer. Chiyo wondered if Hiroshi had wielded the hammer this year. She felt a pang of jealousy for not being able to witness it.

Even during the long walk on the beach, both Hiroshi and Sueko kept their distance.

"Hiroshi, sit down here and tell me all about your work. The rotary engines and the transistors," she said when they returned from the walk.

He smiled benignly and told her what he thought she could understand about the experiments at Toyokogyo and his successes and failures with the machinery for Asahi Electronics. "And I've been promoted to a higher managerial position," he told her.

"Wonderful, Hiroshi! Have the rest of you heard that?" But yes, they already had. His mother was the last to know.

"And the house is coming along well," he said. "Uncle has bought a piece of land adjacent. Just in case Fusako and Toshio want to build out there. And of course we're adding a special room for you when you decide you want to come and live with us."

Chiyo ignored those implications. "Well, Nakayama-san and I will certainly want to see it even before it's completed. Maybe we'll take a trip over there. Let us know the next time you go out."

He nodded politely, looked at his lap, then jerked his head up.

"Oh," he said, "we have another appointment. We promised to meet Uncle Isao and Toshio in Hiroshima for dinner." He stood up. "Mother, would you mind calling us some taxis?"

After they had gone, Nakayama held her in his arms and rubbed her back. "Time will smooth it all out. It always does."

It did not bother him that Hiroshi had snubbed him, that Isao had refused to recognize him. He did not even pay attention to what the neighbors said, or to the gossip among the shopkeepers. Just before their marriage, Mrs. Suzuki had created a stir when she resigned from Nakayama's shop and took control of another down the street. She told everyone who would listen that Nakayama had broken his promise to marry her and that he had betrayed her in favor of an older woman who was quite inappropriate for him. "I can't imagine how such a marriage will survive," Chiyo had heard her comment to someone in a crowded street.

Nakayama and Chiyo maintained an air of supreme serenity, nodding politely to the distant neighbors at Sugi no Ura when they walked on the beach together, ignoring the nudges and whispers around his shop.

The matter was also difficult at the old neighborhood in Nobori-chō. Most of the neighbors had greeted the news of Chiyo's marriage with polite silence. She noticed it when she stopped by occasionally for a visit with Sueko, determined to keep the lines of communication open even though Sueko continued to maintain her painfully formal exterior in Chiyo's presence.

Mrs. Ikeda seemed not to know what to say to her. She avoided the subject of Nakayama, pretending that Chiyo was out on Miyajima just for a short holiday and that she would soon be back, living in her old house, doing all the things she had always done.

At first Mrs. Yamamoto, like the others, was unwilling to bring up the subject of Chiyo's marriage. And she refused every invitation from Chiyo to come for a visit with their daughter. "The captain doesn't like me to leave him," she said.

But in the early spring, Captain Yamamoto died. Suddenly, without any warning, and completely alone. Yoko was at work, and Mrs. Yamamoto had stepped down the street with Yasuhiro for shopping. When they returned, a half hour later, they found him lying on his back with a strange but peaceful smile on his face. Yasuhiro had touched him, then burst into uncontrollable tears.

"I hadn't realized how close they really were," Mrs. Yamamoto said. "There were so many days when the captain hardly noticed anyone at all. But of course he always paid more attention to Yasuhiro than to the rest of us."

For months afterwards, Mrs. Yamamoto was grief-stricken. Chiyo had expected her to feel some relief, maybe even be glad that the captain was off in the Western Paradise, more comfortable away from the earth and the unendurable fact that his beloved Imperial Navy had indeed been defeated. Yet this was apparently not the case.

Months later Chiyo persuaded Mrs. Yamamoto to come with Yoko and Yasuhiro for a visit. At first she was so polite with Nakayama that Chiyo wondered if they would survive the day. He suggested a walk with Yoko and Yasuhiro.

When they were alone, Mrs. Yamamoto sat formally on a cushion picking relentlessly at a thread that had come loose from the lining of her kimono.

"It's so terrible when I think of how often I wished he would just disappear," she said, lifting her eyes for just a moment, then concentrating on her kimono again. "I even wished the house would fall and crush him the way it did Ikeda Yukiji!" She gasped, covering her mouth with her hands, ashamed of having allowed such a horrible thought to pass her lips. She stared at Chiyo, expecting a reaction of horror.

"Of course you feel that way," Chiyo said. "It's all right. We all think awful things about the ones we love sometimes."

"But now I want him back," Mrs. Yamamoto said, daubing her eyes. "I am so lonely without him. I can't believe I miss him as much as I do." She swallowed back tears. "I'm just so grateful for Yoko and Yasuhiro, you know. I don't know what I'd do without them."

"Well, she's lucky to have such an understanding mother-in-law."

Nakayama and the others burst back into the room from their walk, bringing fresh *nigirizushi* rice balls bought from the woman who ran the general store down the road, a large bouquet of flowers, two huge baskets of ripe strawberries, and a bottle of sweet cream.

"Come on," Nakayama said, "everybody out to the veranda so we can watch the boat races while we have lunch."

Chiyo brought Mrs. Yamamoto a cold, wet *oshibori* towel to wipe her hands with as she sat in the fresh spring breeze, her legs dangling over the porch. Nakayama suggested a glass of beer, and when she refused that, he poured her cold *mugi-cha,* wheat tea. When the breeze grew colder, he brought her warm green tea.

Mrs. Yamamoto, after a lifetime of waiting on a husband who could hardly lift a cup of tea to his own lips, was completely won over.

"He's wonderful!" she whispered to Chiyo when they left at

dusk. "I can understand now. It's not often anyone gets to have a romance this late in life. I'm very happy for you."

After that, it seemed that the whispering and gossip diminished. Or maybe Chiyo, like Nakayama, simply stopped noticing it. And gradually the neighbors and old friends began to visit her. Hiroshi was more solicitous. Once he and Sueko invited her and Nakayama for dinner. Everyone rejoiced in her good fortune.

Everyone except Isao.

Chapter Forty

IN THE FALL OF 1969, WHEN SHE WAS thirty-four years old and Yasuhiro was seven, Yoko announced her plans to marry a young man ten years her junior, an accountant who worked with her at Toyokogyo.

"But there must be something wrong with him," Kazuko said when Chiyo called to ask her what she thought. "Otherwise, even in spite of Yoko's charm, he wouldn't want to marry a woman who is so much older and already has a child. There's something in his background he's trying to hide."

The family, searching everywhere, could discover only that the young man, Satoshi Higuchi, was predictable and ordinary. There were no dark secrets, no broken love affairs, seemingly no contamination from the bomb.

They discovered, also, that Satoshi's family had sent investigators around the neighborhood in Nobori-chō and Ujina, Inokuchi, even Miyajima, asking whether Yoko had received even the slightest exposure to the bomb. Kazuko had caught up with a rumor that Yoko was in the city the day after the blast. It was said that she had come in on August 7 to be with her mother. Someone had mixed her up with Kyoko Ikeda, and the evidence was so hard to straighten out that for a while it looked as if Satoshi's father would press for withdrawal of the suit. Apparently, no one had discovered that, technically, Yoko actually was a *hibakusha*.

Chiyo and Nakayama decided they should meet the young man in some private, neutral place without even Yoko present. They chose one of the Western-style restaurants that had sprouted up in downtown Hacchobori, gaining instant popularity because they were less formal and faster. Cheaper, too, unless one had steak—the tender, high-quality Kobe beef—which Nakayama was enthusiastically planning to order.

Satoshi was a few minutes late, out of breath when he arrived. "Stupid Bus Center," he murmured under his breath. "So crowded." But when he made his formal greetings to Chiyo and Nakayama, he was placid and calm. There was nothing exceptional about his appearance. In his dark business suit and with a face that had no distinguishing features at all, he looked like an advertisement in a clothing catalog.

As soon as they had ordered dinner, Chiyo asked him straight out why he wanted to marry a widow almost ten years his senior who already had a child of her own. It was very abrupt of her, she knew, but it did save them all a lot of time.

Satoshi Higuchi's face displayed just a hint of surprise. He took a deep breath and leaned over the table, his manner conspiratorial. "Well, to tell you the truth, I'm a little frightened by inexperienced girls my own age, and Yoko is so beautiful and easy to be with. She makes me feel very special. I'm just ecstatic about her, you see."

He lifted his napkin and spread it across his knees, apparently satisfied that he had done all the explaining he needed to do. Then he looked up and saw them both waiting for more information, so he stared at his lap. Nakayama called the waitress and ordered a large bottle of beer, then poured glasses all around and they toasted one another. It seemed to make Satoshi bold enough to confide in them a bit more.

"Actually," he said, "my father is not particularly pleased, but I've finally persuaded him that Yoko is the only one for me. I guess you could say I'm in love. I met her the way Americans meet their wives. You know, at work. And she's perfect for me." His face turned brilliant red for a moment, and he took another sip of beer. "And I like Yasuhiro very much. Even if we don't have more children, we have him, and I can bring him up as my son."

Nakayama looked at him quizzically. "Well, I think Yasuhiro is committed to the Yamamoto family. I believe it's already been decided that he will keep the name and be the Yamamoto heir."

"Oh, yes, I know. That's all right. As long as I can see him grow to manhood. I'm even expecting her mother-in-law to live with us, and she's agreeable to that since, as I'm sure you know, both of her own children died because of the bomb."

The waitress brought their dinner, and they concentrated on their knives and forks and the tasks of cutting the steak, Chiyo wishing Nakayama had not chosen to add this extra awkwardness to an already difficult situation.

But after their plates had been cleared away and the waitress had brought coffee, Satoshi suddenly leaned forward again with an air of even greater secrecy. "The truth of it is," he said. "I think you should know. There's a problem about the bomb. It's a rather special case. You see, I wasn't exposed myself, but my mother was. She was two months pregnant with me when the bomb fell, and she was living in Otake at the time—"

"Otake!" Nakayama exclaimed. "That's where my first wife was!"

They looked at each other, surprised, then exchanged names of relatives and other people they knew, both pleased to discover this new bond.

But Chiyo was alarmed. This young man was the same age as the Ikeda grandchild. He'd been exposed inside his mother's womb, and yet he wasn't mentally retarded.

"And I was already in college before I realized what had happened to nearly all the others my age." He tapped his head. "I had enough brains to finish commercial college and then get a job as an accountant. I'm very grateful. I don't know why I was the lucky one and not those others." He gulped down his coffee. "Of course I have anemia problems sometimes, and I used to worry that my brain would deteriorate, but I guess if I've managed to keep it in order this long—" He laughed. "Well, I—you know, it's better not to dwell on it too much."

"Does Yoko know this?" Chiyo asked gently.

"Oh, yes," he said. "I've told her." He looked around the restaurant carefully, making sure no one was listening. "But my father would be quite upset if he knew I talked to you about it." He was almost whispering. "He doesn't think anybody knows about my mother being a member of the Otake Brigade that day, you know. He's kept it very quiet, and he's been investigating your family, kind of hoping in the back of his mind, I think, that she might have been exposed too. Then we could admit it to each other."

The waitress brought ice cream, the usual watery, vanilla-flavored Japanese style, not the creamy chocolate kind Chiyo had grown addicted to.

Satoshi picked up his spoon and began to eat it with gusto. "I feel so much better now that I've told you," he said. "You see, we don't plan to have any more children, and I've had lots of medical checkups. I'm quite healthy except for the anemia. And almost everybody in Hiroshima has that. Yoko told me I shouldn't tell you until after we're married. She said you'd worry too much about her outliving another husband."

"Well, it does worry me," said Chiyo. "But Yoko's grown-up now and old enough to make her own decisions, and if it's what you both want to do, then—"

"Then you have our blessing," Nakayama finished for her.

Yoko and Satoshi registered their marriage at City Hall, and Satoshi moved into the Yamamoto household the next day. The two of them went on working at Toyokogyo, and in the spring, when Satoshi announced that the company was transferring him to Tokyo to work in the sales office there, Mrs. Yamamoto said she was delighted to go along with them, pleased to leave the old, dark house. "It's like starting a new life," she said with the same kind of eagerness Chiyo had always admired in her in the old days before Yasu died. "You'll have to come up to Tokyo and visit often."

"Yes, and there's always room at Miyajima, you know," said Chiyo.

It was early summer, and Sueko was finally pregnant. They had been married five years and were comfortably established in their house in Hatsukaichi. The whole family had been waiting for a child, and everyone was relieved, especially (according to Kazuko), Isao. Hiroshi was so excited they took one of their rare trips to Miyajima to inform Chiyo and Nakayama in person. "We couldn't tell you such important news over the phone or write you a letter," he said. "We expect the baby sometime in February."

Sueko sat before them, triumphant, looking beautiful and satisfied.

Hiroshi, in his pride, seemed more open and expansive. "Did you meet your first wife through an *omiai?*" he suddenly asked Nakayama.

"Yes, and it was my uncle who arranged it for me. Just as yours did for you."

Hiroshi smiled at him for the first time since his mother's marriage. "Really?" he said. "Well, after the baby's born, we want to have a dinner at Zakuro, you know, where we had our *omiai,* and we want all the relatives to come."

"But what about your Uncle Isao?" Chiyo asked. "I won't come unless Husband comes too."

"Well, Uncle doesn't have much to say about it, does he? It's our dinner and our relatives, and he can make up his own mind about whether to attend or not."

August was the twenty-fifth anniversary of the death of Kenichi and of Nakayama's son, Hidenori, and of his first wife and daughter.

"Why don't I go alone for the both of us this year?" Chiyo suggested to Nakayama. "There's no point in everybody reviving those old memories. We can take turns. I'll go this year, and you go the next. Or we could have our own memorial service here on the island. This is where your wife and daughter were."

He shook his head. "Too hot for either of us to do it alone. And Hiroshima has become such a huge city now. It's hard to get around. You can't just commandeer a taxi and ride it through the empty streets the way we used to. Crowds are everywhere. People faint at the ceremony, you know, and neither of us are that young. Anyway, those boys deserve a special trip for their twenty-fifth anniversary."

Kazuko wrote the next day, saying that Isao had arranged for a ritual blessing for Kenichi, Akiko, and Grandmother at the Peace Park. They had already invited Yoko to come down from Tokyo. "And I think Isao would like a reconciliation," she added. "He hasn't said anything, but I can tell by the set of his jaw when he talks about you. It's softened."

Sueko wrote too, inviting them for special *obon* festival food which she and Hiroshi were preparing at Hatsukaichi for the whole family.

Yoko wrote saying Satoshi had to work, but she would bring Yasuhiro.

> Hiroshi said he'd meet us at the train when we arrive in the morning. And of course we want to stay in Miyajima. We're always more comfortable there than anywhere else.

On the morning of August 6, Chiyo and Nakayama left at dawn, arriving in the Peace Park by seven to burn incense and say their prayers before the crowd got too thick and the day too hot.

Afterwards they found Hiroshi and Sueko standing with Yoko and the others at the appointed place in front of the New Hiroshima Hotel. Chiyo was delighted with Yasuhiro, an articulate, well-mannered ten-year-old who would be in the sixth grade in April. He held tightly to Nakayama's hand as they proceeded toward the row of chairs Hiroshi and Sueko had reserved for them. Isao and Kazuko entered the row behind them with Fusako and Toshio and the two girls. Chiyo felt Isao's presence even before she turned to look at him. Seven and a half years. He had grown older. His hair was completely white now. It had been only slightly gray when she last saw him.

He smiled at her, then caught sight of Nakayama, and his smile disappeared. He nodded formally, as if she were some distant acquaintance. Had he really expected her to come without her husband?

"You've been well, I trust," he said, glancing briefly at Nakayama, partly including him in the statement. "I've arranged the priest's services for ten-thirty at Jisenji, so we can go over there after the ceremony here."

They took their seats just before eight-fifteen, when the pigeons were released over the Peace Park crowd, and the mayor began to speak, as every mayor always did, about the futility of war in the face of annihilation and his hopes that people everywhere would dedicate themselves, with new urgency, to peace.

It was a good speech, but she missed the old mayor, Shinzo Hamai, who, except for a brief period in the late fifties, had been their mayor for twenty years, from 1947, when he was elected, until 1967. He had managed to get food distributed on the day of the bomb, had planned the Peace Park. He was, in fact, the person most responsible for the city's phoenixlike rise from the ashes. All those years he had been consistently, staunchly antinuclear. He had died in 1968.

Humid heat pressed down on them. Chiyo wiped the perspiration from her brow and from around her neck. After the pigeons had settled on the ground and the last voice had shouted over the microphone, the Ogawa family moved from their chairs. Slowly. Greeting friends. There were so many she saw only in August at the Peace Park. The mothers of Kenichi's classmates. Colleagues of Shintaro's. Teachers and classmates from the Girls' School. Mrs. Takano was there. Her face, more than the others, brought back the old memories.

They moved silently to the service at Jisenji. The priest stood outside, murmuring into the rising heat, incanting Kenichi's, Grandmother's, and Akiko's posthumous names, burning the incense. The same heat, the same colors and smells as last year and the year before. Memories fading into memories, extending back for twenty-five years. Chiyo felt dizzy, even a little faint. She was glad Nakayama was there and she wondered if he was thinking about his own children. She was angry with Isao for not including Hidenori's name in the service. She was even angrier at herself for not insisting it be included. But Nakayama was not interested in precedence or ceremony or appearances. Only reality.

Without thinking, she looked up and away toward Zakoba-chō, the place she imagined Kenichi had been that day, and for the first time in years, he exploded into little pieces inside her brain. He climbed back up onto the ladder, then onto the roof. He exploded again and again. Her head was a monstrous, throbbing ache, but he kept exploding. It was the worst attack she had ever had, and she didn't know how she was going to stop it. Nor could she understand how it had started. Maybe she was standing on the place where Kenichi had died? His skull was buried right there under her feet. She sat on the ground, picked up a stick, and began to dig into the large burial mound in front of the temple.

"*Chiyo!* What are you doing?" Nakayama asked gently, kneeling down beside her.

"I'm looking for Ken-chan," she said. "I think he's right under here."

It was all so simple. Kenichi had always wanted her to find him and give him a proper burial so he wouldn't have to wander the streets as a ghost, whispering at them as he had for twenty-five years, his soul doomed to wander endlessly through the streets of Hiroshima. Would they still be the ugly, rubble-strewn streets of 1945? Or could he see their new, bustling city, spread out now across the six rivers and beyond?

"Chiyo!" Isao exclaimed in horror. "We're at the Memorial Service! Everybody's watching you. Do you realize what you're doing?"

"I'm looking for Ken-chan," she repeated. Hadn't she already told everybody that? "He's down here. I can tell, and I've got to find him."

"Stand up, Chi-chan," Nakayama whispered to her. "Maybe he is there, but right now isn't the best time to look for him. We can come back later."

None of them understood. Not even Nakayama.

Isao took her arm and pulled her up, almost pushing Nakayama out of the way, then removed the stick from her hand. "I'm taking you home," he said.

"I will take her home!" insisted Nakayama, taking Chiyo by the other arm. "I think she's had too much sun, and I'll take her back to Miyajima. We can't go to Hiroshi's house. She's too tired. She needs rest."

"No, we'll take her to Hiroshi's and call the doctor," Isao said. "It's the closest place."

"I am taking her back to Miyajima," Nakayama said, his voice rising.

"Just bring her to our house," Kazuko interrupted. "It's close to Miyajima, and you can go home after she sees the doctor."

"But don't you see?" Chiyo tried to explain again. "Kenichi is buried here. His skull is down there. We have to find it." She jerked her arm away from Isao's and reached for the stick again. Nakayama held firmly to her other arm.

Then Hiroshi came, and Toshio, and everyone else in the family —Kazuko and Fusako, Sueko, Yoko, and the children—all surrounded her and pulled her away.

"Just keep her here and I'll bring the car," Isao said quickly.

Hiroshi had taken hold of her arm, and Nakayama was still on the other side, clutching her to him.

"Let me go," she shouted angrily at Hiroshi, jerking her arm free. But the family had closed around her like a steel trap so that no one would see her. "Let me go," she said again. Then the knot of hair at the back of her head came loose. A strand hung before her eyes, and she realized how she looked, saw herself as the others saw her, a senseless, babbling old woman, gone unexpectedly mad. And she stopped.

She allowed Hiroshi to lead her, meekly, to the car. But Nakayama held tight to her other arm, and was pushing her into the back seat, Hiroshi and Isao up front. Then Sueko pushed in, too. And Kazuko. There was no room for Nakayama.

"Everybody else can come in the next taxi," Hiroshi announced.

"No!" shouted Chiyo. "I want my husband here."

"Mother, it's all right; he's coming in the next car."

"I want him here now. Get him and bring him here."

She stared at Hiroshi with such intensity that he got out of the car and went to get Nakayama.

"Sueko, would you mind going in the next car?" she asked politely. "I want my husband here with me."

Her feelings were hurt, but she complied immediately, getting out of the car without a word.

Chiyo did not feel calm until Nakayama was there, sitting next to her.

Driving on the highway to Inokuchi, Isao sat stone-faced in the front seat, staring straight ahead. Hiroshi's hands were folded precisely on his lap. Nakayama held on to Chiyo's left hand, intermittently squeezing it and looking anxiously into her face.

"You're all right now?" he kept asking her.

She only nodded at him, too afraid of speaking out.

Kazuko sat on the other side, tears streaming down her face. "We'll be back in Inokuchi in no time," she finally managed to say.

"We're not going to Inokuchi," Nakayama told her firmly. "We're going home to Miyajima. I'll put her to bed. She's all right now. I can tell by her eyes. If there's anything wrong, we'll call a doctor."

"We'll have a doctor look at her before she goes out there," Isao said. "She might be having sunstroke." They had passed Inokuchi, and before anyone could object, Isao pulled up in front of the hospital in Hatsukaichi, and in no time Chiyo was in a hospital bed, with Nakayama standing over her, watching her with anxious eyes.

"Really, I'm all right," she told him.

"We're here now," said Nakayama. "We might as well see the doctor."

"A touch of the sun," the doctor said. "But not serious. Do you have a headache?" he asked Chiyo.

"Not anymore."

"Well, we could keep her here under observation for a day, but—"

"You think it's all right if she goes home?" Nakayama asked.

"There aren't any doctors out on Miyajima," Isao said. "It's risky for her to be so far away from medical help."

"Just twenty minutes on the ferry, and another fifteen into the hospital," said Nakayama.

"It depends on where she feels most comfortable," said the doctor. "No danger, I think."

"Then I want to go home," said Chiyo.

"And we're going with her too, Uncle. I can help," Yoko said.

The four of them were in a taxi, ready to drive to the ferry. The others peered anxiously through the windows. Isao bowed stiffly.

"Well, no reconciliation now," Chiyo said as they rode along the highway. "That's the end of that." She sighed. "It's funny how crazy I was. I couldn't get rid of the feeling Kenichi was there. I'm sorry I embarrassed you all."

Nakayama grinned at her. "You didn't embarrass me," he said.

"You'd have to be a lot more outrageous to do that. Besides, I've always known you were a little crazy." He looked solemnly at Yoko and the taxi driver in the front seat, then reached across Yasuhiro, sitting in the back between them, and clasped her hand. "I like you the way you are," he said.

Chapter Forty-one

THE TELEGRAM CAME ONE MORNING IN midsummer.

Isao in hospital in Hatsukaichi. Come as soon as you can.
Kazuko

Minutes later, Chiyo was on the ferry speeding across the water.

At the hospital she confronted Kazuko's worried and puffy face. Fusako was standing just behind her.

"Accident," Kazuko breathed. "He was testing out a new car. Seventy-five years old, and he's been out there racing on the testing grounds, trying to get the same speed as the Shinkansen, the rapid express train."

She sighed "Mr. Matsuda was just here. He said he warned Isao not to do the testing. There are plenty of people who can do it. But he—"

"What happened?" Chiyo interrupted

"Mother, you mustn't talk so much," said Fusako. "Sit down and let me tell it."

She obeyed with unexpected docility, sitting on a chair in the hospital hallway.

419

"It was a convertible," Fusao began. "And he had the top down. You know Father. Of course he was supposed to wear a helmet. But he wanted to feel the wind blowing through his hair. And the speed. Mr. Matsuda said he drove out to the edge of the testing grounds and then went right on into the sea. They had to pull the car out with a crane, but Father swam to the surface right away. They pulled him out, and he shook the water off and started to walk away. That's when someone noticed he was bleeding at the temple, and he started getting weak and dizzy."

"They put him in the hospital out by Toyokogyo," Kazuko interrupted, "and the doctors there said it was a light concussion, not too serious. They were going to release him the next day, but I insisted they bring him here where we know the doctors."

"Well, it doesn't seem so bad, then," said Chiyo. "Light concussion. Hiroshi's was a serious one, and he's even—"

"Oh no," said Fusako, "you haven't heard the worst of it. Last night the nurses heard him moaning in his sleep about pain in his stomach. They felt it and it was hard like a rock."

Kazuko looked up at Chiyo. "You know he's always held himself stiffly." She stared at her lap again, avoiding Chiyo's eyes. "So they're doing exploratory surgery for stomach cancer."

"Cancer," Chiyo said. Isao had walked in and out of the city every day during that dreadful time. Except for the illness he'd had early on, he hadn't shown any weakness at all. Chiyo was the one who was supposed to die, always feeling anemic and getting exhausted, having red-and-white-corpuscle checks, going up to the Casualty Commission for tests, being a guinea pig, as Isao had always put it. He would have none of it himself. And now he was the one. Holding his stiff stomach together by sheer force of will. And she and Mrs. Ikeda and Mrs. Yamamoto were all still alive. They had outlived the healthy ones and the strong ones and the young ones.

"So, that's what we're waiting for right now," Kazuko said, standing up and looking vaguely down the hall. "Just to see—"

"Mother, relax a little if you can."

Kazuko looked plaintively at Chiyo. "Stiff stomach," she murmured, sighing and sitting down again. "He's just always had one, you know. It's not—"

They waited, talking sporadically, drinking tea, pacing up and down the hall. Finally, the doctor came.

"Is it—" Kazuko began.

The doctor pulled off his rubber gloves, then his mask. He looked gently at the three women, acknowledging each of them.

"The cancer is spread all through his body," he said. "Frankly I don't know how he endured the pain this long. We didn't try to cut it out. We couldn't have begun to do that, so we just sewed him back up. We can prolong his life, maybe a month or two. Chemotherapy works miracles sometimes, you know, but other times it's worse. And he told me before he went under the anesthetic that he didn't want any drugs to ease the pain afterwards."

He stood a while longer as if he had something more to say, but finally he shook his head. "He's in the recovery room. You can see him sometime late this afternoon." He bowed and walked away. His shoes struck hard on the concrete floor until he turned a corner down the hallway. Even after he had disappeared, the sound echoed back to them.

"Why did you do it?" Kazuko asked him later, sitting on the side of his bed. "Couldn't you have told us? We could have stopped it if we'd known in time."

"Kazuko," he whispered, reaching up and taking her hands, pulling her face close to him and smoothing back her hair. "I'm seventy-five, you know."

She was sobbing, still angry with him. "Why didn't you tell me?"

He smiled. "That beautiful racing car. I just—"

Kazuko buried her face in the crook of his neck. "You drove it right into the sea."

"Kazuko." His voice was almost inaudible, gently berating her. "Of course I—"

He looked around the room suddenly, searching for someone. "Chi-chan! Are you here?"

"I'm right here. We're all here." She reached out and held tight to his other hand.

"Where is he?" asked Isao.

"Out in Miyajima at the shop."

"Get him," said Isao. "I want him to come here."

They called everyone. Hiroshi was already on his way to the hospital. Nakayama came. They called Tokyo, asking Yoko to come and bring Yasuhiro.

They moved in and out of the room, back and forth from the hospital corridors, spelling one another, taking their turns traveling to Hiroshi's house or to Inokuchi to make more food and bring it to the others standing vigil. No one had any idea how many days had gone by, or whether it was night or day.

He seemed to be wasting away, and yet other times his eyes were bright and clear. But too intense. Like fire. At first he refused, but later he submitted to chemotherapy. Some days he was lively and talked of getting out of bed, going out to his office at Toyoko-gyo.

Other days, he talked of going home to Inokuchi and walking along the shore.

"There isn't any shore anymore, Father. Remember they filled in the sea in front of the house?"

"Oh." He nodded, but they couldn't tell whether he really remembered.

At first, taking her turn going to Inokuchi to make food, Chiyo felt wary. She had not been inside the house for more than ten years. It was the same except for the view.

Soon after the merger of Inokuchi with the City of Hiroshima, the authorities had begun considering ways to extend the land, finally deciding, after long and painful discussions with the oyster farmers, that the stretch of coast that passed Isao's house was best.

The Land Reclamation Authorities cut off the mountain and shoveled it into the sea, leaving only a moat of water around their beloved island Miyojin, the rock with the pine tree and the tiny shrine. The sea was all flat land in front as far as the eye could see. They'd made a park around the rock island, fencing it in, and with benches where people could sit and look at the pine tree and the sea far beyond. Chiyo could not bear to look at it. A fake park in front of the old house where she was born and where all the generations had lived.

What had it been like for Kazuko? Watching the steamrollers reach up their arms and pull down the mountain, then push back the precious Inland Sea away from them, making room for schools, factories, real estate offices, subdivided modern houses for small, modern families. But people needed somewhere to live. There were *hibakusha,* even now, hanging tenaciously onto their squatters' property at the edge of the river and around the new castle that had been rebuilt seventeen years ago.

Of course Kazuko would go on living in Inokuchi with Fusako and her family. Chiyo thought she would rather die than live in Hiroshi's household. What would she do if Nakayama went before she did? Hiroshi wouldn't let her stay out on the island alone.

Arriving at the hospital with Isao's granddaughters, Chiyo found tearstained Fusako in the hallway. "It's not doing any good," she said, hugging her two daughters close to her, "The chemotherapy is making it worse. All his hair is coming out, and he can't swallow. He wants to give it up. He wants to go home to Inokuchi."

Chiyo went into his room. Kazuko sat there silent.

Isao's face was emaciated, his cheeks hollow, but he lay staring at the ceiling with luminous, fierce eyes. He turned and looked at her.

"Are the girls out in the hall?" he asked. "Bring them to me."

Fusako came into the room first, sat down on the bed, and leaned forward, clasping his hand. "I'm sorry, Father—" She began to cry. "I couldn't have any boys for you."

He looked at her, puzzled. "My girls," he whispered. "Where are my girls?"

Fumiko and Myoko, both teenagers now, looked at his brilliant, sunken eyes, then sat on the bed and held his hands. "When are you coming home?" Fumiko asked.

"Soon," he said. Chiyo took the girls away.

The next moment he was staring at Chiyo again. "Nakayama," he breathed. "Bring him here. I must make peace with him."

"Ni-san," Chiyo said gently. "You already have. You did yesterday and the day before. Don't you remember?"

"Bring him here," Isao demanded.

They went and got him again, and Isao raised his head.

"I didn't like it, I'll have to tell you," Isao said for the third time.

Nakayama did not seem to mind. He went through the same ritual again, nodding to Isao, shaking hands.

"When are we going home?" Isao asked when he had finished with Nakayama. But the doctors were afraid to move him in his weakened state.

"Keep up the treatment," Kazuko pleaded. "You don't have any resistance, and the pain will be worse."

He nodded, but no one was sure whether he agreed.

Yoko came with Yasuhiro, age fourteen, holding awkwardly to his schoolboy cap.

"Kenichi, come here," Isao said.

No one corrected him, and the boy went closer, in awe and a little frightened.

"You've got to carry on for the family," Isao told him.

"No, Ni-san," Chiyo interrupted. "This is Yasuhiro, Yoko's son. He's grown up a lot since you saw him."

Isao looked confused. "Oh, then. You're a good boy. Take care of your mother." He patted Yasuhiro's hand. "Is Hiroshi here?"

They called Toyokogyo and Hiroshi came immediately. He had been there every day like the others, but Isao had paid no attention to him. Chiyo was relieved to have him singled out at last.

423

"You've been a good son," Isao told him, reaching out for his hand. "For your mother and—" His voice was hardly audible now. "For me."

He lay silent. They could hardly hear him breathing, but he was fighting the pain, concentrating hard on what he was going to say. Nakayama went outside to summon Toshio and Sueko.

"It's just if you have one more son—" With great effort he lifted his head and fixed his eyes on Hiroshi. "You see, Fusako might not—" He lay down again. "Maybe Fumiko and Myoko won't want to marry adopted—so if your second son—"

He was becoming much weaker now. Hiroshi leaned far over the bed to hear him, and the others stood by, hardly breathing. "Just one more Ogawa in the world to—"

He seemed to forget what he was talking about. He was hardly breathing. "So, if we survive," he went on, "and start floating out into the universe, exploring planets and— Something's coming. Some breakthrough. And I want an Ogawa to be around to—"

He watched the family gathered closely around his bed. Toshio had come. And Sueko with the children.

"I liked it here," he whispered. "I liked being—"

He was very frail. How had he managed to look so healthy? And how long had he refused to admit the presence of cancer even to himself?

He was the kind of man who would steadfastly insist on choosing the time and place of his death. He wanted to be home in Inoku-chi. But there was no time now.

Chiyo did not cry for him until after he was gone.

Chapter Forty-two

I N SPITE OF HER FEARS, CHIYO HAD NOT
expected to survive Nakayama. He had spent
years in Siberia, but he was younger, more robust, and seldom susceptible to illnesses, even colds. When he did succumb, peacefully
and in his sleep several years after the death of Isao, Chiyo firmly
refused to move from Miyajima, even after the period of mourning
was over. She wanted to stay on at the beach house. Yuki wanted
her to move down near the shop with them. Hiroshi wouldn't hear
of either arrangement. He called her often on the phone. "I am
your real son," he insisted. "You took care of me all those years,
didn't you? What would everybody say if you lived with Yuki instead of me?"

"Who's everybody?" Chiyo inquired. But she couldn't remember
what the answer had been. "I'm going to live alone," she insisted.
"I'm going to stay right here on Miyajima and help in the shop, and
paint dolls."

"Well, you could come over here and help Sueko with the children. She's just run ragged."

"Then she can get a maid!" Chiyo said, astounded that no one had
thought of it. "You're a vice-president of Toyokogyo. And I've

raised my children. I want to see the grandchildren. Not raise them."

She felt Hiroshi's shocked silence at the other end of the phone.

"You don't care about your grandchildren?" he asked. "Kenji and our daughter, Sachiko?"

Hiroshi called her even more frequently, doggedly continuing the argument. "We can still keep one side of the beach house and go to Miyajima even if you're not living there. We built the room in this house just for you. With the garden around it. Besides, it's safer here. What if you get sick?"

Chiyo waited for him to say "again," in reference to her madness at the Peace Park ten years earlier, but he did not. He had enough sensitivity for that, at least.

"Then I'll take the ferry. As I have told you many times."

"It's not sensible, Mother."

"I must go down to the shop now. Let's discuss it later."

She held out for several years, traveling back and forth to Hiroshima for the Nakayama Enterprises board meetings and to the shop to paint dolls and help Yuki. She was growing gradually more lonely. She thought afterwards that she could have laster longer if Yuki had been more supportive. But he too began to worry about her living alone. "We'd rather have you stay with us, but you would have more room at Hiroshi's. And of course it would hurt his feelings if you lived here."

It was when she sprained her ankle on the road from the beach that she began to reconsider. Everyone in the neighborhood had been off somewhere. Children in school, nobody tending the oyster beds, and the other houses too far away for anyone to hear when she shouted. She could have rented out the other side of the beach house, but she wanted to keep it empty for the times the grandchildren came. If she had been seriously injured, she could have died there and joined Nakayama.

She was angry at him for leaving her. And so abruptly. He had complained of shortness of breath and gone off to rest. When she went in with tea for him an hour later, he had already died, without even calling out to say goodbye. "Died in his sleep," the newspaper said, but how could he leave her without even waking up first?

She had moved through the funeral in a daze. Yoko had taken the Shinkansen straight through to Hiroshima, her husband and Yasuhiro joining them later for the funeral, then staying a week on Miyajima, urging her to come to Tokyo to live.

She had hardly heard them. It was a flat, distant time she could not remember now. The days followed one after the other the way they had after the bomb.

After the ankle sprain, although she managed to keep the news from Hiroshi, she knew it was inevitable. The next time he brought up the subject, she didn't argue, but packed some belongings and said she would visit for a few days.

"It's not a final decision," she said. "Let's just see if it seems comfortable."

She caught sight of Hiroshi smiling triumphantly at Sueko over the top of her head, but she put it out of her mind. Maybe she really could keep her independence intact. It was a lovely house right on the shore, in some ways even more beautiful than Inokuchi, especially now that the flat, dry land was stretched out before Kazuko's view. Hiroshi's house was not as well made, of course. It did not resonate with the skill of ancient carpenters and solid old wood. But the closeness of the sea made up for that. She envisioned sitting in her detached room, looking out on the garden and to the water beyond, painting dolls.

The first two weeks went well. The children were happy to have her attention, but they never intruded when she retired to her room.

"I've told them not to disturb you there. The only time they can play with you is when you're in the family sitting room or the kitchen." Sueko smiled, pleased with herself, as she always seemed to be.

Chiyo moved more of her possessions from the beach house and rented out the unoccupied side of it for the summer.

"Maybe we should rent out the whole beach house," Hiroshi suggested.

"Absolutely not," Chiyo said, surprised. "Our arrangement was to keep one side empty for our own visits. Don't change it, or I'll pack up and go back right now."

Hiroshi sighed. "You are so stubborn, Mother."

She was unpacking her wooden cylinders, clay figures, her varied collection of oils and acrylics.

"What's this?" he asked. "You're still painting?"

"Of course. Why would you expect me to stop? I haven't stopped for thirty-two years."

"What do you do with the dolls after they're painted?"

"Well, the usual. I take them to the factory or to Yuki's shop so he can sell them."

"Mother, don't you see? It looks as if you have to make your living selling dolls. I know you had to do it when we were really poor. But we're not anymore. I can take care of you."

She was holding one of her dolls in midair, looking at the lively expression on its face. It was one Nakayama would have particularly liked. She put it down. "Hiroshi!" she exclaimed. "This is folkcraft. It's art. Like your samurai doll, commanding high prices. It's my own income and I'll do what I want with it, buy things for the children, furniture for the beach house. I should think you'd be proud of me."

"I am proud of you, but couldn't you just make them as gifts to give to your friends like other women do?"

She began arranging her painting materials on the table in her room.

"You liked me better when I was a child, didn't you, Mother?"

It was one of those rare moments when he emerged from the smooth exterior that protected him like the polished hoods that shielded his Mazda engines. She searched his eyes, hoping he would spill out more of himself.

"In those old days," she said carefully, "you always said exactly what you thought and felt. And even when you didn't, I knew from looking at your face. Now I can't tell anymore. You're so buried down inside yourself."

He shrank away from her. "All right," he said impatiently. "Do what you want. If it makes you feel better."

She continued to paint her dolls and took them regularly to Miyajima.

A year after she had moved in with Hiroshi, she decided to attend the Memorial Service in the Peace Park by herself. Hiroshi had told her repeatedly she must never go alone, and he had accompanied her once after Nakayama died. But it was too tiring for her to go every year, he said. He was worried about her health. What really worried him, she knew, was having her go crazy again in front of Jisenji Temple.

On August 6, she awoke in the dark, crept downstairs, and unlatched the door, sliding it open a centimeter at a time. Hiroshi and Sueko were light sleepers, their ears having been attuned to crying children, but the sound of the sliding door blended with the whispering wind. Early dawn outside, the air just turning gray. No one would know she was gone until at least ten, when Sueko always came to her room. And she had written Sueko a note saying she was out for a little early morning shopping and didn't expect to be back until at least noon.

Chiyo smiled to herself, out in the cool morning now, walking down the path that led away from the sea and the house toward the bus stop. Hiroshi didn't understand. She had never told him about following the man into the brothel at Maizuru. Or about Kenichi exploding into pieces inside her brain. It would have confirmed his fears that she was a little crazy.

On its way to the sea, water gurgled in the canal next to the path. Seagulls called to her, circling overhead. She was alone in the morning. No one was at the bus stop, either.

This year, if Kenichi had lived, he would be fifty-four years old. His mother was nearly seventy-nine, older than either Isao or Nakayama had been when they died. More than forty years since the bomb. But Hiroshi did not remember such things. He hated, dreaded, going to the Peace Park. Even finding Kenichi's bones near the place she had been crazily digging that day had not vindicated Chiyo in Hiroshi's eyes. They had torn down the old Hiroshima Hotel and were excavating for the new one when the workmen came across a pile of bones and identification tags, some of them so easy to read that there was no doubt about who they belonged to.

On one ID tag, the character for Hara was clearly inscribed. The place where the "Ken" part should have been was obliterated, but the single line which stood for *ichi* was there—number one. First child. The second part of Kenichi's name.

Hiroshi had come to the funeral service. He and Nakayama sat with the families in the background. Chiyo was with two other mothers in the front row, listening to the words of the city officials, going forward, one at a time, like a graduation, to receive their boxes of bones. The others cried. Chiyo did not. She sat under the summer sun, smiling, serene. Kenichi had received a proper burial at last and his spirit, hovering out there along the river every August, was tranquil now.

When the bus came, Chiyo saw that she would be the first passenger. She had ridden a million times on that road bordering the Inland Sea. Every curve of the shore was like a blood vessel leading to the interior of her heart. Memories, whispered voices, and images sprung up with every sight. The stretch from Hatsukaichi to Inokuchi looked more like the shoreline of the old days. Narrow black beaches, and a few oyster floats. There were none at Inokuchi any longer.

This morning was special. All the way to Inokuchi, Chiyo held her gaze steadfastly on the sea, ignoring the burgeoning factories and hotels that almost blocked her view. The bus girl had not begun to announce the stations in her high, singsong monotone. There was no music blasting at them from the radio. It was even too early for the delivery trucks, with their growling wheels, or the sound of motorcycle engines.

When they reached the Inokuchi stop, a few passengers got on, none of them familiar. Chiyo stared at the old family house, ignoring the imprisoned island she had once loved and the dry, dusty land beyond.

At Kusatsu, a few stops before Koi, a group of farm women in cotton *monpe* pants, the kind they had all worn during the war, climbed onto the bus with their heavy bundles wrapped for market in huge cotton *furoshiki*. They chattered with one another, standing in the middle of the bus, swaying to keep their balance. A radio blared. The bus girl's voice rose above it, announcing station names. Neither the bus girl nor the driver gave any sign that they regretted losing the serenity they had shared.

Across the Ota River to Koi. The transfer to a city streetcar. Then the ride across the Tenma River and on up to Aioi Bridge through the middle of the bustling center of the city near her old neighborhood in Nobori-chō. Nowadays, the tall buildings, almost skyscrapers, formed a canyon for the wide, traffic-laden streets. Rows of buses waited for passengers. And the bicycles, motorcycles, pedestrians, taxis and private cars, including Isao's beloved Matsudas, had come alive, weaving in and out, forming the rush-hour labyrinth.

She got off at the other end of Aioi Bridge and walked along the bank of the Motoyasu River, remembering the journey she and the Yamamotos had taken. Now she was the only one of the three still alive. Mrs. Yamamoto had died a year after Isao, leaving Chiyo alone to bear the burden of being a septuagenarian miracle, one of the few left who had walked through the epicenter on the day of the bomb. And she was still walking and thinking, in spite of her anemia and general exhaustion and the crooked smile she had carried with her these forty years. They had hounded her, the radio and TV stations, and the newspapers. "How did you survive? What is your secret for maintaining a long life?"

She had granted them interviews. If it helped to keep another bomb from dropping anywhere else on the earth, she would do it, she said. But she didn't know why she was still living when so many pure ones like Kenichi had died. She was lucky to have relatives in the suburbs who had taken care of her and made her rest, fed her fresh fruits and vegetables, she told them. So many others back in the city had received hardly any food or attention. Yet there were so many like herself who had fresh food and rest, and they had died anyway. So she didn't know. She had no secrets to tell them. The only cure was never to drop another bomb.

After moving to Miyajima, she stopped giving interviews. Mrs. Yamamoto had done it before she moved to Tokyo, and sometimes they sought her out even there. They had called Isao, too, but he avoided them. He had nothing new to tell them, he said, nothing that hadn't already been told again and again.

Mrs. Ikeda, diminished and quiet now, was the only other one who still hung on. She was retired, too, and spent her time at home mending kimonos and underwear while watching her grandson. Her son, Ichiro, was solicitous like Hiroshi. "You don't have to spend your time doing that, Mother. I've got a good engineer's salary now. Do what you enjoy." But a lifetime of frugality was not easy to reverse. Her grandchild, now in his forties, had become less capable of walking. He stayed in the house most of the time, or wandered in the garden. They had taught him to dig weeds, and he set happily about his task every morning during the summers, beaming his Kyoko-like smile. "As if he carries the memory of her better than anyone else," Mrs. Ikeda said.

Once, when she was still living on Miyajima, Chiyo had persuaded Mrs. Ikeda to come and bring her grandson for an outing. It had taken great effort and planning. That had been at least five years ago, maybe longer. But now that she was living in Hatsukai-chi, it seemed even harder for Chiyo to see the old friends. Maybe Mrs. Ikeda would be in the Peace Park today.

People were already selling flowers and incense when Chiyo crossed into the park from the Motoyasu Bridge. Only half an hour now until the ceremony. She would burn the incense for Kenichi and the others, then go straight back to the bus stop. No need to stay for the ceremony.

She bought a small bouquet and a bundle of incense, then stood wavering over whether to burn it near the front steps of the new Hiroshima Hotel where Kenichi had been cremated, or near Jisenji where he had probably died. Everyone else was at the cenotaph, and she decided on that more neutral place. Better for Nakayama's relatives, too. She hurried on, keeping her eyes to the ground, hoping not to see anyone she knew. It would spoil the last trace of the mood that clung to her from the morning. She wanted to be alone with Ken-chan. And with Nakayama, who had been with her at each ceremony during the seventeen years of their marriage.

At the cenotaph, she put the bouquet among the other flowers clustered before the eternal flame, burned the incense, pressed her hands together and bowed, stood a moment longer, then turned and walked away. Too quickly, perhaps. But she knew that her communion with the dead would not come now in the midst of the growing crowd and the swirling smoke. She had felt closer to them back on the highway.

She could go home now. Nakayama wouldn't want her to be there alone in the heat and the crowd. And Hiroshi would be furious if he knew.

She saw the rows of chairs filling up for the ceremony. Almost time now—just a few minutes before eight. If she stayed for the first part, just the mayor's words, she could still catch the nine o'clock streetcar from the end of Aioi Bridge. What was the use of rushing back to spend another whole day with Sueko? At former ceremonies she had heard the messages of each of the different mayors. She had seen the emperor, the crown prince, Eleanor Roosevelt, Nehru, Bertrand Russell, Pope John Paul II, countless officials from Europe, America, Russia, Asia. Why miss the ceremony now that she had taken the trouble to get all the way here? It wasn't stiflingly hot yet.

She wandered in among the chairs and chose a seat in the third row. People were coming from all directions now, filling the chairs, compressing heat into this one compact area. Sleeveless dresses. Perspiration trickling down the neck of the man in front of her. An old grandfather in a cotton kimono holding a solemn six-year-old in his lap.

By the time the ceremony began, the air had grown humid around her and the world dissolved into a mist that floated before her eyes. Music welled up around her. Two women, one foreign, walked down the aisle between the rows of chairs, carrying wreaths, which they laid before the cenotaph. A chorus sang, and the mayor stood up and made one more appeal to the world to work for peace.

At eight-fifteen the white doves flooded the sky and someone rang the Peace Bell. Heads were bowed, and she put her own head down quickly on her lap. She was getting dizzy and a little nauseated.

Someone was shaking her arm. *"Oku-sama?* Mrs. Nakayama?" It was Morishita-san. Lately, she had not been attending the Nakayama Enterprises board meetings, and she had not seen him for several years.

"Come over on the lawn," he said. "Get out of this crowd. Follow me."

They went along a path to a grassy enclave, green, cool-looking, surrounded by trees, and not so crowded. Strange to find such a place in the Peace Park, which she always thought of as barren and vacant, full of white cement. But forty years was long enough for trees to grow. The shadows of the leaves made patterns across the faces and bodies of the people sitting there. Chiyo thought fleetingly of the Manet painting in her high school textbook which had impressed her so deeply.

The ethereal figures obscured by shadows turned and greeted her, and she recognized many of them — people who had painted dolls in those early years, people who had worked in the factory, even people from the Nobori-chō neighborhood.

Mrs. Ikeda was there, and some of her former co-workers from City Hall, setting out their lunch boxes, preparing for a morning picnic.

"What? You too?" Chiyo said. Mrs. Ikeda had not changed. And yet the years had gone by. The Ikeda grandchild was there, sitting on the grass, fingering a rubber ball. "He's over forty now, you know," Mrs. Ikeda said. It was always a shock for Chiyo to realize that he was the same age as Yoko's second husband.

"It was hard to bring him here this year. But he wanted to come, so Ichiro brought him in the car, and we pushed him over in his new wheelchair." Mrs. Ikeda's eyes were misty. "It's just — you know, he seems to get more and more frail every year. His bones are so weak."

Chiyo knelt in front of him and hugged him. "Do you remember me?" she asked. "I'm your Aunty Chiyo."

"Chi!" he chirped companionably, and beamed his smile again, then gave his attention to his rubber ball.

Morishita-san was still standing by her.

"How did you all come together like this?" she asked him. "And why didn't you tell me so I could come, too?"

"Well, some of us from the factory happened to meet each other here a few years ago. Then somehow we made it an annual thing, especially when we noticed that Mrs. Ikeda was always here with her group, too. It helps us to get through the day when we see some of the old faces. We would have told you about it, but your son, Hiroshi, said we'd better not invite you because he knew you'd want to come."

She laughed. "That's Hiroshi, all right. But I always find him out. Now he won't be able to keep me away." She was feeling better, revived from her dizziness, and she went about greeting people, then sat, contentment spreading through her while she listened to the news and gossip about people she hadn't thought about in years. Music from the mobile truck units played in the background. People from the different peace groups were shouting through megaphones. But the group in the glade was oblivious, enclosed in a circle of friendship, ignoring the world outside, spearing morsels of food with their chopsticks. Chiyo had not brought any lunch, and was embarrassed that she had nothing to contribute.

"But don't you remember, in the old days, all the times you brought food to the factory and fed us?" Morishita-san berated her.

A breeze came through the glade, carrying the voices of the dead, whispering and echoing the past. Chiyo shivered a little—as if ghosts had moved in among them.

She looked at her watch and was alarmed when she saw it was already twelve. Sueko would be really worried by now. Maybe she had called Hiroshi and they would be out combing the city for her.

She got up quickly and made her apologies, brushing the crumbs from her kimono. Morishita-san stood up to accompany her to the bus.

"No," she told him. "I'd be tempted to talk to you more. And I can catch the bus from the other side of the Peace Bridge. If I don't get right home, Hiroshi will be so angry he'll never let me come again."

He looked after her, a little helpless, but she didn't have time for final bows. She was almost running now. The heat was relentless. She had to find air to breathe. She stopped at the center of the bridge where it arched high over the river, leaning out to feel the breeze on her face. It was the place she had stood so often at dusk to watch the paper boats carrying lighted candles float out to the end of the river to meet the souls of the dead. Thinking of the dusk made her feel cooler, and she imagined how it would be if she stayed until evening. The tiny lanterns pushed in together, some getting caught on the edge of the bank, some dipping into the water and losing their flames, but floating on anyway. Kenichi, Nakayama and his children, Isao and all the others would be out there. Maybe Shintaro, too. She wondered if he had minded her marriage to Nakayama.

A light breeze touched her cheek, and she leaned out farther to feel its blessing, but the heat was oppressive still. In the river below was a shimmering, unsteady reflection of herself. All sorts of heads were sticking up over the arched bridge, some high above the others, some children hoisted up by their parents and others just barely fitting over the railing. They all looked liked *kokeshi* dolls.

She forgot the heat and the bus and Hiroshi's worried, angry face. How would it be, she wondered, an arrangement of dolls standing on an arched bridge—for a display at Yuki's shop. She began counting the heads, but they suddenly blurred in the water. She couldn't breathe. She slumped against the bridge railing, grasping it with one arm. It seemed she was slipping farther—

Suddenly everything was miraculously clear. She saw all the heads as if they were dolls she had just painted. But one head stood out taller, different from the others. A rangy figure with piercing eyes and a funny nineteenth-century bowler on top of his head. It was Shintaro. There was no doubt about it. The knowledge came to her as if some voice were telling her. He was gazing down at her, smiling. A shimmering, almost blinding light danced around him. He looked so young, the way he had before he went into the army more than forty years ago. He was wearing the clothes he'd worn to school in the early days just after they'd married, and he was looking down from a great distance. She was small next to him. Shintaro had been tall.

"Chi-chan," he said. It was Nakayama's voice. But no, there was something different about it. She couldn't tell whose voice it was. How could she remember? She looked up at him, almost in dread, as if she were trying to stare directly into the sun. "Shintaro?" she asked tentatively.

He didn't answer. Just smiled more broadly, then turned in the crowd and beckoned to her. She followed. He was always just up ahead, his bowler hat bobbing above the other heads, going so fast, the way he had that day she'd found him and followed him along the Hondori. She ran to catch up, and he took her hand eagerly, pulling her along as if he could hardly wait to show her something.

They were boarding some kind of vehicle. It was horse-drawn. But when she got into the back seat, she saw that it was an ordinary taxi with a driver up front. They drove to one of the restaurants along the river. Was he going to take her there? She had always wanted to go and sit in one of those places, but there had never been enough time.

They sat at a table. The river flowed beneath them as if it were carrying them along on its shoulders out to the sea. Lanterns were hanging, and a host of girls waited on them. Twinkling lights came on along the river at dusk. A persimmon tree, laden with bright orange fruit, hung just beyond the window of their restaurant room. The leaves were gone, and the fruit was rich and ripe. But it was August. Persimmons shouldn't be ripe yet. There were fireflies, too, and frost on the window, glistening. Shintaro must have brought this coolness back from Siberia.

They were eating such delicacies. Thinly cut raw blowfish, which Isao had always loved. Transparent. And arranged with such care that it seemed part of the pattern on the plate. Shrimp tempura and cold bean curd mixed with egg to make a custard, garnished on top with fresh ginger. Delicate slices of melon. All varieties. Everything she had dreamed of feeding Shintaro in the days she was waiting for him to come home.

The sun shone brightly into the room, then faded and formed a red sunset, brilliant against the sky. She could hardly see Shintaro. He was misty and half-formed. She tried to reach out and touch him, but her hand went through the middle of his chest. The mist grew hot, suffocating, smothering her. Ichiro Ikeda and Morishita-san were there. She was on the bridge with lots of people around her. She knew them all. They were greeting her. But they looked nervous and worried.

Everything was white. The walls and ceilings. Even the floor. And people's clothing. She was in a white bed. Her hand was laid across the white sheet, thin and wrinkled. Incredibly old.

Hiroshi was standing above her. But he wasn't angry. He looked sad. Somewhere farther away was Sueko. She was weeping, but daintily into her soft handkerchief. As if she were acting on a stage.

At the other end of the room, by himself, was a young boy. Her grandson, Kenji. No, this child was older and taller. Almost Hiroshi's height. But Hiroshi was standing right by her bed. It was Kenichi. He was rubbing his eyes. They were red from studying physics. And from the dust of the demolition crew.

He was beckoning to her, suffering over his science book, pleading with his eyes for her to come and help. Beyond him, somewhere in the distance, hardly visible, was someone else.

She lifted herself from the white bed with perfect ease and moved toward Kenichi, motionless, as if a gust of wind had blown her there. She arrived at his side, straining to see the science problem spread out on the desk under the lamp. But a filmy curtain hung, gossamerlike, between herself and her son. She reached out to push it back, then hesitated.

436

A sweet smell of incense came from the room where Kenichi sat. The air seemed deathly still. Why hadn't he opened a window? Nakayama's voice came to her from behind the mist. "We're waiting," he said.

"Have you seen Shintaro?" she asked, but he was gone.

She looked back toward the bed. Everyone was gathered around it. But she wasn't there anymore. She was over here by the curtain.

"Hiro-chan. Come look. It's Ken-chan. He's been here all along, studying."

Hiroshi did not turn to look at her. He did not even hear her. None of them did. She could not make them hear. But she could feel Kenichi's eyes staring at her, almost piercing through her.

She turned, lifted the curtain, and went inside to join her first-born son.